THE RUN
OF
THE COUNTRY

A Border Station

THE RUN
OF
THE COUNTRY

Shane Connaughton

St. Martin's Press
New York

Library of Congress Cataloging-in-Publication Data

Connaughton, Shane.
    The run of the country / Shane Connaughton.
      p.   cm.
    ISBN 0-312-07077-2
    I. Title.
    PR6053.0465R8   1992   91-37341
    823'.914—dc20   CIP

First published in Great Britain by Hamish Hamilton Limited, a subsidiary of the Penguin Group.

First U.S. Edition: March 1992
10 9 8 7 6 5 4 3 2 1

THE RUN

OF

THE COUNTRY

I

He could see the soldiers coming, hear their shouts, and he saw
the sunlight breaking silver on his father's cap-badge. His father
knew the terrain and scoured it daily for armed Republicans.
Whin-scabbed hills, rocks, lake islands, the low-lying fields by the
Finn were only rooms to him. He knew them like you know your
bed. He swept the land like you sweep your kitchen. Nothing
human could escape his net.

He could hear him direct the soldiers, his barking voice hoping
for prey. 'Keep at it, lads. There's a shed up there in them trees.'

The soldiers carried .303s. From the door of the shed he could
see one of them had a sub-machine-gun. The Captain. He was
from Kerry and was a famous footballer. All his men were from
the South. They were stationed in Cavan town, doing Border
duties until such time as the Troubles ended. When they came on
patrol to Butlershill they parked their jeeps outside the police
station, and while waiting for his father, the Sergeant, to join
them, played football on the lawn. Their weapons and helmets
they piled along the wall. Rifles, Bren guns, ammunition belts lay
on the grass, innocent as a bundle of sticks.

The goal-posts were two rifles bayoneted into the ground. He
was always keeper. The last line of defence, the butt of jokes, the
excuse for defeat. The soldiers wore boots, the Captain shoes.
The Captain loved shooting at him, beating him, charging him,
bundling him to the ground, kicking him without breaking bones.

The games on the lawn were the nearest these Free State soldiers ever got to war. The IRA never fired at their own.

Now they were hunting him, though they didn't know it. His
father was in for a surprise. They couldn't miss him. They were
at the bottom of the field, pouring through a gap in the hedge.

His father had his cap-strap under his chin. He always did this

I

when patrolling. 'It's a disgrace, a member of the Force losing his cap. Accidentally or swiped by a corner-boy.'

The Captain, removing his helmet, wiped his brow with the side of his hand. His red hair lay on his skull like mashed carrots.

'Halt.'

The men stopped; strung out motionless, like a line of scarecrows. One of them had a fit of coughing.

'Shut it.'

From the shed he could see them; all staring up, not knowing he was there; eyes flecks of flint in shards of stone. The scraggy land below him broke his heart. In the distance between two hills – one brown from withered ragwort, the other black from burnt whins – he could see the Finn, gleaming like young skin, snake its way across the Border. He and Prunty had swum it, smuggled over it, fished it, walked it, picnicked along it, watched it for pleasure when the moon was drowning three hundred thousand miles below.

At the bottom of the fields behind him, slipping through the land like a sunburnt hand ruckling silk, was another river – the Annaghlee. Even if he could have seen it from the shed he wouldn't have looked. His heart was broken. His body drained. His brain aching for reason and sleep.

The air was razor-cold. The hard, dry clay freezing. He didn't know how long he'd lain in the shed. Couldn't remember what he'd done with his clothes. They'd see his unwashable body. Let them.

He was at war. It was both secret and visible. It had real wounds but the worst blows came out of the dark in broad daylight. This neck of the woods, the tangled heart of Cavan, Monaghan and Fermanagh, needed lives to fill its watery veins with wine. It ate flesh. Drank souls.

His father led the soldiers nearer. They were spread out and stalking up the hill. He could hear their boots sog the ground, see their breath curdle on the frost.

He was naked as a spider. Just outside the shed doorway was a clump of rushes. That was the true symbol of Ireland. Not shamrock. A bluebottle with green velvet body landed on the fuzzy brown flower asprout a stalk. A heron floated down the sky.

Maybe the soldiers would riddle the shed for practice. Good. Maybe the shock on his father's face would kill him quickly. Good. Maybe his heart would break from loneliness. Now. Before they got to him. The Pontius Pilate bluebottle wrung its hands and was gone.

Two soldiers, crouching over their cocked rifles, burst into the shed. He looked calmly up at them. They were khaki pillars of stone, face flesh rotting in shock. The tiny shed darkened as more bodies wedged the doorway, soaking the light. One of them knelt and made the sign of the cross.

'He's not dead. His eyes . . .'

At the entrance was the chaos of a ruck as those outside, unaware, tried to get in.

'What's up?'

'Stand back, stand back. There's a body.'

'Let the dog see the rabbit!'

'Out. Out. That's an order.'

Into the clearing space came his father and the Captain. In his father's eyes was the terror that comes from shame. The Captain was trying to puzzle out the spectacle – was it one of war or madness?

'Do you know him, Sergeant?'

'I know him all right. He's my son.'

Outside, the soldiers went quiet. In a far field Fay's donkey choked on the silence, a halter of guffaws tightening its neck.

'Oh my God. Oh my God and His Holy Mother. What happened to you?' Realization took root in his father's eyes. Black and white testicles were a proclamation. 'Have you any clothes at all?'

'Fold the ground over me.'

'You have my heart broken.'

'That's what hearts are for.'

His father tried to lift him, but he thrashed like a dying pike. He felt his body was long and cold, his brain up one end, like a lonely calf standing at the far hedge of a field.

They piled on top of him, belted him in coats, then carried him down the hill to the Cavan-Clones road.

Bundled on a jeep seat, he was driven along the hill-and-hollow roads of the sub-district of Butlershill. His father had served here for years. His life had melted into the people's. He was sober with the sober, drunk with the drunks, drove to football matches with the sportsmen and was happy only when he met a criminal. He wasn't often happy. IRA men, smugglers, cockfighters were early risers and as elusive as the wind. The remaining

3

locals were God- and police-fearing; their crimes as petty as their sins. Guilty or innocent, all were punished alike by the land, the water, wind and rain. The drumlin fields were everywhere and had to be walked up, grazed up, ploughed up, sown up, reaped up. They were hard put to find a field flat enough for football. Even the village green sloped. And the houses running along the base of the triangular green were on an incline severe enough to throw the last two out of kilter with the rest.

The soldiers shouted, jeered. The jeep had stalled going up the Red Brae. He could smell oil and boiling water. Engines weren't built for these endless steep ridges. Braes, the locals called them. They had driven round this the long way, to avoid crossing the Border into Northern Ireland. The Irish army weren't allowed into Fermanagh. The British army weren't allowed into Cavan. You had two armies blundering around, trying to avoid crossing over into the other's territory. The land was impervious to maps. What appeared plain on paper was on the ground an orgy of political and geographical confusion. Cavan and Monaghan in the South were locked into Fermanagh in the North, like two dogs trying to cover the one hot bitch.

People, land and water flowed over and back, making nonsense of steel girders stuck in roads and blown-up bridges. 'If Westminster is the Mother of Parliaments,' his father often declared, 'she's also the mother of one hell of a bastard round this neck of the woods.'

The driver shouted angrily, his curse lingering in the air like a hawk. 'The fecking hoor's melt!'

The men, jumping out of the jeep, began to push it up the hill. His father stayed.

Rainwater gulging from a sheugh poured out on to the road. The hill, red from iron ore deposits in the soil, was a rusty river flowing down into a bottom the far side of a blackthorn hedge. A bottom was the swampy land at the bottom of a brae. People used the word unaware of its ambiguities. 'Me cattle's gone into Tommy Fay's bottom.'

In the hollows of all the hills were bottoms or lakes. Great stretches of water or hordes of small round lochs lying shiny like shillings in the sun. He could see one of them now – Lady's Lake, where he and his father swam in summer. An Englishwoman had drowned herself there a hundred years ago. Drowned herself from love gone wrong. A family of swans, slow as mist, breasted out from a cover of bullrushes.

4

It was enough of itself to break your heart with its beauty and its pain.

His father stared at him, his eyes wet with rage. The thin, shiny cap-strap still looping his face twitched every time he tensed his jaw muscles. His full lips were drawn thin, his chin set grim. He was scowling from the effort to keep words bottled up. They knew too much about each other. One slipped syllable and they could be on the floor of the clapped-out jeep, going for each other's throats. A drying tide-mark of mud skimmed his great boots. In his seated position, the cylindrical leather quiver containing his truncheon and hanging from his tunic belt jutted across his thigh. 'I've done more damage with that yoke than Wyatt Earp ever did with his gun.'

His trouser bottoms, furled on his ankles, were held in place by his bicycle clips. The dark blue of his uniform repelled the soldiers' green. No matter where he was – at a football match, in chapel on Sunday, at home or squeezed up in the corner of an army jeep – he always seemed alone. Lonely. Like a great rock sticking out of a grassy field. They stared at one another. Then they looked away. They knew each other's thoughts. A head could only hold so many variables. And hardly any variables at all when the end of the road was near.

The soldiers clambered back on the jeep as it began to freewheel down the other side of the hill. When the engine caught, they grunted, relieved.

When at last they swept down into the village, the convoy of lorries, jeeps and turreted armoured cars stopped outside the post office. He could see the Captain go into the post office; returning with a stamp which he licked and stuck on to a blue envelope. One of the soldiers gave a knowing wink. A love letter.

The letter-box built into the wall of the post office, though painted green, was still emblazoned with the royal insignia, G R, surmounted by a crown. It was a constant irritant to his father. 'That's what Independence gave us – the freedom to give everything English a lick of green. Nothing bleddywell changed deep down.' He hated England but spent most of his waking hours hunting her enemies.

Women and children gathered round the jeep. The news had spread ahead of them.

'Divine God he has, he's arrested his own son.'

'He looks famished. Lord, Sergeant, but you're a terrible eejit.'

'Are you all right, gauson? Never done no harm to no one.'

His father looked down on them. Had he thrown manure over them it couldn't have been more effective than his words. 'Look at them – the gulpins! Away home and sweep your kitchens. If you own a broom.' The soldiers laughed.

One of the women had bare, red-roasted ankles from sitting all day in front of the fire. Slatterns, his father called such women.

'There's no greater hindrance to a man than to marry a slattern.'

'Yes,' his mother had replied, 'slattern or slave, it must be terrible for the poor man.'

'Oh we are smart, aren't we? If we're not careful your tongue will cut our throats.'

His father's tongue was the sharpest knife in the house. It could bleed the statue of a saint.

The women, in a cowed huddle, tried to brazen it out but his father's eyes were killing. He knew and liked the women. Lovely laughers who gave him mugs of 'tay'.

Tethered on a long, much-knotted rope to the pump on the village green was a white goat. One of the women went to it and, squatting on her hunkers behind it, milked it through its hind legs into a two-pound jam-jar. The convoy, revving and clattering to life, drove out of the village alongside the high, ivy-blanketed stone wall of Lady Sarah Butler-Coote's vast demesne. A few hundred yards later it came to a stop outside the police station. Home. The Arctic Circle of the soul. Grates without fires. A table without food. Icy lino. Wet walls. Damp bed. The Sacred Heart above the mantelpiece burning without heat.

His mother . . . if . . . He was crying as they carried him in and sat him on the wooden bench-bed in the cell. Prison. The black hole, they called it.

'I'm sorry,' said his father, 'I'll bring you tea in a minute. You'll have to clean yourself up. Somehow.'

The cell door thudded shut. The heavy bolt, disturbed for the first time in ages, squealed, then grumbled into place. A slit high up in the wall let in a slant of dying light. His run ended, he was snared in his own den. As a boy he had played prisoners here with his friends.

Down in the corner a lead pipe stuck straight out through the wall. Through this vent locked-up drunks were supposed to relieve themselves. By the pipe opening a smudged thumb-print of day lay on the concrete floor. Rats came in that way. He wasn't afraid of them, though they'd ruined his life. But the shadows, the brain-whisperings, queueing up in corners would torment him all night long and he could never send them scuttling.

Dying wasn't easy. He would confront them – altogether or one by one. His pain keeping him alive.

The cell was barer than a confession-box.

2

'Yet once more, O ye laurels, and once more
Ye myrtles brown, with ivy never sere,
I come to pluck your berries harsh and crude,
And with forced fingers rude . . .'

It was his favourite poem. Even though it was summer holidays
he sat at the table reading it aloud, his mother making an apple
pie, pretending to listen.

'Ah, that's lovely now, that bit.'

'Which bit?'

She laughed. 'Go along with you.'

Her hands were caked with milky flour. Plumping out her
lower lip she blew upwards at wisps of hair falling down along
her nose. In the swish of her breath they danced above her forehead like a pony's tail. Her bosom bulged her apron and the
strings tight around her waist were sunk in a groove of fleshy
clothes.

In the range flames battled at the grate bars and roared in
escape up the chimney. He could feel the heat on his face and in
the oilcloth on the table see the trapped light drowning. His
mother loved heat. After cooking dinner, even on hot days, she
tried to keep the fire going. 'No heat, no home.'

But heat was money. Timber. Turf. Coal from England. His
father couldn't look in the grate without seeing his savings burning. 'You'd frazzle a hole in Rockefeller's pocket, never mind
mine. Put it out.'

The week before, he'd taken her by the arm and in silence
walked her out of the married quarters on to the hilly road overlook-
ing the village.

'Look down there. What do you see?'

'What are you at? See what?'

'What do you notice? Don't pretend you don't know.' His fingers, gripping her, were tight as his face.

His mother's big eyes brimmed with innocence and pain. They had been married for years, and she was still frightened because you could never gauge his mood.

'Well, I'll tell you. Look at all them chimneys down there. Not one of them has smoke coming out of them. Not one. Now look at ours. Belching bejeepers like an iron foundry.'

'I've only two sods of turf on. And a block.'

'You have in me hat. That's coal burning or I'm a Dutchman.'

'Am'n't I baking bread sure? For tomorrow.'

'Trust you always to have an answer.' Waving his arm at the trees behind the demesne wall he shouted, 'You'd burn the entire wood in a week if you could.'

They walked back in silence, the studs on his father's boots striking sparks on the road.

The impersonal heat of the range was as good as love to her. Flame was better than a man's tongue. It was the one comfort impervious to rickety chairs, cold lino, damp walls. Hot was a good mood, cold a bad one. It was her only succour. Men were mad with passion one moment, the next a hard frost on your soul. Days of good mood were instantly wiped out by the next bad one. Mood stank. Of sick and sin. Blue mould of the soul. Brain canker. Seat of stupidity. Cause of our woe. Spiritual suicide. Vessel of dishonour. Hysterical rose. Towering Dad. Tower of burning eyes. House of pig iron. Bark. Gate of Hell. Mourning Ma. Sick of the healthy . . . He had a litany of mood in his head. Stone music. Which he spewed out to his mother when they were alone.

His father came to the back window and looked in at them. He was working in the garden, digging. Forcing vegetables out of the clay with manure and rage. Framed in the window, wearing his battered brown hat, an old collarless police shirt and wide braces, he was a picture of peasant malevolence. Seated safely at the table, cut off from him, he sniggered at his father, pretending he was laughing at something in the book he held up to his face. He could see his father's eyes narrow.

Face flushed, his mother mashed flour and buttermilk in the big blue bowl, then wiped her silted fingers gently along a knife edge. She looked at him. 'What?'

He nodded to the window. Turning, she looked and smiled.

'Send that fellah out here.'

Dull as rocks the words came at him through the glass. As shorn of humanity as was possible to command flesh and blood. He wasn't going to budge. He was happy in the kitchen reading, watching his mother, basking with her in the fleshy warmth of the range.

The garden at the rear of the married quarters was a penitential plot in which his father always seemed at war. Clay clogged his shovel. Roots tangled the prongs of his fork. Stones blunted the edge of his spade.

'Ah-ha, ya beggar. You would be there, wouldn't you?'

Each stone he flung on to a pile as high as a wheelbarrow. Clack. 'Cavan clay – you could pave roads with it.'

Over the edge of his book he saw him turn from the window.

'You better go out to him.'

'I'm not. I'm on holiday. What does he want me for anyway?' It was a useless, weak question.

From a cracked jug she poured a long tongue of buttermilk into the bowl. White fluted flesh ending in a splatter. He loved watching her. Her brown eyes that had the moment only in them. That was the interesting thing about women. They never thought of the future. He was studying women, his eyes hungry for them. But he hadn't as yet been able to get close enough to one of them. Girls had quickstep eyes.

His mother's eyes danced a slow waltz.

'What are you thinking?'

'I'm thinking if you don't go out to him there'll be murder.'

'I'll go out in a minute.'

Her forehead was a broad bump of shiny skull, higher on the side of her hair-parting. She hated the gleamy skin and every morning powdered it thickly. She liked her nose. It was straight, firm, haughty. 'It's worth looking down, anyway.'

The gentle groove on her upper lip puckered her mouth to a bow. When she pencilled on lipstick it was a burning bow which could fire arrows into anyone's heart.

'I dreamt last night of poor Emily. I was knocking on her coffin but she wouldn't let me in. Oh, we were heartbroken when she died. God help us, only twelve. The Old Chap went on a terrible batter. It lasted a month. He came in one night and beat us with a stair-rod. He was a demon in drink. He rooted the rods out, eyes and all, and pulled the lino up off the steps. Then whallicked us. I saw him washing his face in his urine one time. Dipping into the pooley pot like it was the basin. If one of us was ill, though, he was very kind. Poor Emily.'

The sounds on her tongue were soft and guttery. Like candle flame. They had the drum of fingers testing new-baked bread. She began to sing a Robbie Burns – 'Ae fond kiss and then we sever . . .' Scotland was her favourite country, though she never set foot outside Ireland apart from a brief honeymoon in London.

Head on hand he watched her through spread fingers, looking for hints, trying to understand women, comparing her with town girls that away from home fed his starving eyes.

She was full to the brim with life. But she slept on her own, the door locked against his father. Passion was stronger than bolts.

As he lay in bed one night reading by the light of a candle (*Henry IV Part 1*), he heard the springs on his father's bed suddenly squeal, then the door, swollen by damp, judder open. Hearing his big bare feet swotting the hallway tiles, he snuffed the candle and lay pretending to be asleep. He assumed he was coming to check he wasn't reading late into the night, wasting electricity and shortening the life of the 40-watt bulb. He sensed him at the keyhole, heard his stomach gurgle. He was up to something. Making sure he was asleep. He didn't want a witness.

Big feet mashing the night, he went back down the hallway. He lay listening. Knocks on his mother's door. Gentle at first, knuckles scuffing the panel. The more urgent they became, the deeper grew the dark. Night disturbed was a bat's wing beating his face to pulp. A burst tar barrel spilling over him. Black blood rushing in his ears. On his bed was a sheet, a grey blanket and a police greatcoat. Night disturbed, and the coat weighed a ton. Through the walls he heard his mother's voice.

'Who's there?'

'Who do you think?'

'What do you want?'

'Ask me an easy one.' Derision came off his father's tongue natural as spit.

Behind the station a fox barked on Brady's Hill. It was a string of yelps hanging over the house. A rosary of pain snapping, the foxy beads cascading on to the slates. The fox barking. His mother crying. Fox. Woman. He heard her door splatter inwards, screws squelch from wood, the frail bolt rattling on the lino, his father's howl of loneliness. Like an animal in a trap. Then a silence, pregnant as a harvest moon.

Flesh was for flesh. Denied, the body withered, the brain turned mad, you rotted in a living death. Or you exploded. He couldn't bear exploding silences. In them his father's blood drowned his mother's spirit. Why? Why didn't they sleep together?

Getting out of bed he dressed quickly, took the greatcoat and quietly opening the window clambered out into the night.

Across the road from the Garda station was the Coote demesne – a walled-in paradise of forested hills, avenues lined with copper beech, regiments of Scots pine, massive oaks standing sentry in open fields, and round by the lake a littoral of sweeping lawns edging up to the mansion in which, alone, lived Lady Sarah Butler-Coote. At night the demesne darkness terrified. That's why he went there. It took one fear to drive out another. Each leaf was a black teardrop washing away his mother's face. Every scuttle in the undergrowth drowned his father's cry.

His father's greatcoat draped round his shoulders, his boots unlaced, he trudged along the gravel path making for the boat-house.

Feeling lonely came easy. It was almost pleasurable. It sharpened his thoughts, whittled them to an essential point. He was in a way envious of his father; at least he had someone engaging his being night, noon and morning. He could put his shoulder to a door and break in. Why did women and men grow tired of eating at the same dish? If only he could meet a girl he would be magnetized to her forever. Flesh was for flesh.

In a clump of rhododendron two badgers grunted. A startled pigeon flittered out from a tree and, the air whinnying in its wake, shot off through the dark. An owl hooted a woody note of hushed music. Night shut your eyes, robbed your body, turned your brain into a bird. A hovering creature with feathery movement eating dreams. Hatching and eating them simultaneously. Dreams were brain fog steaming up your soul eyes. Your mind in the black was a dream of a dream.

Girls. A girl. A body. A soul he could cope with. His mother's soul shone in her eyes. He could cope with that even if his father couldn't. Souls were easy. But they came in bodies. Bare bodies. A bare body was the most tantalizing mystery of them all.

At the start of the holidays he had gone one evening to the well for water. As he passed the Methodist Chapel a woman coming out the pathway laughed when she saw him. Dusk was falling, but he knew immediately it was Tilly Roberts. Her laugh was a peculiar short scream of ridicule and hysteria.

'What are you laughing at?'

'I can laugh when I like. It's a free country.'

Opening the half-gate, he went in towards her. She was wearing a royal-blue skirt and matching jacket. On her head was a small, square blue hat. Like a chalice veil.

He was often in her house when he was a child but since he'd gone away to school he'd never met her on her own. A preacher, she had fierce religion and a husband, Bobby, who sold eggs and insurance. She roamed the Border country spreading the Word of God in towns and villages overdosed on it. Hating Papists, she knew if she couldn't save them she could annoy them. 'I come among you to save you . . . The Whore in Rome will not save you . . . only the Word can save.' She stood on street-corners or on seaside beaches ranting for Jesus. Her husband travelled with her and accompanied her hymn-singing on a hurdy-gurdy. Her pointed bosom, high cheekbones, diamond eyes, slug-thick lips and hanks of flaxy hair could, according to his friend Prunty, 'raise steam from a stone'. Because of her long legs and very high-heeled shoes, she had a walk so tipsy that coming towards you in the street she seemed about to totter into your arms.

'Howaya, Tilly?'

He had ordered from his brain a sophisticated, carefree sentence, but the words delivered by his tongue were jumbled, pathetic, dry, nervous. His heart hammered out of control.

'What do you want?'

'It's a free country. Where are you preachin' these days?'

'I don't have to travel far to find heathens.'

Dusk was folding them up. There was safety in that. He wanted her white blouse of breasts against him. He could smell her. A sweet, mouldy, fermenting smell like old gooseberry jam. She and the dusk were one. A veil of perfume. Night smoke.

Passion blocked his arteries, starved his brain of sense. He stepped into her, his knee touching her leg.

'Would you save *me*, Tilly?'

A light came on in the chapel. She laughed, her chin high, her neck like the arch of her instep. The light behind made a monstrance of her head. He wanted to touch with his tongue the lunette of her lips. Swivelling on her heel with such a snap of speed that her hair whipped his face, she pranced into the chapel.

He stumbled back out the pathway and in the adjoining over-grown garden sat by the well on the upturned bucket. He felt foolish, ashamed. He had tried to court her, the bucket in his hand and wearing wellingtons with the tops turned down. And for all the grand poetry in his head not one word of it came to his aid. The moves of sex were beyond him. He could play chess, quote at least three Shakespeare sonnets, and on the football field trade his body in hectic rough-and-tumble with complete strangers. But in front of Tilly, who was married to a runt, his waxy spirit guttered hopelessly away. And he nearly did some-thing dangerous. He was within an ace of pulling her to the ground, falling on top of her and crying out, 'I love you, Tilly, will you be mine?' What a fool! He hadn't spoken to the woman since he was twelve and anyway she was married to Bobby Roberts, even though he was a runt and wore two pairs of spec-tacles at the same time – one on his nose, the other perched on his forehead. It would have been some sight for Bobby had he come out of the Methodist Chapel and found the Sergeant's son on top of his wife, telling her he loved her. It was a mystery. His head was brimming with the longings of the lonely. Sex drove you to love. Or love drove you to sex. Either way it was enough to drive you mad, and was a courtly game for which you required diplo-matic skills. He was no diplomat; not in wellingtons with a bucket in his fist, he wasn't. And a pair of uniform trousers given to him by his father and roughly cut down to size by his mother. 'Here – they'll do you. Sure no one will see you in them.' 'If that's the case,' he had answered, 'I may as well go naked.' 'That's enough of that,' said his father. 'You should be damned glad to have them.'

The light in the chapel went out, the door banged, the big key turned in the lock. He listened to Tilly's high-heels grating on the road. He dipped the bucket into the well, heard its deep gulp fill to a watery sigh, then sat it brimming on the flat stone. He could hear something clinking against the handle. It was a frog trying to clamber out. He scooped it up and felt its throat pulse against his fingers, its slimy legs kick frantically for safety. Night was fully down. A bat zipped above his head. Bat wings. Frog legs. A hurrying corncrake cried through a meadow. Crake. Tilly's heels.

He had sat by the well that evening trying to plot a path to sense. And now in the pitch-black night he would sit in the boathouse and try and do the same. He walked on through the demesne, his boots clacking on the stony avenue. A violent shaft of light hit him in the face.

'What the frig are you up to?'

'It's a free country.'

'Not in here it isn't.'

'I'd appreciate if you stopped shining that light in my eyes.'

'Oh you'd appreciate it, would you? I thought you might have been the steward. You very near got a clock on the gob.'

'Did I? You and whose army?'

'Oh you're a great man when you're out. Like a donkey's tool. When you're with your oul' fellah there's not a meg out of you.'

In the mouths of the locals words were wasps. Late autumn ones. They sounded lazy but were drunk on sting. Ex-Private Jimmy Kelly had served with the British army in Egypt, returning in triumph with a disability pension. Now his days were spent hunting and fishing and many of his nights poaching in Lady Sarah's demesne.

'Now you're here you might as well lend a hand. Houl' tha'. But don't shine it yit.'

Taking the torch, he listened as Kelly stretched nets over a raised mound of earth and scrub. He could hear him secure the nets with forked pegs which he tapped home with his boot. When above them the clouds ripped and the moon poured down, Kelly became a ghostly figure bending over the silver ground. Tap. His movements were furtive, his aim to kill as many rabbits as he could. The earth smelt of rot and rain and the trees slept in a dreamy swish.

Tiny bells jingled. He could see the long body of a ferret dangling from Kelly's hand. He'd taken it from a box on the back of his bicycle.

'The friggin' moon. If oul' Hopkinson comes, you grab up the nets and I'll deal with him.'

Hopkinson was Lady Sarah's steward. His job was to run her estate, hire and fire the labourers and keep Kelly from annihilating her stock of game, fish and rabbits.

'Right. I'm puttin' her in. When they come runnin' out, shine the light in their eyes.'

The moon heaped his back as he bent with the ferret to a rabbit-hole. Tiny bells jingled. Were muffled. Went silent as the ferret worked deep into the warren.

He had come into the woods for peace, to escape his parents' struggle. Yet here he was, a bare half-hour later, helping to inflict death on poor dumb sleeping creatures of God. 'Edible pests', that's what his father called them. 'You can't beat a young grazer in a stew.'

Suddenly the ground was a thumping panic of scurrying bodies as a flock of rabbits tore out from their burrows. Crashing into one another they hopped and tumbled around in demented circles, but couldn't escape the net.

'Shine the friggin' light!'

The beam hit a rabbit in the eyes, stunning it long enough for Kelly to clump it on the head with the back of a spade. The net bulged with scuttling bodies but the pegs held. Quickly Kelly worked through them, killing them with single blows. He counted fourteen clumps of the spade. The last rabbit alive began to squeal. He shone the light. Mesmerized it stared into the beam, its big glassy eyes popping, lips crinkled back from its buck teeth in terror. Clump. Sleepy Death shut its eyes. An owl hooted. The moon drowned.

He picked a rabbit up, stroked its body. It was still warm, soft, furry, giving . . . A living girl's body might feel the same . . .

Tiny bells jingled. Kelly whipped the nets back and as the ferret emerged from a burrow pinned it by the neck, then popped it into the deep pocket of his army overcoat. Rabbit eyes in the torchlight were innocent beads. The ferret's glistened icicle-sharp. He walked on towards the lake.

Kelly called after him. 'Don't you want a couple, to bring home?'

'No thanks.'

'Frig you then. You'll follow the crows for them yit, lad.'

By the time he got to the boathouse the sky was a stack of soot. For all he could see he might as well have had his head up a blocked chimney. In the country on such a night, the clouds above them drumlin high, darkness was complete. He could smell the heavy sweetness of rhododendron, bullrush, reed, waterlily, the boggy undergrowth, the slightly stagnant water at the edge, but he couldn't catch even a hint of light on the surface of the lake or hear a sound.

The boathouse was an open-fronted log construction with a thatch of reeds. A bench ran round the side and back walls. When Lady Sarah had guests from England they used the place when shooting duck. It provided ideal cover when the ducks came in to land. The lake being completely surrounded by trees, they had to swoop down steeply and always right in front of the boathouse. From there it was easy for sleepy Death to surprise them and shut their eyes.

He sat listening to the doldrum night. Silence beat his ears. The black air lay thick on his tongue, bunged his mouth, trickled down into his heart, pressuring him, weighting his lungs with tar. In his own room with the light out, or here in the boathouse, night could grip like his father's fist.

He was a sitting duck. Afraid of his father and even more afraid of his mother's frailty. Last time his father hit him he went into a convulsion of terror, anger and vengeance. His mother managed to bundle him into the oil-house, not letting him out until he had calmed. Why should he be beaten? A beating was just a conscious bungling of the subconscious desire for murder.

He knew his father's father was a tough man. 'You think you've got it bad? You should have seen Dada in full swing. I saw him winding the jennet with a fist to her guts one day, when she wouldn't move. You see, the people them times . . . they had to be tough.' Why should patterns be repeated? Why should the wheel keep coming full circle? What else could a wheel do? Could a wheel escape the rut?

Out on the lake he heard the flip and plop of a fish. It was a clear, clean sound. Full. Like a cork coming out of a bottle. At the moment it happened it was the only sound in the world. And he, in the silent darkness, was the only person in the world to hear it. It might have been the reason he was alive. To be there at that second, when depth of lake and sky came together in his mind. Flip-plop. Fish music. They didn't need tongues when they could create such beauty with their bodies. Though his friend Prunty had told him a pike could make a noise with its mouth. But only if the pain was great enough.

All his fears left him. He was happy. The best things in life were invisible. Untouchable. But then where did that leave girls? As loud as he could, he hummed the tonic sol-fa, holding the last note for seconds before abruptly cutting it dead. He listened for reaction or echo.

'Are you the Sergeant's boy?' The words were slurred, plummy, very English-sounding, and could only have come from the mouth of Lady Sarah Butler-Coote. She must have been sitting in the boathouse all the time.

'You knocked the heart crossways in me.'

'When I heard you coming I thought it might be lovers. Then when I knew you were on your own I decided to sit tight. Sorry.'

Lovers! In Butlershill they came out only at night. When he got a lover he'd take her on to the village green and in broad daylight kiss her up against the village pump.

'It's not fair. You should have acknowledged my existence. However inferior you consider it.'

'Oh don't be so silly. I said sorry. Anyway you're not supposed to be in the demesne after dark. That's why we lock the gates.'

'I climbed over the wall.'

'Indeed?' It was a short word, but she managed to inflect it with understated privilege and outraged ownership. Her accent was an asset as priceless as her land.

'It's a free country. Your ancestors stole it. No amount of dusty documents in your family vault will prove otherwise.'

'What tosh! Besides, do you think if Chief O'Reilly or some such noble savage was still in possession, you could so readily hop in and out as you please? Hm?'

He loved arguing with her. But he felt ashamed. He was at ease with her because she was old. If she were young – his age? Would he be so teasing, relaxed, then?

'It's a great old tickler, the past. It can still make us laugh till we cry. Hm? What do you think?'

'I don't know, Lady Sarah. It's the present I'm trying to escape.'

'Did you hear the fall of that fish?'

'Of course I did. It was the aural equivalent of a falling star.'

'Hm. Or moonrock clunking before a lunar storm.'

Everyone knew Lady Sarah dreamt of the moon. She had two territories – her demesne and space. Still fit though in her nineties, she lived alone in Coote House, a rambling Georgian pile slowly sinking under a weight of ivy on the outside and a variety of rot inside. She had never married. Over the best part of a century a succession of men had travelled from England with high hopes of a fortune. But those who weren't drunks or mental defectives fled when they saw her face. The rest retreated before the lash of her tongue.

Her ugliness was phenomenal. The tip of her tiny nose curved upwards and pulled her lip into a V, which revealed an upper row of ratty teeth. Over her eyes she had to wear thick lenses; in daylight hours she went round blinking at the world and, unable to see it properly, dismissed most of it. 'God help her,' his mother said, 'but she's got a face like a bat.'

She lived for her trees, her birds, rabbits, cats, fish, and the moon. When as a boy with his friend Prunty he had fished the lake, she often sprang from the bushes to inspect their hooks.

'Much too big, my dears. I cannot allow it. You must only use small hooks. The big ones are too too cruel.'

Even then he liked arguing with her. 'You don't allow big hooks? Yet you allow the ducks to be shot out of the sky!'

'The savage traditions of my visiting friends I must occasionally allow. For fear of something worse if I didn't.'

Lady Sarah lived in her dreams. And when she couldn't sleep she wandered the woods or sat in the boathouse.

'I've had a recurring moon dream. Over fifty years now. There is a cavern on the floor of the Mare Marginis. And in it, chiselled on the span of the roof, is the impression of a butterfly. This impression, inches deep, is filled with gold. How do *you* account for that?'

'Dreams bore me. Even my own.'

'You're rude. Insolent.'

'And descriptions of car crashes. And playing cards. Especially twenty-five. And people who still go round singing "Hot Diggity".'

'Go home now. Please.'

A wind came up the lake, lukewarm with dark perfumes. Resin oozing from pine-tree wounds. Dewy rhododendron blossom. Stirring water. Mulch of leaf and earth piled on the forest floor. Suddenly the mountainous ocean of blackness ripped open. At its heart the full moon struggled to break free. White wispy clouds tangling its face, it flickered, grew, dimmed, then raging up, boiled over like a saucepan of milk, its silvery light pouring down on to the lake. Now they could see the fishbone ripples on the water, the reeds and rushes shiver, the trees sleepwalking, their tattered nightclothes billowing behind. The demesne was both black and white, like a photographic negative held up to light. Two owls flew across, their shadows flitting with them on the water.

Getting up, he walked the logged ramp from the boathouse to the shore. The moon in triumph had turned the night to mercury. His boots still stubbornly untied, he cracked along the avenue, angry with himself. It was something his father did when moody – crash around the kitchen, laces unknotted, studs welting the linoleum, his very feet in a temper. Under the oak trees, brooding shadows knelt like figures at a wake. He could glimpse the horse-eyed moon peeping at him down through the tree-tops, wild and white and roving. Off to the right on the other side of iron railings a rising hill of grassland lay in a sleepy heap. Near the crown of the hill stood a horse-chestnut. In dreamy sleep it slumbered, its massive branches holding up the sky.

He thought of the dead rabbits, the fish, the owls, the hummed notes he sang over the water. He and they and the wood were one. They were all going round the sun along with Lady Sarah's moon. Dizzy or dead before the meaning of existence, it didn't matter which. But for certain he wanted someone with whom he could share the journey.

He looked at the chestnut again. His heart bucked to panic. A man had come out from behind the trunk and stood watching him. The man was completely naked. Pale as snow, rigid as marble, he glowed in ghostly whiteness. Large-limbed, with bulky belly, he could have been the tree's spirit made flesh. It was Hopkinson, Lady Sarah's steward. He could tell from the bald head and the dark shadow of the handlebar moustache under his nose.

Cashiered from the British army, he had come to Butlershill to escape his past. But in the barracks the boy knew his father had a file on him. 'By cripes, it must have been something shocking he did for that crew to get rid of him. The whole class of them are cross-bred from unnatural acts. That's a fact. There was never any homosexuality in this country till the British army brought it in.' 'Well,' answered his mother, 'they didn't have to carry it in in suitcases.'

He walked on, stopped, turned. He was still there, staring after him, his nakedness challenging the night. A slab of moon fallen to earth. Eerie. Sexual. Still.

In the dip of the field lay a flock of sheep. Hewitt's beagle barking in the distance, they shifted from sleep, rumping to their feet, gurgling in their throats, bleating. A pheasant shot past his face, its wings whirring with the intense sound of a horse snorting. He had come to the demesne for solitude and found it full. Killers, dreamers, perverts, the lonely and the lost, all one under the moon, all walking in sleep, trying to murder time. Desire had forced them from their beds.

Back at the station, he lay in bed listening. His father groaned in sleep. He sensed his mother was awake, her big brown eyes swimming in the dark. The house was quiet as the grave. Drifting to sleep, he could hear through the wall the telephone ring in the barracks day-room. The guard on duty slept in the dormitory and with a feed of drink in his belly couldn't be awakened by a bomb.

> '. . . bitter constraint and sad occasion dear
> Compels me to disturb . . .'

He sat at the table, arms folded on top of his poetry book, head down, dozing on his arms. He could feel the heat of the range on one side of his body. And hear the tack-clickety of the wooden spoon as his mother stirred ingredients in the blue bowl. Skim milk splashed into the bowl. His mother's arms were freckled, creamy, and along the inside where the sun never reached, pale and glistening like the flesh of a split-open apple.

'You're sitting there dreaming now. Do you want him to come in for you?'

He looked up at her. Away at school she was the only thing he missed. Her big brown eyes were soft, clear, dancing with honesty and – whenever she got the chance – fun. Her full face was strong and gave back whatever it received. If you said something amusing it gleamed. If his father was in a mood, it darkened, her brow a knit of worry. She reflected light and dark like a lake. On her neck, the colour of burnt toast, was a crumb of flesh with a solitary black hair. Like a wart, it had tiny cracks in it. 'It's a mole, if you don't mind! My beauty spot. A lady's skin is too refined for anything else.'

He loved it when she got cross. You couldn't call it anger. She became girlish, shaking her head vigorously and smacking her lips together. The wisps of hair across her face she slapped away with her fingers to show how angry she was. This always made him laugh. He loved the words tumbling out of her. 'I'm flitterin' mad. I'm so angry I could eat myself. You or him do nothing, me do everything. If them boots are still lying there when I come back in there's going to be wigs on the green. And it's no laughing matter. All covered with mud on them everywhere all over the floor.'

When she raged he hugged her, his head on her shoulder, his cheek by her neck. It seemed to quieten women; well, his mother.

'I suppose I'd better go out to him. What does he want?'

'Go out and ask him. By the time it's tea I'll have an apple pie as well.'

He stood up and put his book in the belly of the sewing-machine.

'I wish you wouldn't do that.'

'It's the one place I know I'll find it.'

He closed the hinged flap down with a slap. The machine was the smoothest object in the house. Apart from his father's truncheon. The wooden frame of the machine was the same colour as the truncheon. Chestnut. His mother kept it polished, and in the long narrow drawer on the left were her spools, thread, needles, buttons, a button-stick and Brasso for his father's uniform, and a tin of bicycle oil with a nozzle like a snipe's beak. In the drawer on the right was a white comb hand-painted with a cluster of red roses, blue spiralled rings for hens' legs, a puce pencil, an American dime, a tin handle with a prick at one end like a bee's sting (for cleaning the oil-hole on the primus stove), a frayed yellow tape-measure, a box of DDT, corset whalebones (which he liked twanging), a faded silver spoon which had belonged to her mother, a roll of crêpe bandage for her legs, a macabre set of plastic false teeth which he'd got one Christmas, holy medals, ribbons for her hair and a spare set of chevrons for his father's sleeve. Both drawers had tiny brass knobs.

When she used the machine it made clickety music. His mother's feet on the treadle, the connector rod came alive like a demented gymnast on a high bar, turning the wheels to a breathy blur, the needle to an insect whirr. It gave off an animal whiff then, a sweat of oil, polish, powder, cloth and his mother's body. In a trellis of metalwork was the machine's name in golden letters – SINGER. Its belly was a fitting place to keep his books.

From the drawer he got the set of false teeth and putting them in his mouth assumed a comic pose. His mother, rolling a slap of dough, pretended not to notice him. He persisted until, unable to resist, she looked fully at him, her shoulders shaking, her face and eyes bright with laughter. She loved him. That at least.

Her golden wedding-ring lay for safety on a jam-jar lid. She always took it off when baking. Flour flecked her blue apron. A wisp of hair fell between her eyes. There was sugar on her lips. It was the last time he saw her happily alive.

When he went out, his father was in the potato shed. Down on one knee searching out rotten spuds and flinging them in a bucket.

The bucket had been a lavatory bucket, with a stout handle and a grip down the side bulging out like a thick upper lip. The shed floor was covered with a scattered mound of old potatoes. They lay on the concrete, a pile of withered skulls. Grey, shrivelled, pus seeping from the cracked skins. A corruption of eyes sprouted from them like stunted tusks.

'What the hell kept you?'

'I was doing something.'

'When I want you – hop to it in future! Don't think you're going to sit in that kitchen the whole summer, me buck. If you do you have another think coming. Empty that.'

Carrying the bucket he went down the path and into the hen-run. The run was in an unused part of the garden sloping down to a swamp but separated from it by a hedge. The swamp lay at the bottom of Brady's Hill. It was a stretch of rushy, undrained land split by a river which rose in a boggy part of Lady Sarah's demesne. The discharge from the nearby creamery turned the turfy water clotty and medicine-grey. He dumped the rotten potatoes through a hole in the hedge. They fell with a splash into an oily puddle. The swamp was also where they buried the contents of their lavatory. After a few days the urine and Jeyes fluid came to the surface. The swamp was a rainbow slick of wet filth, a thriving ground for rats and clumps of rushes.

Pecked clean of vegetation the hen-run was a hard, flattened cake of mud, the colour of wet slate. Hen tracks, in a jumble of incomplete asterisks, were everywhere. In the middle of the run sat a saucepan, the handle missing. A hen drank from it. Pecking into the water, then gulping, raising its head in the air, letting the water slide down its throat. The hens were all Rhode Island Reds, the rooster velvet black with wattle and comb the blazing red of a sinking sun. He watched as it darted after a hen, threatening it to low submission with a squawky cackle. Awkwardly it clambered aboard the hen and, curving its rump down into hers, sexed her for a few trembling moments. Its organ looked like the sprout in a potato's eye.

It was easy for birds and animals. There were no mock civilized rules, just instinct and the right season. If you were a rooster hens lay down for you, spreading themselves to make the treading easier, no bother, dead easy, simple as that.

Tilly Roberts was no hen, that was for certain. More like a bloody rooster. Her sharp beauty its own protection. Her eyes knives. Her tongue a biblical lash. It was a disturbing combination – such severe weapons guarding such an inviting feathery body.

Putting down the bucket he ran after a hen. After a few yards it stopped, crouching before him. Waiting for him as if he were a rooster. Hens did that. If they were being chased by anything greater than themselves they almost immediately submitted, and assuming sex was the object, lay waiting in a sexual spread. God, but roosters had it easy. He picked the hen up. She was warm, soft. With the end of his finger he felt the elastic tightness under her tail. He got a sexual thrill from doing this. An emotional shock. He'd seen his mother doing it. But she was testing for eggs.

'What the hell are you up to?'

Startled, he looked round. His father was on the other side of the netting wire, his face angry as a briar.

'I'm . . . I'm testing for eggs.'

'She doesn't bleddywell need you to tell her if and when she's going to lay. Come on to hell with that bucket. I'm driven demented waiting on you.'

In the shed they knelt side by side ferreting through the whole mound of potatoes for rotten ones. Some were just flimsy balls of skin. Hearts eaten by slugs, they were light as puffballs. Rot was slimy, slug-coloured, and stank of vomit. He hated getting it on his fingers and when he did he wiped them on the concrete floor.

'Quit that. It'll do you no harm.'

'I don't like it.'

'Pity about you.'

His father was crouched at his task as if he were sifting gold. The good he handled like nuggets, the bad, disgust and disdain on his face, he pegged into the bucket where they landed with a squelchy thud. 'Ah-ha, ya beggar!'

It would take ages to go through the whole lot. The mound looked as big as a dead elephant. He hated the job and wanted to be back in the warmth of the kitchen. The sheds were purgatory. All under the one galvanized roof, half were on the police side, the other half on the married quarters side. Since none of the Guards wanted to use them for gardening purposes his father commandeered the lot, apart from the police lavatory and locked fuel shed.

Standing at the rear of the station the sheds were a square mirror-image of the barracks itself. The bungalowed barracks was also divided in two. The main entrance led to the day-room, the Sergeant's office, the cell, the men's dormitory and a tiled kitchen. Round the side was a door into the married quarters. Off the hallway was a kitchen on the left, on the right a tiny sitting-room leading to his bedroom. Down the hallway on one side his mother's bedroom, opposite on the other his father's. In the hallway was a stand laden with overcoats, raincoats, uniform great-coats, capes, mackintoshes, caps and sou'westers. At the back the police garden was divided from the domestic garden by a wall linking the sheds to the barracks. Over the main entrance was the police insignia – *Garda Sioícána na h-Eireann*. Guardians of the Peace of Ireland. His father disparagingly translated it as 'Guardians of a Piece of Ireland'. As on the uniform buttons, in the centre of the insignia were a G and S entwined like a pair of Celtic snakes.

The barracks, purpose-built by the Dublin government, replaced the old dilapidated house used by the British and which they themselves had used long after the RIC departed. 'We're a Free State all right,' said his father. 'We can have any amount of damp for nothing.' The walls swam, the wallpaper was always soggy. Damp loved bodies. Bodies seemed to bring it out. He noticed the bare block walls of the sheds were never damp. But he wouldn't have cared where he lived if the mood of the place was good. Mood was damp. Mood was swamp fever.

His father bent over the potatoes, grunting miserably. His braces, which had worked off his shoulders, hung over his rump like a horse harness. In a temper his face got tight and white. Anger turned flesh and bone to stone. His features – high cheek-bones, stern mouth, pale brow, firm chin, straight nose – might then have been chiselled from marble. The backs of his hands were raw, red, the fingers white and blunt. With the ferocious intent of a badger, he hoked through the spuds as if his life depended on it.

'What are you lookin' at?'

'Nothing.'

'Empty that bucket. And be quick about it.' Crouched, elbow on knee, he adjusted his brown hat. The broad brim circling his head was a ring round a planet of flint.

In the hen-run the hens didn't bother following him in expecta-tion of food. They knew by now there was nothing for them in the bucket. He dumped the fetid mess through the hole in the hedge. It stank like a nightmare from history. His father was from the West. His grandfather had survived the Famine. He and all his tribe had been evicted from houses and land owned by a woman.

'She was a landlady by the name of Mrs Gerrard. If there's justice in the next world if not in this, she's up to the high hole of her arse in hot coals at this very moment. Men, women and children – the Infantry dumped them all on the road. They went a few miles away to a bog, dug holes and lived in them. Till they built mud huts thatched with branches and a layer of clods on top of that. It's where I meself was born. And you can tell that to anyone you like at your grand school. Then when the British set up the Congested District Board, the big estates were split up and we got a stone-built house and twenty-five acres. And do you know where? Back in the very spot from which the people had been evicted. Now who can doubt the subtle workings of God? Have you studied anything about the Congested District Board? I bet you haven't. The only decent thing the British ever done. And you'd swear from what I've seen of your schoolbooks it never happened.'

His father showed no emotion. Feelings. But when he talked of the past he could swell your heart and turn your eyes to springs. The past was stuck in his gut, burning him like ice.

Coming out of the run he paused by the wire gate, noticing the rooster and the hens gathering around it. The rooster, head flushed and jerking curiously, was peeking in the open door of the hen-house. The hen-house was a galvanized affair stuck up against the end wall of the sheds. The door was crudely hinged to the jamb by two strips of faded leather. From where he now stood, through a gap in this arrangement he could see a white egg on the floor. With a fat plop, a rat landed beside it. It seemed to be trying to straddle the egg. Then with its snout it began to push at it.

Not wanting to frighten the rat away, he went over to the far side of the run and waited. The rooster too moved off, squawking indignantly, followed by the hens, one of which he mounted in a cowardly show of normality.

Somehow the rat had removed the egg from a nest up on the roost without breaking it. Now he didn't know what the rat was doing because the open door blocked his view. Then the egg rolled out into the run, the rat nosing behind. The run sloped

26

down to the hedge and it was there the rats nested. It was there the rat was rolling the egg, but because of its oval shape it tended to wobble and spin off the intended course, sometimes curving back up the incline towards the hen-house. But the rat persisted and with scuttling urgency kept guiding it back in the required direction. Its scaly tail swept and twitched, and when at one point it looped in a lazy curl over the top of the egg it reminded him of the G and S in the heart of the Garda insignia. When the egg rolled up against the saucepan in the middle of the run, the rat, as if blind, butted at it but couldn't get it past the obstruction. Belly low, wiping the ground, it fretted about in circles, then – front paws up on the egg – appeared to see the saucepan for the first time. Raising itself on its hindquarters, head flicking quick as a wren, it sniffed at the side of the saucepan.

From the sheds he heard his father calling.

The rat, grey as old hair, ran round the saucepan and, coming to the egg, put its head under the end and lifted it. For a moment it was upright against the saucepan. Then it fell over, spun, rolled free. The rat was in control again and nosed it down the run. Carefully. To stop it racing away it laid its head over it, using the underside of its throat as a brake.

A hen, gingerly stepping away from the flock, risked going to the saucepan for a drink. Another hen, moulting, bellied down in a hollow in the ground and, with a flap of wings and back wriggling, wallowed up a dust bath. The rooster crowed, neck stretched, choking out the sound, its worm of a tongue sticking out sideways from its beak. Over Brady's Hill four wild ducks floated swiftly down the sky, making for the river. The rat, on reaching the hedge, let the egg roll out through a gap; like an old man unsure of his footing it clambered down after the egg, its long dark tail at last disappearing.

All around the run the high fence of wire netting was coming away from the crude posts he and his father had sledge-hammered into the ground. The old nails were rotting to rust in the dozy timber. The wire mesh of netting sagged down like a belly of drizzle. The galvanized sheets of the hen-house had been used for the same purpose in the various stations in which his father had served, from the time he got married. They were battered, the corners turned back like the pages of a book, and had once been painted red. Some of the sheets were in fact tar barrels cut and flattened into shape. These were now so flaky with rust that the flat-headed nails went right through them. In the hen-house the roost was a criss-cross of cranky poles cut from a hedge and the nests were orange-boxes with hay in them. Under the roost a ridge of shit piled up for weeks until it was carted out to the garden dungheap.

Chicken shit was highly regarded by his father. 'It's the best manure going. An onion bed without chicken dung is a cod. The hen not being carnivorous, the droppings hardly smell, compared to us anyway. If it's mixed with clay, no onion will shoot up smaller than an egg. The stinkiest animal on earth is ourselves. I was at an exhumation over in the County Roscommon one time. We had to attend whilst they dug up a suspected murder victim. The stench was killing. I rammed cotton-wool soaked in whiskey up me nostrils. That'll give you some idea. And you could see all the dogs of the country coming from miles round. They'd whiffed it on the wind. Hen manure is pure perfume compared to the like of that.'

On the surface the hen-run was a miserable place. Wet and rats and dung. But when you thought about it, it had mystery. Hens that squatted before you. Rats that could steal eggs without breaking them. Nails sawn in two by the wind and the rain. And often he watched his mother standing there, corn heaped in the belly of her blue apron, her arm flinging it to the ground in a sweep of golden hail.

He went out of the gate and saw his father come thundering down the path towards him. There was a murderous look on his face.

'Come here to hell! What do you think you're playing at?'

As he came, his big thumbs hooked his braces back on to his shoulders. There were two gates in the hen-run. As his father came in the one on the police side, he bolted out of the gate on the married quarters side. It was obvious his father was going to hit him. And if that happened he would spend all summer in a lather of hate.

Running up the garden, he glanced back and saw his father's mad look of anger, his ungainly bounds over the ridges, his big feet trying to land sideways between the drills. It was comic. Clearing the rhubarb he tripped, landing on his knees in the lettuce bed. When he stood up there were two deep dents in the clay. He wanted to laugh, but that would have only compounded whatever crime it was he had committed. His father came on, bent forward, his neck sticking out, rage spearing from his eyes. He looked like a giant cockerel. And he was the hen. He could easily escape by running out of the barracks and across the road into the demesne, but he'd have to face the music when he returned at night. Anyway, why should he be beaten? He was seventeen. Why should he be afraid? Anger drained his limbs. He could feel his face going white. Let him come on. He'd run no longer. By the tall privet hedge separating the garden from the lawn, he stopped dead in his tracks. At the end of the onion bed was a muck fork, the prongs stuck deep in the clay. His father saw him look at it. With an enraged howl he was on him, gripping him round the throat. Choking him.

'Ya pup, ya. Stick the graipe in me, would you? You deliberately wouldn't come when I was calling. Who the hell do you think you are? Hah? Hah?'

His father's big hands were round his frail neck. His eyes, under the brim of his hat, were two small rotten potatoes. His teeth were in a white grind, his face distorted by his muddy feelings. He remembered his father telling him of a fight he had stopped at a football match. One player was attempting to strangle another. 'His tongue was out and hanging and him gagging to perdition.'

He stuck his tongue out as far as he could, hoping it would frighten his father to sense. The grip on his neck slackened. Now his father was shaking him. 'Ya whelp, ya. Deliberately taunting me.'

He heard his mother's worried screams. Seeing them from the kitchen window, she had come running, desperate to separate them.

'Stop it. Stop it. Do you want to kill the child?'

'Child my arse.'

'You'll end up in Green Street one of these days.' Green Street was where murder trials were held in Dublin.

'If I'd had sense I'd have ended up in America years ago.' Clearing his throat, he spat into the privet hedge in anger and self-contempt.

'Well go on to America, for God's sake. No one's stopping you.'

'It's too late now, woman, and well you know it.' His father looked at Brady's Hill and at the sky, which was full of faded dreams. As a young man he had been all set to return to New

York with his sister who worked there, but she stayed on at home to get married to a local farmer. His hopes dashed, he went to Dublin and joined the police.

When his father let him go he staggered away, rubbing his neck, pretending he was badly hurt. He caught a glimpse of his mother's face. It was a flush of blood from chin to forehead. Her eyes were wild and weepy. Her shoulders sagged. A wisp of hair fell across her nose. More hurtful than a fist was his father's talk of America. Had he gone there, he would never have married who he did and he himself would never have been born.

He grabbed at the muck fork, knowing his mother would stop him using it. When he turned to face them, she was hanging on to his father's blue shirt and he was looking angrily down at her, his hands raised away from her, not wanting to be touched by her. But the expression on his face changed as she slipped slowly down along his body, her fingers powerless to cling. In horrible nightmarish motion she fought for a few seconds to stay upright but, her knees buckling, she fell in a heap across the onion bed, her head hanging over the edge of the ridge. He and his father exchanged frightened looks, checking on reality. Then his father was on his knees beside her, his hand lifting her head, his face a terrible mixture of innocence and pain. He looked like a drowning child.

'Quick. Doctor.'

He noticed his mother had only one shoe on. Earlier when he'd watched her baking she had kicked both off under the table to ease her swollen feet. When she needed them again she usually retrieved them with the sweeping-brush. Because of her blood pressure she didn't like bending down. When she had heard them fighting, in her rush to separate them she must have taken time to put only one of the shoes back on.

He rushed round and into the barracks day-room and shouted at Guard Ryan, who was sitting by the empty grate reading *The Dandy* annual. 'The doctor. The doctor. Mammy's fainted or something. Ring quick please.' By the time he ran back to the garden his father had carried her into the house. Like a sinister shadow the impression of her body was heavy on the clay. The onions, planted in triangles, were shooting up, but where his mother had fallen the green sprouts were crushed. On the soft edge of the ridge was the crumbled track of her neck.

When he went into the room she was lying on the bed, his

father kneeling on the floor, holding her hand and stroking her forehead. His big wellington boots were caked with clay and chevrons of dried mud had fallen on the lino from the soles.

'Don't tell anyone there was a row.'

'No.'

Guilt and terror crippled him. His heart dunting madly, icy feelings frosting his soul, he knew that were his mother to die he would have to die himself.

She looked dead. Her face, smudged with worry, was still as a mask. Her eyes were shut. He wondered, was Death laying perpetual sleep on them? On her upper lip the downy line of fair hair glistened with sugar. She had a sweet tooth, his mother, and a sweeter tongue. He looked at her swollen legs. Cursed with varicose veins, every morning she had to wrap them in puttees of crêpe bandage. Her own mother had died with a clot to the brain. It was a death she feared. 'The old blood pressure's at me today. Say a prayer.'

Above her bed was a picture of Jesus, head crowned with thorns. Every time he entered the room the first thing he did was glance up at it. To check that the face, with its holy grimace of unbelievable, perpetual pain, was looking at him. Pain for which he himself shared responsibility. All men did. But not women. Not mothers. Not his mother lying there, her blood slowing down, her fluttery heart weak as a dying sparrow's. Women who loved the men they brought into the world cancelled out the Crucifixion. The blood shed on the Cross saved the world. And women carried on saving it with womb blood. At school the priest who taught him English said it was pain that made the blind see. Like in *King Lear*. The empty pursuit of security and pleasure were the goals of fools. It was a chilling thought.

Pain made him cry. Tears began spilling down his face. He had slept with his mother and suckled her warmth well into boyhood. He would have flung himself down on top of her, but his father was in the way. He hated himself for noticing the hole at the big toe of her stocking. It also made him feel much worse, because it frightened him all the more. Her toe looked so frail . . . it couldn't possibly combat Death. Her toe looked dead already.

His mother had told him that her youngest sister, Emily, had died as a child. On her deathbed Emily had promised she would return from heaven to help her when it was her turn to go. 'She was so lovely, Emily. So calm in spite of all her suffering. She had hair to her shoulders like a golden shawl. She'd reach down from heaven to hold my hand when I'm dying. And if she could, she'd get a choir of angels to sing for me. No pain could blot out that music. You'd go straight to Our Saviour without feeling a twinge. Poor Emily. She was one of the chosen.' He found himself looking round the room to see if anything celestial stirred. Out on Brady's Hill a grazing cow moved slowly past the window. He listened for angels but all he could hear was his father groaning hopelessly, half in prayer.

'Say an Act of Contrition in her ear.'

His body shaking, he began to cry out of control. Emotion gripped his throat tighter than his father's fingers.

'That's enough of that. We don't want that carry on. She's not dead yet.'

He bent to his mother, his tears falling into her ear. 'O my God I am heartily sorry for having offended Thee . . .' His mother had never offended anyone in her life. 'O my God . . .'

Her eyes were shut but the closed lids flickered. One of her hands rested on her stomach. On the back of it was dried flour, cracked along the knuckles. Between her fingers paste still glistened. Her face was pale and dull as dough. The prayer wouldn't leave his tongue. He couldn't utter the words. Not words for the dying. His heart rebelled. He fell on her, clinging, shouting.

'Mammy. Mammy. Don't die, please. Please Mammy, don't die, please.'

His father tore him off and plonked him down on the commode in the corner. 'Don't make an ass of yourself. If you can't help, don't be a hindrance.'

His father got mad at rusty nails that bent under the hammer. At potatoes that dared go mouldy. At his bicycle bell if it didn't ring properly. At the world, if when tying his boot the lace broke . . . Yet faced with the greatest nuisance of all – Death – he was a rock of calm. He knelt by the bed as he had done before the mound of rotten spuds. Strong, crouched over one knee.

'Mum. Mum? Can you hear me? Mum? It's me. It's me. It's . . . We've sent for the doctor, Mum. It's me. Don't worry, you're going to be all right, *a grá*.' *A grá*. It was an Irish expression meaning 'my love'. He never used personal endearments in English. They would have been too unequivocal. In Irish he could fudge his feelings. He rarely called her by her christian name. It was always Mum. Or Mammy. As if, like him, he too was only a son.

32

On the dressing-table he could see her hairbrush. It was white, with bluebells painted on the back. Beside it was her powder compact, round and golden. The lid was sprung open and he could see the round mirror. His mother had opened it, and he wondered if she would ever close it again. Things were never affected by people. People were affected by things. In the bottom of the compact you put the powder. On the powder rested a gauze filter which, when pressed with the puff, let the powder through. The puff was soft, firm, plushy. Like a tongue. Beside the compact he could see the velvet pouch into which it slotted neatly. All his mother's things were warm, personal. He liked touching them as he watched her apply her make-up.

'I got that on our honeymoon. In London. He bought it for me. We went to Madame Tussaud's, the waxy place. Oh, it was wonderful. And they had Marat stabbed in his bath by Charlotte Corday. We stayed with a lovely lady in Harlesden. Mrs Peel, 74 Riffel Road. She loved us. Each evening we came in she had Ovaltine and sandwiches ready. My legs were killed walking. The first night we got into bed, and I'm only telling you this because you're big now, I was in first. "I want to sleep on that side," says he. Imagine that? He bought me the compact from a huckster's cart at Baker Street station.'

His father now had both knees on the floor and was holding her hand pressed to his forehead. He was a rock, she a dress draped on it, drying in the sun. He was a tree stump, she fruit. He was a fist, his mother a kiss. His father sleet, his mother light. His father boots and braces, she powder and suspenders. His father the earner, his mother without a penny. 'He's hard because he's had to be. No one ever gave him a penny. Remember that.'

Getting up from the commode he went to the dressing-table. He picked up the compact, sniffed its sweet familiar smell, looked in the mirror. His mother's image was in there somewhere. She had looked in it every day for over twenty-five years. He snapped it shut. Tock. Hearing his mother gurgle he turned to look at her. A seed of blood pipped out of the side of her mouth. On the forehead of Jesus in the picture above her bed were beads of blood from the crown of thorns. It looked as if one of the drops had fallen on to his mother's lips. His father groaned. A desperate, useless croak, like a rooster choking. 'Jesus help us. Mum. We're bucked now, me boyo. She's dead.'

3

There was a rat in the cell. He could hear it scratch and scutter across the concrete floor. Feel the plump vibrations when it gnawed the wooden frame on which he lay. Its whimperings eked his brain. In the dark the sounds were a picture. A rat picture. He hadn't the strength to frighten it away. The rat knew he was no threat. Now it was nosing at his ribs, then, nails pricking, pawing up on to his belly where it sat warm and wobbly and sniffing at his skin. Rats could sense danger. Slithering down it plopped on to the floor, skittered out the conduit and was gone. A second later he heard his father's footfall on the tiled hallway. The bare bulb snapped on. The switch was on the outside. His father's eye filled the spy-hole.

'I've got a mug of tea and toast for you. And clothes. Put them on.'

'Let me out of here. I'm not a criminal.'

'Only to yourself.'

He heard him put the mug and plate down on the tiles, so he could wrestle with the big door-bolt. The bolt was a long, heavy shaft of iron with a hasp coming off at right angles. It always put him in mind of a revolver. Tight in its socket and staples it screeched, gave a damp grunt, then hammered back with a clunk against the stop-piece. His father put the mug and plate on the bunk, then stood in the doorway. There was no way he could get out past him. Not that he wanted to, even had he the strength. Maybe a few days in the cell would rest his body, give him time to make sense of life since his mother's death. And he was rat-proof.

His father now wore shoes and had his best uniform jacket on. The knot in his tie was small as a thrush's egg. He jutted his jaw out to relieve the tightness round his neck; his Adam's apple

34

flicking above the collar then disappearing. He could never do the knot just right. 'Man alive, show here, before you strangle yourself.'

But now there was no woman's fingers to do it for him. He'd obviously done himself up for some reason. He could smell the Palmolive shaving cream. There was a dried scab of it caked on his ear lobe. His greying hair was brushed back, the thinning quiff darker than the sides. He used the shoebrush on his hair, letting the residual polish blacken the grey. This always amused his mother. 'He's the only man in Ireland polishes his head.'

His father was vain. Tall and handsome, he looked well in the dark-blue uniform. But a boyish humility made him grin shamefacedly whenever people admired him. It was probably guilt and fear of being slapped down. He was afraid of words, not blows. Blows had been bred into him from his own tough childhood. He had once seen a drunken tinker hit him full flush on the jaw. He took the punch, shook his head and flailed the tinker and his clan out of the village with truncheon, boot and fist. When that evening he sat taking his supper – a pint of hot milk and a digestive biscuit – he told them about the incident with a mixture of pride and sheepish humility.

'It was the Wards and the McDonaghs. I heard one of the women saying, 'God help us but that polisman is a stallion cuttin' loose.' The one of them that hit me had a fist like a sledgehammer. But he couldn't put me down. No siree.'

'Well,' his mother said, 'it proves you've got a head like a donkey. With as little brains.'

The words stung.

'When you first heard me bray, you came running quick enough, that's one sure thing.' It was worth dying for, the last word. Words were swords. A sentence was for life.

In the day-room the telephone rang with an alarm-clock clatter. His father, stretching his neck, pursing his lips, ran his finger round the inside of his collar.

'I'll have to answer that. You'll stay in the cell here, till we know what we're going to do with you. I'll bring carbolic soap.'

'Who is "we"? Stop saying "we".'

'There's more than me involved. You've upset half the country.'

The big door closed with a no-hope thud.

The tea was hot, sweet and hard. He bit into the toast. Stale bread. It was one of the reasons he had left home. Food. For a few days after his mother died it was cooked by relations who stayed on after the funeral. But soon they returned to their own homes. Then neighbouring women helped out, but eventually came the day they were on their own and had to get dinner themselves. Sunday dinner. On the Saturday his father told him to catch a hen. 'The oul' one with feathers missing. I'm full sure she's stopped laying.' He caught her and put her under an upturned tea-chest. Hours later he watched from the kitchen window as his father killed it.

The slaughter technique was all his own. Wedging the squawking hen between his knees, he trapped the spread wings along his thighs with his forearms and with one hand held the outstretched neck. In his other hand he already had his penknife. Short, slender with white ivory casing, he'd had it for years. The ivory was secured to the frame by tiny black rivets. The blade, narrow with use, the point broken off, was a shiny steel fang for cutting twine, quartering apples, paring pencils, sharpening matches to toothpicks, ending lives. 'Sheffield. The best steel in the universe bar none. And I'm including Toledo.' The knife was a tiny piano playing for Death.

Crouched, tunic hanging open, knees close, feet splayed wide apart, the hen's neck sticking out to the front, its yellow feet to the rear, his father looked comic. He was always lethal then. With his teeth he opened out the blade. Beak and neck pressed in a crook of fingers and thumb, the hen's head with its blunt comb was arched tight – proud for the knife. Nicking the head once, testing for a vein, he then sank the blade deep and drew it across as if slicing along the rind of an orange.

Outside on the sill was a box of geraniums. The spurting blood was a scream of colour. A macabre burlesque of flowers.

The hen struggled, tried to flutter, flexed its toes, squawked. Its grey crinkly lids opened and shut in the desperate surprise of pain.

'Ah-ha, ya beggar. Easy now. It'll soon be over.'

'His father held it over the drain, his feet wide apart so that his boots wouldn't get splashed. The velvet cord of blood snapped to a scatter of drops, hitting the drain grating like a handful of haws.

The hen hung dead in his father's hand, its wings tumbled open. So dead it might never have lived. Carefully wiping the blade clean on the feathery strop of its neck, his father shut the knife against the side of his thigh.

He sat in the kitchen, staring stubbornly at the wall. He was lonely for the hen. For his mother. For himself. There was no eye ever blinked that couldn't be shut by sleepy Death.

That evening his father told him to pluck the hen. 'Soak it in lukewarm water first. That's the way Mum does it.'

For a moment the present tense hung in the air then gonged down on them, ringing their heads and the whole house with deadly silence. They sat and looked, face to face. The position was hopeless. She was dead. Dead dead. But they were alive dead. A pair of zombies moving round a cemetery with chairs for headstones, the table a tomb, the sewing-machine, the old armchair, weird monumental masonry. The inside of his head was a heap of dried potato stalks set alight by sorrow; the acrid, drifting smoke and crackling flames useless against the plague of his mother's death.

'Get on with it. We've got to face facts and that's all there is to it. We can't sit and rot here like this.'

'Can I put on the wireless?'

'Not if it's music.'

'I'm not plucking the hen then.'

'All right, but keep it low. We have to mourn for a full year. Though I know we'll mourn forever. She was the best woman in the world. Bar none. She was everything a wife and mother ought to be, and more. If I walked the world from pole to pole we couldn't find her match. We both know that.'

'We.' He didn't like to be included in his mourning. He didn't want a rope slung between them, tying them together.

By the time he had plucked the hen the kitchen was covered with feathers. They floated up on to the mantelpiece, landed on top of the wireless, swirled around the light bulb. They were everywhere under his feet. The hen's skin was torn where the feathers wouldn't come out easily. Feathers were frail, yet tenacious at root. Like most lives. His father, sleeves rolled up, began to gut the corpse. The kitchen filled with stench as the slimy lights and bubbly coil of gut came out on to the table. The innards had the strangeness of all things pulled for the first time into open air. The gizzard with its coat of suet was a scrotum the colour of a drunk's nose. The black-red liver was sticky Turkish Delight. The intestine had the deadly whiteness of a root pulled out of clay, or the thistle growing in the dark corner of the hen-house – long, pale, deprived of sun.

'Why are they called lights, can you tell me?'

'Because light can't get to them?'

'No. Because they don't weigh much. Like lungs.'

The egg-sac burst, yolk squashing over his father's big fingers.

'Cripes, she was still laying.'

The air reeked. He retched, watching his father sever the neck with the bread-knife.

'Bad cess to it but we forgot to singe her.'

Rolling up a length of the *Irish Independent*, his father lit the end and let the flame lick along the blue ripped skin, burning unplucked fluff and bits of quill sprouting round the arse. A blazing strip of paper burnt free and landed on his father's hand.

'Oh feck. You would, would you?'

Throwing the hen on to the table, he trampled the flame out on the floor. Feathers melted to twists of black smoke. Bits of ash sailed round the room.

'Get that ointment.'

'Where is it?'

'She keeps it in the drawer somewhere.'

The present tense again. He'd have to escape. But not back to school. Next day his father cooked the dinner. It was late afternoon by the time they sat down to eat. The meat was red raw on the bone. The cabbage swam in water. The potatoes were soaking. The kitchen was a wreck of pots, pans, towels, cloths, cutlery, basins of peel and leaves, pools of water on the lino, condensation up the walls. For dessert they had a tin of pears. They tried to make conversation, to pretend they weren't deep in a nightmare.

'If the weather holds up we'll be in with a chance.'

He had no idea what he meant. His weather conversations were another language. Bordering on the philosophical.

'Hail in June is far too soon. So they say. And I'm inclined to believe them. But thank God it hasn't happened yet. If we get frost now there won't be a stalk left standing. The wind will tell us. DV.'

Jesus. The dinner was bad but this was worse. He watched him sharpen a matchstick with his penknife. Blood at the hilt caked the imprint – 'Sheffield Steel'.

'I see in today's paper, prayers have been asked for the canonization of Blessed Oliver Plunket. I bet my bottom dollar if he'd been an Italian he'd have been a saint years ago. If the end of the world arrived in the morning post and all the nations had to queue up to get into heaven, there's no prize for guessing which country would be the last in line. Despite our near-perfect record.'

He was expected to reply but couldn't think of anything sensible. He decided on flippancy couched in a serious tone.

'Why doesn't the government object?'

'The government of this country has less influence on world affairs than a tailor's cat has on the price of wool. I'm telling you that straight.'

But if he left home, where could he go? What could he do? His father was staring at him.

'You'll have to learn to cook for us.'

This was a doomsday proposition. His father's eyes were hard, steady. His upper lip was back off his gum as he probed his teeth with the match.

'Me? I can't boil an egg. I've never wet a cup of tea in me life. I don't know anything about cooking. I know more about zoology. A subject with which I am entirely unacquainted.'

'Don't be smart. If you can spell it you can learn it. One of the women can show you the tricks of the trade. I'm too busy. It'll keep your mind occupied. There's nothing to it. Cooking. All you need is the knack with the ingredients. And I don't like too much salt.'

It was the first time they had sat alone at table. The old scrubbed table with its dividing line of crumbs and waxy dirt was the most personal item in the house. When his mother was alive. Not as personal as the bed. But a more sociable focus. The family trough. But unlike dumb creatures, they could talk as well as eat and look at one another with love and hope. When his mother was alive.

Now his mother's place was empty. A gap in the hedge. An empty fireplace. A derelict house, the roof caved in, the cold stars visible a million miles away. At mealtimes, when she was alive, he could feel her warm glow. When she passed food or drink their fingers touched or their elbows rested together on the table. Even on a freezing day his mother's touch was warm. That was the thing about women. They had pools of heat within, sloshing about, looking for use.

His father shifted his gaze. It was lonely for him too. Hell. But he hadn't seen him cry yet. He looked to see what he was staring at. His eyes seemed to be staring at the blue apron hanging on the

39

back of the door. Subconsciously his father was measuring him up for it. His stomach kept him going. His dinner on the table at one o'clock was an ordered universe. Dinner on the table at 1.05 was disorder. No dinner at all was anarchy, revolution. The sun dropped out of the sky. There was no sorrow could stand in the way of his food. He came from a hungry people.

'My grandmother's sister was pregnant during the Famine. The child within her ate her alive. Yes. They found her dead on the side of the road, the baby moving in her belly. God help us. I must show you her grave one day.' Hungry words came out his mouth like bees from an empty hive. 'You've no choice. It's cook or fend for yourself.'

'Thanks very much.'

'I can always go to the Widow McGinn. She's already offered.'

'Can't I go as well?'

'What? You? No. She's only got five chairs. There's her, three of the men and me. If I go. You'll have to knuckle down. Then come September you can go back to school.'

'I'm not going back to school. I couldn't get me fill there.'

'What do you mean?' His father stopped probing his teeth.

'I . . . spiritually . . . there's a gap in me since Mammy died. I want to stay here.'

'In that case I'll get Mrs Gargan to show you the ropes. We're lucky with our own vegetables and I'll give you the money for meat when the van calls. Fish on a Friday. Mum fried herrings in butter.'

He had it all worked out. He was to step into his mother's shoes. The butcher's van came from Cavan on Saturdays and the fish-man called on Friday mornings. They would be the high points of the week's social intercourse. The elderly butcher's complexion was red blemished with white, like a lump of mincemeat. His small pink eyes opened wide only when he spoke to the younger housewives. The fish-man stank of his trade and handed you the herrings in brown paper bags. He'd often carried them into the house for his mother and by the time he'd got to the kitchen they were slithering out through the soggy holes.

'I'll go back to school.'

'You can go back September twelvemonth. I've arranged it with the Principal. You can have a year off. It'll do you no harm. Father Austen will send out books to you.'

'So you've gone behind my back?'

'No, I haven't gone behind your back.' His father spat the words at him. 'I've done what's best. You're in no fit state to plan anything. A year will give us time to get a grip. A year is a long time. Nothing lasts longer than a year and a day. Who knows what might happen then? God willing.'

The hope in his father's voice enraged him.

'Yeah. Maybe you'll even meet another woman. That'll settle everything. Life can go on as if Mum never lived.'

The words came gulging out of him, angry, nervy, weepy. He braced himself for flight. But his father didn't strike. Instead he held him in an optical grip, weighing, judging, reducing him. Coldly pondering a course of action. Calculating the consequences of knocking him senseless or leaving him to marrow in guilt. When his father raged and ranted he always did it on his own terms. Other people's outbursts he undercut with silence. Till he was ready to spring. When he felt a splurge of anger would do him good. Nodding a few times, he cleared his throat.

'The emotions aren't something we can throw in a weighing-scales. So I'm not going to argue with you as to which of us loved Mum the most. I know I was there years before you were. God help us, she hadn't a penny to her name when I met her. Her father had long before bankrupted himself and put them all on the street. All I wanted was love. And she gave it. And I returned it a hundredfold. Years before you were born, me buck. You're too young to know the price of anything. How much pain costs. Where it hurts most.'

'Your pocket.' The words leapt through his teeth before he could clench them.

His father's fists tightened. But he carried on, digging deeper for sympathy, understanding. Prepared to try a little harder. In his hand was a chicken leg, a skim of meat along it the colour of gingivitis. On a side-plate heaped with skins, a sliced potato revealed the squashy body of a slug. Slugs were perfect tunnellers. Through anything soft. Potatoes. Fruit. Flesh . . .

'Before I met Mum I could have married a teacher over in the County Leitrim. I was a bit of a hero, them days. When I got the Scott Medal. I wasn't a lot older than yourself. The moon was streaking down when I heard them coming. I could see the glint on the rifle barrels. I could see the Parabellums in their hands. They left the road and went into a field. In the corner was a hayrick. We had information, you see. That day they'd robbed a post office in Carrick-on-Shannon. Up they went to the rick and were hiding the weaponry when out I hurtled from the ditch. Them days after the Civil War the country was full of Irregulars. A law unto themselves, pleading politics for self-gain and roguery. You could tell them by their new suits and boots. The Sergeant with me made sure he was well behind when I made me move. "Hands up," I roared. We didn't have guns at all. A calf came round the rick and started nuzzling me. Up went their hands in the air and in two shakes of a lamb's tail I had the handcuffs on them. A wrist each. Afterwards, of course, the Sergeant got the praise and a gold medal. And eventually the Sam Browne belt. I got a piece of silver. Dangling from a tricolour ribbon. Them days I didn't care. I stayed single. Until I met Mum. It was love at first sight. I was blind until that moment. We went to the Theatre Royal in Dublin on our first date. A character on a mandolin thing sang 'Greensleeves was my delight'. And wasn't it a coincidence, wasn't she wearing green sleeves? Her best blouse. I noticed it in her wardrobe last night. I always felt lucky when she wore it. The Lord have mercy on her gentle soul. The morning you were born I was the happiest man in Ireland.'

His father's eyes misted, then hardened. Like ice on top of the rain barrel. He had never seen him cry. Yet he could move stones to tears. Putting his penknife back in his pocket he stood up, stiff, then with a scything swipe of his right arm, cleared the table of everything on it. Dishes, plates, mugs, bowls, saucepans, knives, forks, spoons, the teapot, the milk jug – all went clattering against the wall and on to the range. For a moment after the deafening noise he could hardly believe it had happened. But there on the floor were the broken pieces of crockery, in a comic stillness inversely proportionate to the force that had moved them.

Now his father's voice was thick, his throat bunged with feeling. 'Don't tell me, don't bleddywell tell me what I think. Or by cripes I'll crucify you with kicks. I know what Mum thinks. So don't tell me. And if I did get married again it's none of your business. Or if I went to America itself, where be rights I should have gone years ago. Just because someone dies doesn't mean we all have to don a shroud and jump down into the grave after them. It's the living have to resurrect themselves and not the dead.'

Bellowing like a bull he went out, smashing the door behind him. The bulb and Chinaman's-hat shade swung from the ceiling in the draught of his departure. The bulb, stippled black with fly dung, at night shed sticky nicotine light. He knew if he cleared up the mess he'd become over the months his father's servant. Their hearts were broken, but they'd never mend together. He stepped over the chicken carcass and with his foot righted an upended saucepan. A potato sent flying on to the range sizzled as it dried out. A drift of sugar crinkled underfoot.

In his mother's room he opened the wardrobe. The green-sleeved blouse was in at the back on a hanger. Silk. He sat in the wardrobe, his head amongst her clothes – the navy-blue two-piece suit; a brown overcoat; summer frocks; skirts; the fox fur with glassy eyes, dangling in the dark. On the shelf sat the jumble of her hats, all of them with pins. Her best pillbox and veil she kept in a big paper bag. On the floor of the wardrobe were her flat-heeled shoes. Some of them had holes in the soles. She'd worn them for years. She had no money of her own. Together, neatly in the corner, were her black suede high-heels. Her best. Women's feet were tongues, necks, spouts of cream. Only a few months ago he had washed his mother's feet. She sat on the form at the back of the house, her feet in the aluminium basin.

'I'll wash them for you.'

'Oh, that's grand. Don't forget between the toes. That's nice, that's gentle.'

'Service with a smile, Madam.'

Her ankles were swollen, gorged with water and blood. The knotty veins rippled beneath her skin like blue barbed-wire.

'I was as light as a bird one time, now I can hardly get them into my shoes. The dancing I did, the dancing.' She laughed with joy at the memory.

Smell was the sister of memory. His brain whiffing the past, his nostrils prickly with the fusty odour of old clothes and dying perfumes, he sat trying to say goodbye to her, to her room, the one oasis in the cold barracks. The tallboy, the dressing-table with tilting mirror, the big bed with curved headboard, the wardrobe, were the one suite. All veneered with lacquered plywood. A strip was missing from the headboard. He himself had pulled it off when a child. The legs on the furniture were bull-terrier cabriole.

A dull breath of dust had already gathered on the surfaces. Man-made objects were often in themselves plain, ugly. But love transformed them. His mother's touch increased the power of chairs, lino, sideboards, mantelpieces, the bedroom suite. The sentimentally hideous statue of the Virgin she charged with flowers. But sleepy Death had shut her eyes and the bed she slept in, the tallboy with her stockings, brassières, corsets, underwear, gloves, her clothes in the wardrobe, the commode by the bed, all of them had already begun to die. Death's snow – dust – was falling everywhere. He looked at himself in the mirror. He was wearing black shoes, red socks, and because it was Sunday his charcoal grey suit, white shirt and maroon tie. As he went down the hallway he grabbed his heavy woollen overcoat, draped it over his shoulders and, like a sheep in search of a shepherd, went out of the station gates. He was a disciple looking for a Jesus. A tall thin soul of sadness seeking a heart-mender. A woman. And if he couldn't find one he'd settle for politics or religious belief. He hadn't a penny in his pocket but the sky was blue and a fresh wind pushed his back. Going down the hill he met Tilly Roberts coming up. She was in her chapel-going best – a white frock, blue high-heels, a pale blue wide-brimmed straw hat and white net gloves up to her elbows. Viced in a grip of fingers was a thick Bible. For the first time in his life she stopped before him. Her beautiful hard face softening, she reached and touched his face.

'You poor boy. All things come to pass.'

He smiled.

She smiled, then laughed; her head back, her neck arched to the wind. There was something insane about her. Her beauty so great, her beliefs so bitter. She walked on and he heard her heels click and crake in the path of the Methodist Chapel. She had come down from the North to marry Bobby Roberts and brought her fierce views with her. 'The Wages of Sin is Death' was her slogan. And 'Rejoice in the Severe Mercy of the Lord'. You saw them pinned up in all the little chapels and meeting-halls along both sides of the Border.

'The wages for them. Death for the rest. That's what they really believe,' claimed his father. 'But they're too bleddy cute to say it aloud.'

The Border was the edge of belief. Living along it cut.

He came into the village. The goat on the green was tethered and crying. A can swung empty on the pump. Not knowing where he was heading, he went out over the humpy bridge across the railway tracks.

In the distance he saw coming towards him a clatter of horses.

Leading them from the back of a big white mare was his friend Prunty. There was no mistaking the head of blond dancing ringlets, the weatherbeaten laughing face. His big freckled hands were a tangle of ropes and reins. Only Prunty would dare take to the roads with seven horses in his sole charge . . .

Out in the day-room he could hear the phone ringing again. He bit hard on the toast left by his father and to soften it swilled it round in a mouthful of tea. Stale bread and hard, cold tea. Perfect prison cuisine. The bitter taste at least helped to plug his leaking eyes. He remembered his father saying someone was coming to see him. 'You'll know who it is. He's got an attractive proposition to put to you.'

A last wild scheme, no doubt, to clip his wings. He was a chicken under a tea-chest, awaiting execution. He'd only be released if he promised to lay one egg per day and submit to the cockerels who ruled the roost in Butlershill. No doubt the proposition was a job. Learning the bar trade in Cavan or Clones, perhaps. For £1 a week – if he was lucky. Or go away and become a monk. Or – even worse – work for a 'small' farmer. The three inner circles of pain, poverty and misery. Inevitably leading to a life of alcoholic, sexual or economic paralysis. Probably all three.

For the moment he was safe in the cell. Safe from everything but memory. In the coming hours he would let himself die or ponder his way to freedom. Feed the rat with stale toast.

4

Prunty and he had attended the village school. Prunty was two years older and finished all formal education on his fourteenth birthday. Legally free then, he couldn't be persuaded to spend a further five years in a secondary school.

He was a man even when he was a boy. An only child, his mother had had him when she was forty-five. Shortly afterwards his father had died – it was said from the shock. Prunty from an early age had to run the small farm, which consisted of twenty-five acres of hills, one soggy meadow – a bottom – and a turf bog. A snipe could live on it. Just. Its location, however, was superb. It was right along the Border. To live decent it was necessary to smuggle. Living well came with practice. In Prunty's house there was always chocolate, sweet cake, butter, and in the big kitchen bin, bottles of whiskey and razor blades. Blades fetched good money in Dublin. In the recess of the kitchen window sat a television. Outside, above the thatch, an aerial picked up the fantastic pictures from abroad. In his spare time Prunty did jobs for Castle Finn. Its owner, Colonel Bridge, had an American wife – Sophie Kay – and occasionally employed Catholics. It was the Colonel's horses Prunty was taking along the road.

'Where are you headin'?'

'I don't know.'

'You should niver walk so far you can't walk back. Hop up.'

Folding his overcoat he threw it across the withers of a black mare that even to him looked docile. Grabbing a fistful of mane he managed to haul himself on board, and when safely seated was surprised to find how high he was above the road. He could see over the hedge into a field covered in ragweed.

'Mind that fecker beside you. He's a kicker.'

The horses were all old farm animals on their way to the

knacker. The castle estate had long since been tractorized, but for sentimental reasons of his wife the Colonel had kept them on in retirement. Now, though, his wife away in America, the Colonel had decided to get rid of them before they fell dead in the meadow. The Colonel and Sophie Kay had, according to Prunty, an up-and-down relationship. 'Up is drunk in front of the fire. Down she's fecked off to New York again. Last week, I'm not coddin', she threw a sod of turf at him, bruk his reading-glasses.'

For this latest twist of a stormy marriage, the horses were paying the price. Once in the knacker's yard they would never come out alive. That was the law. They were old, half-shod and skittery on the road. They looked at every telegraph pole as if it were a potential enemy and every time a house loomed up shied by it, jinking sideways. A black stallion, a white blaze on his face, constantly nipped the necks of the horses alongside him and any horse dropping back he tried to kick. Prunty gave him plenty of rope, hoping he'd drop behind, but when he did it was never for long. 'Hit him a slap on the snotter if he comes near you.'

They were a shambolic collection of nags. A white draught mare. A black mare. The black kicker. Two bays with long tails. A big piebald like a tinker's horse. A sandy-coloured jade with tufts of feathers hanging from its fetlocks. The jade's back was scabbed with ringworm. All of them had a good deal of grey in their manes and on closer inspection their natural coat colouring was bleached by age. Round their mouths and under their chins the light shone through wispy whiskers, making them stand out like the spikes on binder twine. The piebald had lumps all over her back caused by warbles. All of them had oozing eyes and dribbling noses.

From the tangle of reins, Prunty had thrown him a single rope with which to steer his mount. Prunty was as much at ease on horseback as he was on a bicycle. He himself sat as best he could, leaning forward, gripping the mane. His horse had a peculiar sideways gait, half prance, half stumble. Her head turned sideways to the hedge, she seemed to be navigating by ear. 'Prunty, what's wrong with this quadruped on which Fate has placed me? I think she needs glasses.'

'Wha'? Yeh. She's blind as a feckin' bat, lad.'

'You're joking?'

'I'm not. She rubs against the rest of them, and gets along by listening. That's why her oul' head's cocked crooked all the time.'

The Kicker, long yellow teeth bared, lunged at his trouser leg. 'Get off. That's my good suit.'

'Hit him a crack on the snotbox.'

Turning left off the Butlershill road they took a narrower one leading to Currinstown. It was untarred, and soon a cloud of dust billowed hedge-high behind them. Bare hoof clattered on stone. He was lost in a fleshy shell filled with echoing bone-music. The sandy jade had a loose iron swivelling in and out on its one holding nail. Through the general clop you could hear its buried clang. His horse now had her chin resting on the rump of the horse in front. As if she were being guided along. It was a sick joke. Running away from home on a blind mare. Were his father to come along he wouldn't be able to look him in the eye.

'Prunty, I've left home. I'm not going back. I'm not going back to school either. Can you put me up?'

Prunty, flapping at his white mount with a fistful of rope, twisted round to look at him. The words came sideways from his mouth askew. 'I know what you want – your hole.'

'Pardon?' He'd heard well enough. Prunty had no regard for his or anyone else's finer feelings. Blond ringlets bouncing along his forehead, a lopsided grin on his face, he was a picture of crude mischievousness. 'Look, Prunty . . . my mother only a few weeks dead . . . do you think I have any time to be thinking about . . . and I've just walked out on my father . . . wanting "my hole" as you so vulgarly put it is the last thing I . . . well, ah . . . in fact it's the first thing, ah . . . I want, yes I have to admit it.'

'Didn't I tell you? Do you pull your sausage in bed?'

'No I don't.'

'You're a liar. Don't worry, it doesn't make you go blind. If it did, half the country would be going round on white sticks.'

They passed a house, an old man in the gateway leaning against the pillar; a white cane in his delicate hand; in his head, eyes white and dead as marbles. Prunty laughed. 'Maybe I'm wrong.'

Head back and tilted, the man shouted, 'Are youse a circus?'

'If we were a circus,' shouted Prunty, 'you'd hear the wheels. We're going to the knacker. But only me and me friend are coming back.'

'Ah I was thinkin' . . . thinkin' right enough.'

Prunty's shirtsleeves were rolled up tight to the bulge of his biceps. His arms were covered in freckles. His bulky thighs resting plump on his mount's back stretched his trousers to bursting. A slash of flesh was visible through a rip along the seam. His big feet were in wellingtons rolled down to his ankles. Sucking air against one side of the roof of his mouth he made wet clickety sounds. 'Up. Up there.'

When they came to a farmhouse with a line of guinea-hens perched on the garden wall the horses pranced, tossed their old heads, arched their backs and refused to go past. The Kicker lashed out with his heels and caught the piebald in the belly. The piebald, neighing in shock, plunged wildly, ending up on the bank of the roadside ditch. For a few moments all was stubborn chaos. The blind mare, sensing the general truculence, swooned and staggered about as if drunk. Tufts of mane in his hands, he hung on. 'Stop it. Behave yourself. Please.'

Prunty laughed at him. 'You know all about horses, lad, except how to ride them. I hope you know less about women.'

The guinea-hens on the wall stood up, spread their wings and unperturbed by the mayhem sat down again.

Prunty reached back and tugged at his mount's tail. The white mare, bucking, shot by the house. All the others decided to follow. The Kicker, coming alongside again, long teeth snapping, bit at his trouser leg, nearly yanking him off.

'Stop it.'

Prunty dropped back on the white mare. When he saw him coming, the Kicker went out at the rear.

'Holy God, lad, don't worry. If me mother doesn't put you up on the settle, you can lie down in the hay shed. Or sleep along with me.' His voice was low now, sincere, the look in his eyes honest, deep.

'You're a pal. Thank you.'

'I dar you shout VAGINA out loud.'

'What? Pardon?'

'You heard rightly.'

He had. But . . . why should he shout that word aloud? Why? That was the trouble with Prunty's dry, quick-shifting sense of humour. You couldn't tell if it was humour. He was probably, for some mad reason of his own, being deadly serious. He'd have to distract him from relentless sexual guff. He had no wish to talk sex from the back of a blind nag. In wide open country. And he certainly wasn't going to shout . . . VAGINA . . . to empty fields, scattered trees and bovine faces staring at him over farmyard gates.

'Don't you ever talk about anything else?'

'When I'm not talking about it, I'm thinking about it. I'm very highly sexed, did you not know that? I'm probably the most highly sexed man in this part of Cavan. Any woman round here will tell you the same. Up there, c'mon, that a girl.' With a length of rope he lazily skelped his horse's rump. 'Your name is a famous name. People went from these parts to England. And changed it to Brontë.'

'Aye, I mind the teacher telling us that. When women see me coming they run.'

'Hm, well I wouldn't boast about that, Prunty. It could mean they can't stand the sight of you.'

'Not at all, lad. It doesn't go be sight. It goes be smell as well. Smell bates all else. With animals and women. I always carry a few cloves in me pocket.'

He'd wondered about the brown trickle at the corner of his mouth. Now he knew. At least Prunty had a theory about women and how to attract them. Unlike himself. Cloves? He'd try anything. 'Can I have a clove, please?'

Two cloves lay on Prunty's welted hand, the colour of plug tobacco. The tang of the Orient on their tongues they clattered along the Border country.

In a garden in front of a slated cottage gladioli stood like spears above the wilderness of weeds. Fuchsia grew through box hedges on either side of a path leading to the front door. Wodges of moss edged the roof slates. A woman looked out through a tiny window, her sad eyes set in a weepy face. Out at the back of the house a baby screamed. A dog yapped.

The gladioli were white, stained lightly with red in their hearts. He and his father had put some on his mother's grave a few days after the funeral. It was the first time they'd returned to the cemetery. His father knelt on his big white handkerchief, fingers entwined in his rosary. Rigid as a headstone he prayed in utter silence. A bitter wind tore in over the graveyard wall, whistling, jeering, so pernicious it rattled the bolt in the gate. His father, hands going raw in the cold, never flinched. He walked away, and from behind a monumental angel he peeped at his father, trying to guess his feelings. He gave up. The wind died, as if it too was defeated by the chiselled face, the pale eyes burning with secrets.

What would he feel when he realized he had left home for good?

In front of him Prunty, the ropes and reins in his hands, was a puppeteer, the horses he dragged along his marionettes.

'Did I tell you I'm visiting a widdy woman? Honest to God. A Protestant. A widdy is your best bet. Single ones you couldn't get their drawers off with a can-opener. A widdy is safe and ojus willin'. Up. Up there.'

'I'll believe you, thousands wouldn't.'

'I'm friggin' telling you, lad. Mrs Kincaid. You know the one with the prize Jerseys. Twice last Sunday, yah boy yah. Onest in the morning. And onest that evening after me dinner.'

'Jerseys as in ganseys? Or the creamery cans on four legs?'

'Wha'?'

'Forget it.'

Prunty turned and looked at him with smiling I-wish-I-wasn't-telling-lies eyes. Though the smile could be the smile of truth. Nothing about Prunty was straightforward. Lies and truth slipped off the tongue the same way. Whenever he went to the pictures in the Luxor cinema in Clones, the screen throbbed with men and women telling each other, 'I love you,' and 'I love you too.' Yet everyone in the audience could see they were lying in their teeth. That was the cinema, where everything was clear. In reality though it wasn't so simple. Words were eels. Too slippery to catch. And Prunty bred his own variety. Niver for never. Onest for once. Bates for beats. Dar for dare. Widdy for widow. Be for by . . . the list was endless. In school, poetry was easy. It was all explained to you in the notes at the back. Out in the open, on the back of a horse, away from home, it was different. Like the country they were riding through. One minute it looked ugly, the next beautiful . . . Christ, but words could rip your brains to tatters.

'Do you dar me ride buff bollock through Currinstown?'

This really was alarming. Why on earth would he want to do such a thing? Looking at him he could see he was in earnest.

'No, I don't dare you. Your hair isn't long enough to do a Godiva. You'd catch cold. Apart from being arrested.'

'There's no barracks in Currinstown. I've niver had a cold these years. The best man agin colds is nettle soup. Back, yah mad dope.'

Raising his fist he threatened the Kicker, who was coming mouth agape for another bite. For an old animal it still had plenty of fight left, its flashing white eyes moons of madness desperately trying to avoid eclipse. The other horses had gentle eyes with long grey lashes. Innocent eyes. Innocent ears too, rippling with veins. And their rumps moved gracefully, skin quivering as they walked. Horses were flowing blood in shiny skin, warm to the touch. Women. To nibble at a girl's ear . . . her lobe in your teeth . . .

A rushy field, water glistening between the scraws, rose away to slabs of red rock coated with green, black and grey moss and lichen. Further up were spiky whins, the wasp-yellow blossom stinging the hillside with colour. Curving along the skyline a ragged line of trees.

'It's lovely country.'

'See don ash fornenst that gate up there? Billy Leonard hung himself from the big branch sticking out. Aye man, surely.'

Two donkeys in a field ran down to the fence, the jack braying in agony, desperate to break out and join them. The straggle of barbed wire and rotting posts were just enough to deny him freedom.

The spine of his blind mount cut like a blunt knife. Whenever he tried to shift position he had to resist a tendency to slip off. Everything about the ride was pleasurable except the ride itself.

'Are you going to shout it – vagina?'

'Don't be an eejit, Prunty, all the days of your life.'

'If you say it you're free of it. In the dark of the roads at night shout, "Fear. Fear." When I'm hungry I shout "Belly. Belly." It loses the spell then. I didn't see you at the rails this morning.'

'I didn't see you.'

'I've given up puttin' me tongue out at the priest. It's bad manners.'

His laugh, starting in a private chuckle, rasped up into a hard public bark. The horses reacted in alarm, bucking, bumping and trying to run past Prunty on the white mare. 'Back, yah shower of hoors. Can youse not take a joke?'

From a blackthorn bush a blackbird rifled out and away, a panic of glassy notes breaking from its orange beak. The fear in its beady eye was as intense as the fear in the eyes of the horses. Or in his own when he looked at himself in the mirror. Everything was equal to everything else. The braying donkey looked and sounded rocky. As if it were choking on stones. In the distance rain fell on a high hill. The light in that direction was steamy grey, like the cigarette smoke streaming from Prunty's lips. The horses walked with a rumpy flick. Like Tilly Roberts in high-heels.

He decided he was going to shout the word. If he did perhaps it would keep Prunty quiet. Besides, there weren't any people about. What had he to lose? 'Say but the word and my soul shall be healed.' The priest had said as much at mass that morning. Maybe Prunty was right. Saying it might free you from the fear. He cleared his throat.

'VAGINA.'

Like the screak of a strange bird the word rang out and fell across the empty fields. Beneath him his horse did a scattery dance but quietened quickly. Prunty, grinning, looked at him. He felt foolish.

'VAGINA,' he shouted again.

Around a bend in the road came an elderly woman on a bicycle.

'Oh, that's nice. You scut. I heard you.' Getting off the bike, she struggled up on to the ditch bank to get out of their way.

'It's the nag's name, missus. My one's called Dick,' said Prunty.

The woman, her long black belted coat hanging on her thin frame, a hat stuck down on a pile of grey hair, looked like an abandoned scarecrow as she stood on the bank looking after them. 'Do youse think I was born yesterday?' she shouted.

'No,' replied Prunty, 'nor the day before ayther.'

Below them lay the Finn river. It came twisting round a bend, then ghosted straight across a stretch of flat fields. Two black-and-white cows, Aberdeen Angus, grazed the wet land. A heron the colour of light and water slowly stepped along the bank. Hearing the clatter of horses it turned towards them, then tilting forward on its spindles, great wings bending to bows, lumbered into flight.

'Are we nearly there? I think I'll have to get down and walk. My backside is killing me.'

'Hang on. It's just the other side of Currinstown. Up there, come on now, that a girl.'

The cobweb-coloured Finn divided the North from the South. But the country on each side showed as little difference as the two sides of your face. The country was one. It was the people who were divided. It took so little to split us. A few quid. A bedroom door. Six feet of clay ... At last they clattered down into

Currinstown; their arrival increasing the nature of the place by a multiplication of seven. It had one Catholic church. One Protestant church. One shop. One pub. One tree on the corner of the one L-shaped street.

The horses, clopping to a halt, looked about, then staring at the ground in front of them seemed to go to sleep. Prunty furiously tried to budge them onwards. Then the big piebald, long tail swishing, went up on the pavement, the sandy jade following. There they wheeled, pranced and rubbed noses as if delighted to be on a footpath for the first time in their lives. The Kicker, looking with disdain at the few buildings, yawned and went peculiarly quiet. He may have decided the place wasn't worth the attention of his angry heels.

A man came out of the private entrance to the shop and stood watching them. He was squat, with broad shoulders and a solid crew-cut head that didn't have a neck to it. A barrel of a belly sundered his braces. He shouted to them in a corncrake voice, low and intense. 'It's about feckin' time. They're waitin' on you up there these hours.'

'They can wait a while longer,' snapped Prunty, annoyed.

'No they can't. They intend killing today.'

The jade, coming off the pavement, had left her only shoe behind. The man waddled across, picked it up and returned to his doorway. 'I'll stick it up for luck.'

'You can stick it anywhere you like,' shouted Prunty.

When they were clear of the place Prunty told him the man was 'the Butt' Smith, known all over the County Monaghan for his strength and temper. 'A friend of mine was caught in a hay shed with his daughter. Buff bollock except for his wellingtons. One night the Butt and his cronies lay in wait for him, stripped him, held him down, tarred and feathered his danglers. Bet all. She went to England and was niver seen again. I'm telling you, lad, single girls are no sport.'

'What happened to your friend?'

'Went to Enniskillen and joined the army. Never been seen since. Last year the wife gave up sex for Lent. He threw her out of the house.'

'Your friend did?'

'No. The Butt. She's in England as well. I'm telling you, lad, widdies are your oney safety. Hup there, that a girl. Give that hape of bones a crack.'

Having you danglers tarred and feathered was a terrifying thought. Circumspection would have to be the order of the day. And night. He wasn't interested in 'widdies'. Someone his own age, yes . . . with long legs, eyes like daisies . . . What – little yellow things? Well, big brown ones and lips like . . . Daydreams. He just couldn't imagine how it was going to happen. His flesh against the flesh of a living girl!

It all seemed so simple for Prunty. Only two years older, yet he knew, experienced so much more. His father dying when he was a baby meant he grew up his own man. There never was a shadow in his path, even on a bright day. The roads were quiet on a Sunday – they hadn't met a single car – but who else would have ventured forth with seven horses? One of them the bloody Kicker? Surely he'd be safe with him. He knew the run of the country better than his father did. Hm. He'd see. And if it didn't work out he could always go to America. God, another dream. His father's dream in fact.

Prunty was sweating. A dark triangular patch soaked through his blue shirt across his shoulderblades and down his spine. The bull's wool jacket tied round his waist by the sleeves draped to the horse's crupper. In a pocket he kept a packet of Gold Flake. His lips were rarely without a fag, even when he was chewing cloves. Blond curls hung down his short powerful neck and over the rim of his collarless shirt.

'See that one you're on? A champion Irish draught at Belturbet one year. I seen her plough when I was a kid, often. She was some horse. Weren't you, Bessie?'

The old nag, as if recognizing her name, tried to turn her head but stumbling into the piebald had to turn again to the nearside hedge. Her remaining vision was in her right eye. The effort of going forward head sideways must have been a great strain. Slobbers of froth falling from her mouth, steam rising from her foaming neck, nostrils flaring, she looked half mad.

An apple tree stretching generously over the road dangled clusters of Cox's pippins above their heads. Prunty and the Kicker grabbed one apiece. Though right in front of her nose, old Bessie couldn't see them. They hoofed up a steep hill, dust spurting behind them. They could see for miles the country spread before them. In dark waves, the fields unfurled beneath the racing clouds. Across the valley he could see the spires of the Catholic and Protestant churches in Clones. They looked side by side. Separated by dogma, they were twinned by distance.

'Here we are.'

They went up a lane hemmed by thick blackthorn and bramble. On the grassy track the hooves fell silent. The horses plunged and dunted for space in the clogged laneway. A bluebottle landed on the jade's ringworm. The oozing scabs glistened in the sun.

Abruptly they turned into a gateway, the gate clanging behind them. A grinning midget looked up at him. The midget, a man, bolted the gate. They were in a stony drive alongside a two-storeyed house with sheds growing out from the far gable. The drive descended steeply between the buildings and on the other side a four-foot wall of bare concrete blocks. The midget wore a red cap on a thick mop of curly hair, a white shirt and black trousers tucked into cut-down wellingtons. Round his waist was a big-buckled thick leather belt. The sight of the man was a shock. When he spoke he had a thin piping voice that hissed out along the roof of his mouth.

'We thought yiz weren't comin'.' Grinning happily, he was obviously pleased by their arrival.

Prunty and he dismounted. The horses' ears were cocked, nostrils dilating, frightened eyes rolling. The Kicker looked wildly about, a desperate expression on his face. The midget went in among them, gently slapping them, calming them. Stroking the Kicker, he scuttled between his legs and emerged unscathed.

'That's "the Goblin" Gilmour,' whispered Prunty, 'the only man in Ireland too small to be a jockey.'

Crammed in an upstairs window of the house were a woman and two girls. The girls had yellow ribbons in their hair.

From the bottom of the driveway a goat came up to meet them. Looking at the horses it gave a low gurgling 'meh-eh-heh'. 'There's Nanny,' piped the Goblin to the horses, 'saying welcome to yiz.'

The horses looked at the goat, not entirely convinced. The woman in the window called down. 'We saw you way beyant coming up the brae. They're ready below. Just drive them down.' The woman had a big laughing face.

Prunty removed the ropes and reins. Without them the horses looked even more isolated. They stood not knowing what to do, slobber spilling from their mouths.

He stood to one side, his arse and legs aching after the long ride. Weak, he leaned against the wall, his overcoat across his arm. The midget minced over to him. 'The slaughterhouse is down there. Yes. Yes.' When he grinned, the corners of his mouth turned up.

In complete contrast a tall, heavy man came into the driveway from round the back of the sheds.

'How's the men? How's she cuttin'?'

'Like a mowin' machine,' replied Prunty.

'Seven, is it?'

'Seven, Daddy,' piped the Goblin.

'Who's the gauson?' His eyes weighed him up but his words were to Prunty.

'The Sergeant's son from Butlershill,' said Prunty, undoing the jacket sleeves from round his waist.

'Go way? That's a good one.' Looking up to the woman in the window he shouted in a rough, booming voice, 'Hear that, Bella? The Sergeant's lad. Butlershill.'

The woman smiled down. 'Aye? He's a good cut of a young fellah.' When the girls smiled their faces lit up as if a bulb had been switched on in their heads. They were all looking at him. Even the doomed horses.

'Whatever ails you, gauson, don't worry.'

How did he know anything was troubling him? Maybe men could be read as easily as animals. Trapped as easily too. The midget had taken them by surprise and, along with the goat, calmed them for disaster. For a horrible moment he felt his fate was going to be the same as the horses'. The massive man was Bill Gilmour, well known for his knacker's yard. 'He's six foot four in his hobnails,' said Prunty, 'and can stun a pony with his fist.'

The piebald, long tail raised, hind legs straddled, let go a gush of urine which ran down the gravelled drive in a foamy rush.

The goat leading the way, they drove the horses down and at the bottom of the drive came into a big yard. The yard was bounded by what was now the front of the sheds and the rear of the house, and by three six-foot-high walls. A galvanized gate closed off all retreat. The gate was painted red and the sheets along the top had been crudely cut into jagged spikes. Painted on the gate in dribbling capitals were white words: 'GILMOUR KNACKER'S YARD. Phone Currinstown 10'.

The yard was rough concrete, pooled with urine, rain, dung and rainbow skids of Jeyes fluid. The sheds were makeshift – clinkered planks of wood, felt and tin. One shed, though, had solid walls and double doors. At the far end of the yard was an abandoned beachball, its innocent colours at odds with the prevailing smell of piss and death. The place was a mixture of slaughterhouse and circus.

'Which lad will we take first, Daddy?' piped the Goblin.

'That lad with the high notions.'

For a moment he thought they were referring to himself. The midget, picking up a hessian sack, handed it to Gilmour. Gilmour, arms outstretched, went towards the Kicker. 'Aisy, aisy now. That's the boy. Whoo. Aisy.'

The Kicker stood for him and allowed the sack to be put over his head. Then Gilmour, hand on the mane, led him in for slaughter. Had Gilmour put the sack on *his* head and led him in, he supposed he'd have gone as quietly. What could a rabbit do, a hen, a horse, a two-legged runaway, when it was decided their time was up?

Through the double doors he could see iron rings secured in the walls and chains hanging from them. Two men stood side by side. One of them held a rope, the other leaned on a sledgehammer.

Into the yard from the back door of the house came a one-legged man on crutches and a young boy carrying a curved dagger.

'The money,' said Prunty to Gilmour, 'and we'll be going.'

'Aye. Go up to Bella. Two pounds apiece, tell her.'

'The Colonel said three. Twenty-one quid.'

'He's coddin' you. Fourteen. Or you can take them back.'

'Frig you,' said Prunty.

'And you,' replied Gilmour.

They left the yard. Going out, he patted the blind mare by way of goodbye. Her old head hung sideways. The warm feel of her bony form was still along his thighs.

As they turned up the driveway Prunty whispered to him, 'See the oul' fellah? He got his leg kicked away be a stallion. No luck, see, killing horses.'

They had closed the galvanized gate behind them, and were going up the driveway when suddenly Prunty stooped down. Knee-high in the shed wall was a small window with a wooden panel instead of glass and a curtain of wire netting. Prunty prodded through the net and the panel swung back. In silence they knelt, looking in the window, which on this side of the driveway was high up in the slaughterhouse wall, almost level with the ceiling. They had a full view down on to the killing-room floor. The window was to let in extra light if needed. By law, the slaughterhouse doors were supposed to be shut in case other animals or children under sixteen could see what was going on.

The Kicker, head still in the sack, now had his feet in hobbles. A long rope made a collar round his neck. On the rope were two rings, one on each side of the neck. The rope ran from the neck and round to the hind leg pasterns in a twist and back to the neck, the ends passing through the rings. Gilmour had one end of the rope, one of the men the other. Standing behind the horse they began to pull. The Kicker's neck was gradually forced down and his hind legs forward. Bit by bit the hind legs moved closer to the front ones. The horse was caught between the pressure on his gullet and the struggle to keep his balance.

'Aisy, aisy. That a boy. Aisy.'

When all four legs were unnaturally close, Gilmour put his hands on the shoulder and hindquarter and pushed. The Kicker, whinnying pitifully, crashed down on to the concrete floor. Quick as a spider the Goblin darted from the shadows and sat on the head.

'A child could hold a horse's head down,' whispered Prunty. 'It can't get up.'

Gilmour's hobnailed boots clacked the floor as he and the men circled the stricken animal. The Goblin whipped the sack from the head and sat again. The one-legged man carried in a bucket of water. The Kicker struggled, trying to rise, its unpared hooves thrashing the floor. Gilmour, on his hunkers, stroked it, calming it down.

'Aisy. Sure there's nawthin' to worry about, hah? There now, aisy.'

The Goblin, looking up, saw them. He grinned, winked. The Kicker's eye, watery white and rolling, was a planet about to crash. When he fell over the shed shook. Up at the window he and Prunty had felt the dull vibrations in their knees. The great black body lay heaving, wet with sweat. It was the underside colour of a mushroom frying in a pan. The Goblin was now on his knees beside the head, and with a magician's flourish produced an iron bolt in a metal holder with a flat projecting rim at one end. Removing a hank of mane he placed the holder plumb in the

59

middle of the forehead and held it there with his stubby, deft hand. The man with the sledge-hammer moved in and got ready to strike.

'Excuse me,' he heard himself shouting down, 'shouldn't you be using a humane killer?'

From the slaughterhouse floor, faces looked up.

'Shut up for frig's sake,' said Prunty from the corner of his mouth.

Gilmour wiped his mouth with the back of his hand. 'The humane killer's lost. Or stolen. This way's just as quick. The state of these animals is against the law. This fellah's got glanders. They've got to be put out of their misery. Or do you think, gauson, we should let him lie a while longer?' Gilmour, head cocked, eyebrows raised, waited for an answer.

A loaded question couldn't be answered. Gilmour had been killing animals all his life. He knew what he was doing. He felt foolish. Gilmour turned away. The Goblin replaced the bolt dead centre on the forehead. The man with the sledge-hammer stood close to the horse's head, shifted his feet for balance, touched the end of the bolt with the sledge, then raising it brought it down with a full-force wallop which drove the bolt into the Kicker's brain.

As if electrocuted, the horse shuddered, legs kicking, tail flipping, then lay utterly still. Its milky eyes frosted over.

'He'll kick no more now,' said Prunty.

The boy with the curved knife went quietly over and knelt by the horse's neck. He placed a porringer on the floor. Making the sign of the Cross, he bowed in prayer. Then he raised the curved blade.

Gilmour reached up and banged shut the wooden panel with a long pole. The wire netting trembled. It was like having a tabernacle closed in their faces. In silence, he and Prunty got up and walked away.

'Him, the wee boy, he's got the cure for bleeding. He drinks fresh blood. And he's got a prayer his grandfather gave him on his deathbed. It stops women bleeding. People from all over go to him. Go you up to Bella and get the money. I'm bustin' for a pish.'

Was life a circus performed in an abattoir? The slaughtering of the horse had comic elements. Watching his father kill the hen had the same feel. On her deathbed his mother's big toe stuck out

60

from her stocking . . . If the worst events were funny, did that mean the best were going to be sad?

He followed Bella upstairs. She was humming 'Hot Diggity'. Her bare legs were strong, brown. She wore flat shoes and ankle socks. From under a brass bed she got a white enamelled basin. It was full to the brim with money, all in notes. On the top were mostly big white hundred-pound bills. For such money his father would have to work a lifetime.

Bella's face was big, rough, handsome. Make-up caked the down on her upper lip. Brass rings hung from her ears. When she scratched under her armpit, he saw a glistening tuft of black hair.

'Have you a girlfriend?'

'Yes. No. No, I haven't.'

'Don't worry. You will.' As she counted out the fourteen pounds she smiled.

'Can you tell the future, Bella?'

'I can. It's the same as yesterday.' She laughed.

In the doorway the two girls stood looking at him. Their smiling faces would grow rough and tough like their mother's. She held his hand and put the money on his palm and closed his fingers across it. 'I've given you a pound extra. For yourself. You'll be lucky. I can tell that.'

'Yes? Can I have it in writing?' He was joking, but she took him seriously.

'I haven't got a pen.' No, maybe she was joking too.

The room, apart from the bed, had modern furniture and plastic flowers.

A pair of wooden crutches leaned against the wardrobe.

'Thank you, Bella.'

He and Prunty walked home. When it began to rain they sheltered under a tree. The soft rain fell with a ticking sound against the leaves. The country was a wet clock.

That night he shared Prunty's bed. In the kitchen he could hear the old mother clucking and scolding to herself – 'What will the Sergeant say?' A fag glowed intermittently in Prunty's mouth.

He was tired, drained.

'Prunty?'

'What?'

'Will you fix me up with a widdy?'

5

From the bed he could hear Prunty out in the byre, milking. The bucket was a tin drum when the milk splashed fresh from the dug. Filling, it turned conch, foaming with the swish and swoosh of creamy lullaby. Swallows zipped by the window, and across the road between hayfields and a distant scraggy hill the morning sun splashed diamonds on a silvery lake. In the kitchen rashers sizzled, the smell seeping into him through gaps in the planked oak door.

'Are you getting up, young fellah?'

'I am.'

Mrs Prunty moved about, the shoes loose on her old feet. 'Your father knows you're here, young fellah.'

'Does he?'

'You were noticed. The squad car from Cavan called this morning to check.'

He was relieved his father knew his whereabouts. He might leave him alone for a while. Give him time to fight his way out of the nightmare. He sat on the edge of the brass bed, letting the cold of the concrete floor calm him, earth his thoughts. He had taken a course of action and would have to be man enough to carry on with his plan. But he hadn't got a plan . . . Action was accidental happenings . . .

The room was sparsely furnished. The bed, a chair, and a solid oak wardrobe on top of which was a horse harness – a collar and hames, saddle and breeching. The inside of the collar was rubbed shiny by horseflesh. Straw stuffing protruded from the underside of the saddle. The leather strap of the breeching had at some time come apart and been re-joined with a crude twist of wire. The hames rested at an angle against the wall. With its slender curves and tapering ends it reminded him of a lyre. The harness, abandoned at the end of an era, still had power to move. Often the humbler a thing was the greater its music.

A small mirror hung on the window latch. He looked into it and saw someone resembling himself looking out. Pale face . . . his father's eyes . . . mother's nose . . . black hair from one of a score of uncles . . . hidden soul. We are camouflaged by bits of others.

At breakfast Mrs Prunty listened to Radio Eireann. On another wireless Prunty listened to the BBC. They commented continuously on what they were hearing. Out of politeness, he felt he had to keep the two conversations going.

'Some government, young fellah, what do you say?'

'It was the IRA blew it up. Sure who else could it be, lad?'

'What do you think of this Macmillan fellah?'

'Yes. Yes. I don't think about him . . . at all.'

'Do you think they'll get in next time, young fellah?'

'Whist! They found your man. The murderer. Hah, did you hear?'

'They might . . . I did.'

He was caught in a crossfire of voices; sniped at by mouths. He tried gulping food down in between questions.

'Hangin's too good for them, smashin' up a cinema, hah?'

'Flour up – bread up! Who'll suffer, lad, heh?'

His mouth was full of rasher, egg and mushroom; they looked at him, awaiting an answer.

'Ah . . . yes . . . no.'

Mrs Prunty's grey eyebrows wriggled up her forehead. She turned and stared up at Dublin, perched above her head on the mantelpiece. Prunty, crouched over his plate, had his head cocked towards London on the dresser. The BBC voice was clipped, dry, confident the world and his wife were listening. Radio Eireann sounded homely, wet, hopeful.

High on the wall above the fireplace hung a picture of St Patrick. The glass had a skim of greasy dust. The cardboard backing bulged away from the frame, ruckling the image, giving it a wavy look, as if the saint was turning into one of the snakes fleeing before his raised crozier.

'Whist,' said Prunty.

'Hisht,' said his mother.

The radio voices came together for the weather. Words and tone differed, but the outlook was the same. Ireland and the

63

United Kingdom were united under a blue sky and the foreseeable future would continue fair. Mrs Prunty, stretching to the high mantelpiece, switched off Dublin. Prunty, without looking, reached back to the dresser and shut down London.

A cock flew up on to the window sill and crowed in at them. The black feathers, flowing down its neck, swept across its body and up over its back in a dangling velvet gush. Brazen head flicking, it tried to focus on its reflection in the glass.

'Ah-ha, yah boy yah, I hope you have as much to say for yourself in the ring.'

'Is it a game-cock?'

'Aye. There's a big battle coming up.' He wiped his plate with a crust of home-made bread.

'Can I come?'

'A fine thing,' said Mrs Prunty, 'if the Sergeant raided youse and found him there.'

The cock crowed again, its high note shrill as the sound from a toy bugle. Mrs Prunty shook a dishcloth at the window. 'Get down, you blaggard. I'll be sorry to see him gone all the same.'

'He's going to win, Mammy, I'm telling you.'

Mrs Prunty wore black woollen stockings, a blue skirt, a black cardigan, a red blouse and on her head a white scarf decorated with a tangle of horseshoes and shamrocks. Her face was sallow, wrinkled – like an old nun's. Lifting an axe she let it fall gently on a sod of turf, breaking it to small pieces which she fed to the open fire. The flames guttered blue, spurted to red and green. Hooks and crooks hung from a crane which Mrs Prunty swung out into the kitchen. Beneath clear water potatoes shimmered in a heavy iron pot. Clunking a lid over them, she hooked the pot to the crane and swung it back in over the flames. Pale blue smoke curled round it, fiery tongues throbbed up to lick. Ash, piled at the back of the hearth, was the colour of Mrs Prunty's face. Milky tea.

Out of the rear window a sow rooted the hill rising sheer from the back door. There wasn't any grass – just mud churned up by cow-hooves. The hills were so steep that cattle never grazed sideways along them; always up and down or at oblique angles.

'That's your good suit isn't it, young fellah? I seen you wearing it at your mother's funeral. You'll need a pair of trousers to knock around in. Skip home and get a pair.'

'I'm not going home.'

64

'Holy God but this is troublesome.'

'He can borrie a pair of mine.'

'You're too butty forbye him. Take him down to Rinty's and get him a pair of jeans.'

Raising the hinged lid of a huge wooden bin, she bent into it, sighing with arthritic pain. The vertebra track along her skinny back was visible through her clothes. She emerged from the bin with a tea-caddy, from which she handed Prunty notes and silver.

'You'll have more than enough there. Wash yourselves first.'

Outside, they scooped a basin of water from a barrel and with cupped hands washed their faces. Prunty sprinkled water on his blond hair and dragged a comb through it. The teeth harrowed glistening tracks from the rim of his narrow forehead to the back of his head. The morning sun lit his pale blue eyes, dancing them in his freckled face. A droplet clung on his temple, then ran at an angle into his sideburn. He looked rough yet handsome, boyish and bursting with energy.

'I do hate tap water. Your only man is the elements. Shampoo yokes make you go baldy. And toothpaste rots your teeth. I'm not coddin' you, lad. And if you need medicine get it from a bush, not out of a bottle. By the way, lad, I've got just the widdy for you, did I tell you? We'll be towering turf today; I'll introduce you then.' Fantasy or reality, he looked as if he believed his own words.

The rainwater was soft on the skin, the sun warm on the back of the neck as he bent over the basin. A hen and chickens coming out from under a clump of bushes went to a puddle and drank. The tiny chickens on thread-thin legs looked light as ash. A cat crossed the yard, pretending not to notice them. The hen clucked her brood back under the bushes and, sitting, hid them in her plumpy feathers. Beside a shed, nettles grew through the wheels of a motorbike lying abandoned on its side. It was a BSA registration number ID 12. Adjoining the house was the byre and attached to that another shed. The yard between the back of the house and the butt of the hill was only about five yards wide, the surface a thin screed of concrete and in places hardened mud. An attempt had been made to tame the hill by planting along the yard-edge privet, box, elder, holly, broom. But they had long since grown wild and now gave shelter to hens and turkeys scratching around on the bare clay. A span above the shrubbery straggled a barbed-wire fence, put there to stop cattle falling down into the

65

yard. House and sheds had been gouged from the hill, but the hill looked as if it could at any moment roll forward and squash the farmstead flat.

It was a beautiful morning and his soul was easy. Life could be simple. All you needed was a thatched roof, whitewashed walls, a turf fire, a hill to your back, a lake to the front . . . And a cow, a sow, a hen . . . If it was alive and gave you food, warmth, the sex was female. Heaven on earth was love and when you died the nettles grew through you; didn't matter who or what you were – man or motorbike. The hills of the world would one day roll forward and squash all the palaces and houses flat. But not today. Today he'd take his chances with the 'widdy'. Whatever happened to him from now on could only be an improvement.

On Mrs Prunty's ladies' bicycle he rode alongside Prunty towards the Border. The ladies' bike was old, with curved down-tubes. Prunty's was a sturdy three-speed with an extra-large carrier over the rear wheel.

'I got them extra bits welded on be the blacksmith.'

'What for?'

'You'll find out soon enough.'

The road was the main road North. 'And the longer you go the mainer it gets.' 'Mainer' was a play on the word 'mean', which the locals pronounced 'mane'. They changed the word 'beat' in the same way, pronouncing it 'bate'. 'Heap' came out their mouths as 'hape'. Language was churned, vowels and consonants shifted until mood and meaning matched. 'There's nawthin' clane about pigs 'cept the money.'

A black Ford Prefect came by them. The driver swivelled to scrutinize them, slowing down as he did so.

'What do you think you're lookin' at?' shouted Prunty.

The driver's head was bald. Moon bare.

'The skull of you,' shouted Prunty, 'and the price of turnips!'

The driver and his passenger, pleased they had drawn him, accelerated away laughing.

'See don boy with the specs – he's head beefer in the Customs in Clones. The driver is Hughie Sloan, the manest fecker ever wore dentures.'

'Is it not a bit dangerous this, Prunty?'

'They're goin' home. They arrested Packie Reilly smugglin' pigs. That's where they're coming from. Trying to persuade him to plead guilty.'

66

'How do you know?'

'It pays to know. Wait'll you get the jeans. The women will ate you alive, I'm tellin' you, lad.'

Their freewheeling bikes whispered over the dry tarred road. Saddles creaking, spokes blurring, they were ghosts ticking through the silent land. When they pedalled Prunty favoured the right pedal, pounding on it hard so that the crank gave a clunk against the chain-case at the start of every revolution. Back arched, handlebars gripped in close to the stem, Prunty affected the pose of a racing-cyclist. Shoulders and head bobbing in unison, his eyes took in the countryside and everything that moved. He lived by his eyes.

On their right the land was a rising, drumlin roll of Christmas-pudding hills. The fields were divided by thick hedges of blackthorn, bramble and a variety of trees. The old grass lay in overgrown clumps, jagged as choppy water. The land was too steep and wet to plough. The fields had lain untilled for centuries. Not even the English could cultivate them. They left them to the Catholic natives. In the sheltered corners of most of them a few cattle huddled knee-deep in cloven muck and dung. In places you could see clumpy rocks sticking up, fringed with whin.

'I've ploughed rock, lad. Bruk me heart. Along with many's the coulter bruk as well.'

A hare came lolloping down towards them, eyes just visible above the grass. Turning tail it bounded away, its long hind legs perfect for the hills.

'It wipes its scent on every blade of grass. The bagles love it the way we love the smell of buttered toast.' 'Bagles' were beagles. Prunty had two of them which he kept locked in a shed until needed for the hunt.

They could see another hare, this one much closer. It stood erect, motionless, its brownish fur merging into the background. They stopped and watched. Baring its teeth, it hissed in their direction. Then grunted. Ears in a V-sign it hopped lazily towards them, to an open patch of ground where it paused so still it was hard to believe you were watching flesh and blood and not a tuft of grass. Its buck teeth were like the row of white control buttons on Prunty's wireless. It grunted again, moaned, then began grinding its teeth. Hopping forward it drummed the ground, front paws blurring.

'He's one cheeky boy,' whispered Prunty. 'He must be a Monaghan hare.'

Like a shot it blurred to speed, disappearing in a necklace of spurting leaps, its flight to its stillness as steam to water. An entire transformation, like words on a page suddenly spoken.

'The leps and bucks is to break the scent trail.'

They rode across the Border into Northern Ireland. The road was slightly wider, a thick lip of tar the dividing line. The land was the same. Nailed to a tree a poster proclaimed in bold black letters: 'REPENT THAT YE MAY BE SAVED'. A broken signpost, twisted from its true direction, leaned out of the ground at a crossroads. Confusing the British army was a Republican ploy.

When they got to the Finn bridge two jeeps were stopped in the middle of the road. The soldiers were out looking at the big map spread on the bridge parapet. An officer with a thin moustache looked up as they approached.

'Is this the way to Newtownbutler?' he asked in an accent dry and clipped. He sounded just like the BBC announcer.

'Aye, 'tis, all the way. In both directions,' replied Prunty.

The officer stared blankly at him. A short, stout corporal stabbed two fingers in the direction of Castle Finn rising in the distance above the seeping countryside.

'The RUC said keep the castle on our left, right? So we must be heading right. The right way. Right?' The corporal's fingers, brown with nicotine, were tar-black round the nails. His accent was Cockney, his face pasty but tough.

'Yiz keep it on your left all right,' said Prunty, 'but not if yiz are facing south. It all depends which side of the castle yiz are on.'

'Are we facing south?' said the officer.

'No,' replied Prunty.

'Well then,' said the officer, his face blank, eyes narrowing.

The soldiers looked at them. Most of them were as young as themselves. The corporal folded the map. The officer made a snout of his lips and stroked his chin with finger and thumb.

'Daft bugger,' said the corporal in Prunty's direction. 'You'd get more sense from that river down there.'

'Well,' said Prunty, 'you wouldn't get a dry answer anyway.'

A baby-faced soldier smiled. The others looked at the officer. When he smiled, they smiled. The corporal looked grim and opened the map again. The castle stood on a hill above a graceful bend in the river. With its decorative battlements, towers and chimneystacks, it looked like a tiered wedding-cake plonked above a swamp.

A girl came through them on a bicycle. Because of the jeeps he hadn't seen her approach. None of them had. The soldiers eyes brightened as they watched her pass. Flaxen hair hung down her back in hanks. He didn't turn his head but she was in his mind, snug as thought. Soft as bare feet on lino he could hear the receding tick of bicycle wheels. Each man's face had been transformed by her sudden arrival. A soldier lit a cigarette. She was gone.

'Get in,' ordered the corporal.

The men scattered into the jeeps, two of them clunking helmets as they scrambled for their places. Uniforms and weaponry were different from that of the Free State soldiers calling at the barracks, but the faces were the same – eager, innocent, far from home. Yet no matter how far away they lived, they were nearer home than he was himself. Where was his home? In the barracks in Butlershill? In the cemetery with his mother? In the fields? Along the roads? Wherever, he felt miles from it. Possibly centuries.

The officer sat in the passenger seat of the leading jeep. 'This *is* Fermanagh, I take it?' he said to Prunty, with the careful, amused air of Hamlet to the Gravedigger.

'It's a good question,' Prunty replied. 'The river is the Border and you're parked dead centre. Another smidge on and you're in Fermanagh all right. But then again another fifty yards and you're in Monaghan.' Prunty was delighted with the geographical confusion he was spreading. 'To my mind, if you don't know where you're going, you shouldn't be going at all.'

Prunty, his left foot on the road, his right thigh resting on the crossbar of his bicycle, leaned on the handlebars, easy in himself, unafraid. His shirt collar lifted away from the back of his sweaty neck. His hair there was matted against the skin, wet and slicked down like hen feathers in the rain. His freckles were the colour of the nicotine on the corporal's fingers.

Leaning out of the window, the officer smiled, winked, but not to Prunty. He slapped the jeep roof with his fingers and the engine roared into action heading away along the indeterminate country.

He and Prunty leaned on the parapet of the Finn bridge. The stones were warm from the high sun.

Prunty laughed. 'You shoulda seen your face when your wan rode by.'

'My face? I was the only one didn't gawp.'

'You were the only one *did*, you mean.'

Maybe thoughts were ripples on a clear surface. Your face could always betray you. If you were full as a tick with longings. Like a breeze through corn, your soul shifted for all to see. His face was a soul-mirror. He was in it all the time. Like his mother's face trapped in the powder compact. Until freed by someone else.

The land on either side of the river was scrawny with dock, marsh ragwort, spearwort, nettles, rushes. Paling edged the water, the posts leaning in rotten angles, reeds plaited through the barbed-wire strands. On the Cavan side a telegraph pole with a crosspiece gave the landscape a Calvary look. A wagtail bobbed lazily over the water, landed on a stone. Down from the castle, they could see near the river bend a semicircle of weeping willows drooping towards the water. A cow and calf hurried for shelter from the clegs and flies.

'See don big oak between the willows and the castle? That's the coven-tree. Where the Colonel's father met all the labourers.'

The Colonel lived in the castle with Sophie Kay. He'd seen her drive through the village once in an open-topped car. She wore dark glasses and a headscarf. A whiff of America hung on long after she'd gone. Prunty swore she went round the castle sometimes with nothing on but her perfume. That would be a good day to call.

'Are we going to the castle today? With the horse money?'

'No. We'll bring it tomorrow. We'll use it first.' Prunty winked at him.

From a wedge of bullrushes an otter swam silently out, a silken V rippling back from its slicing snout. It went right down the centre of the river, the V reaching both banks. Only the snout was visible. It looked like a big insect trailing gigantic watery wings.

'It's a wonder,' said Prunty, spitting into the river, 'with all the water about the place we weren't born webbed.'

He liked Prunty. He liked to be country cute, but for all his winks and nudges, which he couldn't resist, his intentions were always clear. He was going to use the horse money to buy goods in the North, smuggle them South and sell them, so making a profit. And he was his partner in crime. The opposite of life with his father. Smuggling was a custom of the country. Prunty, he hoped, was going to be the catalyst for transformation in his life. The love-bringing excitement-maker. A cleg landed on his wrist, settled with sluggish ease. He felt the surgical probe of the tang into his bloodstream. Clegs lacked the buzzing intensity of flies. They liked to bloat themselves in the sun. The pain grew sharp, deep, thorough. He welcomed it. It confirmed him and cancelled greater pains. He was leaning on a bridge above harsh, divided, yet beautiful land, his heart pumping dreams of lust, on his own, for a moment free. There must be fellahs like him all over the world, dreaming with him, their universal blood sickening with mad passions, clotting for the want of love. He could stand it no longer. He brushed the cleg away and it fell full and dead into the river. He was part of it now. A drop in the ocean. The Finn flowed into the Erne, the Erne flowed into the sea.

Riding on they turned down a lane at the bottom of which, tucked into the side, stood a shed with whitewashed walls, a shiny new galvanized roof and a small window on either side of the open door. This was Rinty Reilly's. On the 'street' in front were piles of furniture – armchairs, settees, chairs, tables . . . bicycles, washing-machines, fridges, televisions . . . the armchairs were upside down on the settees, the televisions were on the tables, the bicycles stacked against everything. Inside the shop was a bedlam of pots, pans, delph and cutlery loose in boxes, basins, buckets, brooms, imitation brass fenders, sacks of flour, meal, sugar, boxes of butter, razor blades . . . A dozen shiny kettles hung together from the one bit of binder twine looped through the handles. From nails along the rafters and in the walls hung suits, overcoats, skirts, dresses, trousers, jackets . . . piled on a table were ladies' hats, nylons and men's shirts . . . By their whangs from hooks above the door dangled clumps of hobnailed boots and clogs. The clog uppers were fixed to the wooden soles with shiny flat-headed tacks. The half-soles and heels were shod with iron, the nails sunk in the grooves. It was the only part of Ireland, this, where people still wore them. When the farmers came into the village the pavements rang, and at night sparks flew from their feet, kindling the dark. Clog whangs were the colour of plug tobacco. Cloves.

At the back of the shop a stout middle-aged woman bent over a heap of corsets lying on the cement floor. Beside her stood the proprietor – Rinty Reilly. He was a dapper man, with a head of silvery hair swept back from his forehead. Slap between his eye-brows, big as a thimble, was a shiny red carbuncle. The thumb of his left hand was missing and the first two fingers seemed to be joined by a flap of skin. As if webbed.

'Ah, the hard men,' he called jovially to them. 'How's the lia-troidie?'

'Oh, dangling nicely,' Prunty replied with a grin.

The woman laughed and selecting a corset from the pile wrapped it about herself.

'A dead-on fit, missus. The fat's held in without damaging the skin. It's a new design altogether.'

'Is it, has it bones in it?'

'No. Completely boneless. Sure that's the beauty of it, missus. It fits snug over the hips, yet it's elastic enough to stretch where required. I'm wearing one meself sure. For the oul' hernia. That's no word of a lie, missus.'

The woman looked at him. The humble look of his blubbery face, fleshy nose and the red carbuncle diverted attention from his eyes. He had a face hard to get used to.

'I'll have a couple of brassières as well,' said the woman, sticking the corset into a white flour sack. 'Have you any in?'

'Begod I have. These Equalizers are just the job. They're revolutionary altogether.' From a shelf he took down a cardboard box and on top of the corsets tipped out six brassières. 'They're designed for the larger figure. Like yourself. Or me own, missus. The subtle contours give you ojus confidence. Because they're strong enough to withstand any pressure.'

He held one of them up so that his right fist was in one cup, his deformed left hand in the other. 'See these cups, missus? They're in four sections, double-stitched. They're the best I've ever had.'

'Don't tell us,' said Prunty, 'you're wearing one yourself, Rinty.'

The woman laughed. Prunty winked and whispered. 'He's a desperate rogue. He'd sell holy water to an Orangeman.'

There was no counter or cash-till in the shop. Rinty conducted business beside the goods in question. The woman stuffed two Equalizers into her sack as well as four slabs of butter and a stone of sugar. Holding her hand out, Rinty slapped it. As in cattle-dealing. When she paid him, he poked the grubby notes into the belly of his shirt, the coin into his trouser pocket. Her sack twisted to a neck, the woman went out carrying it on her back.

'Well, men, what can I do for youse?'

Moments later he was standing trouserless beside a knee-high mound of jeans, his hands cupping his shirt round his privates, Rinty's eyes exploring his long pale legs.

'He could do with a pair of underpants,' Prunty observed.

'They're the one thing I haven't got. Fellahs tell me they only get in the way.' When he laughed the upper plate of his false teeth moved away from the gum.

The woman with the sack came back in, looking worried. She wore a blue dress belted round the middle with a piece of black elastic fastened with a safety-pin. Her huge bosom billowed out the top half of her dress. Her face was tough, weatherbeaten. Her eyes were tender.

'I only need the one bra, Rinty. Two's too many. Here, give us back the price of it.' She held out an Equalizer. The cups looked big enough to carry turf.

Rinty's blubbery face hardened. 'Sorry, missus. You know well – once the bargain's struck, it can't be bruk. Business is business, sorry.'

The woman sighed. Pausing by the door, she looked over at him. His hands were still tight round his privates, his bare legs so white he felt ashamed of them.

The woman grinned at him. 'Well, you're holding your own anyway.'

Her dry words drew a great wheezy laugh from Reilly. The woman went away pleased. Prunty didn't laugh but he saw him smile and turn away, pretending interest in a toaster on top of a tea-chest.

He tried on a pair of jeans.

'Pure American. They come in on a boat landed be mistake in Derry only last week. And I've got a pair of boots just the job for you as well. You'll need them, hanging round with his nibs.'

He was too taken up with trying to get into the jeans to cope with the idea of boots.

'How are they? They look . . . snug,' said Reilly.

'They look to me,' said Prunty, 'like the ballroom in Butlershill.'

Reilly looked at him. 'There's no ballroom in Butlershill.'

'And there's none in them jeans ayther.'

Reilly, looking deadpan at Prunty's grinning face, shifted his false teeth from his gums. 'Try this pair.'

He couldn't move. In agony, he crouched, immobile, desperate. It was his first encounter with a zip. His foreskin was meshed in the grip of tiny metallic teeth.

'Agh. Agh.'

What the hell was wrong with buttons? Why did flies have to be modernized? Speed. Zips were speedy. He turned away from Reilly's livid carbuncle and shifting teeth.

'What the feck's up with him?'

'He's caught his dangler in the zip,' Prunty replied.

'Jaze, is that all? Here, come here and I'll free you, gauson.'

'No thanks. Agh.' He had no intention of letting his private go public. Pain was embarrassing enough of itself. He didn't need the complication of Rinty's webbed hand anywhere near him. Struggling into a corner, he managed to wedge himself between a bundle of spade handles and a barrel of delph.

'Will you come here outa that. Sure I've seen more cocks in me time nor an army doctor.'

'Yeah? Well, you're not seeing mine.'

His most sensitive flesh was trapped. The troublesome core of his being. The flesh that rooted dreams. It looked comic now. He couldn't compare it with others. When he played football, before the match they all stripped in a shed, carefully hiding their danglers by turning their sinless backs on one another. When they urinated at the back of a hedge they cupped them one-handed, as if sheltering cigarette butts from the rain.

Reilly was still behind him, tugging his shirt-tail. He heard Prunty shout, 'Leave him be, Rinty. He'll do it himself. Give us two hundredweight of Indian meal. And I want razor blades as well.'

When he unsnicked himself he nearly fainted with relief. He was on his own now – Prunty and Reilly having gone outside. Carefully he tried on another pair of jeans. They fitted. He sat on a sack of flour. Heat thick as syrup came in the galvanized roof. The clothes hung from the rafters dead and warm. A funnel of light beamed in the window, revolving with dust. A trading-post in, the African bush couldn't have been more higgledy-piggledy than Rinty's. In a dim corner a mouse nibbled at a sack of corn.

A woman came in with her son. He was about fourteen, tall, pale, the side and back of his skull shaven, the top hairy. She wanted to buy an overcoat for him. He shyly looked about, his glance shifting quickly. With his black cap of hair and white face he looked like a willy-wagtail.

74

'In summer I do always buy for the winter, I do, Mr Reilly.'

'I know you do, missus. And fresh and well you're lookin'. There's not a day on you from when last I saw you. Put this on, son. Summer bargains for winter wear. He'd look well in a pair of swimming trunks. A caseload came in be accident with a load of frocks.'

'No, God no. He's afeard of water and'll not go within an ass's roar of it, will you? An overcoat is all we want, Mr Reilly.'

The boy stood dumbly while Reilly fitted him into an overcoat which had been hanging on the back of the open door, along with a string of saucepans. The sleeves hid his hands, the shoulders drooped down his arms, the hem was at his ankles. It looked big enough to cloak a horse.

Rinty buttoned it up on the boy, stepped back in an admiring pose and without a trace of irony said, 'Suits him down to the ground, missus.'

'Looks a bit . . . stretched . . . hah, does it?'

'Not at all. It's feck-all use to man nor baist buying too wee. Sure he'll grow into it. A coat the like of that will last him a lifetime. For a start, feel the wool. It's thick enough to stop bullets.'

The woman opened her purse. Head sideways, eyes narrowed, she pecked into it until her beaky fingers wodged with notes flew up to Reilly's big soft open hand. The boy peeked out from the overcoat like a scaldy from a nest.

Mother and son walked away, she scolding him, reassuring him, tucking at the overcoat, patting it, her touch already making it part of him. Her son walked with his arms held out in front of him as he examined the coat, trying to find something about it to like. It was a horrible colour – rusty red, with two rows of big green buttons, a thick seam running down the back, and a belt dangling from the loops almost touching the ground. It was a 'Rinty special' all right but the big scaldy was walking home beside his mother. She was alive, she loved him, the sun shining on them, blessing them together.

He liked the jeans. This was what they wore in America. This was fashion. When his mother made rice pudding, as an ingredient she added nutmeg. The zip made the same sound as the nutmeg on the grater. He wondered how long it would take for her image to fade from his ears and eyes. Through a rear window with iron bars, he could see out to a field. Two men crossed in the distance, crouched, hurrying. They carried rifles. One of them wore a wellington on his right foot, a shoe on the other. His trouser leg was tucked down the wellington and inside his sock. The other man wore a long black oilskin, the sun skidding all over it. The odd footwear was to confuse pursuers. Every few weeks men died. Bullets tore holes in their hearts and brains, their blood dripping on to the poor grass. But all the blood in the world couldn't make good hay in the fields along the Border. 'Agriculturally both sides are blind,' his father said.

The two men, on their hands and knees, disappeared through a hole in the hedge, dragging their rifles behind them like tails.

Reilly came and stood before him holding out a new boot. 'I'm going to let you have them for half price. Try it on, son.'

Prunty came in and winked at him. As if he had put one over on the world. 'What's the damage, Rinty?'

'Includin' the boots . . . let me tot her up. He could do with a pair of swimming trunks as well.' From a suitcase he pulled a pair of huge yellow trunks. 'They'll double as underpants. Try them on if you like.'

'After you,' Prunty laughed.

'It's not me needs them.'

'That makes two of us.'

'Some people don't know what they're missing.'

'I do, Mr Reilly. I do.' His heart was an empty suitcase.

When they went outside, Prunty had the bikes loaded. The meal bags were slung on the frames across the pedals; the carriers laden with boxes of butter and razor blades. The blades were 'Max Smile' with a trademark picture on each box – a bald head and stubbled face, or if you turned it upside down a clean-shaven face and stubbled head. He tied the cardboard box with the boots on to Prunty's bar. Prunty leading the way, they wheeled the bikes out past the heaped furniture and stacks of electrical goods. The spread-eagled load was heavy and hard to keep upright. Copying Prunty, he had one hand on the handlebar, the other gripping the back of the saddle. They bumped over the uneven laneway, the load tending to tilt one way, then the other. Under the weight the tyres ran flat along the ground, tracing a thin patterned rut over the baking mud.

'How much do I owe you? I've only got the pound Bella gave me.'

'You'll owe me nawthin' be the time we've sold the male an'

blades. And the buthur.' The language shot out of Prunty's mouth rough and rich as forkfuls of dung. After he spoke you could sow thoughts in the air. 'When we're back in the State, any Customs come – down in the gripe, yah boy yah. Bike an' all. Do you want a clove?'

'Not now thanks.'

Chewing a clove and smoking a Gold Flake, Prunty plodded steadily ahead.

'There's a dance in the Freemasons' Hall in Clones on Saturday. We're goin'. A whole gang of us.'

'Yeah? Who? I can't dance.'

'Away to feck. If you can walk you can dance. Anyway, it'll be fightin' not dancin' we'll be. Turnip McQuade outa Belturbet and his mob want to battle us. They sent word. The bastard. There's thirty of them. And they've got the Scud Gillaspie from Newtownbutler. He's done three years in the Irish Guards. His sister's married to Turnip's first cousin. There'll be me and you and the crowd from Wattlebridge agin the whole of them. We'll give them lanty, don't fret. The feckers. Last time they pumptured all our bicycles.'

Dancing was one worry, but fighting was even worse. The only boxing he'd ever done was at boarding school. One of the priests had boxing gloves. He saw himself as a James Cagney figure. He'd sparred with this priest and once accidentally bloodied his nose. Come Saturday in Clones the Marquis of Queensberry rules wouldn't apply. But what could he do now? He was with Prunty and had to go along with him. Or retreat to the barracks. And his father; who had fists hard enough to drive in nails. Mind you, the Scud Gillaspie sounded terrible. Like a giant from a fairy-tale. 'Gillaspie' was the way Prunty pronounced 'Gillespie'. It was a Protestant name. Prunty and the Scud obviously didn't care what foot you kicked with, so long as you kicked.

Prunty could fight. He looked tough. He wheeled the bike along, his strong arms and stocky build an easy match for the cumbersome load. The sacks had two 'pig's ears' on the top end so you could get a grip when lifting. They hung in a slump across the frames like dead swine.

The sun was high in the duck-egg sky. It was the best weather they'd had for a long time. You could see the country drying out; the sullen greens in the hedges cheering up; the rushes in the fields gleaming; the grass trying to look healthy. The veins on the dock leaves ran sharp as herring bones and the hogweed and ragwort were white and yellow flags flying over the battered face of the land. Wrens, robins, finches, linnets, tits, yellowhammers, scattered seeds of song into every hawthorn bush. A crow, jagged wings outspread, floated lazily down the air, landing with a hop on the worn ground of a gap between two fields.

The sun's best gift was light. It reached into death corners, flushing out damp black days. It bled the colour out of loved faces, blurring them like bad photographs; giving you a chance to forget.

'Prunty . . . I believe the sun is an old circus clown, who's seen it all before.'

'Heh?'

'He can make you laugh . . . till you cry.'

'You've got some brains frying in that pan of yours, lad.'

He was perspiring, aching with the effort of keeping up with Prunty. But would he, then, have swopped places for anywhere else in the world? For London? New York? His father had a dream of America. It was a perpetual thirst on his tongue. But men went to those places and died of hunger for Ireland.

Across a couple of fields, sticking above a clump of trees was the ivy-clad gable-end of an ancient ruin. Prunty in vouching for its historical importance had no problem joining the past with the present. 'It was the home of kings. The Chieftains of Fermanagh. There was a king there could battle agin swords with his bare arms. He could put his fist through a shield. He used take to the wars with the English in his buff bollock. Nawthin' on but his crown. It was ojus altogether. He could sit a creamery can along the length of his dangler. Bet all. When Crumwell came to Ireland it took five hundred and sixty cannonballs to finally kill him. But on a moony night you can still see him stalking about the place, looking for his lost kingdom. Maguire was his name. Aye man surely. Me mother would be a distant relation. All the land round here is theirs be right. But most of it's Protestant now. And they'll only sell to their own.'

They crossed back over the Finn and were now in the Free State again. The Free State was what the people along the Border called the Republic. It was a term left over from the partitioning of the country in 1921. Partition was a legal fact, but along the Border fact melted into fantasy. Maguire still was king. Especially on moony nights.

'Do you think smuggling is a sin?'

'Go way and take a runnin' jump for yourself, lad. God niver said a hate about it, did he? God is God. Politicians are a different kettle of fish entirely.'

'Do you believe in God?'

'I go to mass on a Sunday. Isn't that enough for you? God put us on this world to destroy it. I believe that for a fact. Aye man surely.'

Prunty walked faster now, in an urgent crouch, his head cocked for any sign of Customs men. The road was tarred, straight, and sheltered by high hedges. It was an unapproved road – you weren't supposed to traffic along it, but people did. The official route added miles and time to a journey as well as enforced stops at a British Customs Post going north and an Irish one returning.

'Hisht!'

Hearing the noise of a car, Prunty dived for the ditch, slung bike and all down into it, then quickly helped him secrete his load.

'Aisy. There's water here. Keep down.'

The bottom of the ditch was about four feet below the level of the road. Long beards of grass draped down, nettles – the roots bare – grew out from the bank, and on the hedge side yellow primroses smiled up towards the sun. The bicycle wheels were sunk to the hubs in dock and bramble. From the clayey bank a flute of water whispered out over a tuft of watercress.

A car slowly approached. It went past on the far side of the road, then stopped. Reversing into a gateway, it came back along the near side. They could glimpse the black roof.

'It's them all right.'

'I thought you said they were going home?'

'You know what thought done? Stuck a feather in the ground and thought he'd grow a hen.'

They listened until the car noise faded away. On his hunkers, Prunty urinated, the gush splashing a moss-covered stone. Even his dangler was freckled. A wren, head and tail cocked, flicked frantically through the thick hedge, brazen with defiance. A long-legged spider pegged across the bar of Prunty's bike and, lowering itself on a line of web, ambled over the bag of meal.

'We'll chanst it.'

They hauled and clambered out of the ditch. His good suit was scratched, the knees muddied, his shoes soaking. Wheeling along the road, the tension added weight to the load. Over a field a kestrel dived, landed, returned to air, a dark smudge of dying life in its claws. The mother bird, arriving too late, flew up the sky, soaring in despair, her cries against the blue drops on an ocean. Soaring, swooping, wheeling, misery at last brought her to earth, grounding her beside the empty nest.

'A sky-lark. You can tell by the white tail feathers. They breed on the flat under tufts of grass. But the hawk has an eye could spot the ring through a brack.'

It was all a question of balance. Keeping your feet on the ground. Or landing on them after flight. Learning to walk on edges. The road they were on was a tightrope. Cavan one minute. Fermanagh the next. Customs men lay in wait. Squad cars patrolled. His father's eyes scowered the land for his precise location. A lark, a hare, a stone . . .

The closer you were to the ground, the more dangerous it was. Yet danger sharpened the senses. He could see the caution on the back of Prunty's neck. It was a short, thick neck, ready to take a blow from any direction. He lived by his wits, survived by his strength. Baffled with words. Were they true or false?

'The thing about a widdy – they know the ropes. "Flog me for being naughty," says she to me last week. "No better man," say I. It was powerful. We buck-leapt all over the kitchen. It was cat. Then she flogged me. With a sally.'

'Sally who?'

'I'm not coddin' you, lad,' he shouted back angrily. 'And you better not tell anyone what I'm tellin' you. I'm tellin' you.'

The bag of meal seemed to be getting even heavier; the tyres so flat he could feel the wheel rims on the road. His legs and arms ached, trembled with fatigue. Was smuggling worth it? Smuggling goods . . . smuggling yourself?

Fly high, lie low, sing dumb. Your head was a carrier for dead images. The past was dead. But it never stopped fogging up the back of your skull. And then you had to try and put words on it all. Lark, hare, stone. Sense had to be smuggled out into the open, on the back of language. But the sky was full of hawks. Hawk was experience. Death. The invisible eye with a hidden beak. Death – the sun's bastard brother. The eye-closer. And then nothingness. Past. By then, though, maybe your image was in someone else's tortured head. But for that, first there must be love. But according to the poets, love and pain were hand in hand. He'd have to slip into the barracks and get his book from the belly of the sewing-machine. There was a whirring image. He could see his mother's face blurring in the spokes, in his mind behind his eyes, beyond words. But the challenge was to tame thought wordwise. To plant words like seed potatoes, every letter an eye, and hope the blight didn't strike. Famine. It still stalked the land. Every time you looked into a mirror there it was, lurking, at the back of the glass. He could see the fear of it in his father's eyes when he stuffed food down himself. The idea of city-dwellers going out to a restaurant was, to his father, laughable nonsense. Blasphemous. Food wasn't something to be toyed over, dressed up in French words, teased down your throat in the semi-dark of candlelight. Food wasn't a plaything. Food was deadly serious. Food was the best word in the dictionary. Famine the worst. Famine was the curse of God. Famine was lack. An empty plate. But worse, an empty soul. Loneliness. He was walking on the Border, loaded yet empty. He was high at the top of the tent on a tightrope. The circus was always in town. It never left. Today, now, the big top was on a passage of land looping into womby Fermanagh. And if you fell you could, according to the law, land in any one of three counties, two countries. The land shaped you, made your destiny before you were even born. The circus acts never changed. The circus is in town. For one life only. Lark, hare, stone . . .

Prunty was what he was because he was what he was. He was doing what he was doing because he was what he was doing. So where did that leave him – the motherless whelp searching for a bone?

They were coming up to Brady's pub at Legakelly. Prunty ploughed on in front, back bent, arse waddling, his stride restricted because of the bag of meal. In his turned-down wellingtons and his short, mincing walk he looked comic.

'How long more, Coco?'

'Shut your gob. It's not funny, lad.'

'How's your dangler, Coco?'

Prunty stopped, lay across the handlebars and began laughing, his head shaking, one foot kicking the meal bag in a spasm of mirth. 'Yah hoor yah, lad, yah ojus hoor.'

A rat scurried across the road, bumped into the grassy verge, scuttled down into the ditch, the undergrowth rustling like fire. Only a few weeks ago he had sat by the range with his mother, listening to the silky flames tearing up the chimney.

Prunty recovering, they walked on, but within seconds their hearts had practically stopped. Hidden by the far gable of the pub was the Customs car, a Garda squad car and an army jeep. The men were out of the vehicles, casually leaning against them. Waiting their arrival. In the middle of them stood his father.

Prunty groaned and stopped dead. Wilted, he no longer looked as if he owned all the fields he walked through. They were caught, trapped. There for the taking. The men grinned, his father showed a sardonic glint of teeth. His father, resplendent in his dark-blue uniform and silver buttons, hands behind his back, stood in the 'at ease' position. He was enjoying the moment.

Prunty turned to him, a hopeless, helpless, amazed look on his face. Suddenly he had become a child. A boy, his lips stained with cloves.

'Keep walking.'

Prunty looked surprised at the steely bitterness in his voice. He turned, and head shyly down, waddled with his load past the eyes of all the Guardians of the State. His father had arranged the ambush. To teach him a lesson. To let him know that nothing he did would go unnoticed. His father's eyes were a barbed-wire barrier in his way. The country looked empty. Yet a crow couldn't land on a cow-pat without somebody writing it down. He was in a lather of sweat until he saw his father. Then his body went cold with a mixture of hate and shame. The moments it took to walk past seemed to expand into hours. He could hear the leather soles of his shoes on the tarmac, hear the ticking of the bikes, the comic squeak in Prunty's left wellington. Forcing himself to turn, he looked sideways into his father's eyes. They were as hurt as his own. Famine-mirrors.

They were allowed to pass because it was a humiliation. A squashing. A clipping of wings. When at last they were clear round the bend in the road, Prunty began giggling nervously. 'I'm niver goin' smugglin' with you agin, lad. Or I'm niver goin' without you. I don't know the which.'

'If they'd arrested us – what's the fine?'

'Seize the load and twice the value in a fine. Seize the bikes as well, a coorse.'

He'd have lost the boots. And his American jeans. The jeans were on Prunty's carrier, between a box of butter and a box of blades. He was counting on the jeans for a change in his sexual fortunes. The jeans and a white shirt. Maybe with a slim black tie. Combine mourning and fashion. A bit of chewing-gum and learn the words of a few songs. 'It's Only Make-Believe' and 'I Guess It Doesn't Matter Anymore'. They were on the lips of every girl over ten. Lips and eyes. Words and images. Sounds and silence. The only thing he wanted on lips was kisses. Empty lips – that was famine.

When at last they reached Prunty's, the mother was snapping with worry, annoyance and relief. His father had called on her. 'The Sergeant's been here, been here. In here.'

They wheeled the goods into a shed and covered them with hay.

'We won't be making turf today, lad. I'm bet to the world. The widdy will have to wait.'

He went into the bedroom, put on the jeans and then tried the boots. The right one he knew was perfect. He'd had it on in the shop. But when he took the left one out of the box he could see there was something odd about it. The leather of the right was black and shiny. The left was black, but dull and crinkled round the toecap. The welt was thicker than the right, and wider. The upper seemed to sit on a plump lip of leather. The right was as perfect as a boot could be, but the left reminded him of the nursery-rhyme shoe in which lived the old woman and all her children. It was always a boot in cartoons. The boot fitted, was the right size – eight – but it looked somehow grotesque. A nightmare boot. A touch of the surgicals. It certainly wasn't the twin of the other. A cobbler's bastard of a boot.

When he showed it to Prunty and his mother, they stared at it, shaking their heads, the mother sighing.

'That Rinty Reilly, he'd annoy a nation. He once sold me husband, RIP, a jacket and when he got it home it only had the one sleeve. When we complained he told him to cut the other sleeve off and he'd have a powerful winter waistcoat. He'd annoy a nation.'

'Once the bargain's struck, it can't be bruk.' He was stuck with the boots. But the jeans were grand. He liked the look of them, especially the stylish turn-ups. Just having them on made him want to click his fingers to imaginary music. With a pair of jeans on, the world was a better place.

All evening they watched television. It was the first time he'd seen it close up. They didn't have a television at boarding school, and at home his father wouldn't dream of getting one. He claimed it was bad for the eyes. And was coming from London – 'the city of sin'.

'Go long with you. The only thing worrying you is the cost of the electricity to run it.'

His mother was right. His father couldn't bear the thought of a bulb left on one second longer than necessary. And he always listened to the wireless turned down low, because he thought it used less current that way.

Mrs Prunty sat silently in front of the screen as if she were sitting reverentially in church. Her ashen face was tense, her lips moving as if in prayer.

'It'll kill all travelling,' said Prunty. 'You have the whole world in your kitchen.'

The screen was a terrible confusion of creatures pretending to be flower-pots; cowboys shooting Indians; the Royal Family waving to African men, naked except for dishcloths over their danglers. A car horn beeped. Prunty went outside. They could hear a van back into the yard. A few minutes later Prunty returned with a ball of crinkled notes in his fist.

When they were in bed, Mrs Prunty answered a loud knocking on the door. It was the Colonel looking for his money. He sounded drunk. 'I'll be pleased to disturb you . . . Mrs P. . . . young Prunty in? Sophie Kay, you see . . . the little matter of the horses . . .'

Mrs Prunty sent him flying with a broom. 'Away off with you, damn your soul, and see us in the morning. The civilized world's in bed a time since.'

The engine continued throbbing outside the house, then the car drove away.

Mrs Prunty rattled about the kitchen complaining. 'Sophie Kay within in the car with him. She wasn't long in America then. The hussy. You could see the moonlight on her peroxide hair. He'd annoy a nation, the Colonel. When he's drunk.'

'It's a known fact,' whispered Prunty in the dark, 'American women have bigger tits and bigger mouths than women elsewhere. It can only mean one thing.'

He didn't inquire further. The inside of his head was a television screen cavorting with spit-coloured images of larks and hares and stone . . . Prunty's big hairy arse was warm as a stove. Falling asleep, he could hear the clock in the kitchen limping round the never-ending track. Life must have a meaning. Otherwise why would your brain ask questions all the time?

6

He got up early and made for the barracks. Since the funeral, each weekday morning his father went to eight o'clock mass. The house would be empty until nine. He'd have plenty of time to rescue Milton from the belly of the sewing-machine.

The sun was edging over the hills, jagging the rim of the high lands to flame. Down on the lake a veil of mist lay inches above the water. By a phalanx of bullrushes a swan floated in sleep, head under wing, its neck a scarf. A heron stood beside it. He rode up to Brady's Cross, turned left and, pedalling slowly up Killybandrick brae, now had lakes way below on either side of him. The lakes were elongated balloons of water pinched in the middle by juts of land. Two scald crows flew across the road and down towards the trees on a small island in the biggest lake. The trees grew right to the edge. One had toppled in. Bark stripped, the white trunk and roots stuck out of the water like the neck of a beheaded monster.

He could see across the valley to Prunty's house. Neat, white-washed, roses round the door, it was a postcard cottage despite the television aerial rising above the thatch. Mrs Prunty was up. Smoke began twisting from the chimney. At first white, as it rose against the hill behind the house it turned blue, then white again, drifting higher up the air. Smoke was hope. The sun, getting the better of all the hills, lit the fields, dazzled the mist from the water, woke up the sleeping swan.

Unwrapping its neck, it shook its head, raised its wings, beat and settled them, then glided in among the bullrushes. Swans reminded him of piano music. The heron clambered up the sky, swept on to the top of a tree, only closing its wings when sure of its footing. Reaching the top of the brae, he let the bike freewheel down the other side. The fresh morning air rushing into his lungs made him dizzy. The dewy smell of hawthorn hedges, roadside primroses, wild plum trees; the perfume of mown hay, the whiff of turfy water, the tang of a dung hill; all combined, lodged in his throat – a secret language of innocence. There for the taking on any morning just like this. It was a drug you suckled through your nose. He was amazed by the fields. One day they looked wet, bitter, raddled. This morning they looked virginal, beautiful, full of promise. This morning the Border country looked a land worth fighting for. Life in the open, on such a day, was swan music. Inside damp walls, life was a dirge. How could we forget our mother – Nature – the old lady bulging still with honey?

As he rose towards the village the tops of the pine trees by the railway station came into view. Rounding a snaking series of bends he could see the drop-arm of the signal, then the gravelled platform, and lastly the tracks sweeping past on their way north. The tracks in the sunlight were a steely smile across the land. On Prunty's bedposts hung rosary beads and a pair of spurs for fixing on a game-cock's legs. The shiny tracks and the spurs were the same silvery colour.

Wooden fencing painted white ran along the back of the platform. A rectangular sign screwed to the fencing proclaimed in large black three-dimensional capitals: BUTLERSHILL. Under the sign was a seat for waiting travellers. Wallflowers and geraniums in boxes grew against the fencing. The waiting-room, the station-master's office and the metal public lavatory were distempered green and yellow, the windowsills painted black. The drop-arm of the signal was white with a band of red. The cosy station nestling up against the pine trees and flanked on one side by the hump bridge carrying the road across the tracks looked fresh and perfect as a Christmas toy.

As he reached the bridge he heard voices down on the platform. Still astride his bike, he leaned against the parapet. His heart lurched. Talking to Billy Gartlan, the stationmaster, was the girl he'd seen only yesterday when he and Prunty were with the soldiers. Though now she was wearing a black beret and a long green coat, he couldn't mistake the hanks of flaxen hair, or her pale face. It was definitely the same girl. The annoyingly loquacious Gartlan was making her laugh as he tied a parcel to the carrier of her bicycle. She'd either come off the eight o'clock train or was picking up delivered goods. The train had departed some time ago, but Gartlan could detain anyone with his stories and delaying banter.

'You can't beat the bit of binder twine. You could tie a bull to a gate with it. Or a young one to an oul' man.'

He was in his fifties, unmarried, big-boned, with a raw laughing face. His railwayman's cap sat sideways on a clump of thick grey curls. His big hands jerked the binder twine as he knotted the parcel to the carrier. 'Are you sure now you'll manage? Or do you want me to give you a lift home on the bar of me bike?'

'I'll manage on my own, thank you.' Her accent was quick but soft. Female Fermanagh. She looked serious, but then she smiled. Her teeth were whiter than her skin.

'I betcha you're no good in the kitchen, are you? They say, "the better they look, the worse they cook"; what do you think about that?'

'*If* I thought about it, I wouldn't think *much* of it.'

Gartlan laughed and looked up. 'Ah begod, the Sergeant's son. How's she cuttin', young fellah?'

The girl turned her head and looked up at him. For a moment he could feel the pull of her eyes. He jolted back from view, pretending his attention had suddenly been attracted by something desperately important. As if the President of America had materialized on the other side of the bridge, wanting urgent words with him. 'Howdy, buddy . . . gauson . . . Eisenhower's the name. Sure would appreciate it if you helped us beat the Russians into space.'

He was a shy coward. He didn't have the guts to bandy words with Gartlan. Not with the girl there. If only he could shower down on them seductive words of politics and love. He was dry-mouthed with the fear of failure. She might laugh at him. Rather than risk that, he retreated into fantasy. He was a sucker for a beautiful face. He'd glimpsed her yesterday; had looked on her for little more than a minute today; he didn't even know her name; yet he was already madly in love with her. It was crazy. He could hear her wheeling her bicycle up the station path to the road. Sitting on the bar of his bicycle, *á la* Prunty, he tried to strike a nonchalant pose. Turning out from the station path she came up the bridge towards him. She wore long black boots, the tops hidden by her long green coat. His heart was drumming. His tense fingers gleamed tight on the handlebars. Black boots. An extraordinary coat. A black beret. He'd never seen anything like it, not even in the pictures. Her hair was thick as a sheaf of wheat, her face pale as unglazed china.

87

She was only a few yards away. Blue eyes. He could smell her. She walked demurely, pushing the bike without effort. She was looking at him. Now was the moment to say something. Her face was at an angle to him. But his tongue was dumb as stone. In place of words he felt a shy, sickly smile creep round his mouth.

Her liquid eyes were on him. Clear, honest, lake eyes. Her lips opened as she drew breath as if she were going to reward him with words. Just as well she didn't; he'd have fainted.

Stepping astride her bicycle, settling on the saddle, tucking her long coat in about her body, she pushed off, pedalling away. Piano music. All the clothes, though, looked a bit silly for such a fine day. Maybe she didn't like sun. Like a fish. No doubt about it – Nature was full of gifts. But how did you get the one you wanted? The parcel on the back of her bike looked like a roll of material.

She got lost among the hills and hollows of the Fermanagh road. He licked his lips and the inside of his mouth, getting the saliva back. From the far side of the bridge, down on the railway lines, he could hear shouting. He crossed to the other parapet. In the distance a woman hurried along the tracks, waving her arms, roaring, hysteria kept at bay by the struggle she had in walking along the sleepers.

'Murder. Murder. Help! Help!'

Elderly, wearing a black skirt and cardigan, her legs were bare above her cut-down wellingtons. The wellingtons were cut to the size of ordinary boots.

'Murder. Jesus this day. Help! Gauson, get the Guards.'

The sleepers not being equidistant, she couldn't get rhythm into her stride. She hopped along in an irregular series of long and short steps, back bent, her eyes fixed on the permanent way. When she drew nearer he could see a white comb in the bun of her hair.

'Murder!'

From the vantage point of the bridge he looked down on her as if she were on a stage, as if her terrible cries were coming from the mouth of an old actress. Way behind, the railway lines ran through a deep cutting gouged from a hilly farm. The fields on either side were scenery. Backcloths. The tracks stretching away beneath the old woman film going through a projector. The vision of the girl had cut him off. Made him go dreamy in the head.

The old woman looked up hopelessly at him, her face tormented. She might have been a wasp trying to get out of a bottle. He heard Gartlan the stationmaster shout, and she went in under the bridge towards him.

If the sight of a girl could boil your limbs, scupper your senses, what would the touch of one do? He shook his head to unscramble his brains, then scootered on one pedal down the road and round into the station. Pine cones littered the path. The smell of resin thickened the air. The old woman and Gartlan were in the office, Gartlan on the telephone.

'Are you trying to phone the barracks? There's no point. My father is at mass now. And Guard Ryan's at the Widow McGinn's having breakfast.'

The old woman began pacing over and back. The cut-down wellingtons were tight on her big feet. Her face dripped sweat. 'Holy God, it's a holy terror. The poor man's skulled. I seen him with me own two eyes. Down by the railway bridge over the river.'

Gartlan replaced the receiver. 'Go you and get your daddy. Ride to the chapel. Ride like the hammers of hell.'

To show willing, he ran from the office and rode as fast as he could up the incline to the road. But going through the village he took his time. Passing Bobby Roberts' house, he saw Tilly upstairs leaning out of a window, cleaning it. Only a Protestant would be up so early working. When she saw him she smiled and blew a kiss from her finger-ends. Then she laughed, her head hanging back in space, her plaited hair dangling like a tail. Another time and he'd have been excited. Imagined all sorts of possibilities. Tilly was a sexy woman, that was for certain. Nothing in the Bible could blot it out. But she could lead a fellow on, then lash him at the last moment. Bible zealots were a strange mixture of madness and repression. He waved to her, his arm aloft in triumphal salute. He was free of Tilly. She couldn't disturb him any longer. There was a different face in the sky.

He stopped at the barracks and went round the side to the married quarters and in the hall door, which was only locked at nights. In the kitchen the range firebox door swung open. The fire was out. Nothing there but ash and dead cinders. On the table was the teapot, empty, and the lid missing. The picture of the Sacred Heart looked down from above the mantelpiece. Beneath the image was a prayer dedicating the family to God, and golden lines along which were written his parents' and his own name. The ink was blue, police ink, the hand his father's – cranky, sharp, clear. At the bottom of the picture it said: 'The family that prays together, stays together.'

A lie. They had prayed together every night. But his mother was dead, years before her time, and he himself had fled. Maybe religion was a dream. Like the girl at the railway station. The old sweeping-brush leaned into its corner by the dresser, so still, it might have been there undisturbed for a hundred years. 'What goes round the house and round the house and sleeps in the corner at night? The sweeping-brush.' It was an ancient joke his mother cracked every Christmas.

Taking his book from the belly of the sewing-machine, he felt the familiar green cardboard cover and was glad. Opening it at random he read aloud the lines:

> 'Ay me! I fondly dream
> "Had ye been there," – for what could that have done?
> What could the Muse herself that Orpheus bore,
> The Muse herself, for her enchanting son,
> Whom universal nature did lament,
> When, by the rout that made the hideous roar,
> His gory visage down the stream was sent,
> Down the swift Hebrus to the Lesbian shore?'

The cold kitchen full of hushed words was a confession-box with God gone out of it. He got a stab of pain in the heart. He cried out what used to be the best word in the language – 'Mum'. It fell with a dead ring down the green walls, on to the black range, over the worn blue lino. That was it. Done. Had his mother's life been a waste of time? Time would tell.

He went down the hallway to her bedroom. Her bed had been slept in. On the floor beside it were his father's shoes. It was cruel on his father. He was at last sleeping in her bed. Now that she was dead and gone. If only the old ghost stories were true . . . if only the dead came back . . . like Hamlet's father . . . Maybe that's what dreams were – the life to come when you escaped the clay . . .

He left. The Creamery opposite the barracks was rattling awake. Farmers unloaded cans from horse-drawn carts and tractors on to the raised concrete platform. When the cans were tipped into the tank the milk gushed out in fluted slaps. Seconds later it came lolling from the separator in creamy tongues.

The road to the chapel alternated between glorious swoops and penitential climbs. On high he could see down over the scabby land and into Lady Sarah's demesne, with its acres of good grass and forest of oak, ash, beech, elm and serried ranks of fir. A high stone wall ran for miles around the estate. At a point between the wall and the quarry road, the simple two-storeyed building of the Orange Hall stood in its own grounds. Its austere look and leaded windows gave it the appearance of a church. Ahead on a massive hill of rock was the Catholic graveyard. It dominated the country-side. You could glimpse a few of the high stone crosses sticking darkly into the air. The graveyard had so little clay that some coffins never got lower than three feet. He remembered his mother's coffin at one point being tipped sideways to avoid a jutting rock. On the hill down from the cemetery nothing but whins grew, and fern. Only goats were at home there, and boys collecting burnt whins for the school fire.

When he reached the chapel, mass was ending. Because it was a weekday only a handful of regulars were in attendance – a worried mother, two elderly women trying to storm heaven with prayer, an old man who had persecuted his wife when she was alive, a young pretty girl, the local lunatic, and his father. Father Gaynor was at the altar and, in the absence of an altar-boy, his house-keeper, Miss Tackney. Being female she had to remain on the near side of the rails. Only men and boys were allowed on the altar while mass was celebrated. Strictly speaking the housekeeper shouldn't have been serving at all, but the priest made his own rules. He remembered when attending the local school, once a month all the children had to come to the chapel to Confessions. Instead of confessing them one by one Father Gaynor absolved them collectively. 'Quietly say your sins to God . . . *Ego te absolvo in nomine patris et filii, et spiritus sancti . . .*' This procedure took minutes, saved hours. Canon law was putty in his hands. No one could remember the last time the Bishop visited the parish. Father Gaynor got on with what he loved best – history. He spent hours on his knees in cemeteries trying to decipher the inscriptions on old headstones. His father claimed he was a saint.

He stood at the back of the chapel and waited until the priest came down the steps, bowed to the tabernacle and exited alone to the sacristy. He wore a red chasuble – the symbol of fire and blood. His father rose from the pew, genuflected, turned to leave. When he saw him standing at the back he stopped abruptly. For a moment his surprised face looked happy. But as he walked down the aisle he looked grim, his shaved face fresh as a knife.

He wasn't afraid to face him. He was the bearer of great news. For his father, the best news possible. Murder. It was his father's dream. A dead body. A criminal to be hunted down. Arrested. Charged. Tried. Found guilty. Hanged. No hard feelings. Just a job well done. 'I'm sick to death of neighbours going to law over trespassing cattle. Fed up charging drivers for having no tail-lights. It's not why I joined the Force. More fool me. Why on earth I never went to America I'll never know.'

In front of his father he walked out through the porch, dipping a finger into the font as he went. By the pebble-dashed wall against which his father's bike rested, he turned to face him.

'You've got to come quickly. There's been a murder. The body was discovered by a Mrs McKenna, down by the railway bridge over the Finn. A man's been murdered.'

His father's face changed from anger to amazement. His eyes beamed. His mouth opened, trying to form words. He couldn't believe his luck. 'Who? Who is it?'

'Mrs McKenna didn't say. Billy Gartlan sent me to get you quick as you can.'

His father gripped the corner of his lower lip in his teeth. He was trying to suppress a smile, trying to appear reverential.

'Come on.'

Grabbing his bicycle he swung round, but the local lunatic blocked his path. Mouth dribbling, eye twitching, he looked up into his father's face.

'Will we . . . will we have rain, Sergeant?'

'Yes,' replied his father, 'but don't quote me. Now outa hell of me road.'

The man jumped back, giggling, tugging the end of his tattered jacket. 'Ah, das a good one. Don't coat me, hah? Coats for the rain, hah? Hah, Sarge?'

His father rode like fury. Normally when he came to a hill he dismounted and walked up it. 'Why rush? The man who made time made plenty of it.'

He had a job keeping up with him now. His father had forgotten everything – wife, funeral, runaway son. Homicide. Dreams were at last becoming reality. The silver buttons, buckle, badge, whistle-chain blinked brightly on his dark-blue uniform. The sun swam in the polished toecaps of his black boots. His trousers were clipped neatly round his ankles. The chiselled chin, cheek-bones, were geometrically sharp, the eyes piercing. Prunty rode through the countryside looking at the landscape like it was a friend. A friend that could rebuff, but on the whole could be touched for a few quid. His father viewed the fields warily, as possible enemies. He X-rayed hedges, saw under stones. In his early days in the Force, as a plainclothes detective, he had worked on murder cases. 'All family affairs. Brothers and sisters blasting each other to perdition over a few snotty acres. Men and women all the same. And if you saw the land in question. Up the arsehole of the County Leitrim where the land was so poor the pigs had to wear galoshes. I'll tell you one thing, me buck, the peasant will kill quick as a king when it comes to property.'

When de Valera took power in 1933 his father was put back in uniform. De Valera wanted his own men protecting him. His father had joined the Guards after the Civil War in 1923. Joining was a political statement. It meant you had accepted the Treaty partitioning the country. De Valera stood for the Republicans. His election was victory for his father's enemies. Back in uniform, his father was posted to the Border country and served his humdrum time along the political line that first created his ambitions, then circumscribed them. He was a village policeman dreaming of past glories. Now the glories were about to be relived. He was glad for him. His father had waited on this day for years and years. 'No ill-wishes on potential corpses – but please God send me something to get me teeth into.'

They rode through the village and out the Currinstown road. The bridge could be reached that way. The railway lines went over a road bridge before crossing the Finn.

He assumed as they rode along that his father's head was full of the crime and how he was going to solve it. But you could never take him for granted.

'The cut of you in the odd boots. Rinty Reilly seen you comin' all right.'

He was wearing the boots and jeans and feeling good in them. The left boot looked bigger on the pedal than the right. He wondered had the girl noticed?

'Some runaway. You won't get far with a club foot.'

'I'll get further than you got with yours.' His father's boots were huge. He could see him tensing his fingers on the brakes, contemplating stopping and splattering him for his insolence.

93

'I'm sorry, Daddy.' He hated having to apologize when he wasn't in the wrong. But when his father got angry his mood was so black it blinded him to justice. 'I'm sorry.'

His father's fingers relaxed. They rode on. His father had gears on his bike, but he never changed them. The technical intricacies of mending broken gears would have been torture for his blunt hands. His policy was to leave well enough alone. He rode only in second.

'You're some whelp to walk out on me the way you did, without as much as a word. And the fix I'm in. And every tongue in the place waggin'. Well let me tell you, I'm not begging you to come back.'

'Maybe . . . maybe a break from each other . . . would do us both good.'

'Hah? Such ramaish I never heard.'

A gripe ran along one side of the road. Every twenty yards or so a flat stone had been placed in it at a sloping angle. If a cart wheel slipped into the gripe, which was about six inches deep, the stone gave the driver a chance to steer the horse away from the edge by raising the wheel for a moment to road level. Prunty was a stone in a gripe. He had got him out of a rut. And he wasn't going back in – no matter how much guilt his father engendered.

They rode on in silence. Dogs barked after them. A cock crowed on a dunghill. His father's mood was black as his boots. It shone like the peak on his cap. His face drowned the sun.

When they reached the bridge and dismounted, his father looked at him and winked. The moment was bigger than the mood. They were almost at the scene of the crime.

Leaving the bikes under the arch of the bridge, they scrambled up the embankment and on to the railway tracks. In the distance the tracks spanned the river. They could see something lying on the viaduct. Walking towards it, his father's boots whallicked the sleepers, ringing echoes out of them with every step. He had the side of his lower lip gripped in his teeth and was half humming, half laughing to himself. This was usually a prelude to derision.

Lying on the viaduct was the body of a man. The body was on one side of a railway line, the head the other. The head was completely separated from the shoulders. The man's feet were by the parapet, the shoulders and a bit of neck lying up on the ends of the sleepers. The head lay in a gap between two sleepers, face down. The hair, thick and grey, was at the nape caked with

94

blood. Raddled like a marked sheep. The gravel between the sleepers was an oily red, as if someone had spilled paint. The man's clothes were an old black jacket, a waistcoat, brown corduroy trousers and clogs. On his chest a watch-chain looped from one pocket into another. The jacket lapels were food- and drink-stained. The man's body looked peaceful, lying in the morning sun. His hat lay a few feet away on the other side of the tracks. In the hatband was a small green feather. His right hand, like a claw, was up towards his shoulder, as if he had tried, too late, to keep his head on.

His father stepped over the body, stared down at it. Bending, he picked the head up by the hair. Holding it up, he slowly turned it to look on the face. His father looked at the deadhead without flinching. The face was small, wrinkled, pale, with big bushy ginger eyebrows. One eye was open, the other shut. The upper lip had a droopy ginger moustache. Still clenched in the teeth was a curved tobacco pipe, with amber stem and a silver cap over the bowl. In the grin of the man's mouth, the teeth were rotten – black and brown; the pipe was wedged in the gap between two missing ones.

'You know who it is, don't you?'

'No.'

'You don't? It's old Johnny McCann from below Ballyhoe. He always walked the line home.'

'It's . . . it's not murder, is it? It was the train, wasn't it?'

'Murder me foot! You can smell the drink on him still. He lay down alongside the track to sleep it off with the rail as a pillow. And his feet up on the parapet there. He forgot to wake up. RIP. The eight o'clock train got him. Neat as a bacon slicer.'

They looked at the head in his father's fist. It was grotesque. The one staring eye was frightening, the pipe in the corner of the mouth horribly absurd. Yet it also looked meaningless. The pale face was drained of blood. Life was extinct. It could have been a pantomime mask. Sleepy Death had descended, shut one eye, and for a joke left one open, false as glass. The scene was akin to that in the kitchen when his father gutted the hen. A living thing was no longer. A smeared suitcase was all that remained. But the case was empty, as if it had never been full. As if life had never lived. A drop of blood hit the silver railway tracks.

The severed neck on the shoulders was terrifying. An open gash of raw flesh, fierce as meat on a butcher's block. It was hard to look on. He could look on the poor man's face, because he wasn't really seeing it at all. In his mind, deep down, was the face of the girl at the station.

The train was an angel of life for him, an angel of death for Johnny McCann. In his head was a mixture of perfume and the steely whizz of slicing wheels.

His father pulled the pipe from the mouth, then placed the head at the neck. For a moment the body took on meaning. The one eye stared unblinking at the blazing sun.

He and his father sat together on the viaduct wall. His father looked at him, weighing him up. Making sure he was all right.

'Are you feeling sick?'

'No, no.'

'I've seen worse. God works in mysterious ways. Wouldn't I have been the fool had I stopped at the barracks and phoned the Superintendent and the Murder Squad, hah? I'd have been the laugh of the Division. Not an act of murder at all. Not even a suicide. Only a grisly accident. That oul' doxy McKenna – the soft eejit. That's a certain class of woman for you all right. They see a feather on the ground and think the fox has been.'

He turned and spat over his shoulder down into the Finn. The land on the Fermanagh side was held in a long loop of the river. Even in summer the fields lay in a watery embrace. The boggy land stretched for miles without a house in sight. 'Flat Fermanagh,' said his father, 'and lookit will you at Cavan – a humpy oul' horse knee-deep in a sheugh.'

The dead body lay on the Cavan side of the Border. His father sat, back straight, hands gripping his knees. He looked grim, disappointed.

'Well, Johnny McCann, you'll never lick the porter out of your moustache again. You lived a lonely life with neither wife nor chick to your name. And you died a strange and lonely death.'

A soft breeze lifted the quiff of hair on the dead man's forehead. A bluebottle landed on the bridge of his nose. Velvet green and blue. It turned round a few times, wrung its front legs, then walked down on to the upper lip.

'The beggars,' said his father, getting up and flapping his cap at it. 'They come when they smell the blood. Go you and phone the doctor and alert Guard Duffy. Tell him to phone the RUC in Newtownbutler. They'll have to inform the relatives. If only he had lain down a few yards further on, it wouldn't have been my problem at all. Not even a suicide. That's just the luck that's dogged the best part of my days.'

The green of the bluebottle was the same green as the feather in the dead man's hat.

Leaving his father, he walked away. The old sleepers were splintered, wrinkled, grey as dead skin. Before going down the embankment he looked back. His father was down on one knee beside the corpse, the rosary trickling through his fingers dark beads of blood. His father didn't believe in politicians. Wasn't afraid of death. He believed in God.

7

Prunty was outside with the Colonel. He was inside with Sophie Kay. She had poured him a flute of champagne. A silver necklace of tiny bubbles sprouted up the glass. It was the first time he'd tasted alcohol. It was cold and sweet. Or sour. He couldn't decide which. The taste was tart, like a gooseberry not quite ripe. He'd refused at first, telling her he was a Pioneer.

'You're always giving things *up* in this country. Wouldn't it be better to *do* something rather than *not* do something? You give up drink. You give up smoking. You give up sex. Why are you all such *"not-doers"*? Was it a religious decision too made you *not* fight in the last war? Hm?'

He sipped and smiled at her. His foot with the big boot was back under the chair he sat on.

'There's plenty drunks. Plenty killers. They need balancing out.'

'That's funny. What would you know? So nice and innocent.'

'Am I?'

'Unlike your rough and guilty friend. Prunty the incorrigible.'

He didn't see Prunty that way. He let it pass. Prunty was with the Colonel, haggling over the horses.

He couldn't believe his luck. Here he was in the drawing-room of Castle Finn. When the Colonel's father ruled the roost it was the seat of the British Establishment in this part of Ireland. None but Protestants were employed. When there was a pheasant shoot on the estate the kitchen staff was augmented with Catholic scullions. According to local lore old Lady Sarah's ancestors had always been 'good gentry'. Castle Finn, though, was always rigid, unyielding, brutal when British Rule had to be defended. The castle was first constructed in 1695 after the land had been cleared of natives. Until 1920 they lived as they pleased. Then the IRA burnt the outhouses and drove off the cattle. In 1921 there was a pitched battle with the Crown forces in which the Colonel's father, on horseback, was wounded while leading a charge. The horse was a grey. For the rest of his days the old man was known as 'the Grey Hussar'. On the establishment of the Free State, the Grey Hussar summoned a member of the RHA from Dublin to come and paint his picture, seated on horseback, in full military regalia. The result still hung above the first landing on the stairs. The old man on his grey charger looked down on all who entered the main door, fixing them with a fierce, commanding eye. In his raised left hand was a pistol and the reins. His right hand was in the act of drawing his sword. His face was peppery red, the moustache thick under a blunt nose but tapering to needle-sharp waxy points. The horse had its tail cocked and front foot raised. The painting was a caricature of man and beast. The action false, the soul blown up.

But in 1924 the old man was content with his great stretch of canvas. He had the old horse put down and took to the bottle. He died in 1939. Prunty pointed out his headstone beside the private chapel which they passed on the long drive up to the castle. There was a headstone, too, with the horse's name on it, and one dedicated to the memory of a dog. Slates were missing from the chapel roof.

The estate was now in the hands of the old man's son – Sophie Kay's husband. He was known as 'the Bare Hussar', having walked home one night from the pub stark naked save for shoes and socks. When money ran low he went to America to find himself a rich wife. 'It's a holy terror,' said Prunty. 'When the English have no one to order around they go to pieces.'

Sophie Kay sat opposite him, on a Chippendale chair with ball-and-claw feet. Her elbow rested on a mahogany desk which had a tooled leather inset top. On either side of the open marble fireplace were two Chesterfield settees. Between them was a coffee table laden with whiskey, gin and tonic bottles. None of the bottles had more than a finger of liquid left in them.

All the furniture was Georgian, Edwardian, Victorian. The bare polished floorboards were covered with Chinese and Persian rugs. In front of the fire lay a tiger's head and skin. It was a long way from India to Cavan. A glorious chandelier, diamond-ripe, swung from the ceiling. The ceiling itself was leak-stained, the plasterwork in places missing from the naked laths.

Through a big window he could see down on to the lovely bend in the river Finn. It curved through the fields like a bevelled mirror full of sky. Beyond was the bridge on which he and Prunty had met the soldiers. Outside another window were the lawns and coven-tree. Under the tree were the crocked remains of what Prunty told him was a Pierce Silver Arrow car built in 1933. The body was shaped like a turtle shell, especially the tail. The head-lights were faired into the front wings, and the rear wings, Prunty said, were 'spatted' to conceal the upper part of the wheel. The once elegant car was now rusty, covered in bird-shit, the tyres flat and disintegrating. The branches of the tree spread along the roof, pale thistles reached the windows. It looked as if tree and land were devouring the car, eating the metal, rubber, glass. Returning it to nothing. Like the earth and nettles munching the motorbike on the ground outside Prunty's shed.

Sophie Kay wore slacks and a hairy white V-necked sweater. Slung about her neck were strings of pearls. Her blonde hair at the roots seemed reddish-grey. Her feet were bare in her high-heels. He liked women's feet. Bare and raised high, the insteps were swan smooth. The whole body ran into feet. When the weight was on them you could see the strain on veins and toes.

Her face was sharp, clear-cut, the corners of her almond eyes sloping upwards, giving her an edgy beauty. Her clear skin was tanned. Her drinker's mouth was gashed with blue lipstick, the full lips narrowing from years of mean sipping.

'I've seen you drive through the village. We can smell you on the air above the exhaust fumes after you've gone.'

'That's funny. What do the natives say about me? Not that I give a damn.'

'They say you're twenty years younger than the Colonel.'

She laughed. 'Only in years.'

He finished the champagne with a final gulp.

'Anything good – sip it.' Her smoky voice was treacly low.

In an attempt at relaxation he stretched his legs, concealing as best he could his left foot with the right.

The most extraordinary thing he ever saw was the turf lining the two outer walls of the room. Piled high from floor to ceiling were brown, dark and black sods. At first he thought they were some kind of brick- or stone-work. Then he noticed a beetle shifting through mould on the floor. Except above the two windows, the turf covered the entire wall area. From a solid base on the floor the sods were stacked neat as a rick to the ceiling.

Out on the lawn he saw Prunty being chased by the Colonel. Running round the coven-tree, a grin on his face, he easily kept ahead of the Colonel, who was roaring, waving his arms, looking on the point of collapse.

Sophie Kay refilled his glass.

'Why the . . . the turf . . . why?'

'This damn dump is damp. It's the only way I know to block it. I have the turf carried in in summer, burn my way through it in winter. Keeping warm is my only goal. Turf and whiskey. Without them this country would go back to ice.'

'My mother loved heat. She died a few weeks ago.'

'I *am* sorry. That's all any of us want – heat.'

A piece of plaster whirled down on to the mantelpiece. Sophie Kay emptied the remains of a bottle of whiskey into her champagne. Her ham-coloured tongue ran wet around her glittery lips.

The Colonel, coming into the room, staggered to a Chesterfield and lay full-length. 'Your beastly Prunty is a crook. I'll say no more. Who is this one, honey?'

'He is the Sergeant's boy from Butlershill.'

'Just the job for me – Sergeant. Maximum power. Minimum outgoings.'

The Colonel's cavalry-twilled legs were ! .g and thin, his big brogues sticking well over the end of the settee. Head resting against the settee arm, his chin sunk to his chest. Dark grey receding hair swept back from his forehead. His long sallow face looked weak. His hands, though, were broad, gnarled, the big knuckles rhubarb-red.

'Pour us a bumbo, honey, for Christ's sake. You look a college boy – any ideas for making money?'

'Sell this place. Build a bungalow. Rear pigs.'

The Colonel and Sophie Kay laughed. 'That's funny.'

'This is a land of paupers,' said the Colonel. 'Only people with money nowadays are the yellowbellies. The slanty folk from the Orient. I can see them here one day. Castle Finn in the hands of Chinks or Japheads. Won't the locals laugh?'

His ears were pointy. Two white spots of daylight shone on his bright-red cheeks.

Prunty was at the window, peering in.

Sophie Kay turned with a tumbler of drink. 'My lovely horses dead.'

'My wife is one of the Studebakers. Was. I thought she was going to save us. But that's not what love does.'

Sophie Kay laughed. 'That's funny.'

Her beauty was on the verge of ruin. He liked her. For the moment anyway. The crusty Colonel wasn't as handsome as his father but he was relaxed, his devil-may-care eyes looking straight and unafraid at any face or doom.

'Who . . . who were the Studebakers?'

'They made better cars than Henry Ford, boy.'

Prunty was still at the window, his face pressed to and distorted by the glass. 'Cumontahell.'

The Colonel, without looking, aimed two fingers above the back of the settee. Prunty stuck his tongue out.

'What poets do you do at college?'

'Milton.'

'Christ. Excellent. What good news! The natives have got round to the greats. Yeats was a middle-class moaner. I'm certain he had syphilis. Is he still alive? I can't remember. Joyce too, he had the clap. And Shakespeare. He was so poxed up the only thing that could kill the pain was dipping his quill. 'Nother bumbo, honey, please.'

He raised his glass to the Colonel and his wife. '*Sláinte agus saol agat.*'

They looked at him and at one another. Sophie Kay followed him out. At the door they lingered. Her fair eyelashes were long as spider-legs. He didn't know why they stood speechless and staring. Her face was so still he could see the blood pulse at her temple. Her feet were a tangle of slate-blue veins. He smiled and turned away from the big studded oak door. He was shy before her eyes. 'Thanks'. Prunty waited for him by the bicycles, scowling. His shirt, open to the belly button, revealed a chest bare and white as a scrubbed pig. He hadn't shaved for two days. His bacon-rind lips bristled with fair hair.

'Let's get the feck outa here.'

'I've had champagne.'

'It was far from champagne you were reared.'

They let the bikes do the work, rolling down the long driveway to the gates. He was happy and feathery in the head, the drink smoking his brain. The curving river lay on the land like a run of mercury. The coven-tree bowed with age. A peacock strutted the lawn, tail fanned out in a vertical circle of raging blues and greens and eyes. He let his bicycle veer off on to the grass, on which he lay giggling.

Prunty stood over him grinning. 'Holy God, he's drunk as a judge at the Quarter Sessions. On your feet, yah hoor yah.'

'If only I could tell you . . . this girl I saw.'

'Who?'

'Who who? If I knew I'd tell you.'

He beat the grass with his hand, laughing. Prunty hauled him to his feet.

'Did yah see the oul' bollocks chasing me? I diddled him out of a pound. She's a quare one, Sophie Kay, hah?'

Castle Finn was in Monaghan, the drive in Cavan, the gates in Fermanagh. It was a drunken geography in which you had to have your wits about you, even stone-cold sober. The people moved through the land like starlings. Always on the look-out. Like hares. Like larks. Like stones.

Prunty rode alongside, his hand resting on his shoulder, guiding him, ready to grab should he suddenly veer. If perfume was a city, Sophie Kay was Paris. He was lucky to meet her, and for the first time ever, drink champagne. Not porter.

'The oul' Colonel,' said Prunty, 'would drink Loch Erne dry.'

The sky was virgin blue. Fluffy, sheepy clouds were scattered along the horizon. They passed a farmer driving cows. The bag-pipe udders swung full. A black collie trotted at the farmer's heels.

'How's she cuttin', lads?'

'Like a mowin' machine.'

The farmer's scabby ashplant gently thwacked a cow's dunged rump. Words burbled in his head. Worrying him. Something the Colonel said about love.

When they reached the house Mrs Prunty ran about the kitchen scolding them and blessing herself. 'Holy God, stocious. This puts the kybosh on it altogether.'

'Ah, don't be such an oul' barger, Mammy. He had his first lick at the magic dug, that's all.'

Prunty lugged him to the room and threw him on the bed.

'He's kicked the traces right enough,' said Mrs Prunty.

The freedom in Prunty's laugh was golden. He was putting no pressure on him, giving him space. Late in the night he heard Mrs Prunty poking the fire with the big tongs. She was singing about love. Love was lord of all. Love was a song of heart's desire. Her mouth was old, her lips lined and withering. But the words didn't care. They came sailing out like bees from a hive. Soft searchers for the ears of a summer's night. Words were frightening. On the page they lay dead, but given tongue they resurrected. Words came and went like ghosts. Words were soul honey. 'I love you.' What on God's earth did they mean? He was desperate to find out.

8

Protestant dances were held on Saturdays, Catholic ones on Sundays. They had their own music, their own bands, their own halls. Catholic music was everything plus sentimental Irish and Republican airs. Protestant music was just everything. The two persuasions had a number of rogues who didn't care when, where or what they danced as long as they got their money's worth.

The Freemasons' Hall in Clones, Prunty claimed, had the best maple floor in Ireland. 'Wait till you see, lad – she's sprung. You go round like a bird.'

On the Saturday evening, dusk falling, he rode with Prunty to the pub at Legakelly. Nearing it, they could see a clot of men all with bicycles, awaiting their arrival.

'*Hoi-hoi-hoi-agh-howw-how-hoi,*' roared Prunty, imitating a hunter calling beagles.

When they rode up to the pub the men, faces to the moon, rang the night with answering calls – '*Agh-howww-how-agh-hoi-hoi-agh-howwww!*'

'Wha' kept you, Prunty?'

'You'll be late for your own funeral.'

'Come on, yah hoor, it's time we weren't here.'

'Who's the gauson?'

'He's me friend. The Sergeant's son outa Butlershill.'

'We'll have the law on our side so.'

'He's handy with his fists.'

'I'm not.'

'You will be after tonight.'

Prunty led them out along the road. He counted fifteen boys, all round about his own age. They looked bigger, stronger, though, and the two who were smaller had wide shoulders and cropped heads solid as the stone balls on the gate piers leading into Castle Finn. These two he knew by sight. One was 'the Rock' Gargan, the other his cousin 'the Stumps' Smith. They rode on either side of him, squinting at him, their legs pounding the pedals up hill and down.

'We'll look after yah,' said the Rock.

'We'll look after yah,' said the Stumps.

When they got to Drumully Church, boys from Wattlebridge were waiting.

'*Agh-hoi-agh-hoi-hoi-hoi-agh-hoi!*'

'Whose the donny fellah?'

'He's with us,' said the Rock.

'He's with us,' said the Stumps.

There were five Wattlebridge boys. Two had red hair. One was an albino. One was tiny – smaller even than the Rock and the Stumps. The fifth was a tall, handsome, fair-haired smiler in a sharp blue suit.

Nineteen hands held nineteen cigarettes. The Rock offered him one. Matches spat light in the dusk. A cloud of smoke swept up over the hedge. Prunty gave them a pep-talk.

'There's twenty of us. I hear tell there's thirty a them. And as well as the Scut, they got Bouncer Patterson home from Canada. Give them plenty of shoe when the fun starts, and any man run he's nothin' short of a coward. Come on, yah boys.'

As they rode towards Clones the wind fanned the glow of their cigarettes. The Rock and the Stumps were the only ones with bicycle lamps. They gave out a feeble amber light which dribbled on to their front wheels and no further. Bicycles creaked, clattered, sighed over the tarmac. Birds shrieked from the hedges. Prunty rode at the front, on his own. No one was allowed past him.

They sang 'What Do You Want To Make Those Eyes At Me For?', roaring it out high and mighty at the starry sky. The cool pure air, the sweet smoke mixed in his lungs, went to his head. He gulged energy, his body taking strength from Prunty and the eighteen pelters alongside. To meet a girl at the dance . . . He felt good enough to leap and hang on the handlebars of the moon. The night was a tree of dreams. As they passed a house a frantic collie tried to break from its long chain.

They all had nicknames. Apart from the stumpy pair riding beside him, there was 'the Cuggy' Dolan, 'Sticks' Brady, 'the Cock' Carolan, 'Bad' Hughie Fay, 'Jook-the-coffin' Sheridan, Charlie 'the Pound' Kemp, 'the Rope' Rennicks, 'Dandy' Cusack, 'Juicy' Sexton, 'Badger' Tilson, Harry 'Cloudy' Gillespie,

'Slasher' Warren, Terry 'the Wick' Wilson, 'Grunter' Howe (the albino), 'Tar' McAdam, 'the Pike' Maguire. 'The Wick' was only slightly taller than his bike. 'He's no height at all,' said Prunty, 'except the height of nonsense.'

'Hoi-hoi-hoi-agh-hu-hu-hoi-hoi!'

'I can't wait to get at them.'

'We'll kick them into the middle of next week.'

'Any chance of the ride, do you think?'

'The hall will be full of bullin' women.'

'Any chance of a drink first?'

'No, Juicy, not till after.'

'I feel that good,' shouted Prunty, 'I could bull six women against that hill over there.'

'Yah boy yah. Agh-hoi-hu-hoi-yagh!'

'Hughie – you're lookin' after the bikes. In case they pumpture them.'

'I'm feckin' not.'

'You feckin' are.'

'Out of the way, you hoors. We're kickin' down your doors.'

'Fermanagh for the Sam Maguire.'

'Up Cavan.'

'Heh, Prunty, your back wheel's goin' round.'

'How's your mother for buttermilk?'

From all over the dark country hounds answered them, their anguished howls muffled by sheds, walls, barn doors. Barking, distant, black lamps of noise.

The Rock and the Stumps were wearing clogs. He could see moonlight glinting on the strips of tin along the toes.

'I've got a Novena,' said the Stumps, 'she's never let me down. Yah say it nine times a day for nine days and anything you request will be granted.'

'Would it bring back the dead?'

'No,' said the Stumps.

'Do the Novena,' said the Rock, 'and get a pair of clogs.'

He was quite happy with his boots. Especially in the dark. And his jeans and black T-shirt and suit jacket.

The Wick Wilson was panting and out of the saddle trying to keep up. 'You see . . . you see Dandy Cusack there? He's goin' out with a . . . goin' out with a policeman's wife from the Skea. And his sister's . . . his sister's a nun.' The words wheezed from the corner of his mouth.

'Any woman lets me tonight,' roared the Rope, 'I won't charge her.'

'Any woman lets you will have fallen out of a hearse.'

Water gurgled deep in a ditch. The moon melting in the Ulster Canal spread through the water like toasted cheese. The lights of Clones twinkled out to them. They could see the electric glow on the face of the Protestant clock.

Faint music strengthened as they left the black land and came into lit streets. The air came steamy from their mouths. They wore dark suits, tweed jackets and grey trousers, white shirts and cotton ties. Prunty and Dandy had bicycle clips. The rest had their trousers in their socks. Each head glistened with Brylcreem, except Grunter Howe's; his shocking white hair looked dry as twigs.

They hid the bicycles behind the Ball Alley, Bad Hughie guarding them.

'He can't be risked in a fight,' whispered Prunty, 'he's got TB.' Looking back, he could see a cigarette dangling from his lips. Bad Hughie was thin as a spoke.

A gravel path led from the road up to the door of the hall. High on the porch he could see the square-and-compass insignia of the Freemasons. For a Catholic to have anything to do with the Masons was almost a mortal sin. His father detested them. 'Oh ho, they're the villains. They own every damn thing worth owning in this country. If it's not worth it – we can have it.'

When his father attacked, his mother always defended. 'Well, I bet they paid for everything they've got. If our ones can't band together for the good of all then that's their own mean fault.'

'Oh but you're always quick with the sharp answer.'

'Will you look who's talking?'

In the porch two men sat at a table on which was a faded biscuit-tin. He couldn't see the bottom of the tin for pound notes and coins. When he paid over the price of admission he was handed a blue numbered cloakroom ticket and told if he left the hall he'd have to produce the ticket to get back in again.

'And if there's a hint of trouble, lads, the Guards will be sent for.'

'There'll be no trouble,' said Prunty, 'sure we're all Pioneers.'

'Yes, and I'm a double Dutchman,' replied one of the men.

'Well, you were one time,' said the Wick Wilson. The remark was an allusion to the man's Orange ancestry.

'Trust you, Wilson,' he called after them, 'your tongue was always the longest part of you.'

In the hall, couples danced. The floor shone like a new coffin. On a stage at the far end a band played. Stencilled on the big drum were the semicircular words: 'BILLY DIXON'S DANCE BAND'. Dixon, an elderly man with spectacles, played saxophone and sang. The drummer was 'Sticks' Brady, an uncle of the Sticks in Prunty's gang. A middle-aged lady in a summer frock played the piano. A banjo, trumpet and accordion completed the line-up. The men wore white shirts and dicky bows, and dark trousers held up with braces. Fresh flocks of girls in bright blues, greens, reds, yellows, stood along the wall. When Prunty entered they moved away towards the corner by the stage. They were expecting trouble. Right round the hall hung framed pictures of former Freemason dignitaries, all of them wearing moustaches and bowler hats.

'Tek your pardners now please for a wee waltz.'

An elderly couple swept round the floor. Scuffing feet raised resin dust. The resin pellets strewn on the floor looked like incense. A young man and woman moved slowly, pressing close, the man's hand flat on her rump. That's how it was done. Eyes everywhere, but convention allowed. Within ritual you could get away with murder. In a room off the dance area was a long trestle table on which sat a tea-urn the same faded colour as the biscuit-tin. Cups and saucers stood rank and file beside a regiment of glasses.

'Tea and cold orange – that's their pleasure all right,' his father claimed. 'That sums up the whole lot of them.'

'It does in me hat,' muttered his mother.

Clumped on either side of the door were a grinning gang of young men. When they became aware of Prunty they crowded out on to the dance floor, pointing and laughing.

'The big frigger with the red face – that's Turnip McQuade. And lookit the Scud beside him.' Prunty tapped his foot to the music and chewed the corner of his lip as he surveyed the enemy. The Scud wore drainpipes and a black jacket reaching his knees. With them was the tall, pale-faced youth he saw in Rinty Reilly's shop. He was wearing the hideous overcoat. It looked stout as chain mail. No longer the shy wagtail, he was staring at them, threatening them by touching his eyes, nose, mouth, chin, with his clenched fist.

'He's yours,' said Prunty, 'don't kill him.'

'Ah, where's the ah . . . lavatory?'

'Don't worry about nawthin',' said the Rock.

'Don't worry about nawthin',' said the Stumps.

Dandy Cusack was dancing with a woman who looked old enough to be his mother. He was laughing and making her laugh. That was a gift. Hand on rump, make them laugh. School was no help in such matters. Making a woman laugh he felt sure was half the battle.

Turnip and the Scud and all their men looked tough and seemed eager for the word.

Prunty gave it. 'Yah dog's melt, McQuade.'

'You're nawthin' but a sack of rashers, Prunty. You'd look well in a frying-pan.'

A general slag ensued.

'Heh, Scud, is that your sister up be the band? She's so ugly she'd put a horse off its oats.'

'I dar ye say that again.'

'Away outa that. You couldn't burst the skin on a boiled shite.'

'Look whose talkin'. Yah cowardly hoors.'

'Who's a coward?'

'Away before I knock three kettles a piss outa yah.'

'You and whose army?'

'Big and all as you think you are, we'll find a coffin to fit.'

'I wouldn't drink outa the same drain as you.'

'Away you quilt.'

'Away yah hoor.'

'How big is your feckin' graveyard?'

'Skull the fecker and be done with it.'

'I'll wring the leg off your body.'

'You won't, for you'll not be fit.'

'Hit him a dunderer and have done with it.'

'Give them lanty.'

'I've seen better snouts on a pig.'

'What did you say?'

'I don't boil me cabbage twice.'

'The last time you had cabbage you got it from another man's field.'

'*Now gentlemen, if there's any trouble I'm calling the Guards. Cut it out now.*'

'Cut it out and be a lady.'

The dancing couples steered clear, moving in restricted circles by the stage. The band played 'Only Sixteen'. Dixon blew his saxophone, a wary eye on the two factions, now moving closer. The insults became more personal.

'Your mother's the Border bicycle.'

'The British army discharged you. Thief.'

'Turf-stealer.'

'You can tell they're from Wattlebridge – be their yellow gills.'

'What's that big lump in your sister's belly?'

It was madness. A strange lunacy in the blood. A few yards away a bunch of girls stood waiting to be asked to dance. Maybe they were more frightened of them than they were of each other. The music stopped. A daddy-long-legs flew round a light bulb. He could hear the tinklings of its clumsy flitters against the enamelled shade.

'The next dance now, folks, will be a Ladies' Choice.'

He didn't know how, but he was on the floor in a mill of feet and fists. He could see McQuade wielding a turnip in a scarf. Sling-cum-cosh, it was his trademark. Scud Gillespie was chopping round him with the back of his hand. It looked professional. Bouncer Patterson had Prunty by the danglers but let him go when the Wick Wilson landed on his back, knees first. A turnip smashed on Pike Maguire's head. The Rock and the Stumps were clogging men to the floor. At least he was on their side. Suits tore, shirts ripped, noses bled. Prunty, bull-bawling, punched all heads within reach. He was definitely enjoying the evening.

Slasher Warren made hound sounds. *'Agh-hoi-hoi-hu-hoi-agh-hoi-how!'*

He tried getting to his feet but kept getting knocked to the floor. Women were screaming. He began to crawl to safety somewhere, but the big wagtail jumped on him. It was impossible to get to grips with him through the overcoat. He was pinned under, the wagtail's pale boy's face leering over him in mad triumph.

'Yah fecker yah.'

'May I return the compliment?'

'Wha'? Hah?' His breath was a buttermilk reek.

Managing to free an arm, he grabbed a green button. When he tore a second one off, the wagtail could bear it no longer. Outraged he dived amongst the scum of bodies searching for them. The coat he had hated he now loved.

The Rope Rennicks bit the Scud's ankle. The Scud bit the

Rope's ear. Grunter Howe (the albino) was savagely beating what he thought was a body, with two bicycle pumps. It was only a pile of coats and hats dumped on a form along the wall.

'Behind you, Grunter. For Jazus' sake someone point him in the right direction.'

The seat was ripped from Badger Tilson's trousers. A man sat on Juicy Sexton's face. The Cuggy Dolan aimed a kick but his shoe flew off and smashed the glass in one of the hanging pictures. Outside a fisherman's tin, he had never seen such a knot of bodies. Only two men were left standing – the Rock and the Stumps. They strutted like cocks, their iron heels rapping the maple floor. 'Butlershill, Butlershill!'

Billy Dixon struck up 'The Soldier's Song' – the Free State national anthem. Everyone got to their feet and, exhausted, were glad to stand to attention. The Catholics couldn't show disrespect for their own anthem in a Protestant hall. The Protestants, whose secret allegiance was to the Queen, had on the southern side of the Border, to pay respect to Dublin or risk the consequences of their peculiar political position. Dixon had come up with a musical master stroke. The fight was over. It was a ritual. Like Sunday mass, or a football match. Once ended it couldn't recommence. For a week at least. The girls, no longer afraid, took to the floor in flowery bunches, pressing against the bodies of the men.

A girl stood in front of him. Plump, round-faced, smiling. She had a parting down the middle of her short black hair. He could see the line of scalp. Dark sloe eyes. Blue frock, buttoned all the way up the front. Bare arms, white as suet.

'It'll still be the Ladies' Choice. I'm askin' you.'

She wasn't what he had in mind. But she stood bang-slap before him, close in, her nice plain face held up to him. He knew he was blushing. By the door into the tea-room he could see Prunty and McQuade were now laughing together and queueing up for orange.

The music commenced: 'Who's Sorry Now?'. He put his arm round her waist, in his left hand held her right. Her bosom was against him. He could smell powder and perspiration. Sweet and musty like a tomato stalk. He shuffled his feet along the floor so he wouldn't tramp on her toes. She was the first girl he'd ever danced with. 'I seen you noticing me all the time. So I dandered over to you.' He'd never set eyes on her. He wasn't sure if he wanted to make her laugh. Why bother? She wasn't the girl for him. He knew that already. He decided to practise on her.

'Who do you like the best – Billy Dixon or Elvis Presley?'
She looked at him, her face dead as stone. Then she let her head back and shrieked. Her chin and her neck were jug-shaped. 'That's a good one. I thought for a horrid second you were in earnest.'

'I like rice pudding, do you?' Her laugh was a splutter of anguish and mirth. Could it be that easy? Perhaps.

'The look on your face . . . Go on, say something else.'

When they danced past Prunty he saw him straightening his tie and slip something into his mouth. A clove. He didn't want to say anything else. He wanted to escape. Then he decided to say something so ordinary she couldn't possibly find it funny. 'Did you come on a bicycle?'

Now even the lady playing the piano turned to look at them. How could such a warm, soft body produce such a hysterical sound? A mixture of donkey and hen: '*Henkey-henkey-he-haw-he-henkey.*'

'Did you come on a bicycle?' Nothing could be more ordinary than that. Comedy was as personal as tragedy. There was no such thing as a common language. Maybe if someone liked you they dodged sense, to please you.

'You're going ojus,' said the Rock.

'You're well in,' said the Stumps.

The Ladies' Choice over, he left the hall. He wanted fresh air. She followed him out. 'Hang on till I get me coat.'

She walked behind him to the Ball Alley, where Bad Hughie helped untangle his bike.

'Who won?'

'I think the tailor. For there's not a suit without a tatter.'

'Their bikes are around the other side. I let the wind out of every last one of them.' Bad Hughie lit a cigarette, his pale face in the match flare a moon-skull yellow. When he saw the girl in the shadows he whispered, 'Don one goes the whole way. And I don't mean home.'

She walked beside him out of the hot town into the cooler country. He didn't speak to her. Her high-heels clattered on the road. Wheels ticked. A bat zicked overhead. The isolating night gave sounds full worth.

'I live out this way, so I do.'

'Do you?'

He hadn't asked this girl to come with him. She was tagging

113

on. But why didn't he jump on his bicycle and ride away? You
didn't need words for conspiracy. Silence for bodies was loud
enough. She stopped. He saw her dark form go from the road. A
gate bolt clunked back. He let his bike fall against the hedge and
followed her into the field.

The moon glinted on the brooch on her coat. She spread the
coat and lay on it. A hen before a rooster. The dark was made for
this. But he didn't know what to do. No one had told him. He
hadn't been able to get his hands on an instruction manual. Bulls,
buck goats, roosters, in the fields and farmyards gave him ideas.
For a start, none of them wore trousers.

'What are you doing?'

'Taking my trousers off.'

'Wha'? Don't be mad. I'm going.' She didn't move.

Now what? The light lay watery across the land. He could feel
the pressure of the enormous sky. At night the damp land could
suck the nails from your boots.

He knelt between the girl's open legs, raised widespread knees.
He felt for her breasts, found them, naked. Warm, soft, alive . . .
and his mother was now the opposite – cold, bone, dead . . .
Pulling him down, she kissed him. Her tongue in his mouth,
warm and rough, went round his gums and tried to grip his own
tongue. Pulling away from her and kneeling still, he put his hand
between her legs. Desperate to know. Her innards were soaking
hot. Her moans deeper than mystery. This was the word shouted
aloud. The word made flesh.

He thought of his father gutting the hen. He thought of his
mother putting on lipstick.

'Here, put on this yoke.'

She handed him something that felt like chewing-gum. He
knew it must be a French letter. He put it in his pocket. He was
full of curiosity. But not desire. He didn't even know the girl's
name.

'What are you doing?'

Her plump rump and the back of her thigh glowed like the
near side of the moon. Her deep, wet womanhood exerted more
pressure than the land. The moaning noises in her throat, sensual
and frightening, throbbed the night.

He undid one stocking from its suspender and peeled it down
her thigh, over her knee, along her ankle, and hooked it past her
heel. Her shoe dropped off. He eased the stocking along to her

toes. Her instep was bare in starlight. Raising her foot to his mouth he kissed where the flesh and veins curved and pouted on her instep. She was up on her elbows watching him. Her naked thigh was pale and dark as wet flour. He stood up.

'Where are you goin'?'

'Home. Thanks.'

Jumping up, she hobbled after him.

'Are you playing a game or somethin'?'

'No.'

Her sloe eyes were flashing, wary, angry. Standing right in front of him she lashed a punch into his solar plexus.

'You're not making a fool outa me.'

Winded, he staggered back against the gate, doubled over.

'I knew you were dodgy from the moment you asked me.'

For certain he hadn't asked her. Lifting her coat from the grass, she hopped out to the road. He watched her pull her stocking up, then clip it to her suspender. It was beautiful. Her skin was the colour of the moonlit clouds.

She packed a punch. Probably a farmer's daughter. It was lucky she hadn't been involved in the fight. There were no games with women. Everything was deadly serious. Especially their bodies. She walked back to the town. To the dance again, more than likely. Her retreating heels made lonely music. Had he been cruel to her? It was no good feeling guilty for what he had done and not done. A hen didn't lie before a rooster for nothing. He couldn't explain himself to himself. Curiosity and fear had overcome desire. He was mad. The word could have become flesh. He could be going home now with the secret revealed. She was an innocent girl giving off maternal heat. Too close for comfort.

A dog fox barked. His wheels bumped over moon-filled potholes. 'It's the only way they mend the roads in Cavan,' his father said. The night air was creamy. Flowing. Warm. Wet. He sucked light from ditch-water, spokes, the shiny bell on the handlebar, the trees skidding starlight. He could hear furry animals scurrying across the road in front of him. Away in the distance an explosion rumbled. Another Customs Post blown up. In the morning he'd hear the details on the wireless. His vest was sticking to his sweaty chest. The world was a vast place. But apart from his clothes and a few books, he didn't own a tiny bit of it. There was freedom in that anyway. His head was bigger than the world and plagued with hopes, fantasies and fears. It was torture at times.

Heavenly bodies – they had to be explored. No doubt about it. He'd just had his first geography and astronomy lesson combined.

The seven stars were tipping down the sky like a runaway pram. A meteor crashed through past and future, simple as a lump of coal falling from the fire.

9

The rat was in the cell again. He woke up just as it came in the conduit. Its fat, humpy body swept the floor, nose whiffing towards the plate and mug. He'd drunk the tea his father left him and eaten the toast. There wasn't a crumb left for the rat, now squatting on the plate. The light from the bare bulb fell like snow on the rat's grey back. He should have been afraid of it. A rat had caused his downfall. He couldn't remember falling asleep. Heartbreak was the worst disease. TB and cancer, if they couldn't be cured, killed you in the end. Heartbreak killed you but wouldn't let you die.

His father opened the cell door. 'There's someone to see you. And if you take my advice you'll grab the chance he's offering.'

He had no idea what he was hinting at, but he followed him out into the day-room.

A stout, middle-aged man with beetroot cheeks and gaps in smoky teeth sat at the end of the table. He shook his offered hand. He'd never seen him before. He looked like a rough farmer dressed for an outing. He wore a baggy tweed suit, brown boots. A big buckled leather belt held up his trousers. A football medal dangled on his lapel from a chain running through the buttonhole into his breast-pocket.

'Gauson, me daughter's baby will soon be here so I think it's time you did the dacent thing now.'

This man he'd never seen before.

'A fellah sows a lock a wild oats but the time has come now when you have to take the plunge. She's waiting on you in the house now.'

His father standing by the fireplace, hand gripping the mantelpiece, looked at ease, immaculate in his uniform.

'You'll be well looked after. They have a big farm along the

Border. Your future would be assured. Besides, it's a pernicious sin leaving that poor girl in the lurch.' It was always a wild hope of his father's that the future could be assured.

'What girl?' For a mad moment he thought the man might be an uncle of the girl killing him second by second . . .

The man cleared his throat, swept a thick eyebrow with blunt fingers.

His father stepped closer. 'You told me yourself that you took that girl into a hayfield. And may God forgive you, because I won't.' God could forgive, men, never.

'After the dance in the Freemasons' Hall. The whole world knows it now,' added the man.

He wanted to laugh in their faces but didn't have the strength. Handcuffs hung from a line of hooks screwed to a batten on the wall. Keys were attached to the cuffs by coarse green ribbons. Two truncheons dangled from their thin leather straps. Police caps, a black cape, a tunic, hung alongside.

The floorboards were bare, scrubbed. The surface of the table was grainy, ink-stained. The hinged legs were held steady by iron stay-pieces, collapsible if required by the removal of two pins on chains. On the table was the police diary, a ruler, an ink-bottle, a puce pencil and a nibbed pen. The telephone with wind-up handle was in a corner by the window, fixed up on the wall. Above the mantelpiece hung a map of all the townlands of the sub-district of Butlershill. The day-room smelt of ink, uniform, cigarette smoke, Dettol.

It was as good a place as a church for torturing the spirit. That's what they were doing to him. The man was in earnest but he was sure his father was playing some kind of game. If he agreed to marry the girl, problem solved. He would no longer have the run of the country. His father could forget him. Mend his own losses. Get married again. There was no shortage of candidates – elderly teachers, widows, spinsters home unmarried from England, all of them with bankbooks. He stared at the man, trying to glimpse an image of the girl at the dance. It was a time ago. The sloe eyes were the same. Maybe the roundness of the face . . .

'I didn't make your daughter pregnant. We didn't have intercourse at all.'

The man flinched at the word. His father suddenly smiled and looked at the man. He could see he was on the spot. There was conflicting testimony. It could be as good as a court case to his father.

'I'm telling you, Sergeant, me daughter wouldn't tell a word of a lie. She was an innocent girl till she met him.'

'And so was he innocent,' said his father, 'till he met her. I don't think you're claiming she went into the hayfield against her will?'

Outside a car went down the road, light-shafts battering through the dark. His legs were weak. He hadn't eaten properly for days. He could remember ending up naked in a shed. That shed . . . He couldn't remember putting clothes on. If not death, he hoped something would happen to release him from the curse of destroyed love.

'You whelp, you've brought shame on me and on the sacred memory of your dead mother. Look at that arrogance, I ask you.' The words were harsh but his father's voice was strangely soft. There was contempt on his face as he looked at the man's dull face, cute sloe eyes. 'According to my information the real culprit has skedaddled to Glasgow.'

'He needn't think now he's getting away with it now. I've got support.'

This was a threat. Evil. Rats couldn't be compared with it. When carried out. Carbolic soap was useless. He went cold, blind with fury. He screamed. The man flinched. His father looked amazed, troubled. His scream had an iron echo in the day-room. He lunged at the man but his father caught him. Perhaps he was fainting with rage. His father carted him out.

He lay in the cell. Tears gulged up in him. Tears of shame. He heard the man walk out through the tiled hallway and the slam of a car door. Later, the Widow McGinn brought him a cooked meal on a big plate covered with a plate upside down, to keep the heat in as she walked up the hill to the barracks. 'Wedgwood Etruria', it said on the covering plate. Her best delph for the poor prisoner. Women were kind. They had to be. Married to a girl he didn't love – at least he'd avoided that fate. Salvation, if it came, lay elsewhere. Maybe America. Saved from hell was ordinary; saved from heaven was hell. All he had left was his father. The little peep-hole door opened. His father peered in at him.

'No more bloody games,' he shouted at him. 'You're in a bad way. How you didn't die out on them hills I'll never know.'

'You'd have let me marry that girl, wouldn't you?'

119

' "Let you"? Grow up, man. You're not a child any more. You've got to stand on your own two feet. We both have.' He shut down the little door, slotted home the small bolt.

He saw the bar of carbolic soap. He wedged it into the conduit opening. Mind you, rats ate soap. Rats could gnaw through steel, eventually. How could frail bellies stand the shock of them? They couldn't.

He went to sleep staring angrily into the light bulb. Trying to let the pressure burn his brains out. He could hear the tubercular wind lash snotty rain against the pebble-dashed barracks' wall.

10

Go into a hayfield with a girl and you're guilty of something. But he wasn't going to be guilty of guilt. His mind was clear. Coming out of mass the following morning his reputation was already made.

'I hear you're a fast worker,' a smiling girl said to him.

'You're not backwards coming forwards anyway,' Pike Maguire said. On top of his head he had an egg-sized lump. The lapel of his jacket was missing.

Prunty especially was pleased for him. 'Now you know. The wonderful works of a wheelbarrow.'

The more he protested, the more convinced they were of his seductive powers.

'Oh, he's desperate altogether,' said Dandy Cusack's sister, 'no woman is safe from him.'

'Thank God,' added her friend.

It was amazing the way rumours spread. Mrs Prunty gave him a withering look as she prepared dinner.

'What, Mammy?' Prunty inquired.

'The lad with the sheep's smile – that's the lad would cod you to your eyeballs.'

Taking a pot of potatoes from the fire she teemed them out of the back door. Then she emptied them into a white aluminium basin on the table.

'They look lovely and floury, Mrs Prunty.'

'If they're any good they'll be enough. If they're not they'll be too many.' From a flat pot with a heavy iron lid she lifted a duck, roasted.

'Hm. Grand, Mrs Prunty.'

'Too big for one, too small for two. That's duck for you. And there's three of us.'

Mrs Prunty wasn't pleased. Prunty winked.

'And you're no better, leading him astray. What'll his father say?'
Rumours spread like damp. No one said anything direct. The
Border motto was – 'Don't say anything – till you hear more'.
But you could never hear enough.

Later, in bed, Prunty wanted to hear all. He was burning to
know, yet pretended he didn't care.

'You don't have to tell me if you don't want. I couldn't care
less. A coorse I was there meself with the same lassie, months
ago. Did I not tell you that? Oh aye. She's had more rides nor a
tinker's donkey, the same girl.' In the dark, lies dripped from his
tongue.

He told him the bare truth.

'. . . and then I kissed her foot.'

'Yah wha'? Her foot? You kissed her foot?' He sat up in bed, a
fag in his mouth, the ash burning long as he weighed the words.
He seemed pole-axed. 'Jazus . . . that's ojus altogether. Her foot?
Are you sure?'

Prunty had a big black eye from the fight. With one hand he
held a lump of steak to it; when he lay down the steak was kept in
place for the night by a length of cotton-wool around his head. In
the kitchen they heard Mrs Prunty saying her rosary, the words
whistling through her scattered teeth. Then they heard her go to
her room on the other side of the kitchen. A great silence came
down on the house. The walls creaked. Mice scuttled. The cat
struck. Out at the back the hens roosting in the bushes clucked in
sleep. Rain clanged on the shed roof, hissed into the thatch.

Prunty, from deep thought, muttered, 'Yah can't bate the college boy for dirty tricks, hah? It's times like this I wish to God
I'd had an education.'

Tell the truth and you became the devil. All week he swaggered
in new-found confidence. He began to believe his own myth.
When he combed his hair before the mirror he was quite proud of
his image. When he rode the roads on Mrs Prunty's bike he took
his hands from the handlebars when he saw women coming in the
distance and when they went by he was convinced they looked at
him with hope in their hearts.

He couldn't wait to see his father. To see the look on his face.
He was bound to have heard something. He wanted to show him,
without being in the least explicit, he was a man at last. Like him.
A man. The urge proved fatal.

A few Sundays later he went home. His father wasn't in the kitchen. The teapot on the range was warm. A wisp of steam rose from a half-empty cup on the table. Silver coins were arranged in a single pile beside the cup. His father sometimes counted his loose change after eating. He went down the hall and called 'Daddy?'. He went into his father's room. The iron bed was bare to the skeleton springs. The thin mattress, doubled over, rested against the wardrobe. The room was at the back of the building. The sun never reached it. The lino in the light shone icy. His father no longer sleeping in the room, the peculiar smell of holy poverty was gone.

He crossed the hallway into what had been his mother's room. His father's boots and shoes peeped from under the end of the bed. His chamber-pot was there too. Spread on top of the bed was a police greatcoat. It lay like huge black wings suffocating the past. There was no longer the smell of powder, perfume, soft body. The room stank of damp, mass cards, Vick, boot polish. A length of string looped from the light switch by the door over to the bed.

The string was his father's idea. For years they had relied on oil lamps, tilleys, candles. Electrification when it came at last was welcomed by his mother. She had gone round the house joyfully flicking the switches on and off.

'I'm delighted.'

'No you're not. You're the opposite, aren't you?' said his father.

Electricity was progress. His father was dubious. Apart from the quarterly bill, electricity had one great snag. His father liked to read the *Sacred Heart Messenger* or *Wide World* in bed at night. When ready for sleep he only had to reach to the bedside table to extinguish the oil lamp. But with a light bulb you had to get out of the warm bed, walk over the cold lino to the switch by the door, then get back into bed in the dark. His father pondered the problem before coming up with his 'string solution'. He screwed a hook into the wire casing above the switch, got a length of string, made a noose for the switch, then ran the string through the hook over to the bed. He could then lie in bed and pull on the string when he wanted to put the light out.

'Now who has the brains, hah? I think I'll register the invention with the Patent Office. String and a hook – I could make me fortune.'

'Haven't you heard of the bedside lamp?' said his mother.

A lamp cost money. They had to adopt the 'string solution'.

His mother's commode was still by the bed, its padded lid closed. Opening it, he removed the seat and the rose-patterned chamber-pot from its base. Reaching through the base he felt in the corner of the commode. It was where his mother hid the few pounds she could scrape together. He was in luck. He found two five-pound notes. He went to the dressing-table and from a drawer pocketed his mother's powder compact. Her image was still in there somewhere. He needed a new face to obliterate it. The mind was a mirror. A hidden one.

At his mother's funeral the close relatives – 'the aunt' and 'the uncle' – had searched frantically through all her personal possessions. Anything they considered worth having they grabbed . . . a leather purse, a golden guinea. Her wrist-watch. A pair of high-heeled shoes. One ear-ring (they couldn't find the other one). But they missed the money in the commode and ignored the compact.

Worst of all, he watched, horrified, as they tried to remove the golden wedding-ring from his mother's finger.

'It's all right, darlin,' said the aunt, 'this ring was your granny's. Your mammy would want it to stay in the family.'

Even in death his mother's finger was swollen. They couldn't get the ring off. He stood in the death room watching them tug, turn, soap, pull at the ring.

'Jesus, Mary and Joseph but it's stuck.'

'Leave go. Let me,' said the uncle.

After trying for a while the uncle glanced round the room as if hoping to see a knife, a pair of pliers maybe. They looked mean and malicious enough to sever his mother's finger.

He went to the kitchen to tell his father what was going on. He was sitting at the table stuffing himself with ham sandwiches.

'Daddy, come quick, the aunt and the uncle are trying to take mammy's ring.'

His father was in a lost, fatalistic mood. He didn't budge. 'Ah-ha, that's Ireland for you all right – the relatives turned up to rob the corpse.'

That was another thing he couldn't understand – how his father could eat and a dead body in the house.

Back in the bedroom, the aunt was practically astride his mother.

'Leave her alone, leave her alone, leave her alone,' he screamed.

'Have it your own way then. Let the bloody undertaker get it, if that's what you want,' said the uncle.

Annoyed, they left the room. The uncle, a sallow-faced man, had a white handkerchief crumpled in his fist. It was there all the time. He used it to dab his forehead and the bald spot on his greasy head. The aunt went round the house all day, dripping rosary beads and drinking tea. After kissing his mother's stiff, cold hand he went out and hid in the hen-house. He smashed three eggs against the corrugated sides. Sitting on an upturned box he watched the yokey slubber sliding to the ground.

Replacing the pot and seat, he closed the commode and went out to the back of the house. His father emerged from the lavatory, braces, belt, boot-laces undone. Holding his trousers in the grip of his hand, he shuffled up and down the garden path, glowering, downcast.

'What are you doing here?'

'I came to see you, Daddy.'

'When all fruit fails welcome haws.'

'What's up? What's wrong?'

'I'm constipated.'

If his father's bowels didn't move at the same time each day he assumed something was wrong. If they didn't move at all he panicked. More than two days without success and he was convinced death stared him in the face. Hourly gulping pills, Milk of Magnesia, Rennies, cod-liver oil, he waited in cranky mood for relief.

Going to the lavatory was a serious business for his father. It was the only time he smoked. He believed a cigarette relaxed him and at the same time killed the odour. He was the only man in Ireland who smoked for his health's sake.

'It's the Widow McGinn's food, God blast it. I'm finding it very binding. The Lord have mercy on the dead.'

'Amen, Daddy.'

A woman cooked for you for years; your stomach was used to it. Another woman cooked for you, your stomach rebelled.

He watched him walking up and down, the clothes loose on him, ready to dash, if God ordained it so. In a corner by the drain was a baited rat-trap; a bacon rind tied to the plate with white thread. His father hated rats. You couldn't get rid of them. They emerged night and day from every nook and cranny, laden with history and disease. 'They thrived in the Famine.'

His father looked cranky as briars.

'Have you tried taking . . .'

'Don't annoy me, I've tried everything. This is the third day. And what are you doing here? You must be looking for something. What do you want?'

'Nothing.'

'Take it and go.'

His father was hard. Depressed.

'I'll give you dancing . . . in my day we mourned for the full year. The whole place laughing at us. Every tongue out and wagging like a cow's tail at flies.'

So he had heard about the dance. Good. Holding up his trousers, boots untied, shirt hanging out, long johns showing, braces dangling, his father looked like a comedy act. He retreated as he clattered closer.

'What's bleddy funny?'

'Nothing. I think I've got something would maybe work. I'll give you a fiver if your bowels move.'

His father stopped, stared at him, a glint in his eye. 'Where would you get a fiver?'

'Mammy gave it me before she died,' he lied.

Money was everything to his father. He saved and scraped every penny. Money was a pot he sat on day and night. He believed that the way his father crouched over food and when counting money was somehow connected with the workings of his gut. It stemmed from a fearful drive that present benefits couldn't last.

His father came to him, hand out.

'No, Daddy. Afterwards.'

Annoyed, his father looked at the fiver, a shy grin on his face. Turning abruptly, he went into the lavatory, banged the door shut and bolted it. Who would have wanted to interrupt his efforts? But the shot bolt was part of the ritual. Lavatory – bank vault. Smoke drifted out over the top of the door.

A bluebottle landed on the bacon rind. The trap was grey iron – rat-coloured, mouth square, blunt teeth crushing cruel. A chain was linked to the handle. When his father used the trap at the potato pit in the field next to the barracks, he staked the chain to the ground so that a rat half-caught couldn't drag the trap away.

He went into the kitchen and waited for his father. The crockery in the dresser, the chairs, the table (with new oil cloth), the armchair, the press (underwear, shirts, sheets in the top half, his father's law and crime books in the bottom), the tilley lamp hanging out-of-date on the wall, the wireless on its ledge, the sewing-machine – all were in order and obviously dusted from time to time. A local woman came in once a fortnight. But the place was soulless.

His father came in, smiling, clothes now in regulation order. He looked up at the Sacred Heart picture above the mantelpiece, then closed his eyes in relief and thanksgiving. Taking the fiver, he kissed it before buttoning it away in his hip pocket. He was in control again, strong, cool, handsome. Danger had passed.

'It's about time you and me had a talk, me buck.'

'Who told you I was at the dance?'

'I heard it on the wind.'

'Did you hear anything else?' He had a mad urge to draw his father, deluge him with tit-bits.

'Should I have?' His eyes were narrow now, dead set on his soul. He wished he hadn't come. He wanted to escape. He was a fool. He made a move to the door but his father stood in his way. He was concerned. His father turned the wireless on.

Every Sunday afternoon Radio Eireann broadcast a ceilidh and Old Time dance. Accordion, fiddle, banjo, tin whistle, piano music suddenly flooded into the kitchen. Rising up the damp walls, it crept across the yellowing ceiling.

'Let me see you dance, then. Come on. An Old Time waltz, what could be simpler?'

'You need a partner.'

'I'll be your partner.'

His father stood stiffly right in front of him, tunic hanging open, whistle-chain dangling free. His big boots could murder music. His face was a mixture of anger, scorn and smile. His teeth were bared, cheekbones sharp, neck muscles tense. The whole head was set like a rasp. He was nearer stone than flesh.

His father grabbed him, gripped his hands rigidly in waltz position. His father led, so making him female. He could feel his fingers digging into his back.

'Come on. One-two-three. One-two-three. Let's see what you're made of, me buck. Now.'

Tunic buttons pressed into him. He was that tight to his father. He could smell soup and cigarette on his breath. His fists hurt.

'Let me go.'

'One-two-three. One-two-three. I was the boy could do it in me time.'

Powerless, he was pulled, pushed, dragged round the floor in a cruel approximation of a waltz. He was a marionette tangled up in a humiliating passion. Great boots trod his toes, eyes bored his soul. Angry, embarrassed eyes. His father wasn't happy doing what he was doing. But he was doing it.

Gritting his teeth, he hung on, hoping the dreadful music would end soon. It was the most bizarre event. He couldn't understand it. You were the same flesh as your father but mediated by your mother. This was far too near the original source for comfort. He had never been so close to him.

'Let me go.'

His father laughed, head back, strong as a horse. 'One-two-three.'

'If Mammy saw this, saw you, she'd . . .'

'Mammy's not here to help you now, me boy. Don't drag her into it. Stand on your own two feet. Be a man. Not a cowardy custard.'

The damn music was endless. It would have to be one of those forty-eight-verse dirges about going to 'Amerikey'. Jesus. He struggled to free himself. His father's bony knees jabbed his thighs. His raw hands were vices.

'Let me go or you'll be sorry.'

His father let him go. The music ended. In a twinkling he had reeled backwards into the armchair, his father having pushed him in the chest. Leaning down over him, hands gripping the arm-rests, face inches away, his words hit him like a shower of hail.

'Sorry, will I? I'll knock the swagger out of you. Coming in here, throwing your weight around. I'll knock your bleddy block off. You dirty thing, going into a field with some poor trollop knows no better, God help her. And your mother not cold in the grave. Have you no respect? How could you? Saints have mercy, how could you lower yourself? How, hah? Tell me. What have I done wrong, that you want to ruin me? Jesus, Mary and Joseph help me, save me this day.'

Saliva splattered on to him. He couldn't move. His father's pressure squashed him like a ton of greatcoats. His mood was almost touchable. Mood was soul damp . . .

Desperate, he dived out sideways from under him and ran to the other side of the table. Raging, he caught his father's tone.

'Yes, I went into a hayfield. It was smashing. She's no trollop, but a queen. I'm in mad love. So is she. We're getting married next month.'

For a second his father's face relaxed in boyish surprise. He should that instant have darted out of the door. Too late. His father drove at him, missed. They circled the table. The tea sloshed out of the cup . . . this was nightmare. He was sweating with fear.

'Where did you get it? That money. Come on, out with it.'

He circled, jumped to the other side of the armchair, grabbed it, turning it to keep his father away, darted back to the table, circled . . . hell had come . . . on the radio a woman sang un-accompanied . . .

His father, gripping the table edge, with brute force pushed him back into the corner, driving him, crushing him against the wall. 'Where's the rest of the money? Out with it.'

His father flung the table across the kitchen and was on to him, dragging at his jacket, his hand now in one of the pockets. The French letter the girl had given him in the hayfield . . . there it was, between his father's thumb and index finger. He stared at it, mesmerized, as if it were the living symbol of Satan.

'Heavenly Father, blessed Mother.'

He saw the punch coming. Had it landed . . . His father swung again. This time he dived out of the way under the table. He began to scream a mad, convulsive splurge of fantasy and lies. Snatches he remembered from the lives of the saints. Anything to stop his father beating him.

'I'm going to be a priest. Don't touch me. A priest. I've applied to Maynooth. The Bishop said he'll have me. I've always wanted to be a priest. Or join the Guards. But it's a priest I'm going for. I've an interview with the Bishop in Cavan tomorrow, Daddy. Don't hit me, Daddy. I'm going to be a saint. I mean a priest. Definitely. No two ways about it. My vocation is absolute.'

On the radio the ceilidh band played a jig. His father went to the range and with his bare finger lifted the hot iron plate. He pegged the Frenchie into the flames. With a rough twist he turned the wireless off. Under the table, frozen with fear, he couldn't run to the door. He was crouched and waiting for Fate to destroy him, with less fight than the Kicker in the knacker's yard.

His father staggered to the armchair and sat head in hands, howling. Misty-eyed, raging, sad . . .

The glasses in the dresser rang. The Sacred Heart lamp flickered. The house vibrated in a tremor of unplugged emotion. His father hadn't even cried at the funeral. This was it now, howling, gulging, tumbling, a river sweeping all before it – furniture, cattle, the kitchen, the past, the future, the sky . . . his face was a tearing mask of fury and pity. That was the trouble with him – he was never one *or* the other. Always *both*. You never knew how to take him. Wild heart pumping, he dived for the door and on Mrs Prunty's bike rode towards the Border like the hammers of hell.

His father would have to cry alone.

11

He lay in the turf bog with Prunty, head back on the heather, above him the eye-blue sky. Prunty sensed something wrong but didn't pry. A blue dragonfly, head stripy yellow, helicoptered over a dandelion. 'Devil's needles, I call them lads.'

A velvet-green bug puzzled its way through the hairs on his wrist. An earwig raced over the ground, stopped, swivelled, raced on. A knitting chorus of grasshoppers laced the day. The breeze swished through a hazel bush. The more troubled your soul, the more you needed peace. Yet peace gave you too much time to think . . .

The turf bank was chocolate brown at the top, dark in the middle, black deep in its heart. The water in the hole was treacly thick, a scum of green floating at the edge. A hunk of bog oak stuck up from the bottom. Just above the waterline the bank had a bluish tinge. Earlier, he had watched Prunty dig out from that part a lump of turf that was half coal. 'Looka that,' he said, 'black as a Cloverhill Protestant.'

The turf cut previously, now dry, they stacked in round towers, wide at the base, tapering to two sods at the top. The towers were about three feet high, hollow in the middle to let the drying winds defeat the rain.

The bank, cut into for years, stood more than a hundred yards from the laneway running into the bog from the Belturbet road a mile away. Behind them reared drumlin hills, the hay cocked, new grass already growing fresh and gentle green. In the far distance the Cuilcagh mountains blurred to the sky, clean and dreamy and coloured Cavan blue.

They drank tea from a bottle corked with a fold of newspaper, now soggy. The air was wonderfully pure. Prunty, belly bare, rolled on the turf mould, playful as a cub.

'Yah can tell me if yah want, lad. What's up?'

'I'm going to become a priest. I am.'

Prunty could tell he was serious, so didn't laugh. 'Is that right? When? Why?'

'I'll have to finish school first. Then.'

Prunty lay still, the sun dazzling into his blond hair. Prunty had survived without a father. As far as he could tell, survived well. He wasn't churned up night and day trying to understand him . . . Was it a law that fathers couldn't melt?

'You'd look a right article in priest's clothes. You'd no more make a priest than that sod of turf.' Picking up the sod, he flung it far into the water. A green plume of spawn flared, died. 'Quare too the way the sinner wants to turn a saint. I can't see it, lad, no way.'

'What makes you so certain?'

'I know the class of animal you are and it's not a priest.'

When they came that morning to the bog Prunty said he could smell fox. 'Hisht. He's about. Or just gone. I can smill him.' When Prunty wanted emphasis he narrowed the words.

Two small blues, four whites, a red admiral, three tortoise-shells butterflew across the bank face. A dozen or more blue, green and grey dragonflies zipped and hovered above the heather.

'You know the way you see some polismen and the uniform doesn't fit? Not your father, a coorse. They're just not cut out for the job. The same with the clargy. I've seen priests come out on the altar and the garments hangin' on them like they were scare-crows. If you don't look right for a start, you're on a hidin' to nawthin'. Come on we'll go up to the chapel and you can try on the vestments and see how you look and feel in them. If you pass the test, at least you'll know you're on the right road OK. If not, if you look an oul' cod in them, you'd be as well to think again. 'Cos if you don't look right, you won't feel right. And if you don't feel right, lad, you're only pissin' agin the wind. You know what I mean, lad, don't you?'

Prunty's eye still bore a mushroom puffiness from the blow he had received at the dance fight, as if his assailant had left a knuckle under the skin.

They walked up the drumlin field, the bog below and behind them a calm wilderness of heather, rush, grass, bushes, sally and hazel saplings. On the clear patch away from the bank, the towers of turf looked like strange black beehives from some other age.

Preserved forever underneath the spongy ground were trunks of oak and deal and lumps of coal ... The land destroyed you or held you. Forever.

Prunty whiffed, contented, at a cock of hay. Passing two grazing cows, he slapped one of them gently on the rump. 'Mother and daughter, them two.' Going through a gap in the hedge he stopped and pointed at a beaten track. 'Look. Fox.' A paw-mark in the mud. Toes. Round like a dog's.

In the house, to quench their thirst they drank buttermilk in pongers, then rode to the chapel.

Prunty's idea wasn't bad. Clothes did proclaim the man. Fine feathers made fine birds. The sacred uniform might transform him, give him the feel of the future. If he became a priest his father would for certain sure forgive him. For anything. A direct family line to God ... On ordination day his father would kneel before him for his blessing ... What a moment! Each day he'd celebrate mass, his father in his thoughts, his mother always in his heart. Brain – thought. Feelings – heart ... But then there was the body, and that was the trouble because that's where it all met and mixed. Your body was a churn. He liked watching Mrs Prunty pounding at the milk, loved the conchy cranching seaside agony sounding in the upright churn. A wooden lung, a plain pounder and liquid changed to solid. Maybe you had to be battered to produce good. If that were so he must be bloody brilliant already ...

They rode up and down the braes and along the flat where between high hedges the air lay in balmy pools. Wild fuchsia, growing out of the banks and ditches, dangled through the thick blackthorn, which everywhere kept the fields back from the road. The dark green hedges, haw-heavy, looked as if someone had gone along with a paintbrush splashing them with red. By the side of a field an abandoned plough, rusty handles tipped up askew, lay half buried in the clay. The earth seemed to be sucking it slowly under.

They walked up the steep hill to the chapel. The priest's car wasn't outside the parochial house. To check the housekeeper wasn't about either, Prunty went to the belfry, which stood in the open, grabbed the chain hanging from the wheel and pulled. The great cup heaved and struck the iron tongue, the clang throbbing out over the woods and valleys way below. Not a soul stirred.

'Come on, yah boy yah, the coast is clear.'

He wouldn't have dared ring the bell. It was only rung for mass, funerals and the Angelus. Prunty was lawless.

The chapel was a rectangular building with a protruding porch. The walls were grey pebbledash, the roof slated. Above the porch was one round window flanked by two small ones in the Gothic manner. The windows in the sides of the building were long, slender and Romanesque. The chapel had recently been renovated, the materials used all smuggled across the Border. 'I brung a stone of nails one night,' Prunty said.

Round the back of the chapel they opened the sacristy door and entered. He knew the lay-out well from the days when he was young and served at mass. The room was large, sparsely furnished.

Prunty opened the door of the big wardrobe. 'Now, your reverence, get into some a them and let's have a gawk at you.'

Opposite the wardrobe was a long, deep chest of drawers in which were kept the different chasubles, all laid flat on tissue paper. When you opened the drawers the action was smooth and snug. By a small table with a crucifix was a prie-dieu on which the priest knelt in moments of quiet reflection before mass. Hanging on a hook was the thurible. Directly underneath it, on the shiny wooden floor, lay the incense boat. On the back of the door was a pair of men's trousers. When the priest's housekeeper served mass she had to wear them. A concession to canonical law, it gave her a mannish appearance and made her acceptable whenever she had to venture on the priest's side of the rails.

Reaching into the wardrobe, he took out the amice and draped it over his shoulders. The amice was a white cloth with strings which tied around the waist. It was a reminder of the blindfold Jesus was forced to wear by the mocking Romans. Next he put on the alb, a long white linen dress, and round it tied the cincture, the symbol of holy purity.

Prunty by now had discovered what he termed 'the sparger' – a holy-water bucket and sprinkler. The sprinkler had a perforated metal knob which held the water and allowed it to escape when shaken. In mock ceremony he sprinkled all around him.

> 'Ashes to ashes, dust to dust
> If God doesn't take you the Devil must.'

'Don't, Prunty. Quit. This is serious.' The vestments had power. He was in awe of them and the eerie silence of the chapel.

He put the maniple on his left arm and round his neck the stole. He was now ready for the chasuble. From the chest of drawers he selected a green one, Prunty helping him into it. Green was the colour of hope. The material reminded him of the chevrons on his father's uniform. Embroidered on the back of the chasuble was a cross to remind the priest he was bearing the yoke of Christ. He walked up and down, feeling the weight of the vestments, enjoying the power they imparted. Kneeling on the prie-dieu, he closed his eyes, contemplated, rose, and turning to Prunty made the sign of the cross over him.

Prunty looked at him, half-impressed, half-cynical. 'Holy suffering Geronimo, you look a cross between a big altar-boy and a stuffed parrot.'

'Thanks very much.'

'No, no, lad, you look grand, but . . .'

'But?'

'It's just not you, lad, honest to God. You're like something from the top shelf of a toyshop.'

White wax tapers for lighting candles lay on a window ledge. Leaning against the window was a long-poled cone-shaped snuffer. The snuffer was forever streaky black from flame and smoke. Prunty found a cardboard box of unconsecrated communion hosts. Taking a handful he stuffed them in his mouth.

Green was for hope. And Ireland. Red was for blood. The red on the neck of the headless body along the railway track. Black was for mourning. The priest wore black at his mother's funeral mass. Turning the key in the door of a press, he opened it to reveal a collection of sacred vessels and accessories. A chalice, a paten, veils, a burse, the corporal, a ciborium and the glorious, golden, sun-flaming monstrance.

Holding the monstrance aloft, he threatened Prunty with its magnificence. 'Repent ye, Prunty, of your fleshy sins. Committed, we hear, with one widdy woman, wicked and unwise. Beg for forgiveness, you devil's pup.'

'Away and fuck yourself. Where do they keep the wine?'

'No, Prunty, come on. We'd better go before we're caught. Come on, we've done what you said. You've proved your point, haven't you?'

Prunty's turned-down wellingtons looked odd in the calm, sacred surroundings. His blue shirt was stained with bog mud and patches of sweat. Pleased with himself he lit a cigarette, tossing the spent match on the floor. Prunty was profane and without fear.

What had the exercise really proved? The vestments made him feel good. Proud. Arrogant, even. Frightened. He could see himself as a priest, but would it solve his problems? A collar would contain feelings that one day might explode and blow his head off.

As he replaced the monstrance they heard a loud knocking on the sacristy door. If it was the priest they were as good as dead. But the priest would hardly knock on his own door. Still as statues, they stood listening. They could hear a man's voice.

'All right now, daughter, aisy. We're here now, aren't we? Aisy.'

Prunty, finger on lips, confused-looking, decided to investigate. Opening the door slightly, he squeezed out so that no one could peer in. He waited. The chasuble forced you to stand in a certain way. It represented the robe Jesus wore when crowned with thorns. You couldn't slouch in it. Arms half-raised in priestly gesture, he waited for something to happen.

He could hear mumblings, then Prunty's raised voice. 'He'd be no good to you, he's only visiting. You'll be wantin' Father Gaynor.'

'He'll do rightly, no bother.'

'But he's only just ordained.'

'All the better. Aisy now, daughter.'

What on earth was going on? A big moth flew out of the wardrobe and beat at the fearful day with panicky wings.

Grinning from ear to ear, Prunty stuck his head in the door. 'You're wanted out here, Father.'

Prunty, cheeks puffing with repressed laughter, wouldn't answer his mouthed question. He just followed him out.

A farmer stood on the gravelled path, beside him a big fat pig.

'Good day, Father. I want you to bless me sow, she's about to litter any day. The wee prayer Father Gaynor says over her always brings us luck. Aisy, daughter, aisy.'

The sow, with a heaving belly of chalice-sized tits, was restrained from moving by the farmer flicking her neck with a long sally rod. Her snout was massive, her weeping eyes tiny. The tips of her dirty lugs were bent. She reeked of urine, dung and straw. Even her curly tail was caked with mud. The farmer was no cleaner. Clogs, dark trousers, green gansey, white shirt, tweed cap were filthy. His big belly was as impressive as the sow's. The sun gleamed on his greasy cap. He hadn't shaved for days. Only his teeth were white. False.

The sow's nostrils were bigger than her eyes. She was whiskery under her snout, hairy all over her body. Pink snout, pink eyes, pink nipples. Sow and man looked up at him.

'Perhaps you'd prefer Father Gaynor. I'm . . . new. I don't feel . . . equipped.'

'Fresh out of Maynooth, Father, sure what could be better?'

Prunty had told the farmer a pack of lies. But how could he confess the truth to the man? He was looking at him, a hopeful, servile smirk on his face. It was plain he loved his pig. She was his wealth, his future.

'Aisy, daughter, aisy.'

'Holy water, please.'

Prunty went into the sacristy, his face a tight mask of seriousness.

When requested, animals were blessed by the Church. As a boy he remembered a priest making the sign of the cross over a basket of eggs. The farmer was waiting. He couldn't not bless the sow. How could he tell him he was a fake? The sow was waiting too. She'd been through this kind of exercise before. Prunty returned with the aspergillum, head on chest to hide his mirth.

He took the sprinkler, shook it over the sow, dipped it back in the water. This he did three times. When he sprinkled he copied the priestly movement of one strong forward action, followed by two shorter ones. It was the watery equivalent of a hand blessing. 'In the name of the Father and of the Son and of the Holy Ghost . . .' A good deal of the water landed on the farmer. Blinking, he blessed himself, his fingers black with dirt.

Prunty shook, lip gripped in his teeth. The sow was staring at him.

'Knio, knio, knio. Dominus vobiscum. Kyrie eleison. Christie eleison. Gaulia est omnes divisas in partes tres. Knio, knio. Alleluia. Asperges me Domine hogwash et mundabor. Oremus. Go in peace, gentle sow and thrice gentle farmer, may thy bonhams have full suck upon thine ample tits. Knio. Kneel and pray.'

On one knee the man crouched, head bowed, arm resting on the pig's back. Prunty, groaning, went into the sacristy.

'Aisy, daughter, aisy.'

'The blessing of Lug and Crom and the waters of Life pour upon thee soon. Knio, knio. Lycidas et Julius Caesar, amen.'

Prunty stood in the doorway, holding out the golden monstrance.

'That won't be necessary. Put it back.'

The farmer got to his feet, blessing himself.

'Thanks, Father, she's well and truly blessed now. The best ever. How much do I owe you?'

What price the blessing of a pregnant sow? He had no idea. 'Ah ... um ... some rashers, perhaps? A pound of rashers. A few sausages maybe as well? Half-dozen eggs? Is that reasonable? And some black pudding, too, if you could manage it.'

The farmer, a crafty look on his face, tugged at the peak of his cap, shifting it up and down a few times on the brink of his forehead. 'A few rashers, no bother, Father, if that's what you want. No eggs, though, I haven't a hen about the place. A few rashers, aye, no bother. When we kill in a while or so. Thanks, Father. Come on, daughter, we'll hit home.'

'How far have you come?'

'From the other end of the parish. But it was worth it.' Guided by the sally rod, the sow turned and waddled away. 'May you rise to be a bishop, Father.'

One side of the sally rod was mud-stained, as if it had fallen in farmyard dirt, the uppermost part of it remaining clean.

In the sacristy he quickly removed the vestments, he and Prunty reeling with hysterical laughter.

'I'm telling you, lad, you're some hoor the way you carried it off. Knio, knio, knio ... ah Jazus, that's the best ever. "Oink" backwards.'

They left the sacristy and jumped on their bicycles. Mudguards rattling, they flew down the untarred hill to the main road. At the cross they just managed to break in time as Father Gaynor, driving in a hurry, swung off the main road right in front of them. Skidding to a dusty halt he lowered the window and, lip trembling angrily, stuck his head out.

'Are you looking for me?'

'No, Father,' said Prunty. 'Why?'

'Don't be so bloody cheeky, you cur. I thought you might have been up to the house and I wasn't there.' His lip always trembled. He wore his temper like a crown of thorns.

'Sorry, Father, no offence intended. Fresh and well you're lookin' anyway.'

The housekeeper sat in the passenger seat, looking straight

ahead. The locals claimed she 'wore the trousers and the collar'. Her head was broad, the chin pointed. Like an anvil. Her bosom was as big as a sack of straw. In looks she was on a par with Lady Sarah.

The priest looked at him. 'What's the matter with you?'

'Nothing, Father.'

'What do you think of the world situation, Father?' Prunty asked. 'Do you think the Russians will ever drop the atomic bomb on this country?'

'Hopefully,' Father Gaynor replied, before accelerating up the hill to the parochial house.

History and world affairs were the priest's interests, which was why Prunty had asked the question. The man had a fearsome reputation. He once announced from the pulpit that he possessed a sword, and if rowdies continued to cause trouble after dances in the parish hall he would 'stick sixteen inches of shining steel in their guts'. Tinkers camped in the area. On the Sunday morning about a dozen of the women and children came to mass. Dressed in their gaudy frocks and finery, they marched up the aisle and sat in the front pew. Father Gaynor ordered them into the sacristy, where, door open, they had to kneel in quarantine throughout the service. People were angry with him but nothing was ever said. He ruled the roost. He and his father. The Church and the Law.

If they ever found out what he and Prunty had got up to there was sure to be an Inquisition. Sacrilege, theft, blasphemy, personation, violation of the Disturbance of Worship Act, cursing . . . they could be charged with a whole slew of crimes under canon and State Law.

He didn't feel good about hoodwinking the farmer. What victory was there in fooling the ignorant? And the look of servile piety and faith on the man's face was humbling. Faith. It was a gift. You either had it or you hadn't. At school Father Austen had told him as much. He felt bad. Had he the gift or had he lost it? Thrown it away, most like. Father Austen had talked to him about moral absolutes. Trouble was, they weren't absolute at all. Everything was absolute on paper, but as soon as they stood on legs they kicked out all over the place. Even the country wasn't absolute. He'd seen with his own eyes the British army, full of confused purpose, searching for the edges. Were maps any good at all? The land was only absolute in that it buried you in the end.

Flesh – how could flesh be absolute? If flesh was absolute then so were dreams.

He felt bad. Now what was he going to do? What was there that he could do? Surely he wasn't empty of all ambition? What about fighting for his country? Didn't he want to free Ireland? Be the man who at last united Dublin and Belfast? He'd be famous for evermore. Yes. And if he died trying, he'd be a martyr. They'd name football teams and pipe bands after him. Yes. Even his father and Father Gaynor would forgive him then. Why was he always looking for forgiveness?

'Prunty, I've been thinking . . . I want to join the IRA.'

Prunty, giving him a sideways squint, dismounted, and pushing his bike along the road said simply and seriously, 'Why?'

'I'd like to fight for my country. That's why. Take part in the struggle to get the British out of Ireland. Once and for all. Do you know who I get in touch with? I'm serious.'

'You were serious about being a priest a while ago, lad.'

'That's the thing about whiles ago. This time I might be right.'

'The Sergeant's son in the IRA, that'll be one for the books all right. Him trying to catch them, and you in them! Be some chase when he gets wind of it.'

'He's chasing me now anyway. I don't care about him.'

'Don't you?'

He had never seen Prunty so serious. He walked along head down, brow furrowed, lips pursed. Why? To join the IRA was a natural wish, so ordinary as to be banal. The jails on both sides of the Border were full of Republicans. The struggle for Independence had gone on forever. There weren't many blades of grass without blood. That morning Prunty had taken him to a secret part of the bog and shown him a pile of mossy stones. 'There's a Black and Tan buried there, lad. Don't say I told you. He was shot by the IRA in 1921. After a court martial. The old people know his name, but no one will say. You're on holy ground, lad.'

The entire country was holy ground. The people who killed and died for it made it so.

They passed a farmyard. Cattle stood in a shed entrance. Such was the depth of dung on the floor their heads touched the galvanized roof. Why didn't the owner clean out the beasts every day? Why give them comfort when they were only bred for slaughter? Sleepy Death couldn't be too far away . . . Jaws moving sideways, the cattle cud-munched, big eyes looking hopelessly from the shed on to a world of manure and soggy fields.

'The man in charge of Sinn Fein is Peter Joe Reilly. He might be able to put you in touch.'

'Peter Joe Reilly? Which one?'

'This one doesn't come from about here. But every Friday he goes to the pictures in the Luxor in Clones. You'll meet him there.'

'How will I know him?'

'At the National Anthem everyone rushes from the cinema. But not him. He stays until it's played out. You'll see him standing to attention, his hat in his hand.'

In the Luxor they played a crackling 'Soldier's Song' as a tricolour fluttered on the screen. No one listened to it. Political reality was no match for Hollywood fantasy. Obviously, though, there were men like Peter Joe Reilly who couldn't be hood-winked.

'I'll go on Friday and meet him.'

Prunty threw his bike against the hedge and, fists up, came towards him. Circling like a boxer, fists moving, he seemed to want to fight. What on earth was he up to now?

'Come on, yah boy yah.'

What had happened to spark Prunty off like this?

'Come on, lad, bike down and mitts up.'

'Why? What's the matter with you?'

'Nawthin's the matter with me! You're the boy lookin' for a fight. I'll give you plenty of it then, if that's what you want. You want to take on the British army, don't you? And the RUC? And the whole crew of them up there, don't you? That's what you're talking about, isn't it? Well, try me for a start. Let's see the cut of your jib. If you can make a fist of me maybe you'll make an IRA man, hah?'

Prunty's fists were so big he couldn't get them easily into his pockets. He usually stood thumbs hooked into the pockets or on the rim of his belt.

'What are you trying to prove, Prunty, for God's sake?'

'There's two kinds of men. Fighters and talkers. And I'm damn sure I know the kind you are. If you were a fighter, lad, I wouldn't give a tuppenny damn what you did. If you disagree . . . come on. I'm dying to get a crack at that chin of yours. Always cocked up like a rooster's bake.' When he wanted to disparage, he flattened the language even more.

'I can fight. I fought in the Freemasons' Hall, didn't I?'

'Away and shite. You never threw one punch. All you did was pull two buttons off the Wagtail's overcoat. And him only a gauson. And you want to fight the English army? You wouldn't bate your way out of a wet paper bag. You couldn't kick snow off a rope, lad.' Prunty's eyes were narrow, lips tight; the weather-beaten skin taut over chin and cheekbones. It was a look his father had when angry. 'You want to end up in a coffin draped in a flag, do you? Like Sean South and O'Hanlon?'

'That wouldn't be the object of the exercise.'

'No? What would the object be, then? Do you think if you die for Mother Ireland you'll meet your real mother on the other side, do you? Is that what you want?'

'To die? No. I'm allergic to death.'

So why the hell did he want to join the IRA all of a sudden? Prunty was boxing him into a corner. The priest's vestments idea was his. Now this. He wouldn't dare hit Prunty. He had to admit it, there was a strong possibility Prunty was on the right track again. Was he the type of man brave enough to swear a secret oath, to train, to lie in wet fields at night with a .303, waiting for an enemy armed to the teeth? Was he prepared to go to jail for ten years at least, if caught? Was he prepared to die or spend the best years of his life on the run?

But he was on the run. From his father, who was armed only with piercing eyes, a sharp tongue and bare knuckles dipped in the acid of an ancient personal history. Prunty, without any formal education at all, had sore answers. Damn him. It made him angry. He wanted for once to get his own back on someone.

'You're not the man for the job, lad. If you were I wouldn't stand in your way. Come on, tay will be ready be the time we get home.'

'Tell me honestly, Prunty, do you really have a widdy woman at your sexual disposal?'

Prunty, only just on his bike, jumped off again, enraged. Good. 'Yeah, flick your quiff back, fancy boy. Yah know nawthin'. I'm tellin' you when I go into a hayfield it's not to stick her foot in me gob anyway, that's one sure thing. The same widdy wants to marry me, yah boy yah, so she does, so she does. Now. Stick that where the monkey stuck the nuts. For all I care.'

Ginger stubble glistening on his chin, he angrily shook his head, stamped the ground and kicked the front wheel of his bicycle. Men's emotions were always boyish. Was there even such a thing as mannish?

'OK, Prunty, you've only got to take your wellingtons off and women's suspenders go twang. I'll believe you, millions wouldn't.'

'You're not with me all the time, are you, smarty pants? Aye, flick your quiff. Love yourself, don't you?'

Prunty did go out some nights alone. Coming back at dawn, tumbling into bed, a runty rucking figure in the ghostly light.

'All I want to know is, have you smuggled your goods across female borders, that's all.'

'You'd annoy a nation, do you know that?'

'Sorry, Coco.'

'It's not funny. You're mental. You don't know what you want. And I'll tell you something else. Women aren't angels, you know. They'll take what you give them. And if they want what you won't give them, they'll go mad. Even your mother wasn't a saint.'

'Leave my mother out of it.'

'She is.'

They rode home sulking. The warm air was thick with tiny black insects. They landed on his arms light as thought, and could bring lumps up out of all proportion to their size. He wasn't going to be a priest. He wasn't going to join the IRA. And Prunty was in a huff with him. Great, wasn't it? And what was that he said about women not being angels? His mother not being a saint? Surely a mother was different to a woman?

That evening, in silence, they drove the cows into the byre and milked them.

'Oh come on, Coco, say something.'

'No, feck you. You'd annoy a nation. You'd worry a hole through a pot. You're stubborn as a jackass. Milk the fecker, not pull her spins off.'

The byre had stone walls and a galvanized roof. Up on the rafters cobwebs hung thick and dirty. Big snotty cobs, old billowy webs. A white hen came in, cackled and flew up to a joist. Other game fowl followed. The black rooster, looking indignant, was last in and last to fly up. For a moment two swallows with red throats, creamy breasts, joined them, then flew out again. Round the byre walls were old mud cup nests. The fowl lined up above their heads, looked down as the milk whooshed into the pails. The hens when they didn't roost in the bushes, used the byre.

His head was against the cow's side as he milked. She was warm. He could hear deep gurgles in her belly. She was gentle and looked round at him when his tired fingers lost the milking rhythm. Only a woman could match the heat of an animal. Jesus in the stable could not have been cold against the body of a cow. He knew what he wanted. He wanted the heat that warmed the marrow of your bones.

Later they sat in the kitchen watching the news on television. News from London. A tube train had crashed, laden with passengers.

'That's a fret,' said Prunty.

'A holy terror,' said his mother.

In the byre the hens were roosting; the cows back out in the fields. The fire was burning low. Dusk falling. Out of the window he could see the swallows flit and swerve, dive and curve over a ragwort field. There was so much ragwort it looked like a cultivated crop. In the half-light the colour was deep gloomy yellow. The hills were ragwort and whin, fern and rock. Dusk was webbing down over hills and lakes, rivers, hedges, trees. Next time he looked out, night was in. The dark tent pitched over them and they hadn't noticed. The circus was always in town, for one life only . . . the larks were asleep on the ground, so were the hares, and the stones were impervious to day or night. He had tried to fly high, thought of lying low, but Prunty had clipped his wings. Who wanted to be a stone? The television screen was the colour of slate and spit. A fat man with a bow tie glowered out at them.

'What do you think of Winston Churchill, young fellah?'

'My mother always said he was a great man for his own family.'

'True for her. A woman and a half, your mother. RIP.'

On the dying flames Mrs Prunty boiled milk. Pouring it into three mugs, she then broke bread into the milk. The blobs of bread were mushy-white. Softy-hot in the mouth. They ate and drank, staring into the grate of glowing ash. At the back of the fire was an iron sheet, protecting the brickwork from the heat. The blackened hooks hung empty from the crane. The heavy three-legged iron pots were over in a corner of the kitchen on the floor, ready for morning.

Outside, a car screeched to a halt. Prunty was instantly alert, worried. 'If that's anyone for us, Mammy, we're not in.'

They made for the bedroom. 'Sounds like the priest's car,' he whispered.

It was. Father Gaynor had come into the kitchen, Mrs Prunty servile before him in word and deed.

'You'll have a drop a tay, Father, you will. Or a wee sniff of the cratur itself.'

'Where's your brada of a son? And his sidekick? I haven't time for blather or plamas. Where are they?'

'You tell me, Father. Haven't seen them all day. Why?'

'You'll know soon enough. Tell them I want to see them immediately. And so does the Sergeant. They're in trouble up to the gills.'

'Saints alive, what? What, Father?' Mrs Prunty's voice was strangled high with worry.

'They impersonated me today and blessed a poor man's pig, that's why.'

'What? They were impertinent to a man's pig?' Her voice was now a croak of sheer bewilderment and confusion.

'No, you amadaun. They dressed up as me. As a priest. A farmer came to have a sow blessed and they blessed it.'

'I see. And what was wrong with that?'

They could hear the thump of Father Gaynor's fist on the table, his enraged shout. 'What? What was wrong with it? Are you mad entirely, woman? On the way home the sow was killed and the distraught farmer came to me to get his money back. Then the whole story tumbled out. I know it's the two of them, because I met them coming from the chapel.'

Father Gaynor's waspy voice buzzed with malice. Mrs Prunty couldn't comprehend him. 'Did they kill the pig, the two of them?'

'No. No. God protect me from the stupidity of oul' women. The pig was killed otherwise. After they had blessed it.'

'Saints alive, but this is ojus altogether.'

'Ojus is right. And they're going to suffer for it.'

In the dark bedroom he could make out Prunty, staring at the floor. After the priest had gone and the noise of his car faded, Mrs Prunty chased them round the kitchen with a dishcloth, Prunty hopping like a child. It was amazing to see her power over him. He was like a big baby, manly swagger gone.

'It's a pack of lies, Mammy. One of the good boys must be coddin' him.'

Mrs Prunty grew tired of swiping them and made them kneel and swear on her rosary beads it wasn't them, they weren't in the chapel, they never saw a pig and wouldn't know how to bless one even if asked. This they readily did. Her rosary was black and long as a rope. 'It's not just the sow,' said Mrs Prunty, 'think of all her wee ones, for they must have been kilt as well.'

The cat sat curled by the hob. A beetle crossed the floor. The final remains of a turf sod glowed, then disintegrated to ash.

In bed Prunty chuckled. 'We'll brazen it out, lad. The hoor of a farmer must have told Father Gaynor he paid money for the blessin', hah? I bet he gave it to him as well, for he's not mean that way.'

Prunty put out his cigarette on the sole of a shoe which he held in his hand for the purpose. The shoe hit the floor with a slap. He lay down. His body steamed heat like warm straw. His big hairy arse was warm as the cow's belly. The silence in the house was thick and tense. At least he and Prunty were talking again.

'Coco? What do you think of sleepy Death?'

'It's the sleepy living I'm worried about. Sweet dreams.'

'You know that body in the bog you showed me? I bet it's still preserved. Nothing in the world can be destroyed. All the water is the same water that has existed since time began. You drink a cup of tea and it could have been drunk before by Henry the Eighth. Do you realize that?'

'I realize it all right, lad. But I don't give a tuppenny fuck. Now go to sleep.'

'What'll happen if they catch us?'

'They have to catch us first.'

For days after when they saw his father coming they took to the bog. And when he came to the bog they took to the hills. One night they slept in the hay shed. Which was as well, because the priest and his father searched the house at two o'clock in the morning.

'It's our word agin' your man's. Two agin one. They haven't a shred of evidence. The hue and cry will die down in a couple of weeks.'

They brazened it out and went to mass, and though the priest on successive Sundays spoke about the evil act he didn't mention them by name. 'The two culprits, and we know who they are, condemned that animal to death. God will not be mocked.'

But after mass the girls still smiled at him and their brothers winked. Mothers and fathers, though, stared with holy anger and disgust. When details emerged – via a discreet Prunty – people's attitudes changed. Fellows rode through Butlershill shouting, 'Knio, knio.' There was irony and humour in the story. After the blessing of the pig, the farmer walking it home went into a gateway to urinate. The sow wandered on in the middle of the road. A car came round a corner and ran it down. The driver of the car was a nun from Monaghan. She was known to be a 'holy fright' behind the wheel. The local paper, the *Anglo-Celt*, reported the incident under the headline: 'SOW KILLED BY ROAD HOG.'

The priest and his father gave up the chase.

He and Prunty worked in bog and field, helped smuggle goods and cattle across the Border, played cards in people's houses into the small hours of the night. Prunty always went to play cards well prepared. He had more cards up his sleeves than there were on the table. Some nights Prunty went off alone.

He sat with Mrs Prunty then, listening to her stories. Sometimes she took off her headscarf and washed her hair in the white basin. He rinsed it for her, pouring cold water from a jug. To finish drying it she let it hang over her face in front of the fire. Her hair was grey and long enough to touch the floor. The back of her neck was snow-white. It was a strange sight to see and hear her talk from behind the tumble of her hair.

'I remember me husband every single hour of the day. Everyone about the place always had great braggs of him. He was the image of that son of mine. He's as like him as a rope twisted out of him. He had the best motorbike about this country. A finer wallop of a man never lived. Come on, we'll have a boiled egg before we turn in, young fellah.' She claimed that a fresh game hen's egg was so good that after eating it you could see the wind.

He often sat watching her bake bread and when it was ready, lifting it, round as a wheel, from the iron pot. She let him have the first hot slice, cutting it with the knife against her chest. 'We'll soon stop it from hurdlin'.'

She worried about the state of the world and about his state.

'You're in great danger, young fellah, of wasting your brains.'

'Maybe I haven't any.'

'Oh you have, I can tell. You're as quick as a train.'

Alone, he worried about himself. He still waited for something to happen. Every night he clicked the powder compact in his pocket. Tock. In the morning he smelt it and looked in the mirror. No longer pale, he was tanned from sun and wind and rain. When he went hunting with Prunty he loved it when it rained. At hunts the hills were strung with men and dogs, yelps and cries linking on the bitter winds driving up the drumlins, whipping the rain so hard you couldn't hide from it. '*Agh-hoi-oi-hoi-agh-hoi-hoi-uh-hoi!*'

'See the hare, lad, sittin' fornenst the gate beyant.'

The hare was faster but the dogs stronger. They could persevere. The hungry howling was frightening, the desperate urgency in their throats savage.

'When the hare starts tiring, they can tell that be the footprints. The feet are longer on the ground, the scent heavier. The dogs know.' The hare could for a time string the beagles out for miles, effortlessly bounding ahead, then sitting to listen. It always ran the country in circles. No matter how straight her course she always turned. 'She'll ring yit.'

He had stood with Prunty and thirty men in a country lane. The ground, rutted mud, grass and rock ran between stone walls. The hare came out of a field and turned towards them along the centre of the laneway. The men, with courtly gesture, pressed back against the walls to let it pass. Even the hunt had its rituals. If you were being pursued you were a partner in a macabre dance. When the music stopped you were dead. The hounds came up the lane, necks stretched, tongues dripping, bodies mud-spattered, baying in a two-note howl, desperate to sink their teeth in something softer than themselves. One dog, thirsty, stopped to lap at a puddle but – swept up in the rage of the chase – hadn't the patience to stay and drink properly. It raced on with the pack pouring through the laneway; a river of sleek bodies, unstoppable skulls.

'It's a good hunt now.'

'She'll ring yit.'

When the dogs were far away he stood alone in gaps where thorny hedges pricked cold whistling music from the air. When it rained it came spearing down, hammered by the wind. He loved it on his face, the wet whips of it cutting at his skin until he had to close his eyes and turn away. Under the pelting rain the land turned smoky and disappeared.

He had stood with Prunty on a hill, under a lone and leaning flat-topped bush. They could hear the dogs closing in, excited, for the kill. 'It's quare and aisy to die,' he said.

12

They were scouring the country for the main. Prunty had the cock in a hessian sack. The sack was tied in a thick neck with hairy twine. Even when Prunty rested the sack on the ground you couldn't guess what was in it. The trim form of the rooster was muffled by the thick material. They wandered through one field after another, looking for signs of men, listening for cock crow. 'Hisht! When one pipes up the others answer.'

They walked through a potato field along the drills, making for a hill rising from a lake. The stalks were well up and covered with blossom – white and orange. Maybe a flowering potato stalk – green, white and orange – should be the country's emblem. The morning air was fresh, the potato leaves damp from dew. He crushed a leaf in his fingers, held it to his nose. It gave off an acrid yet dull geranium smell. It was strange the way failure could fill a people's soul. His father claimed that though the people starved in the Great Famine, empty bellies gave way to full and bitter hearts. Hatred of the English landlords was a rotten smell carried all over the world. The country, he said, ever since was fed on that failure and it was a taste that would take centuries to get out of our mouths and other men's conscience.

White butterflies flitted across the drills, landing where they pleased. The hedges were full of singing finches, sparrows, blackbirds, big mistle thrush. Skirting the lake, they walked through long grass, heading for the hill.

'If the Guards make a raid, what'll we do?'

'Run across the Border, what do you think?'

'Well, if the RUC come, what?'

'Run back.'

A fortnight earlier Prunty had trapped the rooster under a

riddle, bagged it and taken it to Herbie Tackney, who bred and trained all the game-cocks in the area. In Tackney's shed, they fitted 'boxing gloves' over the cock's natural spurs and matched it with a rival. Without hesitation the birds flew at each other, but because of the gloves they couldn't cause serious damage. The gloves were leather stumps the size of thimbles. They were allowed to spar to get their blood up, to get them used to fighting. Stacked on shelves around the shed walls were neat boxes each containing a game-cock. Pencilled on the boxes were the owners' names – Cusack, Maguire, Dolan, Rennicks, Warren, Gillespie, McAdam . . . fathers of the boys he went with to the Freemasons' Hall in Clones.

The concrete shed floor sprouted dust as the cocks flew, hopped, fought. Prunty's was the better of the two, always ending up on top of his opponent, pinning his neck to the floor.

'He's a fierce wee hoor,' said Tackney, 'for that red boy's won twice afore now.'

Tackney was a small, elderly man in dungarees and clogs. His voice was deep and smoky. He had a cigarette behind each ear, one a butt, the other untouched.

'Leave him with me, lads, and I'll see what I can do.'

As he spoke to them, holding Prunty's black rooster in his hands, he seemed impervious to the rooster pecking at his bare arm. The rooster gripped the skin, trying to tear the flesh away, but the skin looked tough as old canvas.

'Is he a winner, Herbie?' asked Prunty.

'Well, he's no waterhen anyway. But you can never tell.'

Prunty said that Tackney was the best trainer in Ulster. And he had a secret recipe which he fed to the game-cocks. Corn, milk and an ingredient only Tackney knew; it was given to him by his father who got it in Derbyshire in England, and on Tackney's deathbed it would be revealed to his son.

Cures and kills were handed on just before life expired.

When they reached the top of the hill, the country lying below – tiny fields, thick hedges, scattered trees – looked fresh and rinsed in the dewy sun. Out in the middle of the lake a flock of swans sat still as ornaments on a wedding-cake. On the hill summit was an abandoned shelter for cattle, made from rough pine poles and corrugated iron. Grass grew up the sides; at the entrance the ground was trodden to a hard bare patch.

'Where the hell are they?' said Prunty, disgruntled, 'I was towl'

it was goin' to be about here somewhere in Manzie Rehill's field.'
They came down the hill, watching listening. In the sack the
black cock sang dumb.

'It's a grand wipe of land this, lad.'

Prunty wore a good pair of tweed trousers tucked into wellingtons. The trousers were held up by gealasses.

'Mammy, have you seen me good gealasses?'

'Look for them. It's not me wears them, is it?'

Cockfights were secret affairs. Only Herbie Tackney and one
or two others knew for certain where the battles were to take
place. Often the venue was switched at the last moment. Then
switched again. The police had to be hoodwinked. His father.
Sometimes, though, his father turned a blind eye. If the people
were hounded on every occasion they wouldn't cooperate on more
serious political matters. 'Up to a point you have to live and let
live,' his father said.

They circled the country and coming out on the Cavan road
met a man who told them he'd seen 'a lock of folk' going round
by the back of Castle Finn. 'I don't know a whole pile about it
but I'd say that's where it's at today. Good luck, men.'

When they walked on Prunty told him the man was Sammy
Kincaid from Newtown. 'Oul' Sammy. A Protestant a coorse.'

'Is he?'

'You can be sure of it. Black as the Earl of Hell's waistcoat.'

Prunty knew everyone by sight and by religion. And if you
knew their religion you knew them politically. The names proclaimed them. Dolan, Maguire, Cusack – Catholic. Warren, Kincaid, Howe – Protestant. Some names, like Jackman, Gillespie,
North, Smith, appeared to be one thing but were in fact the
opposite. Prunty knew which. He knew the country. He knew the
boundaries of fields and souls.

Crossing the river, they turned left and headed across a swampy
bottom towards rising ground. Over a clump of trees Castle
Finn reared up shimmering in the morning light. Sophie Kay
was probably still lying in her feather-bed. The Colonel
maybe padding downstairs to embrace his first bumbo of the
day . . .

Prunty let him carry the bag. There seemed to be no weight in
it other than the material itself. Going down a laneway, past a
squat bungalow with hollyhocks growing by the door, they heard
the gurgly call of a game-cock. At once the rooster in the sack

struggled to be free. When he crowed, the hessian muffled his challenging call.

'We're on the right track at last, lad.'

The bugle calls of cocks sounded everywhere. The calls were high, clear, threatening. It was amazing how simple notes could convey such viciousness. Language was redundant. You didn't need it. Just passion. If all you wanted to do was kill. Prunty said the cocks were bred to kill, fed to fight.

The country, so empty before, filled up with people. Men emerged from gaps, over gates, along lanes, across fields, out of ditches. A loaded car sagged, swung, bumped through a hayfield. People hid bicycles in thick bramble or slung them in the gripes. As well as men and boys there were some women and girls.

'It's no crowd at all,' said Prunty. 'The last battle of the season, it's only an oul' shite spar.'

They made for a sloping field, surrounded by thick hedges, in the middle of nowhere. The only building near it was the bungalow down along the laneway. It was a field like countless others. It was hard to imagine it being transformed into a pit for sleepy Death to dance in. When he saw them coming Herbie Tackney shouted to Prunty, 'Go down to yon house, will you lad, and borrie a scythe?'

Prunty tied his sack on the hedge. All round the field sacks dangled from the blackthorn bushes. Hessian sacks, necks tied with string, they hung like strange plucked birds. There were forty sacks. Forty cocks. The best of twenty fights. The black rooster and nineteen others had been trained by Tackney.

'See don fellah with the hairy face? That's Grimley from Armagh. Some boy, I'm tellin' you. Look a' that chest on 'im. Like a wee polly bull.'

Grimley trained the opposition. A stocky man in a dark green suit, he had eyebrows like moustaches, tufts of hair on his cheekbones and coming out of his ears, and on his chin two small bits of paper which he must have stuck there after cutting himself shaving. He was the driver of the car. Opening the boot, he took a chair out and, with the help of others, lifted a crippled man from the back seat. The cripple, in his fifties, smiling, they sat on the chair. Grimley drove the car out of the way, parking it over by the hedge. The cripple was knock-kneed and had very white twisted fingers. In the middle of the field he sat, smiling. His voice when he spoke was Northern, energetic, sharp.

'How's she cuttin', boys?'

'Like a mowin' machine.'

'Are yiz goin' to win today?'

'Aye, we are, Hopper.'

'That's "the Hopper", Grimley's brother,' Prunty said. 'He goes everywhere for the day out.'

They went down to the bungalow to get the scythe. The hollyhocks grew higher than the door. An elderly woman answered their knocking.

'Hello, missus. Can we borrie a scythe, missus? Just for a wee minute.'

'Aye. Aye, gauson. Good lock a people about. What's goin' on?'

'Ah, just collectin' mushrooms, missus.'

The old woman searched in an outhouse for the scythe. On the old door were two new hinges. 'They come outa Morgan's Hardware in Clones. They do a good price in hinges. Look a' the way they've been put on. Clouts instead of screws. Ah now, carry me out and bury me dacent.'

People, the lie of the land, hinges . . . everything was grist to Prunty's mill. The old woman handed them the scythe. It had woodworm in the handle down by the curving blade.

'Look after it now, gauson.'

'Don't worry,' said Prunty, 'we'll even bring it back in a bag.'

The old woman laughed, toothless.

Back in the field about a hundred people stood round in clumps, talking. In the sacks along the hedges the cocks were crowing, trying to outdo one another. Tackney, taking the scythe, smoothly mowed a circular patch in the long grass.

'Stand back there.'

The cut grass men kicked aside with their boots. Ring ready, the spectators crowded to the edge. A van drove into the field. A woman got out and opened the back door. The van was full of beer and whiskey, tea and sandwiches.

Tackney and his men went over to a sack, opened it and took out a velvet green game-cock. For a moment it blinked, confused, but immediately struck with its beak at Tackney's wrist. Tackney held it as a man with scissors clipped its tail, wings and neck feathers.

'That's so they can't fly away,' Prunty whispered. 'And they trim the neck so that they can get at each other clean.'

Tackney, fingering in his breast pocket, took out a pair of

spurs. The shiny steel spurs, about an inch and a half long, were curved like the scythe blade. They were the same silvery colour as railway lines. About as thick as a darning needle, they ended in a sharp point.

'Heel him.'

'Hold your horses,' said Tackney.

A spur at a time was fitted over the cock's heel – the natural spur on the back of the leg, cut the year before to a stump. A washer made from chamois leather held the steel spur to the leg and was tied in place with tape and fine string. The cock up-ended as the heeling progressed, looked angry and indignant. It kept pecking at Tackney's flesh. 'What ails you? Sure I'm not harming you at all,' Tackney said, in a matter-of-fact, gentle tone.

From a distance Grimley shouted over – 'Are yiz not ready yit?'

'Take your time, Bob.'

'We've wasted time enough the year or two trying to bate you Cavanmen. Come on to hell, Tackney.'

'And you'll be wastin' your time today as well, Bob.'

Grimley held a white game-cock, spurred, clipped, neck darting, ready for fight.

'Two to one Grimley, come on, any takers?'

'Five pounds Tackney.'

'A pound Grimley.'

'Will you take a pound each way?'

'I'll take a lump a your face, yah bollix. Come on, a pound Grimley.'

Tackney tied off the second spur.

'It's some skill that,' said Prunty. 'You have to feel the nerve in the leg. And you have to know a right spur from a left. They have to be dead in line with the cock's natural action. If they're on the wrong angle, they can cut their own throats. Like a pig swimmin'.'

The cocks were weighed, surprisingly lying sideways on the scales without a flutter. The green one was four pounds, the white within two ounces of it. Tackney and Grimley walked through the spectators, now jammed round the ring of mown grass. Each outstretched hand had money in it. The betting was straight bets between individuals. Grimley's supporters bet on the white, Tackney's on the green.

The two men held the game-cocks in the air, ring centre, then brought them close so they could peck at each other, getting their tempers up. Their vicious little heads flared red.

'Now, yah boy yah,' said Tackney.

'Come on, down with them,' shouted a man from the crowd.

Backing off, Grimley and Tackney lowered the game-cocks to the ground. Instantly necks out, cackling angrily, they raced forward. Wings wide they flew at each other, rising as if sucked up a shaft of air, tearing at each other beak and claw.

'Strut, now, yah boy yah.'

Strutting, pecking, face to face, not giving an inch, rising up in a white and green velvet flurry they ripped away, their movements so quick you couldn't see immediately what damage they were inflicting. The green gave ground, looked beaten, the white jumping on it, pinning it to the grass, beak in its eye-socket.

'Agh, it's only a feckin' waterhen,' a man shouted.

'Give them a chance.'

'Part them, part them.'

Tackney and Grimley, darting forward, lifted the birds and retreated to a knot of supporters. There was a rip in the green's neck. Tackney put his mouth to it and sucked away the clotted blood. With a splattery explosion from his lips he spat out. A gob of haw-red blood and spittle hit the ground. Swigging from a half-bottle of whiskey, first swilling it round his mouth, he kissed it over the game-cock's wound.

'Come on, let them at it.'

The cocks were held in the air again. A man, down on one knee, counted to twenty. Once more they were placed on the grass. They rose in the air, feathers flying, landed, hopped, pecked face to face, rose again. A snot of blood flew out.

'He's done,' said Prunty.

The green staggered, fell sideways, chest slashed to the heart. Trying to kick, it turned on its back, claws up, dead.

'What did I tell you?'

'A feckin' waterhen.'

'Shut your dirty mouth.'

'I'll feckin' shut yours.'

'That's enough a that. I'll clock the pair of yiz.'

Blood matted the green velvet feathers. There was blood on the grass. Way above, the sky was blue like potato spray. Men settled their debts. Tackney picked up the dead body and flung it in the ditch.

'Stringy as bits of leather. You couldn't make soup with them,' said Prunty.

Away from the ring the cripple sat on the chair, his back to the action, singing. People stood near him, listening, drinking, laughing.

> 'Come all you fighters far and near
> I'll sing of a cockfight when and where
> Along the Finn we made our way
> To see the black and the bonny grey
> With a hip and a hop and a loud hurray
> The charcoal black and the bonny grey . . .'

'He makes it up as he goes along,' said Prunty. 'He'll rhyme and sing to bate the band.'

Another battle began. A grey and a red. A man in the crowd smoked a pipe. The thin shroud of smoke drifted above the ring, the sun shafting through it on to the cocks, burnishing their colours, bringing out the shadows of their bodies on the ground. The birds were light as sods of turf. Compact as fists. Bog-oak knots on legs. Their small heads and feathers blazed ferocity. As soon as they glimpsed each other they longed to kill. A dog saw a hare . . . a game-cock sees a game-cock . . . a hawk sees a lark . . . what when a man sees a woman? Or a woman sees a man? He had to watch closely to see how the spurs did damage. When the game-cocks rose in the air, claws up, the backs of the legs were forward. Which was their natural striking position. Claws up meant the steel spurs were curving downwards. When striking, the game-cock shuffled his claws so that when the spurs pierced deep in the flesh they ripped downwards. The cock striking first and fiercest usually won. Some battles ended in seconds. One rooster ran out between the legs of the spectators. In a strange place, wings clipped, it couldn't escape. It was put back in the ring where it made a perfunctory fluttery hop to defend itself. In a lucky strike it practically severed its enemy's head. Tackney raised it aloft triumphantly. People cheered. When it was put back in its sack it began to crow.

The man who counted aloud in the fight breaks had a cup of tea in one hand, in the other a ham sandwich mustard-yellow along the edge. His trouser knee was dung-stained.

'Why do they fix spurs on them, Coco?'

'They'd only maim one another if you didn't. There wouldn't

be a clear winner. The spurs cut the misery. Come on, ours next.'

Tackney heeled the black rooster with the spurs that had hung on Prunty's bedpost. On the other post was the rosary. Spurs and beads had belonged to his father.

The black, gorgeous, gushing tail, clipped, lay still in Prunty's hands as Tackney armed it. A feather floated down into Tackney's turn-up. Behind his ears were an untouched cigarette and one half smoked.

'I mind these spurs well. Your father and me sat at the same desk, aye man surely. Lord a mercy on the dead.'

'Amen.'

'Is this the first battle you've seen, gauson? Well, what do you think to it?'

'Ah . . . it's very interesting.'

'Aye. Interesting is right. Now.'

The black rooster lay stiff on the weighing-scales. It looked like a hideous manikin. A nightmare doll, comb pared down, black scaly legs thin as briars.

When Tackney held it out towards Grimley's, it looked amazed that there should be another male in creation. Head flushed, raging, crowing, it tried to fly out of Tackney's grip. The crowd roared, laughed. The man who counted slugged at a whiskey bottle.

'Let them at it.'

'A pound on Tackney. Any takers?'

'Five pound Grimley. Five pound the grey.'

A cloud went across the sun. The shallow pit of death dimmed to a black chalice of men, thirsty for excitement, trying through money, drink and blood to raise their mundane lives to magic. Sleepy Death, mean and neat, danced with silver spurs on. Strutted, hopped and struck. The black landed, tipped forward on its chest, throat slashed. Trying to flap its blunt wings, it collapsed sideways and lay gasping as its blood treacled on to the grass. The grey stood back, perplexed that victory came so easily. The dying game-cock, puzzled, blinked . . . tried to keep its eyes open. But gently sleepy Death bent low and shut them.

'Only an oul' fuckin' waterhen. What's the matter with you Tackney, yah hoor yah?'

'Good man, Grimley. C'mon Armagh.'

He lifted the dead cock by the legs. It would never again stand

157

in brazen glory at Mrs Prunty's kitchen window. Prunty told him to fling it with the others in the ditch.

He wanted to get away. He told Prunty he was returning the scythe to the house. The crippled man, the legs of the chair he sat on sunk deep in the earth, recited to a knot of people.

'Had I the power to turn the world
I'd spin it like a top
And keep it spinning so I would
Until I ordered stop.
Then hop I would upon that place
Oh for years I have not seen
Butlershill in Cavan
And its lovely village green.

'How's that, boys? Or would yiz prefer another song?'
'Good man yourself, Hopper. You never lost it.'

Making for the gap in the far corner of the field, he noticed two girls standing near the van from the back of which the drink and sandwiches were sold. One girl was smallish, black-haired. The slender girl with her he was sure was the girl he'd first seen riding through the soldiers at Wattlebridge. The girl he had fallen in love with when he came face to face with her at the railway station. He could hardly believe it. It must be her. She wore jeans stuck into brown boots and a white pullover. It was her . . . the hair hanging in flaxen hanks . . . it was definitely her. What on earth was she doing at a main? He stood in the middle of the field transfixed, the scythe dangling from his hand. Already his mouth had gone dry. He had to do something. Surely this was Fate. Somehow he had to go to her. She and the black-haired girl played with stems of ribwort. Holding the stems out, they took turns trying to knock the heads off. They laughed. Her hair moved on her shoulders. Her lips were only slightly darker than her pale skin.

The nearer he got to them, the weaker he felt. And the scythe was a nuisance. He would never forgive himself if he ruined this chance. He had to think of something witty or wise. Christ. They had noticed him approaching. Well, they weren't blind, were they? What, what was he going to say? The black-haired girl laughed, her red face dancing with merriment.

He stood before them, the scythe, blade stuck in the ground, leaning against his leg. She was pale, delicate . . . creamy skin the colour of Belleek china.

'Do you live here?' Ah Jesus, is that all he could say?

'What, in a field?' said the black-haired girl, laughing, cheeky.

He had eyes only for one of them. She smiled, then looked serious, almost frightened, big eyes shining. She didn't speak.

'I have to return this scythe to ... to ... who lives in that house down there?'

'Why don't you go down and find out?' said the black-haired girl, not laughing this time, just cheeky.

He looked deep at her. She looked worried. Her friend looked set for a fortnight's banter. He had to say something that would draw words from her. He flicked his quiff. 'Will you come with me?'

From the ring came a roar of death and victory.

The friend answered, 'I can't. I have to stay by the van. You go if you want.' Walking away, the friend, looking glum, got into the back of the van. He was alone with her. He couldn't believe it. But she was there. Breathing, her hair moving when she turned her head.

'You could spin linen out of that hair of yours.' It wasn't bad. But his dry tongue mauled the words. So far she hadn't spoken a word. He flicked his quiff again, an action he knew came from nerves and arrogance.

'What's your name?'

'A-N-N-A-G-H Lee. Annagh Lee.'

'After the river?'

The Erne, the Finn, the Annaghlee were the three great rivers of the district. The Annaghlee began and ended in Cavan. It gave its name to the parish of which Butlershill was a part. Lee was a local name.

'Annagh? Come on. Please. Remember at the railway bridge? I saw you there.'

She didn't move or reply. He was beginning to panic.

'Annagh Lee – it's the best name I ever heard.'

'It's the only one I've got.'

'Do you take after it – flow gentle, run deep?' That was glib. God, stupid. Then, he didn't know how, she was walking beside him out of the field. It definitely was her. There on his left. And they were together walking down the lane to the house.

'Do you go to cockfights?'

'No fear. Are you mad? I came with Daphne. Her mother sells the sandwiches. I couldn't look.'

'What school are you at?' Her eyes were light blue. He tried to keep in step with her. He was taller than her but she took longer steps.

'I was at school in Belfast. I'm finished now. My father died when I was thirteen. Unlucky for some. My mother's grown more nervous every year since. So she wants me to stay with her. I'm going to. I don't mind. I like polterin' about the place. I can always go to university later on.'

'My mother died this year.'

'Sure I know. Know all about you. Everyone does. You're as good as a concert.'

Maybe that's what people thought; that he was a bit of a clown. But why? He was in a circus all right, up on the high wire, yes. But he didn't have big boots and his nose wasn't red. Yes, but kissing a girl's foot? Blessing a pig? And what about that peculiar left boot he was wearing? Unless you walked round with a mirror all the time you couldn't see yourself as others saw you. He *had* a mirror in his pocket all the time . . . the compact . . .

He put the scythe down and they stood for a moment in the laneway as he cupped his hands round her hand, holding a flaming match to his cigarette. She kept her packet of Gold Flake up her sleeve. He had touched her flesh. How was this happening? He couldn't believe his luck. Coming to the cockfight with Prunty, he was aware of his surroundings. Watching the cocks kill each other was mesmerizing. But now it had all gone from his mind. He wasn't even aware of his own body. Even when he touched her. Her touch sent a spasm through his spine. Or his soul . . . He was up in the air somewhere, outside himself, like in a dream. Thank God for dreams. What was sleep without them? What was life without them?

'Do you believe in a united Ireland?'

'It is united. It's the people who are divided. The game-cocks in the ring – they don't know what side of the Border they're on. The air we breathe both sides is the same. The land is the same too. God's Kingdom we're told is one.'

'You believe in the after-life, then?'

'That would be telling. At night I still need my teddy-bear.'

They laughed and dragged the smoke deep into their lungs and clicked their fingers and stood and walked on.

'What religion are you?'

'My father was Protestant. My mother is Catholic. So I've got two religions or none. Can never tell which.'

160

'Who's your favourite poet?'

'You tell me first.'

'Milton.'

'Blake. He's easier to understand. Because he has his heart on his sleeve.'

'It's the only place to wear it.' In his jacket pocket he carried the battered copy of *Lycidas*. Great. He had disposed of the religious and political questions at one go. And she liked poetry. God, how wonderful. She was beautiful. She had goodness. She was therefore equal to truth. When they reached the squat bungalow they knocked on the door. The hollyhocks grew higher than the eaves. The old woman came in answer. She took both her hands in hers.

'Ah, Annagh Lee. Annagh, how are you girsha? How are you, Annagh?'

She wanted them in for a cup of tea but they told her they couldn't. Going back up the laneway they heard a shout. Suddenly the laneway was jammed with running people. Laughing, shouting, in a panic to escape. He saw Prunty coming, empty sack in hand.

'It's your oul' fellah, lad. The Guards.'

Through a hedge he saw them – his father and four men. The dark-blue uniforms against the landscape looked massive, threatening, out of place. Silver buttons and badges dazzled in the light like spurs. His father was out in front, pounding ahead, taking giant strides across a hayfield. Big, lethal, comic strides like the day he chased him up the vegetable garden, precipitating his mother's death. Maybe she would have died young anyway. But would he ever forgive his father? Forgive himself? A row over a mound of rotten spuds! And now when his famine was ending, here he was again, hell bent to blight his life perhaps for good and all. Angry, desperate, he ran after Annagh Lee, who was running against the fleeing crowd, trying to catch up with the van which was going off along the lane in the opposite direction. She ran with grace, the hanks of flaxen hair bouncing on her back.

'Will you meet me Friday at the Luxor in Clones?'

'I will.'

Amazed, he watched her go. She'd said yes. He wasn't deaf. He'd clearly heard the shouted word. It came over her shoulder, a troubled smile on her face. Yes. It was hard to believe. He had struck lucky. But his father, now much nearer, could ruin it all.

Some of the boys he knew ran by him – the Rock, the Stumps and Grunter Howe.

'Stick with us,' said the Rock.

The horizon way behind, his father loomed large before him. His chin-strap was in place to keep his cap from flying off. His trouser legs were neatly folded into his socks. The big boots were shiny as the chin-strap. His father was Fate moving in for the kill, mesmerizing. He had to force his legs to work.

He began to run. He could see Prunty in the distance, turning round looking for him. His heels took flight, joy lifting them. He had met her. Annagh Lee. Out of the ring of death – life. Out of chaos – happiness. He had at last something to live for. His days would have purpose. Friday – the Luxor cinema. He had no idea what was on and he didn't care. He would sit beside her in the shimmering dark and he'd kiss her . . . if she let him. Maybe she'd kiss him first. God. Anything was possible when your luck was in. He'd been in a sack for weeks but at last he felt like crowing. Mind you – Mrs Prunty always said it – 'Don't crow too soon.'

He scattered with the crowd across the Finn and into Fermanagh. The North. The other side of the Border where his father couldn't follow. North or South, the ritual was the same – blood would flow, lives finish, money change hands. Less than an hour later sacks hung on hedges and in a ring of men two gamecocks struggled to an end . . .

From the time he first saw her he was in love, but lately he had given up hope. But now love pounded inside him, knotted his stomach, belted songs from his brain. He stood beside Hopper Grimley, the cripple on his chair, singing along with him about young loves and old wars, for all the world like a mature man of the moment. In his prime. Tip-top. A woman-understander. A supreme political decision-maker. The king of his domain. The Chieftain Maguire, out from his ruined castle, back in triumph, loving his enemies, in control, this time forever and a day.

'You know what, boy,' said the Hopper, 'you could do with a good haircut.' The Hopper didn't like a rival. Men were gamecocks. When the crowd fled, he saw the Hopper being lifted bodily and flung into the boot of his brother's car, the chair stuck in on top of him.

You had to be like the Hopper – a survivor. You had to sing in the teeth of the wind.

Look-outs were posted round the field. A man up an ash tree, his head sticking out the top, shouted, 'Polis. The Polis.' Another raid. This time by the Northern police – the RUC. In seconds clattering bodies, laughing, swearing made to escape. Grimley's car left the field, the Hopper in the open boot, smiling out through the legs of the kitchen chair. In seconds the field was empty. trampled grass, a few velvet feathers, a dead cock flung up on the hedge, was all that remained.

Later in the day he and Prunty saw the RUC and his father and men talking and laughing together in a laneway. The RUC uniforms were bottle-green. Black revolvers dangled at their hips. They straddled the Border chatting, cigarettes alight, the smoke from their lips a common pale blue. He recognized the RUC Sergeant. His father knew him. He was a Catholic stationed in Newtown. They met occasionally in the barracks in Butlershill. At night.

His father looming over the land. His dead mother. Blood on the grass . . . A girl's face wiped them clean. Annagh Lee. From head to toe he was full of hope and happiness. He didn't even notice the sky. That night he lay alongside Prunty and had, for the first time in ages, a sleep deeper than the grave.

13

Outside the back door he sat on a sack of meal, a towel about his neck, like a serviette the wrong way round. Prunty was giving him a haircut. His implements were rusty scissors, an old black comb, and clippers which he claimed were used for sheep-shearing. 'If it's good enough for sheep, it's good enough for you.' He kept them in a wooden cheese-box along with a razor and a ball of twine.

'What's the twine for, Coco?'

'By the time I'm finished with you your head might want tying on. Do you know what I'm going to tell you, lad? Annagh Lee. I found out all about her. She's been brought up by a parcel of oul' aunts would ate you alive. I'm warnin' you.'

'I'll steer clear of them.'

'Fallin' in love – you can make a right cod of yourself.'

'Haven't you ever fallen?'

'Aye. In the bog hole, several times. There's no one like a woman to clip your wings.'

His shorn hair fell on to the towel, then to the ground. Hens gawked at it. A cat sat on the windowsill, one eye open.

Mrs Prunty looked out of the back door. 'What sort of a haircut is that? I'd do better with a knife and fork. I have your shirt ironed. And your good trousers pressed.'

'Thanks, Mrs Prunty.'

Her tone was tired, slightly ironic, saintly. Bit like his mother. A mother-of-fact tone. Women got their men ready and their only pleasure was to see their backs going out of the door.

'You'd be as well have a shave, lad. You can't go coortin' with bum fluff on your face.'

He had his first shave with Prunty's cut-throat razor. He knew how to use it from watching his father. Razor in hand, his father's movements were always delicate then, like a priest raising the Host at mass. The clippers going up on the back of his head felt grinding smooth. The razor on his face was scrapy sharp. At the finish he smelt of Brylcreem and Palmolive. In the mirror he could see and whiff his father. Prunty came into the bedroom and slipped him some cloves. 'If women don't like what they smell, they won't like what they see.'

As he rode away from the house Prunty shouted after him, 'And this time make sure it's not her *foot* you kiss.'

He took his time, not wanting to arrive in a sweat. Prunty had given him his three-speed and bicycle clips. Near Clones he hid the bike in a field and walked into the town. The ding-dong chimes of the Protestant clock marked the hour as he reached the Diamond. By the time the gong had struck seven times he was half-way down Fermanagh Street. A minute later the clock on the Catholic church rang out. It was a local joke that Catholic time was a little later than Greenwich Mean Time. It had to come all the way from Rome.

Clones was a two-horse Border town. It had two churches on two hills. Two times. Two hotels. Two banks. Two platforms on the railway station. Two faces for business – one looking North, the other South. At weekends people from both sides of the Border flocked in to the shops. He had often come with his mother and, shopping done, had tea and chicken salad in one of the hotels. He loved those trips. He remembered a woman with a crooked squint-eyed look bumping into them in the crowded street. 'Will you watch where you're goin',' she said to them angrily.

'My dear lady,' replied his mother, 'will you go where you're watching?' She loved her own wit and couldn't wait to get back to the barracks to tell his father.

'Ah-hah, leave it to you, *a grá*, but that beats Banagher. And Banagher bet the devil.'

He knew from his father's face he loved her. His pleasure and pride in her couldn't be denied.

'Don't I know meself what it's like to get the quick whip from the sweet tongue.'

'It's little you get from the same tongue but honey.'

The Luxor was towards the bottom of the street. A shadowy poster in the window announced the name of the film – *Joe Macbeth*. On top of the poster, in lurid letters dripping blood, it

165

said: 'Joe Macbeth deals in death . . . His enemies . . . his friends . . . his own.' It looked a gangster, an old movie still doing the rounds. He didn't care what it was as long as she turned up. Walking on, he stood in the doorway of the Tower Bar. He could hide, yet see her coming. He had half an hour to kill. Fermanagh Street was empty. From the Diamond with its Celtic cross down to the Butter market and the level-crossing it flowed steep and long and narrow. The houses on opposite sides were so close they could almost be spanned with outstretched arms. Some of the buildings were divided by graceful archways leading to back-yards. The shops were well kept, windows large and full. Houses had windowboxes bright with flowers. A horse-drawn cart came out of an alley laden with bags of flour. A boy closed the archway doors after it. The cart was painted blue, the spokes orange. From the open window of an upstairs room came the swelling music of an opera. It was an old record crackling out *Aida*. He often had to listen to it at school in Music Appreciation class. The strange and tragic singing cascaded down the street, drowning the jingling chains and clattering hooves. Behind him, inside the pub, he could hear the clink of bottles being stacked from a crate on to shelves. The jutting walls on either side of the pub entrance were decorated with tiles depicting cosy fireside scenes. A young woman sitting on the floor in front of a blazing hearth . . . alone, reading a book . . . her cup and saucer balanced on the fender . . . It was a wistful picture designed to seduce passers-by. 'Tower tea no other for me' was painted on one set of tiles, 'Tower retreat for tired feet' on another.

Time killed slowly. People at last began to drift towards the cinema. A man and woman gazed at the poster, then went across to the pub opposite. Still time for a quick drink . . . Boys stood on the street corner, hands deep in their pockets, backs against the wall. Three girls went into the cinema. It was open. He chewed another clove.

Still no sign of her. What if she didn't come? What a laughing-stock he'd be . . . He began to find fault with himself. The charcoal-grey suit was out of fashion the day his mother bought it . . . His shoes were plain black. His red tie . . . he snatched it off, rolled it up, stuffed it in his pocket. And the haircut Prunty had given him . . . Was this her coming, walking down from the Diamond? . . . No. The opera was reaching its crackling climax. What an end for Aida. And her lover . . . what's his name . . .

Buried alive in a tomb. Jesus, it was her. Annagh Lee. Coming down the street. His mouth went dry. Better walk up to meet her. He stepped out and . . . wait a minute, That's not her. What was the matter with him? Idiot. Cod. Calm down. The bell pealed out the half-hour. People were crowding into the Luxor now. A goods train sliced over the level-crossing. The big gates trembled, clattered shut. The warning lights on the gates glowed red behind glass thick as bottle bottoms. She wasn't coming, simple as that.

He walked up to the cinema, which had a flat, tiled frontage and bevelled-glass doors leading into a small foyer. He felt sick. What was the point going in alone? A car drove quickly up the street, stopped. A woman got out. His heart dunted. It was Annagh Lee. The car drove on. She was wearing the long green coat, a black skirt, high-heels, a black beret . . . She looked good enough to have dropped straight from heaven.

'Sorry, I'm late. In the end I got my uncle to give me a lift.'

'I thought . . . that coat – I've never seen anything like it.'

'Well, I've never seen anything like your haircut. Did you fall into a mangle?'

'No, no. It's fantastic. Your coat. You look . . . lovely.'

'Do I?' She looked surprised. She had on her lips some kind of pale blue lipstick. There in the street he could smell her. Fresh and clean as apples after rain.

'Better go in, if we're going,' he said, nervous, dry. 'It's either that or stand here for the rest of the evening.' He paid for the tickets with money Mrs Prunty gave him. The foyer whiffed of disinfectant and cheap perfume.

The cinema was more than half full. They stumbled in the darkness as they followed an elderly usherette carrying a bicycle lamp. Martial music blared and a crowing cockerel announced a news programme. Annagh took her coat off, folded it and placed it on an empty seat beside her. Everybody in the place had a cigarette on the go. People coughed continuously, like in church.

Their arms touched on the arm-rest between them. She took off her beret; raising herself, she adjusted her skirt. He couldn't help himself: lifting her hair, nuzzling into her, he kissed the back of her neck and near her ear gently bit the skin. They hadn't been sitting together more than thirty seconds.

'Quit. I want to watch the film.'

'Sorry.' He wasn't. 'I'm not.'

'You will be if you do it again.'

An awkward silence came between them. Tense. But then she reached and held his hand, fingers entwined.

This was it. She was with him. He was starving, dying of hunger. He had tasted her. Annagh Lee. He barely knew her. Love was the only cure for famine. His father was all wrong. Famine had nothing to do with potatoes. He couldn't hear the soundtrack from his heart drumming in his ears. The lights came up. They looked at each other. His staring eyes were wet, dreamy . . . but so were hers. So were hers. The lights dimmed. Without power to stop, they were in each other's arms, wide-open mouths together, tongues probing wildly, sliding, desperate, deep. He was eating her alive. Trying to get at her soul to save his own. Longing could drive you insane. No sex – that was hungry grass.

She broke free, stroked his head. 'Easy. Easy.'

On the screen, guns barked. A man fell to the floor. A nightclub. Blood stains. He had no idea what was going on. Guns weren't as lethal as love. To stop his wandering hands she held them in hers, a tight grip. She looked frail but she was strong. In control of herself. He had no idea how he was going to last through the film. He just wanted to be out in the unfettered night.

At the end of the row of seats, two fellows his own age discussed the film aloud. 'Banky is Banquo, I'm telling you.' So that was it. The film was modernized Shakespeare.

'They're right,' whispered Annagh, 'the old lady selling the flowers – she's a witch, I betcha.'

He tried to take an interest. He knew the play. At school it was Father Austen's favourite. 'It's got everything we fear for ourselves.' The word 'witch' never appeared once in the text. Shakespeare was clever. He wanted to please King James, who was Scottish and believed in witchcraft. But he must have known it was all gobbledegook. Witches were poor old hags, lonely as hell, frightened for the future.

She let him rest his hand on her thigh, just under the edge of her skirt and no further. His blood was burning. Nylon couldn't stop heat. She felt so hot he wouldn't have been surprised had she burst into flames. He always had faith in the future. Something good would come from bad. This was it. Annagh. And at last the film ended. The wife had gone mad. Someone swimming in the lake had been murdered. Joe Macbeth had to face the music of his own sins alone. And when the music stopped . . .

'Not bad at all,' said Annagh, 'a good idea anyway, to do it like that.' She was cool. She had to be to cool his passion. The door to the foyer was jammed with people trying to escape the National Anthem. As the drums rolled and the tricolour fluttered on the screen, he and Annagh were the only ones left in the cinema. Apart from a man standing near the front, the hat in his hand held over his heart. Prunty was right . . .

Peter Joe Reilly had a dream. It was the hardest dream of all, because more than two-thirds of it had come true. A dream like that you could never wake from.

Rotten spuds. Rotten sleep . . . Nothing could hold a candle to Annagh Lee. He was reborn in the Luxor.

They crossed Fermanagh Street and went into a café. It had a juke-box. Local boys and girls sat around talking, shrieking, laughing, singing along with the music. A boy in drainpipes and comically thick-soled shoes was out on the floor showing them how to rock and roll. His arms were thin as bicycle pumps. Red spots covered his face. But he could dance.

They had coffee and fish and chips. In the clear light of the café he looked at her as if he'd never seen her face before. He couldn't get used to it. Everyone, including the man and woman behind the counter, cast looks in her direction. Her hanks of hair were stunning. It was thick and a strange mixture of blonde, dark, light grey, gold. It looked like a sheaf of corn and binder twine. Her big eyes were billiard-chalk blue. Brow, cheeks, chin were clear, very pale but firm.

'I don't like my nose. It's too big.'

'Not for you it isn't.'

Her laugh was soft, serious, deep. She was a year older than him. Good. She could teach him a thing or two. In the cinema he had nibbled her ears. In the café, when she lifted her hair, he could see them. Perfect sea-shell shapes for tongues.

'Can I whisper you something?'

'Yes.' Her ear sideways to him she waited. Women. Women were magic.

'I . . . this moment.' He nearly told her he loved her. Fool.

She looked at him, knowing full well. He could see her brassière through the buttons of her blouse. It was red. God. Red. A red bra. Ah, fantastic. She didn't buy that in Rinty Reilly's. He could understand the expression, 'Taking leave of your senses'. That's how he felt. Brain control had gone. Pelting blood, pounding heart, skittish nerves had taken over. His knee, touching hers under the table, began to tremble. He had to, casually, put his hand on it, grip it, stop it. He was so far outside himself he was away in space, looking back at himself through the wrong end of the telescope.

On the right side of her neck was a mole. A black crumb of flesh. His mother's was dark brown, but at the same spot exactly. The coincidence assumed symbolic importance. They were made for each other. As far as he was concerned.

'I like your eyes,' she said, 'they're nice.'

'My eyes?'

'Have you been eating cloves?'

'Ah, yes. In an apple pie before I came out. No, no. My friend Prunty gave them to me. He swears they're an aphrodisiac.'

She looked with raised eyebrows and, hand to mouth, laughed in merriment and disbelief. 'And are they? I must meet him.'

'You will. What was your favourite subject at school?'

'English. And biology. Do you know our bodies are just bags of fluid and bone? I don't think we have a long-term future on this planet. So there.'

'Well, maybe some other planet will be kind enough to take us in.'

'You know why we're here?'

'Fish and chips?'

'No, seriously. We're here to be destroyed.'

'We're here to destroy, you mean.'

'No. It appears we destroy. And so we do. But the country remains long after we're gone. The land swallows us in the end.'

The way she spoke was lively and intense. She meant every word. When he roamed with Prunty he often thought about the beginning and the end. The land was both. Sometimes he believed they had the run of the country, other times the country had the run of them. He could never work out which. Even when he saw a plough being swallowed into the snake-belly earth. Would God put men on the planet just to be destroyed? But if there was no God – what then?

'Annagh, let's talk about rock and roll.'

'Right. I like it. Do you?'

'Yes.'

'Good. Now let's talk about something else.'

'Why do you wear that long green coat?'

'To stop the wind going up my legs.'

'I wish I were the wind.'

'You are. Full of it.' They laughed.

He poured sugar on to the palm of her hand, then licked it off. The man and woman behind the counter watched him. So did the dancing boy. She looked worried, but her eyes sparkled. She smiled. 'How are we getting home?'

They left the café and walked up the hill. The night air was balmy. As they walked beneath the lights they watched their stubby shadows stretching long enough to climb the buildings. Above the narrow street the starry sky was a blue sparkling river. It would run forever. It would never end. It had flowed for the first man who noticed it. It would still flow up there for the last.

She lived across the Border. Female Fermanagh. He took her home on the bar of the bike. She was between his knees. They laughed and sang, rang the bell and kissed going down the hills. Her lashing hair blinded him in the wind.

Her house was high, substantial, white in the night. A graceful lawn in front. He leaned the bike against the yard gate.

They kissed deep, breathing heavy.

He whispered to her, 'Annagh, I want to put my hand somewhere. Let me.'

'Where?'

'What's that like?'

His hand on her, feeling, they stood for a long while. The night had come to a halt. As if it had crashed on to the trees, the house, themselves. They were two heartbeats lost in the world.

When they parted, he listened to her high-heels corncraking to the door.

14

Life and the days were glorious. Nothing that happened in the past or present could match the future of all the nights he spent with Annagh Lee. After working with Prunty at the turf or in the fields he cleaned himself, had tea, then went off to meet her in Clones, or she rode out to meet him on the way. They walked and talked, went to the pictures, dances in Cavan town, or to the Border pub where they drank listening to a blind man play the *uileann* pipes. Prunty sometimes came drinking with them. He had a sweet singing voice but only knew two songs. 'The notes are aisy. It's the bloody words.'

On a hot Sunday afternoon the three of them walked along the Finn until they reached the point where it ran into the Erne. The river bank baked in the sun. There was a heatwave all over Ireland. The rutted ground was rock-hard, the stones warm when they picked them up to skid across the water. The bank was strewn with bone-dry broken reeds and rushes, shells and mutilated fish. Prunty could tell how they died.

'That's a perch. Skewered by a heron. Like a dagger in the belly. That there's a jack pike. An otter got him.'

'How can you tell, Einstein?'

'The lumps out of the neck. When he's not very hungry the otter will leave most of it.'

'How do you know all these things, Coco?' Annagh said.

'It pays to know. Look.' He pointed to holes dug into the bank just above the waterline. 'An otter's holt. They tunnel in one way and out the other.'

The Finn was at its widest where it met the great sweep of the Erne flowing north to Donegal. They merged without murmur, equal under the cutting sun. On the far side, trees grew down to the edge, and away to the right along the Erne, a green wave of gentle hills rolled into the South.

A rock stuck out of the water, a vein of flint running up one side. It looked worn, shiny.

'Do you know what that is?'

'Yes,' Annagh replied, 'it looks remarkably like a rock.'

'I know that, smarty pants.'

'How do you know she's wearing any, Coco?'

'Shut up, you. It's an altar.'

'A what?'

When Prunty was serious he looked funny. Laughing, they ganged up on him and tried to push him into the water.

'Go way, will youse. I'm tellin' you. It's an altar. It's used by otters.'

'What, to say mass?'

'No. It's a feeding place. And signpost.'

'Oh I see. So if an otter is driving along in his car, he can tell which way to go?'

Prunty laughed and shook his head. 'It's well for you, the pair of you. Not a care in the wide world. Your man there, Annagh, he doesn't care a damn about anything since you came along.'

'He cares a damn for you, Coco. He cares as much for you as he does for me. Well, nearly as much.'

'Yeah, I'll believe you.'

Prunty was pleased. Taking his wellingtons and socks off, he sat on the rock with his feet in the water. 'Ah that's grand. Freezing, mind.'

'Let's go in for a swim.'

'We've no togs, lad.'

'Who needs them?'

'Get in in the buff bollock? Are you mad? Anyone saw us we'd be slaughtered.'

'Who cares? This is Fermanagh, isn't it?'

'I'm game,' said Annagh.

'It'll be one for the geography books anyway,' said Prunty. 'The Erne, the Finn and the Annaghlee meetin' all together.'

With a plait of rushes she tied her hair back, kicked free her tennis shoes and removed her sleeveless frock. Her long legs were bare. With nifty movements under the white slip she removed her knickers and brassiere.

'I'm leaving my slip on.' She looked pale as a ghost. The hair tied back revealed even more of her haunting face. Gingerly she walked over the stones to the water.

Prunty stood naked on the rock, his right fist raised in the air, his left hand holding a big leaf over his dangler. They laughed at him, Annagh shrieking her delight. Despite the freckles, his body looked whiter than Annagh's. His arms, the back of his neck and a V-shaped patch on his chest were tanned. The rest of his skin and hair looked shocked by the light, like a moth disturbed at noon. The sun skidded off him. Grinning like a satyr, he let go the leaf and plunged in the river.

'Agh. It's ice.'

'Agh. Agh.'

'Agh. But it's lovely.'

They swam, splashed, shouted. Annagh, graceful, otter-smooth, was at home in the water. She went out where the rivers met and turned to look at them, her face beaming, happy, pleased. She held her head up, not wanting to get her hair wet.

Prunty did a dog-paddle, his strong arms beating into the water like he was cracking stones. 'It's a mortal sin this, lad, swimmin' dangler-free.'

'Well, we're only mortals after all.'

'What's immortal sin, that's what I'd like to know?' Annagh shouted.

'All sins are immortal if you die with them on your sowl. You'll be in hell forever. That's what we're towl' anyway.'

'Do you believe that?'

'You wouldn't know anythin' about sin, Annagh. You a half-Protestant.'

It was hard to gauge if Prunty was serious or joking. Probably both. Out on the bank they dried in the roasting heat. Annagh sat away from them on the rock until her slip had dried and her body couldn't be seen beneath.

'If they saw us, lad, they'd burn us alive.'

'Who are *they*?'

'Who do you think? The priest. Your oul' fellah. The doctor. They could whip up a storm of spit agin us.'

'Go way outa that, Coco, you're talking through your hat.'

Prunty looked funny, a mixture of mirth and surliness. He was warning them in case they were caught. Prunty knew that what he and Annagh were doing at every opportunity would bring great wrath upon their heads. The priest, the Sergeant, the doctor ... Prunty was right, they ruled the roost. It would be a brave person who stood up to them. You couldn't. Sex. Making love before you were married was the worst sin you could commit. It was more pernicious than ragwort, dock and warble-fly. Father Gaynor was mad enough to read you from the altar. Relatives were crazy enough to tar and feather your dangler. Girls were chased out of the country. He had heard his mother say that the dread of sex was the fear of children. That fear was a legacy of the Famine. A bastard was an unwanted mouth that had to be fed. He and Prunty and Annagh were only children. Half-orphans.

The first time they made love was a few days after they'd met. They were helping Prunty draw home the hay from the hill above the bog. They forked the haycocks on to a cart borrowed from a neighbour. When the load was high enough they made for the house, Annagh walking alongside leading the horse by the bridle. They were at the back, pushing the cart, helping the horse up the steep hill. Coming down the other side was worse. The cart pushed down on the horse, making it want to go sideways and running the risk of toppling over. They dragged back on the cart, acting as brakes. Annagh, a tight grip on bit and rein, kept the horse slow and steady. It was a nerve-racking business. The horse was a young black mare, a white star on her forehead. She didn't mind hauling up but she hated the descent. Sometimes she sat back, her rump almost on the hill, as if she were trying to snap the shafts. Going into the yard with the last load of the day, excited, as if she knew her work was done, she quickened, lurched too close to the hay shed, wedging one of the shed uprights between the cart and the right wheel. At the same time she slipped on the concrete, splattering down as the wheel fell off. Her back legs under her, her front ones up, she sat between the shafts like a dog. She looked pleased with herself, as if she had at last achieved what she'd been trying to do all day. The cart was at a twisted angle, the bare axle on the ground. The right shaft was under the mare's rump. Prunty was aware that if she rose to her feet the weight of the collapsed cart would snap the shaft. Mrs Prunty, hearing the commotion, came running out, terrified until she was sure no one was hurt.

'We'll have to get her out of the harness,' Prunty shouted.

'No,' said his mother, 'I'll hold her, you three lift the cart when I tell you.'

Frantically they cleared the fallen load of hay to one side. Prunty took out the tailboard to use it as a prop in place of the missing wheel.

'Poor Dolly, aisy, that a girl, you're all right, thanks be to God.' Mrs Prunty spoke to the horse, stroking her neck, standing right in front of her, so she wouldn't surge to her feet until they were ready to lift.

'Right, Mammy.'

Mrs Prunty slapped the mare's flank with her hand, urged her forward. 'Up, Dolly. Up now. *Up. Up.*'

The horse neighed, made an effort, decided not to bother. Then suddenly she rumped and struggled on to her back legs, he and Prunty supporting the cart as best they could.

'Stop her, Mammy, stop her!'

'Whoa. Whoa.'

The shaft looked about to snap, but Mrs Prunty managed to stop her going on and Annagh propped the tailboard under the cart frame. Quickly they unhitched the mare and led her from the shafts. The worst had been avoided. The mare, as if nothing had happened, stretched her neck and chomped the leaves on an overhanging bush.

'First thing, Mammy, we're buying a tractor.'

'It'll have to be second-hand then, son. Or third. What'll you say happened?'

'The pin holding the wheel was rotten anyway. Look. It's their own fault. You could never borrow anthin' from them people in pace. I mind the time I borried a graipe and the bloody prong bruk. Sure looka – the crosspiece in front of the wheel is bruk. Only for that it could never have happened.'

They had tea, Mrs Prunty thanking God all the time nobody was injured.

'Ah, poor Nobody,' said Prunty, 'what have you got agin him, Mammy?' He said it in such a dry way, Annagh spluttered her tea, laughing.

'Thank God,' said Mrs Prunty after a time, 'nobody ended up in the Surgical.'

'He's one patient the doctors don't want to see, Mammy.'

'It'd be no laughing matter if the mare bruk her leg. Or one a youse did. Or were kilt.'

'I know one thing. Thank God I wasn't on me own when it happened. Thanks to the lad. And Annagh.'

'Well, that's true for you. We're so used to him about the house now, Annagh, we won't know what to do when he goes.'

He wasn't going. Well . . . he'd have to go sometime. He tried not to think about it. He wondered, was Mrs Prunty giving him a gentle hint? He looked at her. She smiled kindly at him. For the moment anyway, he was as much part of her world as Prunty, the cat or a three-legged pot.

Prunty returned the horse and cart. He and Annagh went back to the hayfield to retrieve the cardigan she'd left behind.

They walked arms around each other, heads close together. They were happy. Drawing home the hay had been hard work, the incident with the horse exciting. Together all day, they hadn't been able to touch or kiss. They went straight through the field and out into the turf bog. The grass was wild and long, the heathery ground springy beneath their feet, a hovering kestrel the only sign of life. Below them on the cut-away section, the round towers of turf stood black and dry, ready any time for carting home.

Jumping down the turfy steps cut into the bank, they made for a sheltered corner hidden by hazel, sally and bramble bushes. They stood for a moment, breathing quickly. When she saw what he was doing she looked shocked. He removed all his clothes, stood still before her. She took off her dress, her slip, her underwear. This was naked. This was flesh. Her drumlin stomach curved into the clump of her pubic hair. She took him in her hand.

'What's this like?'

They smiled, equal in word and deed.

Like the neck of a game-cock he stuck out stiff and ready. Her nipples were the colour of raspberries. On the mouldy earth they joined, groaning with hurt and joy. She was a river of life beneath him, his body and soul flowing in. The word had become flesh. All the memories he ever had were washed away. Love blotted out death. They lay wrapped, as in one skin, crying with happiness. Her tears ran on to his tongue. He put his eyes to her mouth. Her flaxen hair spread over the turf like a burst-open sheaf. Skin was smooth as a lake on a calm evening. Their sailing mouths carried fire. Burning blight. Destroying history. A corner of a turf bog could be a jewel on heaven's table.

'I love you.'

'I love you, Annagh Lee.'

When they were walking home he took the compact from his pocket and gave it to her. Opening it, she looked at herself in the rounded mirror. A lark soared singing up the sky. She clicked the compact shut. Tock. They stood kissing, the dusk filling with swallows diving low. A curlew cried. An owl flapped out of a tree, floated above them, its face for the passing moment a gigantic moth's.

Old images were shattered. His mind was a new sheet of glass. Her face would be there always. Going through Time, like a bird flying above endless water, whenever he looked her reflection would be his own.

15

He met his father on the road. Every second Wednesday of the month was Court Day in Belturbet. Anyone summonsed by him in the previous weeks had to appear on that day for judgement. His father always looked forward to the rituals of Court Day. When his mother was alive she pressed his uniform the night before, and in the morning before he set out he cleaned his father's bicycle with an oily rag. 'Give the rims a good rub.'

His father enjoyed appearing in front of the District Justice, crossing swords with defence lawyers, showing off his knowledge of the law.

'Your honour, the horse and cart had neither front light nor reflector. Had it been engaged in the internal operations of a farm, well and good. But it was on a public road and is therefore, in my opinion, subject to the aforementioned Road Traffic Act.'

'Thank you, Sergeant, I entirely agree.'

His father surprised him, coming round a bend in the road on his way home from the Court-house. He hadn't a chance to escape. They rode up, dismounted, stood in at the side.

'Well?'

'Hello, Daddy.'

They smiled at each other, shyly. His father looked pleased to see him.

'What are you at?'

'Coming from the shop with Mrs Prunty's messages.'

'Well for you.'

They leaned on the bicycles, elbows on the seats, heads down, not looking directly into each other's eyes. But they were as close together as lungs.

'How was the court? How did it go?' He sounded like his mother.

'I saw something today you won't often see in a lifetime. The Justice putting on the white gloves. There wasn't one case before him. Not one.'

He spat out, the ball of spit spinning, gathering dust on the roadway. He looked amazed, as if a joke had been played on him. Sad. Bitter. Crime had dried up. His uniform soaked up the sun. The light screamed at his buttons and badge and glimpse of whistle-chain. He looked well but pale. He knew, looking at him, he would love him forever.

'How are you, Daddy?'

'I've been thinking. There's no future at all for you round here. Maybe you should hit for America. Like I should have done myself years ago. Will I write to Auntie Josephine? She'd put you up until you found your feet. I can't honestly see you going back to school. If you want my solid advice I'd steer clear from your friend Prunty. And come home while you're waiting to go.'

'Why?'

'That's why.'

His father looked up at him, his eyes clear and piercing. In his firm set face his jaw muscles flicked.

'I'll think about it, Daddy.'

'You'd want to. How can this compare with New York?'

They looked into the empty fields. Along the dusty road the tar bubbled in the heat. Down at the Border a sign said: 'Welcome to Northern Ireland. Repent Ye of Your Sins'.

His father got on his bicycle but didn't move away. He sat on the saddle, feet on the ground, arms folded, brooding.

'I had a barium meal test done on my stomach. They found nothing. I've applied to be excused from night patrols. I came into this job after the Civil War and the I R A were at it then. And here I am at the end of me days and they're at it still. God blast the politicians who run this benighted land. What have they ever done but feather their own nests? Hah? If you want a future you have to leave, emigrate. Emigrate. I hope all those behind the shooting of Michael Collins will be up to the high holes of their arses one day in everlasting hell. Beats me how the only men in history who could have saved us were always bamboozled, bought, or gunned down in their prime. Why? Why?'

A herd of cattle romped across a field and stood looking out at them over the hedge.

The way he said 'emigrate' it sounded like a disease. His 'Why?'

was intensely desperate, as if he were cracking his skull against sick logic.

'I can't see any way out. Can you?'

He hated his father's direct questions. There was no answer to them. Not even ones in agreement. When he was drowning in a mood, his questions were ropes thrown from the water. He wanted you to catch one, not to save him but to pull you down into his black bitterness. Collins was his hero. Inside the cover of his Garda handbook (1923) he had written in puce pencil: 'Action. Not words', and underneath, 'Motto of Mick Collins'.

He wanted to get away, back to Mrs Prunty. He was angry too at his father's reference to Prunty. It meant more than just the words. He was implying something. Hinting that Prunty had a criminal reputation.

'I've got to go, Daddy.'

'You'll consider what I said. About America.'

'I will indeed.'

They parted. He was sorry for his father and angry with him. He could churn your emotions, make bits of your peace. Whatever the future held, it would have to include Annagh Lee. He was afraid to mention her. And if he did go to New York, spiritually would it be him going or his father? He didn't want to think about the future at all. Not now. Nothing could compare with the moment. He and Annagh made love in fields and ditches, hay sheds, up against farmyard gates, in the turf bog and on one occasion in her house.

Her mother lived with two unmarried sisters. The farm was managed by an uncle, worked by nephews. The mother and sisters toiled and worried in the orchard and gardens round the house, keeping them neurotically spick-and-span and colourful. Once a year they rewarded themselves with a day out in Bundoran.

On that day, a Sunday, Annagh invited him to the house. He hadn't met her mother yet. She was afraid to introduce him. Her mother was a snob. As far as he could tell most mothers wanted their daughters to marry tuppence ha'penny instead of tuppence. He was too young, and not only was he not tuppence, he wasn't even a penny. He understood Annagh's fear. He was frightened to bring her to the barracks to meet his father. Her house was well furnished, cluttered. You could hardly move without crashing into some piece of Victoriana – whatnots, hallstands, serpentine stools, mahogany chests, upholstered chairs, firescreens, china cows, dogs, cats, Buddhas, thick velvet curtains cloaking every door, standard lamps with tasselled shades, coal buckets, big vases and, swinging head high, chandeliers in clusters.

'God, it's like Rinty Reilly's place, Annagh.'

For all that, it was luxury compared with his own home, or Prunty's.

They lay on a leather sofa, kissing.

'My father's room is locked. She only goes into it on Christmas Day. I know where she keeps the key.'

Hand in hand they skipped up the stairs. The key was inside her mother's pillow. The pillow inside the pillowcase had a zip at one end. Annagh put her hand deep into the feathers. The key was long, dark, heavy.

Though the house was empty, she stood outside the door into what was her father's room, afraid. The opening lock grated. Compared with the rest of the house the room was bare. It had a four-poster bed, a wardrobe, a washstand with jug and basin; on the floor, lino and a small rug. Framed photographs stood along the length of the mantelpiece. A man and woman in wedding dress . . . the same couple smiling through a snowstorm of confetti . . . the couple side by side, serious, in front of the Eiffel Tower . . . the man with his arm around the woman as she held a baby . . . the man holding a young girl's hand . . . a young girl in school uniform standing stiffly beside the man . . .

'Do you know who that is?'

'Skinny legs like that? Who else could it be?'

'She comes in here, Mammy, on Christmas Day morning and bawls her eyes out. I can't stand it. I go for a walk until it's over.'

'What was your father like – as a person?'

'Generous . . . Moody, I remember. Good fun. He got a tumour. And died. Mammy locked the room. I remember when I was fourteen. I had my very first period. I tried to kick the door down to get in. I was beginning to forget what he looked like. She's a bit mad, my mother. And my crazy aunts.'

Annagh didn't want to lie down on the bed but she wanted to make love on it all the same. He sat on the edge and she sat across his knees. Supporting her back with his hands, she leaned away in passion, her long hair touching the floor. Groaning, crying out, they were greedy for all the pleasure they could get. They had a lot of pain to kill. When they'd finished she smoothed out the eiderdown, obliterating the track of his bum and her heel marks.

182

She locked the door. 'I don't think I'll ever want to see in there again.'

Her beauty made her look frail. But you could see firmness in her clear eyes. Her words were full of sharp intentions. When she said, 'I don't think I'll ever want to see in there again,' the way she hit 'there' quashed any doubts contained in 'I don't think'. And she knew everybody. Like the first day they met when she went with him to return the scythe, the old lady knew her. He and Prunty tramped the country; she floated over it. Old and young smiled when they saw her coming. When she smiled back you could see ten top teeth, all perfect, even, ivory white. Beauty was a passport. The morning he saw her at the railway station she was collecting a roll of material for Sophie Kay, who, when the fit took her, made her own clothes with Annagh's help. The green coat she wore was a birthday gift from Sophie Kay. The black beret was given her by Lady Sarah Butler-Coote. Lady Sarah had more berets than she had cats.

She knew that Hopkinson, the steward, wandered the demesne at night, nude. 'He communicates with the trees. They are the only things he has to love.'

'What about the sheep?'

'He's not quick enough to catch them any more. Haven't you noticed his limp?'

'Yes. Got that in India, didn't he?'

'Nonsense. A ewe bit him and it went septic.'

On the rare occasions when the Colonel held religious services in his private chapel, Annagh played the organ, which was a small portable carried down from the castle.

She could cross religious borders. Her face couldn't be shut out. It was a mortal sin to attend a Protestant service of any description, even a funeral. He was beginning to think she wasn't mortal. He could never have a row with her and win. Tears coming down her face crucified him. Her wet cheeks, wet mouth, wet tongue licking wet lips . . . they defeated him easily every time. He'd seen his mother cry.

He wanted to make love one evening in a field of corn, but she wouldn't lie down beside him.

'Why not?'

'That's why.'

She stood, gloomily rubbing the chaff from the ears of corn she held in her hand. He couldn't get her to change her mind. He got

183

up and his face inches from hers, in sullen mood, stared at her hard, trying to hurt her with thoughts.

'You're cruel,' she said, walking from the field, tears falling, her flaxen hair hanging above the golden corn. No touch, kiss, word of goodbye. It maddened him. He thought of his father ... the hurt on his face when he was hurting his mother, who hurt him back. By silence. By looks. There were so many moments between men and women when language was stone dead, yet meanings leapt like lightning in the sky. His father was starting to hop up on his shoulder, instead of the other way about. That chilled him to sense.

When next they met he gave her a jam-jar filled with wild-flowers – honeysuckle, rose bay willow-herb, knapweed, devilsbit, ox-eye daisy, yarrow, meadowsweet, montbretia, clover, lady's bedstraw. What else could he give her? What else could he afford?

She was pleased, held him tight. But she wouldn't say why she didn't make love. Women were like that. They didn't hark back. Emotionally they went onwards. She told him her mother knew they were going out together and wanted her to stop.

'We had a fight. I told her to shut up.'

'What did she say?'

'Nothing then. Just carried on knitting.'

They were troubled, but they had time on their side. They began to use French letters. He got them in a shop across the Border. Prunty told him to ask for 'them yokes'. That was the code. The man who sold them didn't like to use the words 'French letters' or 'Durex'. You asked for them out of the corner of your mouth when the shop was empty of other customers. 'Give 's a packet a them yokes.' It could have been chewing-gum you were asking for. He slipped them to you at the back of the shop where he was sure no one could see. The man was a Catholic.

When the Colonel arranged a Harvest Thanksgiving service, Annagh took him along to the private chapel and to the castle afterwards for supper. He was glad to be in her shadow, sailing with her through exotic doors. Invited as well were Lady Sarah and Hopkinson, Dr Dixon, a Protestant doctor from Enniskillen, the vicar from Newtown and a few local Protestant farmers and their wives.

Annagh played the organ. The chapel was small, with pews enough for about forty people. Pews with cushions on the seats and kneelers. How could you take seriously a religion with such comforts? His father always said if your knees weren't hurting it wasn't holy. No penance, no religion. Protestantism wasn't a religion. It was born out of politics. Catholicism was, by and large, hopeless politically. Where England was concerned. Protestants believed themselves superior politically. Catholics thought they had all the answers religiously. The two could never mix. You couldn't have the Queen and the Pope defending the one faith. The Queen was stronger on the ground. That's why she owned the Six Counties. The Pope was mightier in the air. Around the cold stone walls were regimental colours and brass plaques commemorating the Colonel's ancestors who had died fighting the natives of umpteen countries across the globe. The chapel, shut for most of the year, was cooler than a scullery meat-safe even though the evening sun was streaming in the one stained-glass window. The other windows were small and of clear glass. On the altar steps were baskets of fruit and vegetables. Sophie Kay brought apples – scabby Granny Smiths from the lovely walled orchard at the back of the castle. The trees were old, never pruned, and covered in moss. Everything else was supplied by the local farmers. Not one vegetable was grown on Castle Finn estate.

The vicar, a tiny man with a sallow well-scrubbed face and snow-white hair, thanked the Lord for the year's bumper harvest. Strictly speaking, the harvest along the Border hadn't commenced yet. What corn there was still stood awaiting final ripening.

'Lo what abundance thine earthly paradise doth produce,' the vicar proclaimed, looking up towards the roof beams, from which dangled cobwebs twice the size of anything in Prunty's byre. Three slates were missing, the holes patched with sky light. Two big radiators stood useless on either side of the door, monuments to the Colonel's dream of a heating system.

They sang Psalm 12, 'Let us with a gladsome mind/Praise the Lord for he is kind . . .' The words were John Milton's. He was surprised his favourite poet could produce such cant and doggerel. And that anyone would want to sing it.

As Annagh's feet pedalled and her fingers worked the keyboard, the sun poured stained-glass red, blue, gold and green all over her hair. It looked as if she were wearing a rainbow.

The Colonel went to the lectern. He thanked God, the God of his people, for benefits bestowed. Though the days of strength and glory were seemingly past, there was hope in the life to come.

185

The old must give way to the new; the new in turn grow old. But with the help of He who made the land and the great vault of the sky, no yellowbellies or Japheads would ever set foot in Castle Finn. Lady Sarah and Sophie Kay exchanged amused looks. The Colonel, seeing them, paused grim-faced, then smiled and finished off with the Lord's Prayer.

Protestants said, 'Our Father which art in Heaven'; Catholics, 'Our Father who art in Heaven'. 'Which' and 'who' – two little words philosophically poles apart. If you couldn't agree on that, what could you agree on? No, it was sad; despite his father's hopes and dreams, the Irish people would be divided forever. And at the world's end, they would rise divided from the grave.

Another hymn and the service ended. They emerged to the reality of Rinty Reilly, who wanted to speak to the Colonel. Rinty wore a hat. Between his eyes the big red carbuncle glowed. The farmers and their wives went home. The vicar, doctor, Lady Sarah and Hopkinson followed Sophie Kay up to the castle.

He and Annagh heard the Colonel say to Rinty, 'Come, come, man, not now. See me tomorrow.'

'No, no, I'll see you now, Colonel. Tomorrow never comes. Once the bargain's struck it can't be bruk. Pay up or else. You've had fair warning.'

They felt sorry for the Colonel. Everything he did was half-cocked from the start. But he was fun. He was doomed. The country was closing in on him. The table was laid and supper served in the dining-room by the time he joined them. He had obviously spent ages trying to get Reilly to relent. He looked rattled and was the poorer by a good few quid.

The dining-room was large, the ceiling high, the bare floor polished oak, the walls hung with tapestries. The long table was black oak, and around it fourteen solid oak dining chairs with space for a few more. A small turf fire burnt in the vast fireplace. Above the high black marble mantel was a massive mirror in a heavy gilt frame.

The Colonel plonked himself down at the head of the table. 'I remember the time when this table was always full.'

'It's quality, not quantity,' said Hopkinson, twitching the ends of his handlebar moustache.

The Colonel's hand was lovingly on Sophie Kay's.

'As long as one sticks to one bottle a day, eh?' said the doctor. 'Most Irish livers can take that for a lifetime.'

'How long's a lifetime?' the vicar inquired.

'As long as a piece of string,' Annagh replied.

'Why are all the handsome women Papes?' said the Colonel in a serious tone.

Sophie Kay told him to shut up or he'd get no food.

'Suits me. All I want is bumbo, honey. That despicable Reilly fellow. I know his type so well, yet I tangle with them. Hell. Just because I owe him money he expects me to pay.'

'Yes, terrible, Colonel dear,' Lady Sarah boomed. 'People to whom you owe loot ought to be found guilty of making you a debtor. Hang them.'

'Oh you old fart, Sarah, I thought you were being sensible for once in your life. How's that damn moon nonsense? I want you to clearly understand that's what I believe it to be. Utter bilge.'

'Say what you like, dear, there are whirlwinds even as we speak, blowing gold dust on Serenity Sea. But I am not here to bandy words with cynics. Delicious bit of beef this, Sophie Kay.'

'I keep out of the way. Best thing to do in this life. It's me motto,' said Hopkinson to the doctor, who was drinking, not listening.

The Colonel looked at him, looked at Annagh. 'Annagh, you ought to absolutely and entirely abstain from that boy. Why should he be so lucky? Why should you be so lucky, boy?' His face was reddening. Drink. His tweed tie was whiskey-stained.

'May I humbly inform you, Colonel, that in the last minute or so you have split two infinitives?'

Sophie Kay laughed. Lady Sarah howled with glee. The Colonel was very angry.

'I must say,' said the doctor to Hopkinson, who wasn't listening, 'to be blunt, I wouldn't recognize one if it stared me in the face.'

'I do not split my infinitives.'

'Oh darling, honey, it's the only thing you can split. Can you split logs? Could you split a tenner?'

The Colonel slugged his drink and sulked, but then laughed and winked.

In a corner of the room a white cat sat by a gnawed hole in the skirting. A fly landed on Hopkinson's bald head, wrung its front legs, flew off towards the open door.

'I'll have a wee piece more trifle if I may,' said the vicar from behind his long pale fingers.

After the meal they sat before the fire getting pleasantly drunk. Sophie Kay looked kindly at him, kissed his cheek. Her perfume was sweet and rare. Her long nails painted blue. The doctor and Hopkinson played chess, the doctor's trembling hand dropping the pieces as he moved them.

'No, dear,' said Lady Sarah to the flames, 'I've long since given up on people. Things – trees, spoons, cut glass, hedge-clippers – now they are far more interesting.'

'Hm, my mistake. Things, as you say, never appealed to me.'

'Hence our state,' said Sophie Kay quietly through her narrow sipping mouth.

He wondered for how much longer she could last in Castle Finn, in the cold, the damp, the relative poverty. What was it the Colonel had said about love? Could love save? He wasn't thinking about himself and Annagh Lee.

Later, Sophie Kay showed them upstairs. A bedroom to themselves the whole night long . . . The Colonel was right. He was lucky. The room was thickly carpeted, the bed the biggest he'd ever seen.

'Thank you, Sophie Kay,' Annagh said and kissed her.

'You're a lovely person,' he said.

'That's funny.'

It was the first time they'd slept together in a bed. This was what beds were made for. He lay in her arms, his stomach soft and tight with nervous excitement. Away, lost somewhere in the Castle, they heard the Colonel shouting about infinitives.

He could hardly believe he was a guest in Castle Finn. Every time his father rode past the castle he muttered contempt for it, scorn. 'Ah-hah, their day has come, thank God. The present buck's father – what a bad, mad, bigoted bastard. It killed him when the British left.'

Here he was, deep in the heart of enemy territory. Annagh was magic. She opened doors in stone.

'What'll we do, Annagh? Will we go away? Will we leave Ireland? We'll have to do something soon.'

'Wait and see.'

Through the great window they could see the stars. They twinkled on the river bend, on the castle battlements, on the little whitewashed houses along the Border, on the churches and chapels, belfries, steeples, on the twisted roads and laneways, on the cattle sleeping by the hedges, on the birds asleep in the trees;

turning the dark land of Cavan, Monaghan and Fermanagh into a lovers' fairy-tale that couldn't end till cock crow. Not even a shed of hay could compare with a feather-bed. A bed was an altar. Safe from enemy eyes, they were otters on a heavenly bank, sliding into timeless waters. They made love eight times. Jaded, warm limbs tangled, they fell asleep with the rising sun.

16

On Sunday mornings he and Prunty stood at the back of the chapel, wrists crossed on their bellies, waiting for mass to end. Home then to Mrs Prunty and a dinner of floury spuds, chicken, duck, or bacon boiled in cabbage. Apple pie was a constant, with a mug of milk to wash it down. On the mantelpiece and dresser London and Dublin resumed their wireless clash; dry voice, wet voice, dishing out their litanies of woe.

'What do you make of the world situation now, young fellah?'

'Do you think that crowd should be disbanded, lad?'

'Ah, er, I . . . another teeny bit of pie? Please.'

'Come on, lad, time we weren't here.'

'Goin' when youse are full. Like the tinkers. Who are youse playin' today?'

'Drung.'

'Drung? God help yiz.'

It sounded like the beat of a war drum. The most important part of the Sunday ritual was the football match in the afternoon. He was goalkeeper, Prunty full-back. The field sloped badly but was the flattest the club could find. The goal area was browny-green with cowpats. Normally the field was full of grazing cattle; they liked congregating around the posts, scratching themselves against the knobbly pine. As he took up his position he could see cattle hair stuck under what was left of the bark and in the cracks where the wood was splitting. The goalie was the loneliest man on the pitch. He watched the game ebb and flow, imprisoned in the frame of posts and crossbar. He could see the moves develop but was powerless to stop them. Until it was too late. He was the last man in the last moment. Even when the ball soared over the bar for a point, Prunty, the team, the supporters, looked at him with hurt in their eyes. If you performed miracles they took it for granted. It was your job. If you let a goal in you were useless. 'Where did yiz get that fellah? He couldn't stop a clock.' The spectators, clumped along the sideline, kept encroaching on the pitch. A man went up and down in front of them, whacking his wellington with a stick as he tried to threaten them back. 'Ah come on now, come on, please. Back to hell will youse, the whole a youse.'

Way down the far end of the field the cattle sat quietly chewing the cud. Children picked blackberries in the thick hedges. Football boots with big brown cogs tramped down on ragwort and thistle. Butlershill wore blue-and-yellow jerseys, Drung all red. Red as blood. Drung had to be sent home beaten. They were an ancient enemy. There was a parish history of defeats and injury to be revenged.

So far he hadn't touched the ball in play. Prunty took the free outs. He ran up to the placed ball, arms outstretched, fingers open, in an imitation of wings. As if he were hoping for flight. Round his left knee he wore as a bandage a strip of bedsheet. On his head he had a hairnet to keep his hair in place. His face was a cranky knot of tension and fury as he tried to threaten his opponent into submission by looks alone, or words.

'Burst the hoor. Get stuck into them. Come on the Hill.'

In a tussle of milling bodies Prunty emerged with the ball but in his excitement kicked it over his own bar. The spectators roared their derision. Their collective howl of laughter scared a cow to its feet.

'Yah bollix, Coco.'

Prunty, head bowed in shame, looked up at him surprised, wounded.

'Sorry, Coco.'

He placed the ball for the free out. Prunty stood well back, hitched up his baggy togs. His ankles were thick as poles, knees round and raw, thighs bulging. Wide-arsed, deep-chested, he looked as hard to knock out of the way as a tree stump. The hairnet gave him a weird yet comic appearance. Arms wide, fingers spread, he thundered up to the ball giving a buck-lep as he kicked it, trying to inject it with his last ounce of strength. The ball soared beyond the midfield, came down dead on a clump of rushes. A Butlershill man picked it up and scored. The spectators roared.

'That's better. Come on the Hill. Give them lanty.'

Prunty was pleased with his kick out. He turned to him and said, 'I'm fuckin' playin' them on me own, lad.'

An umpire stood at either post. A man from Drung and Tom Gannon the local man, a white handkerchief in his hand with which he flagged the scores. Because of the cattle rubbing against them, the uprights weren't firm in the ground. Drung attacked. A forward shot for a point. As the ball came flying in, Gannon leaned hard against his post, shifting it at the last moment so the ball sailed narrowly wide.

Immediately a fight erupted. Teams and spectators swung punches. The referee landed on the ground. Prunty clobbered his marker. 'That'll put manners on yah.'

He saw his father come on to the pitch. He took his time approaching, knowing violent explosions often ended as quickly as they began.

'Stop now or I'll arrest the lot of you.' Though the day was warm he had on his greatcoat. He looked massive.

'It was them started it, Sergeant.'

His father drew his baton. 'I don't care who started it.'

The referee got to his feet, blew his whistle. His father called to Gannon, 'Was it a point, Tom?'

'It was as wide as a barn door, Sergeant. As God is me judge.'

The pitch was cleared, the game raged on, the encroaching spectators roared. Prunty got angrier as Drung piled up the scores.

He could see his father watching, worried when play burst round his goal-mouth. Fists, boots, elbows flew, bodies crashed. Sometimes he managed to emerge with the ball, clearing it to safety.

A man shouted from the crowd, 'Good lad yourself. A chip off the old block, hah, Sergeant?' His father smiled, pleased. He knew his heart was beating for him, hard and fast.

At half-time they huddled for advice in the middle of the field. He saw Annagh coming in through the gate. It surprised him. She had no interest whatever in football. She had come, out of love, to encourage him. He was afraid to go near her. He couldn't. Not with his father watching. She saw him looking and returned a half-hidden wave of fingers. And a smile. Smiles lit distances. The field was full of young men. He wondered how many of them, for all their physical prowess, had lain naked in a lover's arms? That was the only test.

Gannon was telling them that unless they bucked up they were out of the Championship. 'Youse are a lock of oul' women. They're walkin' all over yiz.'

'We'll have to change the bacon on the pan,' said Prunty. 'We need a rake a goals.'

Annagh wore her brown boots, jeans, white pullover. She had her hair pinned back just behind her ears. A young girl called to her, hand out, offering blackberries. The way she moved, her fingers touching the girl's hand . . . everything she did was gentle, easy. Each moment intense with graceful, female confidence. He couldn't help watching her.

'Come on,' shouted Prunty, 'get between them sticks.'

He stood under the crossbar which had a rusty nail banged into one end, at the other a piece of rope tying it to the upright. The goal area was brown, bare, cog-marked. At the butt of the posts tufts of grass sprouted. Drung, a mixture of good youngsters and battle-hardened veterans, were fifteen points ahead.

Gannon ran on to the pitch when Prunty took a knock. He saw him slip something into his hand and Prunty surreptitiously sliding it down his sock.

The ball came soaring towards him. Grasping it, he held it tight against his midriff. A forward charged toward him. Side-stepping, he kicked the ball as hard as he could. It landed among the crowd, near where Annagh stood.

'He's trying to give the ball to the girlfriend.'

'Wouldn't be the first ball he gave her.'

It was hard enough playing the enemy. Worse were the insults and quips of your own.

Despite the dirt, the cow-dung stains on his jersey, the murder-ous boots, mean fists, he loved the game. He loved the passion, the ball sailing under the sky, the pressure of his own people willing him to do well, laughing at him but ready in an instant to turn him into a hero. If they won.

Drung scored again. He ran among the cattle at the back of the field to retrieve the ball. Prunty, muttering, took it from him. There was a penknife in his hand. He stuck the blade through the stitching. The air hissed from the bladder but the leather held its shape. Prunty placed it and kicked it out. With an empty thwack it fell flat. The referee examined it. 'Punctured. Drung ball.'

Drung didn't have a ball. Gannon had noticed that their players weren't kicking a ball around before the game started. They had travelled without one. The rules stated that the home team supplied the ball. But if anything happened during the course of the game, the visitors' ball was called for. The match had to be abandoned. The game would be re-played. Butlershill were saved. Drung had to face their drumlin hills of flax and ragwort, victory stolen from them.

'Up the Hill!'

It was said that Gannon was the best player Butlershill ever had. He scored more points or saved them more often than any man playing. Depending which way he leaned against the goal-posts. Bursting the ball was a masterstroke. Machiavellian. With such cunning, how was it Irishmen couldn't defeat their enemies?

They changed in a hayloft, their clothes lying in lumps on the floor. Outside Annagh waited. When ready he went to her. They walked along the road, pushing their bikes. When most of the crowd had dispersed, she stood and stared into his face.

'I'm pregnant. That's why I came. I had to tell you. I'm going to have a baby. I'm sorry.'

He could feel the world caving in under his feet, the blood draining from his face. His insides tightened with fear. He was cold all over. This was doom. It was inevitable. They hadn't always taken precautions. Besides, they got in the way of mutual, thumping passion. Now what was he going to do? Run away to England? Jesus. Jesus help. Tell his father? He'd have to go and see her mother. The mad woman who kept her husband's memory locked in a catacomb. He'd be sent to see the priest. He'd have to get married. At seventeen? He hadn't money enough to buy a sixpenny ice-cream cone.

'Have you told your mother?'

'Not yet.'

That would be some moment when she did. A fly wouldn't be safe on the wall. Holy God. Poor Annagh. He was scuttled. It was his own fault. He clung to her, tried to comfort her.

'It's my fault. My selfish fault.'

'It's as much mine. We enjoyed it, didn't we?'

'What'll we do?'

'Nothing yet. Wait and see.' She shrugged.

Taking the compact he'd given her from her pocket, she looked in the mirror, dabbed her cheeks, wiped her eyes. Women's misery went on and on. Whatever the face, the tears were the same.

They parted. Their youth, he knew, all over bar the shouting. Pregnant. He remembered shouting 'vagina' aloud, to take the mystery from it. He couldn't bring himself to shout this one out. This was a horrible curse word. A word heaped with famine. He wanted to lie in a ditch. Turn to stone.

Prunty caught up with him, his football boots tangled round the handlebars of his bike. He told him the news. He flinched, whistled through his teeth. 'Jazus, lad, I'm sorry. Holy smokes, now you're for the highjump.'

Prunty knew what it meant . . . making a girl pregnant. The trauma. The stigma. Born out of wedlock. A bastard. It sounded medieval. The outrage of family and community. The remarks passed. The hopeless, confined future. You were trapped for good and all. You could never get over it. Now was he a lucky boy? It was an unwritten law that if you took more than your fair share of pleasure you eventually got more than your fair share of pain. He looked at the hedges, at the road flowing beneath his wheels, at the sky, his hands, trousers . . . they all looked unreal, stupid. Hateful. He had planted something in Annagh's belly and it was going to grow and come out one day and sit looking at him, demanding to be fed. He was going to be what his father was. A father. He was going to be stuck dead centre between the devil and the deep blue sea. He had heard of women getting rid of babies before they were born but it was all the stuff of nightmare. There were orphanages, of course. You gave your child to the nuns, they looked after it. Until it could stand on its own feet and scream its way through the world. Would he give his own flesh and blood to the torment of loneliness and longing? If the nuns whipped it, who could blame them? How could they give love to abandoned strangers? Would he, an only child himself, condemn a creature yet unborn?

And what about Annagh? What must she be feeling? His heart was broken. For her. For himself. He was in a black living grave, buried by mood and the stench of famine. Lark. Hare. Stone. He envied them.

Riding up to the entrance at the side of the house, they put the bikes in the shed. The hay smelt sweet, innocent. He could just glimpse the motorcycle lying in the nettles; a skeleton in flaky rust. A cat uncurled itself, humped its back, tensed, stretched out, front paws clawing the ground, yawned, slunk lazily across the yard and sat in the dying sun. Annagh had the sleek grace of an animal. How was she going to jump? Parting from her, he couldn't tell from her eyes what she thought of him. Were he to lose her he'd drown himself. 'He's gone to the lake.' That's what local people called suicide.

In the kitchen Mrs Prunty was in the armchair, asleep, head back, lolling to one side. The table was laid for tea. Ham, salad, scones and jam. Prunty went into the bedroom. His football boots thudded on the floor.

He was going to tell Mrs Prunty. Face her with the truth about himself. She had seen a hundred tragedies in her time. She'd know what was to be done. He went between her and the fire, his back to the flames. He looked at her. Her mouth hung open, grey wisps of hair fell across her eyes. Her hands lay on the armrests, as if trying to grip them. She wasn't breathing. Her false teeth hung out of her mouth. She looked dead.

'Coco. Coco!' His scream rang round the kitchen.

Prunty ran in, frightened, saw him staring horrified at his mother in the chair. Prunty shook her shoulders. Her head fell useless to her chest. Her false teeth landed in her lap. She was dead. You didn't have to be a doctor to tell. Prunty hugged her, stood back, hoping he was dreaming, took her hand. His face crumpled like the knifed football. He staggered round the armchair, howling.

'Mammy. Mammy.'

He went to him, hugged him tight. Dead mothers he knew about. 'Cry, Coco, cry as much as you want.'

He was crying himself. Mrs Prunty had given him refuge, helped save him from his own sorrow. What she had she shared. He loved her words: 'We'll soon stop it from hurdlin',' 'You're as quick as a train,' 'What do you think of this Macmillan fellah?'

At least he had his father. Prunty was now alone. A life went out. Another one was coming in. The flames jumped in the grate. The cat came in the back door, rubbed itself against Mrs Prunty's ankle. She was wearing black slippers, thick grey stockings. A blue dress and black cardigan. She was dead now forever. Her weak heart pegged out peacefully in her sleep. Not a bad way to go.

He could watch it all at a distance. Annagh was pregnant. He was half-dead himself. Prunty asked him to fetch the priest, the doctor, his father. He rode up Brady's Hill. Below, the land lay bare as bones. It was a dunghill of a country now, a bitter place.

Pain, misery, blood stained every blade of grass. Death perched in every bush. The sky filled with clouds.

When he went round to the married quarters of the barracks, his father sat to his tea, the table covered in crumbs.

'What's up?'

'Mrs Prunty is dead.'

'The Lord have mercy on her soul. Ring the priest. And the doctor.' The doctor would examine a corpse. The priest would bless a corpse. For his father there was a corpse with one verdict only – 'No foul play suspected'.

That evening, Prunty's house filled to overflowing. Bottles of whiskey were taken out of the bin. The kettle boiled all night long. The women laid the body in a shroud, entwined a rosary in her fingers. Father Gaynor, Dr Langan, his father, stood for a moment in the bedroom. They were looking at him, not at the dead woman. Surely they didn't know about the pregnancy already?

An old man knelt by the bed. 'You were the best friend a man ever had, Lily.' That was her Christian name. He had never thought to ask. It was the first time he'd been in her room. The mantel and walls were covered with religious pictures, statues, objects. The Sacred Heart burnt in all shapes and sizes. The Blessed Virgin was many times flanked by Popes. Pictures and prayers to Blessed Martin de Pores, the Child of Prague, St Francis of Assisi, Oliver Plunkett, Maria Goretti, St Pelagius, Mother Josepha, S. Sp. S., were on top of every bit of furniture. He picked up a small leaflet. On the front it had a picture of Jesus behind the barred window of a locked door. On the back, written in French, were the words: *'Quel est ce prisonnier d'amour?'* He knew the answer to that all right.

In the kitchen, men sat round the fire drinking. An old woman, a scarf on her head, said to no one in particular, 'We get a life sentence the day we're born.' People tried to console Prunty. Newcomers went to him, shook his hand: 'I'm sorry for your troubles,' 'She had the grand life, RIP,' 'She's in heaven if ever a woman was.'

He followed his father out. He had a notion to tell him there and then. Get it over with. His nerve failed him. His father and Father Gaynor got into the doctor's car. 'Well,' said the priest, his lower lip trembling, 'it puts a halt to your gallop.'

They drove away. He was furious. They were taking triumph

from death. Food. His father knew he'd have to seek elsewhere for his dinner. Prunty was no cook. He'd put a halt to their gallop when he told them about Annagh Lee. If he ever had the guts.

Late in the night men sang. The old kitchen filled with words of love and hope and Ireland. The music of the voices joining in soared round the house and into the dead woman's room. Candles burnt at either side of her head. The sweet songs danced the flames across her face, shifted her body over the room and up the walls. Words and flame. Magic. There was no sleep for himself and Prunty. At dawn he slumped in the armchair. Outside a young cock crowed. His mind was in turmoil. The death had cancelled Annagh's pregnancy, then made it worse.

That day Prunty and the undertaker lifted the corpse into the coffin. Prunty, crying, screwed the lid down. 'Mammy. Ah God, Mammy.'

He walked beside him to the chapel. Stretched out for a mile behind them along the narrow road were all the people who wanted to show the son that his mother's death was part of theirs. The high hedges held in the murmuring voices, the shuffling feet. Murmurs, leather, road.

'Cry, Coco, cry all you want.'

He was tired out. He had helped the men dig the grave. Prunty, not able to face it, asked him to lend a hand. He was glad to get out in the air.

'Lad, lad, I won't forget this. Won't forget what you've done for me.'

'I've done nothing.'

'Begod you couldn't say the same to Annagh Lee.'

They smiled, laughed, cried together. Prunty with his quip was showing he hadn't forgotten. He knew he was suffering on his own account.

Next day Mrs Prunty was buried. Annagh Lee came to the funeral. She wore a black coat and hat. And gloves. Black high-heeled shoes. Black nylons. She looked beautiful. They lowered the coffin down, taking it easy, so the wood wouldn't shatter against the jutting rock. Clay from the shovel landed on the lid, thud.

Over at his mother's grave his father stood alone.

Father Gaynor spoke a few final words. 'She was what I'd call a good woman. What harm did she ever do? What hurt did she ever cause? She kept an open door and an open heart. *Requiescat in pace.*'

'Amen.'

'Poor Lily.'

'I'm sorry for your trouble, son. Aye man, surely.'

He walked over to his father, Annagh by his side. He saw them coming, walking at angles, avoiding the graves.

'Daddy, this is Annagh. Annagh Lee.'

His father looked at her, his eyes shining. He liked a good-looking woman. But sensing trouble, he bit the corner of his lower lip.

'Hello, Sergeant, pleased to meet you.'

His father took her hand. 'I'm pleased to meet you. You look pale. The pair of you.'

'I've got bad news to tell, Daddy. Annagh's . . .' he couldn't say the word 'pregnant' '. . . going to have a baby.'

His face seemed to freeze. Become a block of ice. His eyes glazed, shut. Annagh's head hung down. On the edge of his mother's grave he had told him the worst news a man could hear. In his father's face was the stony defeat of hopes and dreams. How could you hit for America, a pregnant, teenage bride in tow? His father hated sin as much as he loved crime. Sex was sin. The act of sex murdered the Blessed Virgin.

'Go 'way the pair of you. Not now. Not now.'

'I'll call in. We'll . . .'

They left the graveyard, rode away. They said goodbye near the Border. He left her to ride across and face her mother, aunts and uncles, all alone. He was sunk, love defeated. There was no energy in his guts. 'I'll come to your house tomorrow. Come hell or high water.' Christ. He was sounding like his father.

In the emptiness, he and Prunty sat alone. They drank a tumblerful of poteen each and went to bed, utterly exhausted. Back to back they fell asleep. The devil in uniform sat on his head and he couldn't struggle free. His mother, wearing spurs, tried to help him but couldn't. When morning came it was raining. He had never felt worse, more miserable, in his life.

There were lines in his head from school, lines haunting him: 'The worst is not so long as we can say this is the worst.' Jesus help. He loved her but he didn't want to get married. He'd love a child but not now. He couldn't bear to think about life without her, yet couldn't stomach the idea of kneeling with her at the altar rails one morning, bride and groom. It was in his stomach the dilemma raged. He was in pain, agony. All day his stomach gnawed at him, gripping him with the opposite of excitement. It was a boiling pot of dread, hopelessness, worry. He was walking round like a zombie. His limbs moved out of habit. His mind was dead. Sleep was dreadful, food tasteless. He couldn't think without crying on all the ruined years to come. Yet he loved Annagh to distraction. He wanted her so long as he wasn't nailed down. He knew what a wilderness marriage could be from his father and mother and countless others. The scraping and saving, the buying of food, the spade in the ground, the washing on the line, the sewing and darning, the rat trap at the potato pit, the quarterly bills and, in the heel of the hunt, separate beds. You couldn't enter a house without seeing crying babies, the whiff of their piss stealing up your nostrils at the hall door. He was also, simply, afraid. Scared witless. This was an exam he knew he couldn't pass. He was too young for God's sake. You were old enough to do the dirt! Yes, he knew what people would say. What his father and the in-laws were thinking. He loved the flesh but didn't want to take the consequences. He hated himself, his turbid mind, disloyal thoughts.

'You're just going to have to face the music,' Prunty told him.

Prunty, in the dumps for days after the funeral, began to cheer up, organize himself, shave every morning, go to the fields and turf bog. Work. He stayed in the kitchen, fed the hens, tried to sweep the floor and have the kettle boiling when Prunty came in for tea. Most of the time he sat in the armchair, staring out at the lake, the rain, the dripping hedges. Annagh hadn't come near him since the funeral.

He still hadn't been to her home. That was a broken promise. Doom had taken him over.

'You're just goin' to have to take the bull be the horns, lad.'

Days later he did. Shame forced him on to a bike. Mrs Prunty's – he owned it now. On the way he met the Rock and the Stumps. The one had a guitar strapped to his back, the other a drum tied on the carrier of his bike.

'We're startin' a rock and roll band. We want you to jine.'

'We're calling ourselves, "King Knio and the Rambucks".'

'I can't play an instrument.'

'That niver stopped anyone. Half the friggers on the television can't play, sure.'

He left them. Saddened. That's what he should be doing. Becoming a Rambuck. Crazy and uncaring. Whamming a guitar.

Singing. Flinging his life on the wind. He rode on, the blood slow and bitter in his veins. He crossed the bridge where he first glimpsed her coming through the soldiers. He was afraid to stop and lean on the parapet and look down . . . Her house loomed up, white and neat. The lawn was cut, not a flower out of place, not a weed in sight. It was as well ordered as a Protestant cemetery. Heart thumping in the coffin of his body, he crunched up to the door and knocked. For a house so full the knocking sounded hollow. He heard footsteps. The door opened. He smelt Cardinal polish. A tall big-boned woman, grey hair in a bun, looked him in the eye, looked him up and down.

'Are you Annagh's mother?'

Her lips snouted as she stared at him. Not answering, she closed the door but didn't bang it shut. He could hear women's voices, urgent, consulting. He heard Annagh shout – 'If you do! If you do!' Feet flurried to the door. A woman wielding a carpet-sweeper charged out. He just had time to jump back, turn and run down the path. It mst have been the mother. The full joke! Big, nasty, tough as any man. No wonder the husband got a brain tumour. Her hair was in a bun as well. And there was a third woman there too. The three sisters. All cackling mad. He could see Annagh's flaxen hair at the back of the hallway.

'Come back here again, you dirty scut, and it'll be the last thing you do.'

In the farmyard a man stood watching, a pitchfork on his shoulder.

He jumped on the bike, glad to escape. But angry. Unfulfilled. He knew sooner or later he'd have to face them all over again. He was so so really sorry for himself. Oh unlucky boy!

He cried for Annagh. He loved her. To hell with them all. He'd take the consequences. It would be purgatory. But when you got out of purgatory you were in heaven.

He was in a mood to be abused and battered. He made straight for Butlershill. His father. He was in the day-room with Guard Ryan, the two of them sitting in front of the empty grate. They weren't allowed a fire until the first of November. His father rarely sat with the men. He usually worked alone in his office. They could have been talking about him, his father sharing out the sorrow.

'Talk of the divil,' said Ryan.

He was right.

'Well?' said his father. 'Sit. Sit.'

Arms across his knees, head down, he burst into tears. Choking. They watched. The tears fell on to the bare floorboards, widening like drops of rain. 'I went to her house. They ran me. The mother chased me away.'

'If it was me,' said Ryan, 'I'd be on the first plane to America in the morning. You wouldn't be the first man done it. Nor the last, by hokey. They ran you. What more can you do? Leave. Leave. Blast it, man, leave.' He spat into the empty fireplace.

'It's no use crying. Pull yourself together. They'll come looking for you when the fit wears off, don't worry about that. You're not getting away with it that light.'

Ryan rubbed his belly with a flat hand. He was from Cork and lived for drink. In the local pubs he drank after hours, sometimes cracking eggs on the edge of his pint, then swallowing them from the shells. He was tolerated by the authorities because he only had two more years to go before retirement. His father couldn't stand his hopeless, sloppy attitude to the job. Yet here he was listening to his advice. Anything to stem the horror of having to work it all out on his own.

'Your boot shouldn't be off a woman's arse except when you're swinging it. Take the highroad, boyo, while the going's good.'

There was disgust in his father's face. And shame. 'Come on.'

He followed his father to the door. Ryan, winking, slipped him a fiver. He mouthed his thanks. Ryan dismissed him with a wave of his hand.

In the kitchen his father walked up and down, jingling the coins in his trouser pockets. His tunic hung open, the whistle-chain dangling. 'I'm glad she's dead. She must be turning in her grave. You, you . . . she thought the sun shone out of you. You can imagine what the neighbours are saying. The ould cackling harridans. How can I ever look them in the eye again?'

'I'll marry her. I'm not running away.'

'Will she have you? That's the question. If I was her I wouldn't. You've less prospects than a wet week. What are we going to do at all? Jesus help us.'

'I'm sorry.'

'Ah, you stupid fool. Yah big lug. Yah big thick lug. Yah great big double-barrelled thunderin' jackass. You've ruined yourself. How long was the relationship going on?' What he really meant was how long had sex been taking place.

'Months.'

'Sacred Heart. Blessed Virgin forgive him. Get on your knees. Yah pup.' He had to kneel. Together they said the rosary, his father trying to roar his way into God's good graces. It was almost comical, the two of them. Suddenly breaking off, the thought striking him, his father said, 'You'll need to go to confessions. What if anything happened, God forbid, with sin upon your soul?'

'I'm going to go tomorrow morning.' He had to say something to placate him. He couldn't go to confessions. Not to Father Gaynor anyway. They sat at the table in total silence. With great difficulty, his father began to speak his thoughts aloud.

'Jack . . . your uncle. He did . . . the very same thing as yourself. In his case . . . with a much older woman. They lived in the nearby town . . . no one would visit them. Then they cleared off to England. He left poor Dada face all the work alone. Grannie never forgave him. She lit a candle in the window for each one of us every Christmas Eve . . . But she never lit a candle for poor Jack. Secretly . . . I helped them as much as I could. After I joined the Force, I sent them money from me first wage envelope. They survived, God help us, and made a life for themselves in Birmingham. All this I never told a soul. Except Mum. The Lord have mercy on her. Oh my, oh my, oh my.'

His father's eyes were misting over. His fists, tight, were on the table. Jack was his older brother. He had run no doubt because he couldn't face his father every day in the cruel, bitter fields. An older woman needed and gave him love. He was a moth, she a flame. Thank God for history after all. Jack saved him. That's why his father ranted but didn't rave.

Well, he wasn't going to run. Unless he was chased out of the country. That night he slept in his old room. It wept damp. He put on a uniform greatcoat and got under the blankets. But it was useless. He couldn't get warm. Nothing could warm him . . . except Annagh Lee. In the middle of the night he sneaked out and went back to Prunty's house. Prunty wasn't in and didn't return till dawn. Bodies stopped. Smuggling never. Maybe, though, he was with the widdy woman. You could never tell with Prunty.

17

He received a letter from Annagh and pressed in the closed-over page a primrose. Yellow and green.

> Meet me on the bridge, Friday, 7 o'clock.
> To hell with them. Cheer up. I love you.
> From the river that runs and runs but never runs away –
> Annagh Lee

He couldn't wait. The primrose was for love. Indestructible. It could cling to any old bank, stare prettily from any thorny ditch. She was his river. He had run into her and she was going to have a tributary. Or lengthen. In less than nine months. He was nervous waiting to see her. He couldn't sit still; hopping in and out of the kitchen, unable to help Prunty with the milking, hardly able to pour water into the kettle without splashing the fire out. Love made your legs go skittery, your body reject everything but air. His future was cloudy but at least come Friday he'd see a ray of sun.

His finances had increased by yet another fiver. Prunty received an envelope containing his mother's will from a solicitor in Cavan. 'You're included in it, lad. You're entitled to attend the reading of it.'

'When's that going to be?'

'Now.'

Prunty sat at the end of the table, cleared his throat and began to read his mother's handwriting in as formal a manner as he could. The will was full of important-sounding semi-legal jargon. Wills and hymns had their own patterns.

'"... I do hereby leave the aforementioned jam-jars to the friend of my deceased sister, Mrs Polly Tilson, the jam-maker of Wattlebridge ..."'

Mrs Prunty had sackfuls of jam-jars in one of the sheds.

' ". . . my land, my hills and bottom and the bog and house and outhouses I bequeath to my only son and heir . . ." '

Prunty looked moved. He drank a sup of milk, licked his lips, continued.

' ". . . I would wish for a photograph of me to be given to my dear friends, hereto aforementioned, if possible. I bequeath the sum of thirteen pounds to Father Gaynor for masses to be said for me, five shillings per mass . . ." '

Prunty paused. 'That's, let me see, yes, five bob a mass, that's fifty-two masses. A mass a week for a year.'

He reached the part of the will concerning him.

' ". . . Finally I intend five pounds to be given to the Sergeant's boy, on the day he is ordained a priest." '

It was a merry moment – the first for weeks. Someone had faith in him. Prunty, to preserve the dignity of the occasion, tried his best not to laugh. He got up, delved down into the bin. From a big jar he handed him a five-pound note.

'Here. It's yours. May as well have it now as later. Ha-ha. I'll not acks you for a resate.'

'Thanks. Thanks, Mrs P. The Lord have mercy on you. You're even kind to me dead. Thanks, Coco.'

'I'm not coddin' you, lad, she swore blind you were for May-nooth. She said she saw it in a dream. Behind your back she had a world of braggs of you. She writ this will only a month ago. I saw her at it but niver let on. I knew somethin' was up when I caught her a while ago counting them oul' jam-jars. She was ready for to die and wanted nawthin' better.'

He'd be a priest of love. He'd carry the old woman in his heart. That was fair enough. With that there was no law could find a fault.

The morning of the day he was to meet Annagh, he went to the lake, stripped off and washed himself all over with a bar of carbolic soap. The keen air, the cold water, were as good as a cure. A basking pike lay among the bullrushes like a lump of wood. Later in the kitchen Prunty forced him to eat some food. Since Mrs Prunty's death they'd lived on boiled eggs, bread, ham, lettuce, sweet cake and sometimes potatoes.

At last the time came to go and meet her. He was excited, nervous, afraid she mightn't be there. She was. She was on the bridge, leaning over, looking down into the Finn. Wearing a skirt, a jumper. The flaxen hair scattered across her shoulders like light spilling. Hearing the approaching rattle she turned. He jumped off. They ran and clung in each other's arms.

'Darling, darling, are you all right?'

'Annagh, Annagh, I love you, love you, missed you, love you.'

They kissed and clung and laughed and tried not to cry. They went down a laneway into an abandoned farmyard. Outhouses tumbled. A dwelling-house falling in. Only the hay shed was still in use. The farm was right on the Border. The family who owned the place fled, it was said, because of debts. Others said they were threatened out. Who by, nobody knew. Nobody said. 'Don't say a hate – till you hear more.'

They climbed up into the hay. They kissed passionately.

'My mother went round the house screaming. So did my aunties. She tried to hit me. My uncle stopped her. She did hit me. With that bloody carpet-sweeper.' She lifted her skirt, unhitched her stocking. Her thigh was bruised, black and blue and greeny-brown. Like a shot his hand landed on her flesh. 'She locked herself in the room. Yes, my father's room. You could hear her screaming.'

'What are they going to do? What do they want you to do?'

'They don't want me to have anything more to do with you, that's for certain. They think I'm in Clones now seeing the priest. They want the baby to be born and they'll bring it up but I'll be sent away to Canada. Or they want to send me up north to relations in Antrim. And I'll have it there and it'll be put in an orphanage. They'll pay. They don't know what they want. But they don't want me to marry you.'

'What do you want?'

'I don't know. What should we do? Run?'

'I don't know. We could stay with Prunty. He told me we could. Tell me your feelings.'

'I cry sometimes. My face goes all blotchy. Horrible, eyes red. I walk round wanting to wake up, you know? A baby? So what. And then I think – so everything!'

'We've next to no money. Ten pounds is all I've got. We'd have to try England. My father might help us that far.'

'Look.'

She lifted her clothes up. Underneath she wore a red slip. Her belly was white as sugar, warm, beginning to swell. He kissed her navel. Put his tongue in it. She giggled. They tore each other's clothes off, fought into each other's flesh. They were desperate. Their lovemaking gave them hope. Her lips were bruised by his hungry mouth. Her blue eyes closed, calm crept over her face. Her hair merged with the hay. Her long, slender, warm legs wrapped round the small of his back. They could all scream. Go hang. You couldn't stop surging feelings. Love. That was all there was to it. It was a force of nature, like grass growing. But what were they going to do? What was going to happen?

'I'm frightened.'

'So am I.'

'If anything goes wrong – come to Prunty's.'

'I will.'

'Promise you'll never leave me. Never go without me.'

'I promise.'

They came up the laneway, back on to the road. Dusk was falling into the Finn. Swallows lined up on the telegraph wires, getting ready to fly south.

They stood on the bridge eating a bar of chocolate. Then they kissed goodbye. His belly was in agony having to leave her. His legs were heavy, barely able to push the pedals round. His heart was an old bucket flung in a ditch. Soldiers came along the road in jeeps. A police car followed them. He heard shots being fired. It could be the IRA . . . the army . . . men hunting rabbits. You'd never know – till you found out. And even then you wouldn't know for certain. Jesus, what a country! What a state! Poor Annagh, poor Annagh, poor Annagh. The whole world screaming round their heads, yet come the first opportunity and they were at it in the hay, drinking each other, stealing time, blotting out to-morrow.

Maybe the world, the earth, the clay, couldn't destroy bodies . . .

18

Prunty wore a scapular worn by his mother day and night. He took it from her before she was coffined. A Franciscan had given it to her round the time Prunty was born. It was two pieces of woollen cloth, each an inch square, with pinked edges, linked together by soft brown string. It hung over the shoulders so that one of the squares was on the chest, the other on the back. Each square had a stitched-on picture of St Francis. Prunty didn't wear it at night. He took it off and hung it over the bedpost with the game-cock spurs. 'It protected her. You never know.'

They were loading turf into a tractor and trailer with the help of the owner, 'Monkey' Sexton. Prunty swore blind he'd never use a horse and cart again. When he flung the turf sods up over the high sides of the trailer, the scapular, which had worked up from inside his shirt, bounced on his neck.

The wind was cutting. It came down off the hills, across the top of the bog, and loaded with turf mould whipped straight into your eyes if you dared face it. They tried to keep their backs to it as they lifted the sods. Monkey Sexton, bending to the work, farted.

'A bettur sound nor the doctor's horn.'

'Aye,' agreed Prunty, 'better out nor your eye.'

Sexton was small, wiry, with a grin from ear to ear. He wore a cap, the peak pulled down on the back of his neck. The tractor was a second-hand Ferguson with bad brakes. Sexton left it in gear when the engine was switched off.

'Are you the lad's kicked the traces?'

'I suppose so.'

'No suppose about it,' said Prunty.

'I seen you a lock a days ago in Cavan with the girlfriend. You've a good eye for a pullet, I'll say that for you.'

He hadn't seen Annagh for days. He was planning to go that night and hide outside her house. She was bound to come out sooner or later. He was fed up loading turf.

'Are we nearly finished?'

'Nearly never bucked the cat. How are you gettin' on since the mother died?'

'I'll niver over it,' said Prunty, 'niver.'

'Hah? That's a fret, hah? You know that baist a mine?'

'Which one?'

'The one won best bullock at Belturbet Show with permanent teeth. I sowl' him a fortnight ago to a daler from the North. Gave me an ojus price.'

'How much?' said Prunty, winking.

'G'out a that. Holy God, this wind's a scourge.' The way he said 'wind' rhymed with 'blind'.

At last the turf was piled high over the trailer sides. They were finished for the day. Black mounds of turf and grey mounds of potatoes kept the whole country going. And boggy black porter. He remembered a school trip to Dublin. They were taken to the 1916 Exhibition in the National Museum, around Stephen's Green and to a meal in the Ormond Hotel. The thing that struck him most was the sweet smell of burning turf hanging over the city. Dublin was the capital village.

When Sexton got the engine going the wheels began to bog in the wet ground. They tore down branches, ripped up heather and laid them in the ruts. The wheels gripped and they made it out to the laneway. There was at least another load left on the bank. Prunty told him he could have it.

'How do you mean?'

'Since Mammy's dead we won't be burnin' what we cut. What's left we'll wheel out near the lane and rick it. After Christmas you can sell it in Clones, if you're still here. You've earned it.'

If. He still had no idea what fate awaited. He half-expected, hoped, his father would sort it all out. Go to her mother, bring it to a head. Marriage. Two nights before, he'd woken up in the small hours, parching for a drink. He'd gone to the kitchen for a cup of water when he heard a noise outside. A full moon filled the lake with silver. Parked a little way down the road was a Garda squad car. In the morning he told Prunty. 'I thought it was my father come to get me. But I don't think so. He'd have knocked us up.'

Prunty looked thoughtful, worried. 'Maybe they're expectin' smugglin' comin' up to Christmas, d'ye see? That'd be it. Are you sure it wasn't the Customs?'

'I'm sure.'

His father didn't come near him. He was leaving him to stew. Prunty told him that if he and Annagh wanted they could use what was now the spare room. It was an idea. Maybe she could cook for them ... Jesus, what was he thinking? Thinking of his belly. The only one with a belly problem was Annagh. A baby on the way, no income, living with Prunty ... Something had to happen. He was a great one for feeling sorry for himself. He just had to go to her house again. And to hell with hiding outside on the off-chance of seeing her. He was going to force his way in and make them face reality. The reality of him.

The turf unloaded into a shed, he cleaned himself and rode along the Border road, leaving Cavan for Monaghan, then across into Fermanagh. Outside her house he left his bike handy for a quick escape. Just in case. A twist of pale-blue smoke came out of a chimney. They were in. A collie dog, sitting on the concrete of the farmyard, wagged its tail when it saw him and didn't bark. That was something. The dog was on his side. He went up the path to the door, scowling, trying to look determined in case they were peeping out through the net curtains. He wanted to show them he meant business. The knocker was a horseshoe adapted for the job. He banged hard, then gave the door a thump with his fist for good measure. Footsteps. He was going to shout and curse and fight if necessary. The door was opened by Annagh. He was as surprised as she was. Her jaw dropped. She wore a blue apron spattered with flour. Her yeasty fingers went to her mouth in surprise.

'Come on,' he whispered.

For a moment she dithered, then, hands behind her back, undid the apron strings. Her long green coat hung in the hallway. Wiping her hands on the apron she went to get it. Her mother came down the stairs. She looked gigantic. The grey hair scraped back made her big square face fearsome. Inside her thick stockings he could see the windings of bandage. Vein trouble. Like his mother. She must be human after all.

'Where are you going? Where do you think you're going?'

'Out, Mum. I'll be back.'

Her mother tried to close the door. He stuck his boot in, the big left boot from Rinty's. Stepping into the gap he pushed the door back, allowing Annagh out.

'Mrs Lee, I'm sorry. For what's happened. I'm sorry. I'll do whatever you want.'

Anger spilled from her eyes. She was trying to hate him as much as she could. He waited, giving her a chance to soften, not minding even if she hit him. Blows were better than hateful silence. Her soul was black with loathing. He held her stare. Had she been happy in love? Her husband left her for the grave. Why should Annagh be happy?

'I love Annagh, Mrs Lee. Is that a crime?'

'If you go,' she shouted, 'don't come back to this house.'

He couldn't understand flesh and what went on inside it. What made people hate? When he stepped away she banged the door shut.

Annagh sat sideways on the carrier as they rode back to Prunty's. The two aunts and uncle had gone shopping to Clones. If they'd been there she probably wouldn't have been able to escape. No doubt that's why the dog didn't bark. If his master had been around he'd have had his ankles flash-quick.

'They're sending me away to Antrim next week. They watch me like hawks.'

'She said not to come back.'

'She doesn't mean it. She thinks I've ruined my life. She's probably up in the room now, screaming.'

'What am I supposed to do if you go away?'

'I don't know, darling, I don't know.'

'Will you stay the night in Prunty's?'

'I'll be shot. But I will.'

He was a horse being tied for slaughter. Hobbles on, the rope was tightening, the end dawning. How did he walk into this? Couldn't he smell death in the air? Annagh, she was a primrose . . . she could dodge, bend from the worst the wind could offer. A woman absorbed blows better than a man. Her frail wrists were round his waist. You could snap them like pencils. Her fingers playing the organ in the Colonel's chapel looked as if the light was passing through them. Yet of the two of them she was the stronger. Well, if her mother was mad, he was going to be madder. He wasn't going to let them take her away. He loved his mother – she was dead. He loved Mrs Prunty – she was dead. If Annagh went away – he'd be dead. Gone to the lake. What the hell was he going to do?

Prunty was watching television. They sat with him, drinking tea. 'He must be some mechanic can send them pictures down the wires. It'll kill newspapers. The airplanes may pack up. Who'll want to travel when the world can travel to them?'

'God Save the Queen' played. Prunty snapped the set off. The kitchen was dark. He hadn't put the light on. Flame shadows flickered over Annagh. She sat right in front of the fire on a straight-backed chair, hands on knees, staring, hardly moving. You could guess better what the cat was thinking. Women were mysterious when they were in trouble. In sorrow they were fields covered in snow. So what? they seemed to say, one day the snow will melt. One time he thought love was peace.

'Supposing we had to, you did say we could stay here, Coco?'

'For a start anyway.'

A start under thatch, a hill behind them, a lake before.

'But don't you understand, darling, they are going to send me away? I tell you, I'm beat to the wide world. I'm losing the run of myself.' She looked frightened. A minute before, she had looked compact, composed.

'Feck all use losing the head,' said Prunty. 'Away to bed the pair a you. Go to sleep on a question you often get up on an answer.' He bent to the fire, poked at the burning sods, broke their glowing hearts, covered them with ash.

They lay in bed naked, side by side, holding hands.

'There's fourteen pictures of Jesus and twenty of the Blessed Virgin.' He'd been thinking, she'd been counting. 'We could get married. Force them to marry us. Demand. It's our lives.'

'You've never asked me to marry you.' She looked at him, her face sideways on the pillow, watching him, lips pouting, hair flowing back over the bed edge. Her eyes were the colour of potato spray. Soul-blight killers.

'Will you marry me, Annagh Lee?'

'I will. Feel my belly.'

Maybe she could do without him now that she had him in her womb. That happened. Women had to look after themselves. In there in her belly was a separate planet. The man in the womb. Or woman. His own mother – he'd been the apple of her eye. He *was* her eye. His poor father never got a look in.

He got out and switched off the light. He told her about his father's string invention. They lay in each other's arms giggling. There was a hollow in the mattress. They rolled into it, snug.

They didn't make love. One of the Sacred Heart pictures glowed in the dark.

'Was your father religious?'

'When he was a Methodist he was. It was all bare knees on scrubbed floorboards in draughty halls then. And the Bible. I loved the Bible. I still do.'

Death practised on you with sleep. Each night he tested you with drugs. A nervous wreck, he drifted out on to a dark lake, losing contact with Annagh . . .

He thought he was dreaming. He was sick but sure it was a return to childish nightmare. She was sitting up in the bed screaming, tearing the night to tatters. Her screams were away out on the edge of his brain; he was so glad it was only a dream. The screams were tearing out her throat, drowning him in pain. Maybe he was walking in his sleep, making for the lake. He tried desperately to wake up. Was she sitting up? Was she screaming? Something hit him on the head. A mallet? Reality. He jolted from sleep, bang into a wall of screaming dark. Yes, she was sitting up. She was screaming.

'Agh. Agh. Agh –'

Cold with terror, he jumped out and fumbled across the room to the light switch. Her hair snaking round her shoulders, her knees up, she was screeching, staring, pointing to the bottom of the bed.

'There's something!'

He thought for a moment he was being tortured. Demons from childhood had come back to scourge him. It was Annagh's shoulders. Her face. The screams were growing more frantic.

'What is it? What is it?' she roared at him, neck straining, desperate, angry at his lunatic stillness.

Jesus, there was something moving. The blankets were moving. He was either dead or he was alive and there was something real in the bed. Moving. Scurrying. Her screams strangled the house, blew his brains out. He grabbed the bedclothes and pulled them clear. A rat jumped down, plop between his bare feet. He roared, screamed himself. He wanted to vomit. He could see it hurry-scurrying along the skirting-boards, grey, fat, belly wiping the floor, humpy back carrying a plague of dreams. Its nails ticked the lino, turning it into a mad clock. He was scunnered. It had got into the bed. A rat in the bed. The bastard. He looked for his boot to throw at it. Annagh stood up on the bed. Her face was screaming but in silence. She looked terrifying, insane.

'It was only a rat.' Only? Since Mrs Prunty died the cat cleared off most of the time. Going wild.

She let out a low moan, her hands like claws clutching her belly. He saw brown water break between her legs, blood running down her thighs. She stood on the bed, half-crouched, still, crucified in space. The life within her . . . him . . . drained, came away in gobs and clots, mucous . . . something hung from her, broke free down on to the sheet.

'Hold me, hold me, help. I'm having a miscarriage.'

The terror changed on her face. It was a different terror. He was shaking with cold and fear. His teeth were chattering, making the same noise as the rat's nails. For a mad moment he thought he ought to do something about the pool of blood and water staining into the mattress.

'All right, all right, Annagh.' She was weeping. In the freezing night her tears landed warm on his shoulder. Blood gulged from her, then stopped. The rat was trying to squeeze out under the door.

'Kill it. Kill it!'

Grabbing his boot, he flung it with all his might. Writhing, squealing, it tried desperately to escape, its back broken. He grabbed the boot again and hammered it to death with the heel. The rat was dead. So was the baby.

Annagh stood down on the floor, her hands out in front of her, appealing. He didn't know for what.

By the tail he flung the rat out of the back door, knocking a hen roosting in the bushes to the ground. With a screech and cluck, it gathered itself and ran towards the byre.

Prunty's bedroom door was open. His wellingtons weren't by the end of his bed. He looked more closely. He wasn't there. He was glad. With a basin of water and a towel he returned to the room.

Crying, she washed herself. He dried her, cleaned the mess . . . him, her . . . on to newspaper. The blood had come from her in snots, like clots from the game-cocks' necks . . .

'It's over. It's over. It's over.'

'It was horrible, it was horrible.' She sobbed, stopped.

The hollow of the mattress was stained. You could never get it out. When they got back into bed she lay shivering, clutching her stomach in pain. Fear. Loss. Agony. They were all in her face. He tumbled out words of love and relief, but she looked lonely, lost. Her sorrows a man couldn't know. She put a towel between her legs. He got out of bed, made her a cup of tea with a glug of poteen. Then held her until the warmth came back to her body.

They were saved. A nightmare had delivered them from a nightmare. Rats roamed the world whiffing out gaps, holes, slits. Rats spread terror. But this rat was a hero. It had come a long, long way. Old famine rat had rescued them. Dead, grey, horrible rat.

He would never forget her screams. He felt weak, drained. Every bit of him was terror-tossed. He was free. They were free. Life ended, life could go on. Fermanagh. Annagh. Maybe she was born to scream.

19

She was gone. Prunty threw the letter on to the bed. Her innocent hand formed his name, neat, clear, rounded.

> . . . I'll be in Belfast by the time you get this. I'm going to try and get into Queen's but if they don't have me then it's Canada in the New Year. But I'll be home Christmas. Nothing will keep me from seeing you. My darling, my heart is broken too . . .

Summer was over, autumn ended, winter here to stay. In the mornings the windows were iced over. To get a look-out you had to scrape at the glass with your thumb nail. The fields were salty cold, the dunghill frozen over. The windows at the rear of the house stayed icy all day. The low sun couldn't lift itself above the hill at the back door. Most days it rained, pelting down through the bare branches, splattering for hours on the thatch, churning the fields to mud, making every hole and hoof-mark a dirty puddle. A necklace of snotty drops hung from the lintels, swelling, falling, re-forming. The gully in the yard gurgled all day long. When it was really cold you had to take a hatchet to the ice on the rain barrel to get water. The grass then was grey, stiff, crinkly. The ice on the muddy puddles splintered when the cows walked on them. The warm side of a cow on his face was all the female heat he had. Annagh was gone. He thought when she was pregnant he was in purgatory. Now that she wasn't it was even worse – he was in hell. Her family closed ranks. He couldn't get to her. Then her letter arrived . . .

One afternoon he stood at the back door looking at the darkening hill. A flock of wild geese went across the grey sky, heading south. They were the same colour as the sky. Feathery, watery. Honking, chattering, they flew over, all together, all one. He cried with loneliness. What had he done to deserve such heartbreak? His heart was breaking. He couldn't think beyond the moment. Were it not for the cold he'd go to the lake. A magpie landed in the yard and with long hops made for a trough of chicken feed. When it saw him standing in the lit doorway it gave a brazen rattle-cackle. Turning its back on him, it pecked at the remaining feed, its beak beating out a hungry morse code on the wooden trough.

He'd try and hang on until Christmas. He'd try to eat. He'd try to sleep. He'd try not to dream.

'Holy God,' said Prunty, 'you're goin' round like a sick calf.'

Immediately after the miscarriage the clouds had lifted. When he told his father what had happened he shook his head in disbelief and awe.

'A rat? A rat in the bed? Who, tell me, sent it? If it wasn't the Almighty?'

The rat a blessing he thought a curse. If the miscarriage hadn't happened, the chances were that he and Annagh would still be together. Somehow.

Working didn't kill the time. Prunty took him smuggling. Crossing the Border at night, they made for Rinty Reilly's shop. If the Customs were about they went through the fields.

'Ah, good man yourself,' Reilly said when he saw him, 'I hear tell you hammered a job on Mrs Lee's daughter. Fair play to you, gauson. That'll knock the cock out of their walk.'

They brought south butter and razor blades. A shopkeeper in Dublin was a regular customer. No creed could stop greed. If there was a Border there had to be profit. It was a law of nature.

They wheeled the remaining turf from the bank out to the laneway where it would be just dry enough to get a tractor in. The rick of turf they built looked like a medieval monastic dwelling. 'She's sound for an eternity there,' said Prunty. 'Wind nor rain'll not shift her.'

Coming up to Christmas, as they milked the cows one evening they heard a huge explosion tear the sky apart. The galvanized shed roof tingled. The roosting fowl, necks out, looked from side to side until the night went quiet again. The milk, deeper than sea-shell sounds, whooshed into the lullaby pails.

'That'll be the Customs Post on the back road,' Prunty said. 'I'm surprised she hasn't gone before.'

'Do you think the IRA will ever win?'

'Never. But they'll never lose.'

'What about the Protestants?'

'They'll not lose. But they'll never win.'

'What about the British?'

Clearing his throat he spat behind the cow. 'The British? They'll always be the best-dressed mourners at the funeral.'

There was no electricity in the byre. Light was from a tilley. It spread in a golden circle over the dunged floor, conjured massive shadows, floated the roosting hens in space, merged man and beast in a dark plaster on the old stone walls. There was not much hope for himself and none it seemed for his country. Like fighting swans, necks wrapped, they'd try and drown each other, forever. The swans looked the same, sounded the same, lived on the self-same lake, yet like creatures trapped in a spell they'd divide, fight, kill, rather than share.

'It's like a nest,' Prunty said, 'the scaldies will keep squabblin' among themselves till the cuckoo clears back to London.'

'That'll be the end of smuggling.'

'We'll never live to see it, lad. That's one sure thing.'

The only hope for him was Christmas. Every step he took he could see her face, her pale skin, the sheaf of flaxen hair, the long green coat flying behind her as she ran to greet him. He ached for her in his guts. The pain was physical as well as mental. He could hear her soft voice in his head. 'I'll never call anyone a dirty rat again.'

He bought a Christmas card and posted it to her house. Inside he wrote:

> Look homeward, Angel, now, and melt with ruth:
> And, O ye dolphins, waft the hapless youth.

Since her mother was bound to open it, to confound her he signed it 'Joe Macbeth'.

When he received a letter with a Belfast postmark his heart leapt, his fingers went blind trying to open it.

> ... I'll meet you at Prunty's, Christmas Eve night. If I can. The end is nigh. They have booked my ticket to Toronto. What can we do? What can we do? What can we do?

> > He who binds to himself a Joy
> > Does the winged life destroy;
> > But he who kisses the Joy as it flies
> > Lives in Eternity's sunrise.   Yes? No?

> Annagh – the river they're trying to turn from her natural course – Lee.

When his mother was alive they never left the house over Christmas. His father would expect him home. He'd have to think up some lie to tell. The bigger the better. He just had to be at Prunty's on Christmas Eve.

Prunty told him he was spending Christmas Day with Mrs Kincaid – the widdy woman. 'She's doing the dinner. I've already given her the turkey. You can come if you want.'

'Where will you be the night before?'

'I'll be at midnight mass. Why?'

'Annagh's meeting me here.'

Prunty looked at him, worried for him, but didn't speak.

He was dreaming of a white Christmas. Annagh's white skin beside his own on Mrs Prunty's bed. Drifting snow-flesh piling round their heads, blanketing out reality. Love was a torturing mixture of physical hunger and mental thirst. You had to eat and drink the other person to survive. Lovers were cannibals. It wasn't turkey he wanted. Like a dog who'd tasted sheep, he was hooked on forbidden flesh. Incurable. He'd seen a farmer put a pitchfork on a collie's neck and hold it down in the river until the life went out of it. The dog had attacked sheep. The farmer had to lean with all his might on the poor animal. The dog's neck was pinned to the river bed between the two prongs, but it bucked and splashed and pulled so fiercely it almost knocked the man off his balance. The terrified barking gurgled to an end. He knew now what the dog felt as it hunted the country under a wild moon, crazy for the hot drip of blood. Love was a criminal act.

On Christmas Eve morning he went to the barracks. Guard Ryan had stuck a few sprigs of holly round the day-room – one above the map of the district, one thumb-tacked to a shelf, another dangling through a handcuff.

His father hadn't bothered with holly or decorations. His mother kept the decorations in a tin box on top of the dresser. Getting them down, he opened them out, letting them spill like concertinas to the floor. His mother had lovingly handled them every year for as long as he could remember. But it was as if she had never existed. Things were impervious to people. He hung them from the electric light flex in the middle of the room to each corner. Red, yellow, green and blue paper rainbows spanned the motherless kitchen. It was a defiant gesture, nothing more.

A pile of cards lay on top of the sewing-machine. From relations and friends wishing them both the best for the holy season and the coming year. He stood them up on the machine, along the dresser, the mantelpiece, on top of the wireless, and slotted them behind the Sacred Heart picture so the Dickensian scenes of snow and pudding and carriages and hymn-singers were visible, albeit sideways.

His father came in. 'Hah! When all fruit fails welcome haws.'

'What are we doing for Christmas dinner?'

'If I'd left it up to you we'd be doing sweet damn all. The Widow McGinn has invited us.'

They sat by the range. When the fire began to pull, his father stuck the poker through the bars until the end heated to a black-smith's glow. He poured a bottle of stout, then stuck the poker into the glass. The liquid hissed, smoked, throbbed to silence. After he took the first sip a moustache of froth sat on his upper lip.

They didn't speak. They knew Christmas without his mother was a joke. A miscarriage. The house was freezing. It was colder than Castle Finn. Yet if she hadn't died he'd never have met Annagh.

'It's been the worst year in living memory,' his father said simply.

'They're sending Annagh to Canada.'

'They've got the right idea. There's nothing here.' His father had no idea what she meant to him. Or in his own way he was trying to bluster him from future sorrow. 'Have you thought about America?'

'I have.'

His father drank, feeling the porter in his mouth before swallow-ing, savouring it. In a trance he stared into the glass.

'I hit off myself in May 1923. In the small hours of the morning. Your Uncle Mick, God rest him, drove me in the horse and cart to Grangelawn station. I never told Dada I was going. The eggler in his pony and spring cart came along and I continued with him. Mick and I, we shook hands and it was a bargain as well as goodbye. With Jack gone and me leaving, it meant the homeplace would be his. I got on the train and there was another chap in the compartment. We never spoke one word to each other the whole way to Dublin. The Civil War, you see. In the heel of the hunt wasn't he going to the Depot as well, to join the Force. We spoke when the train pulled into the Broadstone. Why, oh why, didn't I carry on to New York?'

'Because . . .'

'I don't want you to mention Mum. I have men to face and duties to perform.'

He was letting ice ring round his soul, to stop the memory of love breaking through and crippling him. Draining the last of the porter, he rested the glass on the range. 'Aye, bedads.'

'I'm going out this evening. I have to rehearse with the choir for midnight mass.'

'Good enough so.'

When he got back to Prunty's there was berried holly all round the kitchen. Stuck to the tongue-and-groove ceiling were paper bells, orbs, stars, fairies. On the mantel was a free-standing Santa Claus: a cheerful cardboard cut-out with white beard, black sack, red tunic trimmed with tinsel, a bobbled hat and black wellingtons with silvery tops. A stocky figure, it looked somehow like an older version of Prunty.

'Here, lad, happy Christmas. I got your card this mornin'. Ojus nice words. Thanks.' Prunty handed him ten pounds. A present cum wages.

Late in the evening Prunty went out, heading for the pub before going to midnight mass. He had on a dark-blue suit, the trousers bicycle-clipped above brown suede shoes. He was chewing cloves.

He went into the bedroom and knelt in the middle of the floor and appealed to his mother to help him. Then he prayed to Mrs Prunty, the Sacred Heart, the Blessed Virgin and every saint in the room. He was a child again, afraid of the dark.

He sat before the fire, waiting. His stomach was a craving pot of nerves. His hands shook with excitement. All over Ireland children lay listening for bells, their stockings hung hopefully at the ends of their beds. Good hearts were full of goodness. It was one night of the year when the good outweighed the bad. It was a night when love had a chance to root.

He heard her footsteps; her corncraking heels. They were in each other's arms, holding, kissing, squeezing, tearing, necks wrapped, faces buried, time stopped. Blind from emotion, he'd barely looked at her. She was the first to break free. Her face was smiling, her eyes blue stars in a pale sky. She wore a fur hat and coat, a dark two-piece suit. She was supposed to be at mass as well, in Clones. She was cold, the night outside all over her. They sat across the table, holding hands. In her eyes he could see the end. He gave her his copy of *Lycidas*.

'It'll remind you better than a photo. Just in case.'

'They wanted me to marry a solicitor from Enniskillen. I never saw the man before in my life. I just hooted at him. He ran. Honest to God, they're mad. I said I'd go to Canada instead. That way maybe we can meet again.'

'When are you going?'

'The sixth of January.'

'The Epiphany.'

She gave him a scarf, gloves, socks, cufflinks. He couldn't understand why they couldn't be together. Yet he knew his position was forlorn. Young love – every pop record hammered home its hopelessness. But he wasn't going to give in. He had to confront her family properly. He had to be heard. That was the killer – not being listened to.

'The day we swam with Prunty, I'll not forget that day. Our first date at the Luxor – I was so nervous.'

'You could have fooled me.'

She began to sob. He fought back his own tears. He felt they were being slaughtered.

They didn't go into the bedroom. He sat in the armchair, she knelt before him. They felt all over each other, their eyes locked as their hands wandered up and down and in; their mouths and tongues searching deep for the food of life because they knew famine was only round the corner. Their bodies were saying goodbye.

'I love you.'

'I love you.'

To hold another person in your heart; to have your heart jump for joy when you saw them approach; to sit silent together drowning in dreamy thought; to be as careless of the world of politics, guns, religions, borders as a pair of swans – paradise!

He went with her when she had to go. On the way it began to snow. Their bicycle lamps were golden shafts in the dark, swirling with mothy flakes. When the wind spurted the snow riddled the beams like bullets. They had to keep wiping the lamps clean. The snow didn't take on the wet road but the grassy verges turned cotton white, stretching on either side like endless beards. They rode hard, keeping warm, sometimes holding hands. In the scattered houses candles burnt in the windows. He thought of Uncle Jack and the light that never shone for him. A love victim. A pariah. If you couldn't shoot the dog you could starve it. In a farmhouse they heard a fiddle and melodeon play. A young girl and boy sang 'Silent Night' in Gaelic. They stopped and listened, and listening, kissed. Their lips were ice, their tongues cold at first.

'Happy happy Christmas, darling.'

'And a happy New Year?'

'I'll never forget our love. No matter what happens.'

'I'll love you forever and a day. And if they cure death before we die I'll love you all my life.'

They were along a barbed-wire border running between their hearts. He'd have to cross it somehow if he could. A dog barked. They rode on. It was after two o'clock by the time they reached her house.

'I'll see you soon. Promise. Somehow.'

'It's tearing my arms off, my heart out, leaving you.'

'Sssh. Goodbye, darling.'

On his way home the snow stopped. Head into the wind, he rode hard for Butlershill. The country was asleep, the lights out in the houses, the sky dark, the only sound rattling mudguards and sighing tyres. His father had left the door open. He got into bed. There was a hot-water bottle in it. His father had put it there. It was still hot. He put it down on his freezing feet. What did he know, lying under a ton of blankets and police greatcoats? He knew Theorem 29. He knew the Murray was the longest river in Australia. London had Shakespeare, Jonson, Marlowe. Dublin had Joyce, Yeats, Synge, O'Casey. They made ships in Belfast. Heat was transmitted by conduction, convection or radiation. And hot-water bottles. They shot James Connolly blindfold in a chair. Which was decent of them. Newton discovered the laws of gravity. Jesus was a Jew. God was an Irishman. His father was a sergeant. His mother dead. And altogether everything he knew couldn't equal Annagh Lee. A woman was geometry, physics, poetry, all wrapped into one. Love – that was education. Love – life. No love – death? He'd somehow survive Christmas, then go to her house and if they didn't let him in he'd cut his throat on the doorstep. Or something.

The mice raced across the ceiling, their tiny nails tearing into sleep.

20

On St Stephen's Night the Superintendent from Divisional Head-
quarters arrived at the barracks with a film projector. Every year
he put on a show for the policemen's children. This year there
were no children as the men with young families had been trans-
ferred elsewhere. None the less, he insisted on coming into the
kitchen and setting up the 8mm projector. With him was a crony
who was going to perform comic turns. Both men were the worse
for drink. The only audience they had was his father and himself.

'Now Super,' said his father, 'are you sure you want to go to all
this trouble?'

'No trouble at all, Sergeant. And Jim's brought along some
performing fleas.'

The Superintendent kept his hat and overcoat on all the time.
Brown leather gloves stuck out from one of the pockets. He was a
smaller man than his father and had a pot belly. Though clean-
shaven, a heavy black stain of beard was visible on his cheeks.
Because of his hooked nose he was known as 'the Eagle'. His
father had a carefully concealed contempt for him. 'He's under
the regulation height. It was political pull got him in. When Dev
came to power in '33 he changed his tune like a June cuckoo. And
they gave him the Sam Browne belt. He couldn't arrest a blind
beggar.'

The Super set the projector on a card-table and plugged it into
the socket behind the sewing-machine. The crony, Jim, helped
himself to bottles of stout from a crate his father had bought for
Christmas.

The Super spoke with a flat Midlands accent but emphasized
all his -*ing* endings. 'We seem to be get*ting* there. We're plugged
in, yes. What's happen*ing*? Switch her on might help. Yes, *voilà*.'

A frame of light hung empty on the wall.

'Anybody for a wee whip of the old madam?' crony Jim asked, taking a half-bottle of whiskey from his pocket.

The Super fixed a reel to the projector and fed film into its sprockety mouth. A man in baggy trousers, bowler, cane, big feet and a black postage-stamp-sized moustache materialized faintly on the wall.

'Lights out, Jim, please. Sergeant, do take a seat.'

The projector rattled, whirred. A creamy cone of light tunnelled the dark kitchen. People and images escaped out of the end and into the mind. It was the same rag-bag of Charlie Chaplin clips shown every year for as long as he could remember. But every other year his mother was alive. Then, the beam of light conjured magic across a table laden with cakes, buns, lemonade. Then, the kitchen was full of laughing children. Now there were only the two of them.

His father lit a cigarette. The smoke made for the beam, turning the cold kitchen for a moment into a cinema. His father was ill-at-ease. He considered the Superintendent's invasion an insult. 'He's damn well forgotten Mum's dead. The thundering lug. And the other putog he's got with him.' 'Putog' was Irish for 'pudding'.

Charlie Chaplin knew his spot on the damp wall well. He cavorted, grimaced, ran, smiled at girls, escaped the police, made a mockery of authority, just like he did every Christmas. Films were dreams. They took place in the dark like dreams. The screen was the inside of your head. Worlds and time merged, shifted instantaneously. Though they had seen it so often, they still laughed when the tramp woke up in hospital and, noticing the striped pyjamas and iron bars of the bed-head, thought he was in prison. Charlie had an eye for girls, pretty waifs who in the end always headed in the right direction. With their fair hair, big eyes and air of innocence they all looked like Annagh in her slip.

The film purred from one reel to another, finally flapping to an end. When the light was switched back on the kitchen had never looked so tawdry.

'Now, boys and girls, what did you think of *that*?'

'Oh grand, Super, grand altogether,' said his father.

'What did *you* think?'

'My mother couldn't stand Chaplin. "The oul' sheep's head of him. And his dirty 'tache." That's what she used to say. Isn't it, Daddy?'

'Oh, ah, yes. But . . .'

'She never said.'

'No. She wouldn't.'

'You can't beat live entertainment,' said crony Jim, standing up and taking a matchbox from his pocket. 'In here, ladies, I've got two performing fleas. Let me see now, are they awake? Open up and – oh my goodness, ladies, one's got out. Oh. Agh. Itch. Come back here. Where are you, Simon? Get back in immediately. There you are, bold boy. On top of the Sergeant's head. In you go now and don't come out till I tell you. Oh. Agh, the other one's got out. Cyril! Come back here, Cyril. Cyril, where are you?'

It would have been obvious to a baby the fleas were imaginary. But the man didn't have the power to make them live in the imagination. Despite his words, his eyes, his mime, were dead. It was embarrassing.

'Who'd like a drop of tea?' his father interrupted, annoyed that the crony had made fun of him.

'I haven't found Cyril yet, Sergeant.'

'Very entertain*ing*, Jim. Highly entertain*ing*.'

The crony sat, disgruntled. 'You need a live audience.'

'Or live fleas.' They looked at him. His father laughed.

The whiskey and stout finished, the Super wobbled to his feet. 'Well, Sergeant, that was an enchant*ing* even*ing*. Thank you.'

'No, thank *you*, sir.'

'Call me Eugene, Sergeant, it's Christmas. Come on, Jim.'

Carrying the projector and reels they left. As they were going out of the door his father, with thumb and index finger, placed an imaginary flea on the crony's head. 'Don't go without your friend Cyril. His family would miss him when you go to bed tonight.' His father guffawed, pleased he'd given as good as he'd got. Because of his own sense of dignity, yet uncertainty, he could never easily take a joke.

His father stood in front of the fire, brooding. Then he began to growl about the Super and the 'head-buck-bummers' who promoted him. 'General O'Duffy made them all. And they stabbed him in the back.'

O'Duffy had been the first Commissioner of the Garda until de Valera sacked him. He formed the Blueshirts, a movement with the trappings of European Blackshirts and Brownshirts, but at heart the failed politics of the Civil War. A priest at school told

226

the class about him – 'He was a good man. But a little misguided.'
After Collins he was his father's hero. All his heroes were fallen.

'At the big rally where he was arrested, he says to the arresting
Superintendent, "Go 'way, you cur. I put that Sam Browne belt
on you."' His father spat the words, heaping them with contempt,
hitting them as if he were punching his political opponents.
Aloud, he nursed old grievances, suckling them, dragging them
out once more into the light for re-examination.

'If I'd wanted, if I'd pushed, I'd be wearing the Sam Browne
today. If I'd your education it's more than three stripes I'd have.
I got the Scott Medal – what did the Eagle ever get? A well-
feathered nest.' He sat on the edge of the old armchair. 'How is
it, why, why do all the wrong people come out on top? Answer
me that, will you?'

'It only appears that way from the bottom.'

'What? Are you bleddywell saying we're at the bottom?'

'No, Daddy, but ... O'Duffy went off to fight for Franco,
didn't he?'

'And why wouldn't he? Franco was on God's side.'

'I think maybe he liked civil wars – that's why he went.'

'Go 'way outa that, you don't know what the hell you're talking
about. Clear off to bed and don't be annoying me.'

'No. Why should I?'

'No? Oh, I see. Think you're a big man now, do you? Go 'way
before I lockjaw you, Christmas or no Christmas.'

Sick in the stomach, he watched his father boil with frustration
and self-disgust. Of course he was a better policeman than the
Eagle. But so what? You made your own destiny, didn't you?

'You tell me how to run my life? You who already, God help
us, have made a botch of your own?'

'How have I?'

'Hah? Go 'way, man. You've been looking for a cross to climb
up on since the day you were born.'

'What? Pardon?'

'If that's how she reacts over a rat, it doesn't say much for her
prospects, does it?'

The rat had drawn blood. He was trying to do the same. He was
implying Annagh's womb wasn't sound, couldn't be counted on.
His father had wanted lots of children. He believed numbers were a
bulwark against misfortune. Instead all his eggs were in one basket.
Him. His mother's womb hadn't been completely rat-proof.

His father's tongue could hurt so easily. But he was like a bee stinging – he destroyed himself as well. He wasn't going to sit around being stung. There were always old bones to be chewed over. The Famine, the Civil War, de Valera, the IRA ... it wasn't history to his father. It was a highly personal unresolved past, colouring the present, shadowing the future. To hell with old bones. He wasn't that hungry. He had new bones to chew.

He cleared the empty bottles into the crate. 'I'm going to bed. Goodnight, Daddy.'

'Oh, going now are you? Go on then.'

He left him sitting in the armchair, staring into the dead fire. His father, concerned, shouted after him, 'There's a bleddy rat in the hen-house. Set a trap for it in the morning, will you? I saw it yesterday when I locked up.'

Next morning he cleared off early, back to Prunty's. Christmas was over. In peace, he could now plot to see Annagh. With luck, thwart Fate. Maybe they could run away. To England. London. They could get a room. A job. And at least he'd be able to watch Spurs play at White Hart Lane.

'If you're goin' to run away you'll need more money nor you've got,' said Prunty. 'We better sell that turf.'

A few days later Monkey Sexton came with the tractor and trailer and slowly they bumped down the laneway to the bog. Prunty, holding on to the wheelguards, stood on the tractor behind Sexton.

He was in the bouncing trailer, looking out through the wooden bars. Prunty turned and looked at him, his face dancing as he poked out his tongue at the back of Sexton's head and made faces at him. Prunty, riding along on the back of the tractor, had the same jaunty air as on horseback when he met him on the road to the knacker's yard. A lot had happened in the meantime. But worse was still to come.

Sexton swung off the laneway on to the turfy ground. The wheels made tracks which soon filled with water. The heather and grassy scraws were oozy sponge. When they jumped down, dark water seeped round their feet. The bog was winter grey on top and bubbling silently from deep down in its blackened heart.

'Better not go too far in or we'll never get her out,' said Prunty.

'She'll be all right here fornenst the rick. When we've got her loaded I can swing round across the heather there. She'll grip no bother.'

228

The ground they were on was higher than the ground immediately ahead. The ground ahead, cut away over the years, was about four feet lower. A boggy drain separated the two levels. The tractor faced the lower level, about three feet from the edge.

They loaded the trailer. It was an effort to throw the sods up over the crated sides. They landed on the wooden floor, thud, then changed their tune, as the trailer filled, to a brittle scratchy rat-note.

'If we don't sell it at one go, we'll sell it by the bag. From house to house.'

He and his father didn't have the knack of making money. Prunty did. Making money was an art-form, Prunty an artist. As the crated sides grew darker he began to feel better about the future. Maybe he'd have enough money for himself and Annagh to escape. The people in the town would have burnt their fuel over Christmas. Dead on cue he and Prunty would arrive. Demand – supply – cash.

They threw the last sods on. The trailer was full, the load a rising mound above the sides. Perfect. 'Didn't I tell you, lad? I knew rightly. One for luck,' Prunty said, flinging up the very last sod.

Sexton, at the front of the tractor, swung the starting-handle. The engine wouldn't catch. He tried several times, bending, jerking, groaning. His wellingtons were gashed at the heels. His feet squelched when he walked. At the controls he fiddled with the gear-stick and a switch.

'I'll swing her,' said Prunty. 'Check the choke. And she's not in gear.'

Prunty, a hand resting on the engine, bent, gripped the handle and swung. The engine spluttering, catching, lurched forward. Prunty desperately tried to get out of the way. But for the few seconds he had, his mind was fatally split. As well as trying to escape he half-tried to push back on the tractor to stop it going over the edge. The engine ploughing on, it plummeted down into the drain, Prunty crushed beneath it. It was all over in a wink. The end of the trailer, at a crazy angle, was still on the bank, but on the lower level the weight of the tractor was on Prunty's chest. Hopelessly, in madness, he and Sexton tried with their bare hands to pull the whole lot back up. It was Sexton's fault. The fool had put the tractor in gear when he was asked to check.

He jumped down on to the lower level. Only Prunty's head, shoulders and upper part of his chest were visible. It looked as if he were planted deep in the earth. His eyes were open, his face a grimace of pain. The ground was soft. He tore into it with his hands, his soul in frenzy.

'Coco. Coco.'

Prunty was only in the bog because of him. He was selling the turf to give him money. It was his fault, not Sexton's. He gouged at the wet ground, his arms going in up to the elbows.

Sexton ran out the laneway to look for help. As he dug with his hands the bog came easily away in big dark clots. He felt something hard. Prunty was pinned between the tractor and a submerged tree stump. His back was probably broken. He was being crushed to death, slowly, in the brown soaking turf. His head lolled to one side.

'Coco, don't die.'

He held Prunty's freckled hand, threw himself down, put his face to his to comfort him, to show him above all he cared. At the hour of death, if it was the hour of death, to show he loved him. He began to say an Act of Contrition in his ear. 'O my God I am heartily sorry . . .' But as at the death of his mother, he couldn't continue. Tears were gulging out of him. His body shook. He was crying out loud in the empty wilderness, frightened, trying to scare Death away.

The front wheels were in the drain, the water black as porter. The end of the trailer rested on the bank above, its wheels in space. The big back wheels of the tractor were just above the water. If the tow-bar had snapped the engine would have sunk back in the drain and he might have been able to release Prunty. But the tow-bar and lynch-pin were the strongest parts of what was otherwise a shambles of a trailer.

Prunty's eyes opened and shut, his face twisted. The engine sagged, settling deeper in the bog. Prunty gasped for air, his breathing short and rattling. His hands went out to the tractor as if he were trying one last push to free himself.

'There's help coming, Coco. Hang on.'

His hands fell limp. His head hung sideways again.

'Don't die, Coco.'

Time was in an agony of slow motion. The nightmare event zoomed in and out, clear and confused, like the image on the kitchen wall as the Superintendent focused the film. Long grey grass hung over the edge of the bank, the turf gleaming beneath like wet chocolate. A crow, a big spud wedged in its beak, flew over, wings flapping in panic trying to support its greed.

Where the hell was Sexton, with his torn wellingtons and stupid cap on his fool of a head? Why were disasters stacking up? Life was an evil rick. Was it because of his love for Annagh Lee? Nonsense. If Sexton didn't come back soon he'd have to go and search for the stupid bastard. Prunty was wearing an old Butlershill football jersey. The scapular stuck out over the collar. It was the same colour as turf. He went dead in his arms, his head hanging back. He must be dead. No. He was still breathing, wheezing, his big chest panting. Strong as an ox, he was trying to hold on to life.

'I love you, Coco.' He did love him. They had shared everything like brothers, even the bed. Prunty had shown him the country but it was only now that its meaning was becoming clear.

'I'm done for . . . am I, lad?' The words squeezed out in hoarse groans.

'I'm sorry, I'm sorry. It's my fault. You came here for me. I'm sorry Coco . . .'

His words dribbled out, useless. They couldn't match the loaded angle of tractor and trailer, hanging over the edge like big toys, still, curious, berserk. He would never be able to rip from his brain Prunty's attempt to stop the tractor and save himself . . . Legs straddled, he hopped backwards, face surprised, desperately trying to get out of the way, to jump clear at the last moment. The tractor's engine cut out as it plunged over. Prunty fell before it, facing it, arms spread, fingers open. His arms flailed as if he were trying to fly.

At least he wasn't impaled by the starting-handle. Not that it made much difference.

He heard an engine and shouts. Men came running in the laneway and down the hill from the direction of the house. At last help was on hand. He could see a lorry coming. A spot of blood oozed from the corner of Prunty's mouth.

'Please, God, please. Don't.'

The sky was an endless sheet, grey as wild geese. Men pulled him off Prunty. He didn't know who they were. Sexton was looking at him. If Prunty was going to die he didn't want to be there when sleepy Death shut his eyes. As if he were only a hare, a lark, a rat in a trap. He wanted to do something. The boy who could cure bleeding . . . the knacker's yard . . . He ran for the house, over the drumlins, his legs heavy, his heart in tatters. On Mrs Prunty's old bike he tore down to the pub at Legakelly where they let him use the telephone. He remembered the number on the gate – 'Phone Currinstown 10'.

The woman, Bella, answered. He told her what had happened, calming himself just enough to speak. Could the boy who had the cure for bleeding come immediately? He'd wait for them at the pub . . .

He waited. He could have told them how to get to the house or into the bog but he didn't want to go back on his own. Not if Prunty closed his eyes . . . for good. That he couldn't bear to see. His wrists hurt. The men had had to tear him from Prunty's neck. There was a piece of collar in his hand. Prunty's football jersey. He hadn't wanted to let go. He could remember that much. In his head the events were whirring, tumbling, the tractor and loaded trailer plunging, Prunty scattering backwards, his body and face crucified in space. How could he live through it all? Why wasn't Annagh with him . . . for help, for comfort?

Bella pulled up in a Morris Minor. Beside her was the Goblin, in the back the boy. In the boy's hand was a porringer. When he sat in beside him he saw a small blue crucifix with a white body lying on the bottom of the aluminium porringer. The locals pronounced it 'ponger'.

'You got a nice girlfriend anyway. Like I told you. Trust in God. For the light shines from Him who is the sun,' said Bella, driving dangerously, looking back at him over her shoulder. The boy didn't speak. His eyes were shut in prayer, his bright red lips moving silently.

'Brave country up this way,' remarked the Goblin in his piping voice, his head just above the dashboard. 'Frost was so bad last night it killed a frog on our doorstep, didn't it Bella? Bad sign that.'

They got to the house as they were carrying Prunty in on the trailer tailboard. His hands flopped over the sides. He was dead. The boy held the blue crucifix aloft. The faces of the men carrying Prunty were grim. Sexton, shocked, kept on shaking his head.

They put Prunty on his mother's bed. The Goblin and the boy stood watching. The boy handed the Goblin a curved dagger with black rosary beads wrapped round the blade. There was blood on Prunty's mouth. Dried.

The boy shook his head. 'Crushings, crashes, guns, I'm not able for. Them's 'ospital cases, sir. It has to be natural bleeding. Illness, himridge or disaze. What God gives, God can cure.'

'He's dead as a maggot anyways,' whispered the Goblin.

'I riz the dead the onest,' said the boy.

Outside, Bella spoke to him. 'It wouldn't be lucky nor right to ask for a donation. Seeing he was dead when we come. If you want your fortune telling, come to the house, young fellah.'

'I know what it is,' he said bitterly, 'if the past and present are a judge.'

'You know nawthin'. God has got you in His pocket.'

He went into the byre and sat on a milking stool. Cry the word and you killed it. But it was no use shouting 'Death'. He began to shake. Then he went cold and still. Stony. Lark, hare, stone . . . he was turning into a stone. For the first time he was afraid. Afraid of himself, afraid for himself. Blindly wandering, he walked through a field to the lake. At the water's edge he stood confused, not knowing why he was there. Lycidas was a student drowned in the Irish Sea. If Prunty was a ghost, he could see him from the house. The first thing Prunty did in the morning was to look out at the lake and tell the weather from what he saw. 'Do you know what, lad, there's goin' to be a week of boilers?' Or if it was going to rain, 'There'll be enough of the wet stuff to float an ark.' Prunty was dead. Dead? How could he believe it? Throwing himself down, he began to wail and tear with his fingers at the rock and muddy shore.

21

The wake was strange. The house was filled with people, most of them claiming to be Prunty's next-of-kin. A tall red-haired man established himself as chief mourner. He said he was an 'uncle by marriage once removed.' The relatives were lining up to rob the corpse. There was a house and farm and cursed bog up for grabs. King Prunty had no heirs. Members of the football team came to pay their respects. The boys they went dancing with at the Free-masons' Hall in Clones arrived. Their bicycles lay thick and tangled against the gable-end of the house. The boys they fought turned up as well. 'We won't see his likes again,' said Grunter Howe. 'That's for sartain,' agreed the Scud Gillespie. They all looked stunned. The entire district was shocked by Prunty's death, and by the way it happened. When the boys knelt at the end of the bed to say a prayer, Grunter Howe faced the wrong way.

In the kitchen men talked in subdued voices. The Rock and the Stumps arrived; as soon as they managed to get into the bedroom, side by side they began to sing a hymn – 'To Jesus' Heart All Burning'. From every room and from the yard outside people joined in the singing until the air throbbed and the walls seemed to shake with sweet, swelling grief. It was a hypnotic moment. Prunty's head was visible in the open coffin, the blond hair slicked back, his face a mask. A stone. His hands had been joined round a big black crucifix which stuck out at an angle from his fingers. The freckles on his face were faded. Two men stood at the head of the coffin, their hands behind their backs. It looked as if they were standing to attention. One of them was Dandy Cusack, the other he didn't know. He couldn't understand why they were there, standing guard.

That night he went to Castle Finn and asked Sophie Kay to get in touch with Annagh and tell her what had happened.

'Sure. Relax. Take it easy. I'll do it.'

She begged him to come in for a drink but he couldn't. He was too unhappy, shell-shocked. He slept in the hay shed. He had to get away from all the people crowding the house. He slept on the hay brought home by Prunty and himself and Annagh.

Next day, when the coffin was carried out into the hearse for the journey to the chapel, it was draped in a tricolour. The green, white and orange flag was a shock. 'He must have been in the RA,' the Rock said from the corner of his mouth.

That was it. Prunty all the time had been a secret Republican, in what precise capacity he'd never know. He had lived with him for months, slept in the same bed, and Prunty never once as much as hinted. Along the Border tongues were stone. 'Don't say anything – till you hear more.' That's why his father didn't want him to have anything to do with Prunty. His father knew. Maybe Prunty had used his friendship as a shield. The Sergeant's son in the house – what better protection? It was enough to drive you insane. It was definitely some kind of betrayal. Yet when he asked that time how you joined the IRA, why hadn't Prunty encouraged him? He must have been protecting him. He must have cared something for him. Prunty was right – he knew he couldn't beat his way out of a wet paper bag. Maybe that's why Prunty wouldn't let him join? He was protecting the movement from a useless recruit. The Sergeant's son – he could turn out a spy ... Prunty was his best-ever friend ... But surely a friend would ... he tried not to ponder it out. His whole being was wrecked. Anyway, deep down, maybe he was using Prunty. Lying low with him, walking in his shadow until he learnt to fly ...

They walked behind the hearse along the narrow roads, just as they had done at the removal of Mrs Prunty's remains. It was the same murmury-leathery shuffle but the atmosphere was different – deep, sombre. A young person had died tragically. A life had been wasted. Crowds waited at the chapel. Among them he saw the farmer whose pig he'd blessed. He stood stout, clean, in an old shiny blue suit.

The funeral next day was the biggest he'd ever seen. Members of the football team shouldered the coffin to the graveyard. He took his turn, carrying it at the front, the priest in surplice and soutane, flanked by altar-boys, walking on before them. Way below the countryside lay watery green. The whins on the nearby hills were bare and black from burning. In the distance across the valleys, Cuilcagh mountain wore a cap of snow. The frosty air came into the lungs pure, cold, sharp as a blade.

In the graveyard his father stood watching, alongside him the Superintendent. Among the crowds, standing between the Colonel and Sophie Kay, was Annagh Lee. Christ, she didn't look all that well; she looked even paler than usual. But his heart was lifted all the same. The tricolour, that potent flag, was removed from the coffin and neatly folded by a young girl. Maybe there never was a widdy woman. Maybe the widdy woman was political business. He would never know for certain, and nobody would ever say. One way or another Prunty had joined Maguire, the Chieftain, who stalked the land looking for his lost kingdom. They lowered the coffin. Clay from a shovel hit the lid with a scattery thud. The people prayed as one, their voices in a seashell chant, rising, swooning, breaking in a holy wave across the headstones. He was fed up with funerals.

At the end he went away with Annagh, the two of them sobbing, clinging together on the back seat of the Colonel's car. It was their funeral too. At least he knew what he had to do. There were no options. He had nothing left to lose except Annagh. He was going to her house. Now. Before it was too late. Before they both cracked under the pressure.

'It's no good now. She's not there, Mammy.'

'I'll go tomorrow evening then.'

'All right, darling, I'll tell them.'

Back in Prunty's he sat alone on the bed. In the kitchen the relations were plotting in low voices. The tall red-haired man came into the room. 'Gauson, you'll not be fit for to stay here any more. You can have tonight, but then . . . you know.'

'Who'll milk the cows?'

'They'll be milked. Don't fret about that.'

A woman gave him a mug of tea and a hunk of stale bread and jam. She didn't speak. They wanted rid of him. On top of the wardrobe the hames rested at its angle against the wall. Lyre. Prunty was a lyre. And a liar. When he was in bed that night, they came into the room searching for valuables. In the morning he put the game-cock spurs in his pocket.

Out at the back a hen stood miserably on one leg. The cat stared from a clump of bushes. The cows had come down to the fence, waiting for Prunty to come and drive them to the byre for milking.

He went up the hill and down to the bog. On the upper bank the ground was rutted deep by the wheels of the lorry and tractors they had used to pull Sexton's trailer and tractor up out of the drain. A cigarette packet floated in a rainy track. The edge of the bank was gouged and broken. On the lower bank he could see the impression Prunty's body had made in the turf. A smooth groove, bodied-in deep, back as far as the now exposed stump. But for the stump, he would surely have lived. The stump was black bog oak thousands of years old. A killer tree. The bog held man's secrets. Prunty had shown him the Black and Tan's grave. He went over to it. Green and yellow moss and grass grew over a mound of stones. Prunty the secret Republican and the Black and Tan from another age were opposites. But the bog had balanced them out. They were wrapped in the final flag of green grass, black turf, blue sky. Green for earth and Ireland. Black for death. Blue for hope.

On the secret spot where he and Annagh first made love he prayed for them all. For himself. He was frail, hungry, his nerves on edge. He could easily shatter like a splintering mirror.

Back in the house the tall red-haired man and helpers humped furniture out on to an open lorry, parked along the road. Two women sat at a table drinking whiskey. They looked at him as he went into the bedroom to collect his bits and pieces. When he came back out one of them said to him, 'It's not that we need any of this stuff. It's just we don't want the tinkers to get it. You know.'

Heart breaking, he left them to it and walked away. He just couldn't accept Prunty's death. He went along the road slowly, hardly knowing where he was heading. That evening he had to get to Annagh's. He slept in a hay shed ... where they'd often slept together.

It was dark when he woke up. By the light of a match he looked at his watch. Five o'clock. He lay smoking, careful not to set the hay aflame. It would take him a few hours to walk to Annagh's. He was cold, hungry, in need of a wash. From an overflowing water barrel he wet his face, dipped his comb, dragged it through his hair.

Cars passed him on the road and though he stuck his thumb out none stopped. One car slowed as if the driver was studying him. Because of the dark he couldn't make out who it was or what they looked like. He had an idea he knew the car. A Volkswagen.

Where had he seen it before? The Fermanagh registration . . .
Then he remembered. Annagh's uncle dropped her outside the
cinema on their first date. That was a Volkswagen. It could have
been her uncle. Why had he slowed down? Did he recognize him?
If Annagh hadn't told them he was on the way, they'd know now.

The clouds cleared. A sliver of moon showed in a sky of stars.
It made the walking easier. Her house was down a by-road,
tucked away in gentle country. He could hear the dog bark as he
turned off the main road. He went on, hoping for miracles. That
Prunty's death would soften them towards him. They'd surely
understand his pain. People weren't monsters. They knew he
loved her. Could they guarantee that of any other man?

A small garden gate led up the path to the hall door. Before
you got to that there was a big gate leading into the farmyard.
The dog was in the yard, barking furiously. He stopped, hoping
to calm it, show he wasn't a prowling enemy. He couldn't see it
but it was very close. Probably just inside the yard wall, which
struck him as odd. Why wasn't it at the gate itself?

The dark bulk of men reared all round him. A flashlamp shone
in his face.

'That's the dirty bastard all right.'

His eyes swimming he tried to run, but they were on to him,
tearing him to the ground, rolling him over to the high grassy
verge. Someone kicked him. A man lay across him, his arm along his
neck, ready to choke him if necessary. In the night form and shadow
danced gigantic shapes. He was terrified. 'Stop. Quit. Help!'

A hand went over his mouth. He smelt tar. No. Not that. Holy
God, they were going to tar and feather him. His danglers. The
uncle, the nephews, the whole gang of them. He couldn't tell how
many of them milled about his body.

'Yah dirty scut, you won't show up here again.'

'Yah dirty fucker. Stick him.'

'Stick the pig and have done with it.'

He tried to kick as they pulled his jeans down his legs. Despite
the mayhem he heard the zip; felt crude fingers all over his skin.
The night was freezing but he could feel sweat running down his
back. They daubed his dangler with a coarse brush of some kind.
Feathers fell like snow. A man laughed. He was sure he heard a
woman's laughter too. It was a sound to break your soul. A huge
man towered over him. In the starlight he saw a blade flash. A
pig knife.

238

'Next time we'll cut them off yah.'

'Yah dirty little hoor-master.'

'Yah fucker. Fuck off now.'

The tar was hot but it didn't burn. His jeans were round his ankles. The faces disappeared. He heard a door shut. The dog stopped barking. They were gone, but the sweaty smells of them lingered. Getting to his feet, too shocked to cry, he stumbled back towards the Cavan road. How was he going to cleanse himself? How could you remove tar? It didn't matter anyway because his mind was going. His nerves. It was all over. Annagh was over . . . dried up, diverted, geography changed . . . He was finished. His mind was dark with rage and murderous revenge. It was no good. He hadn't the strength to stick a thorn in a balloon. He thought his body was shaking. But he couldn't be sure. He wandered, fainted, came to in light, hid in sheds, drank from a wayside spring, got bread from a woman when he bumped into her door. In his head were the faces of his friends at school. Sitting at desks, getting on with books. What would Father Austen say if he saw him now? He sensed he was having a breakdown. The men coming out of the night, attacking him, desecrating the secret part of him, the lover's part, was so horrible he assumed he would soon lie down and die. From shock, shame, grief. They had destroyed his humanity, turned him into an animal.

He wandered the country, clipped, shorn, confused, like a bedraggled game-cock who'd escaped the death pit but was going to die anyway. He got the whiff of Annagh in his brain when he went past places he seemed to know. He tried to wash himself by a lake. The water ran off the tar. He needed oil. Butter. That's what his mother rubbed on his hands when he got tar from the summer roads. He may as well die naked. Where was his father?

Walking up a hill, through freezing grass, not knowing how many days he wandered, he tore his clothes off. There was a shed on top of the hill. A shelter for cattle. As good a place as any in which to die. He knew his soul was ill . . .

22

The cell was both confessional-box and torture chamber. He confessed to himself. Tortured himself. The events, on a loop in his mind, ran non-stop. The same faces, the same actions presented themselves, gripped him all day and most of the night. Sleep was a dream of broken headstones, rats, dog-faced men pouring unstoppable tar over him. He tried to die. Funerals came in threes.

He'd had his – mother, Mrs Prunty . . . Prunty. You couldn't go a second before your time. You were a part of time. It was annoying. Sometimes he'd look at his tall, pale body, trying to understand why it wouldn't snap. On his upper arm there was still the faint trace of a love-bite . . .

His father let him out once a day to the lavatory, escorting him, waiting outside until he'd finished. It was the final irony; imprisoned by his own father. Maybe it wasn't an irony. All people in relationships imprisoned one another.

'You're not getting out of here until I say you're ready.'

'If I'm imprisoned so are you.'

'No danger of your tongue being sick. If you want anything – shout.'

He shouted in the night for Annagh Lee. Guard Ryan, in his pyjamas, looked in the peep-hole. He could smell the porter on his breath.

'You'll be all right, boyo. Love is like the drink. There's withdrawal symptoms. A few more days and the bloodstream will run clean. I'm telling you, I know.'

'Do you know about getting your danglers done with tar? And the bastards getting away with it? I'm going crazy in here, angry.'

'It happened across the Border, boyo, what can we do?'

'If Prunty was alive . . .'

'Prunty, let me tell you, boyo, was on a short rope. He'd have come a cropper sooner or later. Butter wasn't the only thing he smuggled.'

'I don't believe you.'

'Rock bottom he was their eyes and ears.'

'Nothing he saw or heard or passed on was worse than what was done to me. They held me down in the dark of the road and defiled me. I went out of love and they gave me hate. Black tar and chicken feathers. I suppose they ate the chicken for dinner.'

'You're alive, boyo. That's the main thing.' He shut the peep-hole.

His father gave him blankets and a uniform greatcoat to keep warm. The rat ate steadily through the carbolic soap. The rat would soon be back in the cell.

On the hill behind the police station he heard lowing cows. Each evening at the same time their owner whistled them from the field gate. He didn't have to round them up with stick and dog. They came when called, milk dribbling from their huge udders. He heard the whistle of the evening train pulling out for Ballyhaise and Cavan. When he came home from school on holidays, his mother waited on the platform. She was always there. Her lips always warm. Her hot smell – body, heat, powder – was still in a corner of his brain. But howling through his skull was the primrose perfume, apple whiff, creamy heat of Annagh. At least she was alive. Somewhere. Maybe one day they'd meet again. Miracles did happen. The boy with the cure for bleeding said he'd once raised the dead. Bet he didn't have the cure for bleeding hearts ... Love was a sickness. A heavy disease. A plague. Only time could heal it. But you'd always carry the scar. Maybe like bleeding or the secret ingredient for game-cocks there was a deathbed cure. One way or the other that was certainly true.

He was tearing between Prunty's death and the loss of Annagh. One he could have been able to cope with. Perhaps. The two crushed his spirit. Escaping one, his mind went straight to the other. Their voices echoed round the cell. He was ripping in two.

Dr Langan came to examine him. A tall, black-haired, smooth man, he had come home from working in English city hospitals to make his fortune among the rural poor of Butlershill. He lived in a big house, drove a big car, had a big wife. There was money in poverty. The best emigrated. Only the worst came back.

'I can tell by your face you don't like me. You don't have to.

241

I'm paid per examination, not per my personality as you perceive it.'

A stethoscope hanging out of his big ears, he listened in to his heart and lungs.

'You've been a very foolish young man.'

'I suppose I'd better ask why?'

'With your education you ought to know.'

'What?'

'There's the body and the body politic. And to me they are one and the same. Damage one, you damage the other. That's why we have laws and religion. You've transgressed all sexual mores. Ethics we call it. You and Miss Lee. I know her mother. She's not as bad as she's painted. Believe me.'

'You know her? Will you give her a message? Please.'

'Yes. Of course. What?'

'Tell her to go fuck herself. I'm still alive. I'm still in love. Tell her that.'

'No wonder they don't want anything to do with you. You can't run amok forever, you know. Reality is a border. You're bound to run up against it sooner or later. Do you understand what I'm trying to tell you?'

'I do.'

'You do? Well that's something. I've seen it in England. Please believe me. The sick filth of some lives. God help us all. Any rate you're sound as a bell. Physically. You've inherited that from your father's line, no doubt. Are you all right for a few bob?'

'I am, thanks.'

'Good. Good. Bit of a chicken coop this, eh? I'm going to see an old codger broke his hip. Care to come along? You can if you wish.'

'I can't.'

'Why not?'

'I have to get more tar off my balls. And out of my pubes. And my dangler. You haven't got a prescription for that, have you?'

The doctor stared at him and without answering left the cell.

He could understand Father Gaynor going on about sexual mores. But what the hell had it to do with a doctor? Witch doctor. What were sexual mores anyway? A brush and tar and feathers . . . no one mentioned them.

High-heels corncraking on the tiles outside the cell. Tilly Robert's face at the peep-hole, a rectangular miniature of sharp prettiness. She had a Bible for him and a pound of butter. She must have come to annoy his father. Her evangelical rantings were anathema. Her wild words whirled round the barracks like hailstones. 'This is your Damascus, sweetheart. Release him. Hath not the potter power over the clay, of the same lump to make one vessel unto honour and another unto dishonour?'

'Get that bleddy woman out of here, Ryan,' his father shouted from the safety of his office.

'Amen I say unto you we are the vessels of wrath fitted to destruction.'

'Thanks for the butter, Tilly.'

'I know rightly what you need, sweetheart. I've attended these cases before. Amen amen I say unto you . . .'

'Get her *out*.' The office door scraped open. Tilly fled laughing.

The butter was smuggled. Butter was made in the South. Exported North. There by some strange economic law it was half the price. How could this be? The same butter. You had to smuggle to keep sane.

He sat on the edge of the solid bunk fingering the butter on to himself; rubbing, wiping, picking the tar off his flesh. The butter turned black and oily. It was a mess. He smelt like a rancid tar barrel. But it worked. Slowly. Tilly's mad, smiling eyes in the peep-hole made him smile for the first time in weeks. He'd tried to kiss her once . . . felt the swish of her hair on his face . . .

His father looked in and saw him naked. Shocked, he slammed the peep-hole shut. 'Jesus, Mary and Joseph.'

Had you the run of the country? Or did the country have the run of you? You ended up in it . . . or your ashes were scattered over it. A harsh country made a harsh people. Yet some days it looked cruelly beautiful, even when it rained. Love sprouted among rocks, grew in ditches, rose out of briars. It was always there. And people kept on coming. Thoughts were air. You couldn't see them. You could only write them down, bottle them on paper. Annagh said once, towards the end, she was losing the run of herself. That's what happened to him. He cracked. Would he crack again? Maybe not. Maybe from now on the tenderest part of him would turn to stone. He'd look on the world flint-eyed. Like his father . . .

The rat ate its way back in, and was soon joined by a partner. He woke up one morning and saw them gnaw the upper of his big boot. His father let him out of the cell. He stayed in his room, never went out.

The Widow McGinn brought him his dinner. She was a plump woman, rosy-cheeked with greying, permed hair. She had a country face, weathered, smiling, attractive. Her wedding finger half-full with rings. She had no children and would have none now. She was in her fifties.

'Your daddy asked me something.'

'What did he ask you, Mrs McGinn?'

'He asked me to go to the altar with him.'

'You said no of course.'

She laughed. 'I did. I like the single life. He's a fine man your father, but.'

'God preserve us from fine men.'

He read his books. But he could never go back to them in the confines of a school. He had sported with Amaryllis in the hay shed and with the tangles of Neaera's hair. Milton's classical strictures couldn't compare with one loving turn in a ditch. Old John was another fine man no doubt. He read his father's law books – *The Irish Constable's Guide* (1923), *A Digest of the Law of Evidence* by the late Sir James Fitzjames Stephen, Bart., KCSI, DCL. *Crime And Its Detection*, Volume 1, edited by W. Teignmouth Shore (1932). In the latter book a section dealing with the difference between men and women as witnesses was underlined in puce pencil. Women were skilful liars when protecting a lover. They were more primitive in their instincts but had more vision . . . his father saw him reading it. In the west of Ireland, as a detective, he had worked on a murder case where the chief suspect was a woman.

'She poisoned the hubbie. She lived up a mountain. In a half-hovel. I surprised her at all hours of the day and night, trying to get her with her defences down. But she wouldn't confess. The bitch. I couldn't crack her. I knew it was her. Guilty as sin. One night I went out to her house and so she wouldn't hear me coming, I walked up the mountain in my bare feet. I wanted to catch her asleep. To try and understand what made her tick. You can tell from a face asleep if they've got a troubled conscience. I got up there at three o'clock in the morning. She was waiting on me. Up waiting. She said she'd dreamt I was coming to see her. Oh, the witch. Heaven help any poor man in the clutches of an evil female.'

His father was frightened of strong women. He'd married someone soft as butter.

Strong women were considered odd. Lady Sarah ... Tilly Roberts with her Old Testament tongue ... Mrs Lee wasn't strong. She was mad. It was her laugh he heard when they tarred and feathered him. You couldn't get madder than that. Mad and horribly weak.

Annagh was strong. When she made love her eyes held him, gave him secret instructions, until she was ready to splash and melt like honey on a hot stone. She was a deep river. He had drowned in her, then been fished out and left half-eaten on the bank. Otters had two legs, wore hats, went to church on Sundays, broke the law on Mondays.

One morning through his open window he smelt spring. Down the garden a primrose flowered in the hedge. A primrose was common as the sky. Man had looked on both forever. When he was dead, man would carry on looking at them. Eyes no longer looked. Eyes to come would look. Forever. The primrose had green wrinkled, warty leaves, frail pale-yellow flowers.

He knew he was better. It was a sad moment. Life forced you to sprout again. Forced you up through the moody clay. You were a second in the ticking of the country clock. A mere second. But you were needed. Seconds made Time. Forever. Larks were killed by kestrels. Hares were killed by dogs. Stones lay in the belly of the earth or under water. Forever. He'd go to America a stone.

On the kitchen table his father laid out the forms he had to fill. They were a confusing jumble of bureaucratic nonsense.

'I wish it was me going,' his father said, a shy, earnest smile round his mouth.

'You'll be able to get married with me out of the way.'

'What? What the hell are you driving at?'

'You asked Mrs McGinn to marry you. Now who hasn't waited the full mourning year?'

'Get away, man, and have a styme of sense. I only asked her to keep her happy. To pretend I cared. To keep the food coming. I knew damn well she'd say no. I'm not a jackass entirely. You have to soft-soap women. If you think I'm going to bring another woman into this house, well let me tell you – you're wrong-shipped. A barren woman? I thought you knew me better than I know meself?'

Of course. His father would never take seriously a woman who couldn't have children. His father was slow but cunning, always one step ahead.

'Anyways why should you worry? You never asked me, consulted me about your Annagh. Why should I tell you anything? What business is it of yours? Do you think I should go on living until I die alone? Hah?'

'No. No, I suppose not.'

'Well then. I loved like you. And I lost as well. Mum. I know what you've been through. I know it in my heart and soul. The way things are, to be tarred and feathered in this part of the world is to be a class of hero. You'll never be forgotten. What with that and blessing the pig. Hah?'

He signed the papers. His father's eyes gleamed.

'Thank God. You won't know yourself beyant. This place is finished. As long as that Border's there fools' blood is all you'll get in this country. If they wanted peace they wouldn't put a border up, would they? A border is a wall. Misguided fools will always smash their heads against it. Hm?'

His father had smashed his way into his mother's room . . . lonely passion turned you into a wild horse. He knew that himself. Would he not smash his way into Annagh's room?

He'd get a letter one day in America, with an Irish postmark . . . telling him the news of his coming marriage – a young widow . . . or a woman home from England, love-broken . . . His mother would sleep on under the clay . . . It was the only way. How else could man live, rats survive, birds whistle every spring?

They sat by the range, his father pleased, mulling porter. They touched glasses. Drank.

'Since 1923 in this part of the country we've had nothing but peace. We had a short Civil War which produced two democratic parties. And there's never been a decent country in the world but has had its civil war. America. France. Spain. Italy. England never had a just system till they cut the king's head off. And let me tell you they'd have done it again in more recent times. Suppose Hitler had won the war? Suppose he put the buck who abdicated back on the throne? Let me tell you any decent Englishman first opportunity would have cut the skull off him, believe you me. No, a border hems you in, narrows your view. I'm glad you're going.'

'The Border's nothing to do with why I'm going.'

'You're going anyway, that's the main thing. We'll not argue about it. Here's to the coming times. Here's to New York, where there's more Irish millionaires than parish priests at home. Here's to the pair of us. We've had our backs to the wall. But we'll dog it out to the end. God bless you in all you do, *a grá*. Knio. Knio.' They laughed.

He sat drinking, looking at his father. His long legs were the same as his. His fingers were the same – the same knobbly joint on the middle finger of his right hand. His cheekbones were the same. He was the same height. Looking at him was looking into a mirror. His mother's face and Annagh's were in the powder compact. His was in his father's. It was hard to tell which of them was going to America.

When he said goodbye to Lady Sarah she gave him a telescope. Tom Gannon, the football umpire, gave him a bottle of poteen to give to his sister in the Bronx. 'If the Customs ask you what it is, tell them holy water.' He called at Castle Finn, but the Colonel and Sophie Kay had gone away. He rode round the Border roads and up Brady's Hill. Through the telescope he looked down on Prunty's house. The windows were broken, the door kicked down, the thatch caving in. A jackdaw came out of the chimney. Nettles flourished where roses grew. The hill behind the house was closing in. What was once a picture postcard was now a broken dream.

A hasky wind came up the drumlins through the whins, shook the ragwort fields, ruffled mercury drops of water against the breasts of swans. Two wild duck rose from the turf bog. He watched them wheel, fly west towards the mountains, become flickering dots in the cold blue air.

Over the village the new moon hung pregnant with the old.